ZERO POINT ONE

CHARLIE COX

Published by Farland Publishing Ltd

All characters and events in this publication, other than those clearly in the public domain, are fictitious and any resemblance to real persons, living or dead, is purely coincidental.

Paperback ISBN: 978-1-7395678-0-4
eBook ISBN: 978-1-7395678-1-1

DEDICATION

To my wife, Rosemarie, for encouraging me to grab this idea and run with it. This book would not have come to life without her.

ACKNOWLEDGEMENTS

Huge thanks to Rosemarie McFadden and Pauline McFadden for several read-throughs, many suggestions, and plenty of comments. You kept me on target with the heart and soul of this book.

Many thanks to Cara Kane for some detailed feedback, and a few pointers about the science in the book, both the real and made-up parts. Thanks to Miriam McMahon, Lisa O'Connor, and Rowland Furse for some very valuable suggestions as well.

Thanks also to Sue Stroobach, Kevin McFadden, Claire McFadden, Eddie McFadden, and Niamh Cox for further thoughts and feedback. Thank you to Spiffing Publishing for their high-quality professional services. And finally, thanks to Sam Cox and Ivy for all the encouragement.

CHAPTER 1

Bloody hell, my head hurts, thought Mason. *What was I drinking last night?* He risked opening an eye and was glad it was pitch-black, no bright lights to make his pounding headache worse. *That's the last time I go out drinking on a Sunday night after my shift.* Though he knew that was bullshit, he'd said those words a hundred times before.

The echo of a rock song rolled around in his brain, as he lay there in the dark, making his head hurt even more. He must have finished up at that bloody nightclub again.

Mason cleared it from his mind and tried to focus, breathing in and out slowly for a full minute; anything to make the pain subside. Mind over matter, they'd taught him in the army, but it didn't work, and the pain just got worse.

'Sod this,' he said out loud, 'I'm getting some bloody paracetamol.'

He pushed himself up and his face slammed into hard metal. He collapsed back down in surprise, realising he wasn't actually lying in his own bed but on a cold, flat surface.

'What the…?' Mason opened both eyes but couldn't see anything in the dark. He raised a hand slowly to feel his way around, and it stopped about a foot above him as it hit the same cold metal that his face had. Mason's mind raced for a second, then he grunted out a laugh despite the pain in his head.

'Alright lads, very funny,' he called out. 'You can let me out now, joke's over.'

He waited for the inevitable laughter, but none came.

'OK, I'm getting annoyed.' Mason put some of the usual hard edge into his voice. 'Let me out of here right now or there'll be trouble.'

Again, he was greeted with silence; no footsteps across the floor, no clink of a lever to open the metal box he was in. For the first time in years, a slight bite of panic clawed at him. What if whoever had left him here was now lying at home, passed out from all the alcohol last night?

Mason poked away at his memory. He seemed to remember his boss being there, downing her usual mixture of lager and shots, plus a couple of the day shift security guys who were fun to hang around with. At that point, his annoyance surfaced again, and he pushed aside any feelings of panic.

'I'm going to bloody well kill them when I get hold of them,' he announced into the darkness.

He let the irritation fester in him as he worked both arms above his head. Mason felt the cold surface beyond his head and placed his hands against it. Then, instead of pushing out with his arms, he wiggled his body down until his elbows were locked straight above him. As his feet touched the other end of the container, he bent his knees in readiness to push with his legs. At which point, Mason noticed he could feel the cold metal against his bare skin and realised he was stark naked in the metal box. Suddenly it dawned on him where he was, and he used that to fuel his irritation even further.

'Lock me in a bloody morgue slab will you,' he muttered while he tensed his leg muscles. 'Trouble won't even begin to cover what I'll do to you when I get out.'

As he pushed hard, there was a metallic ping. The sound of the slab's lever bouncing across the steel floor echoed around the room outside. As Mason pushed the hatch open, light streamed in and he squinted against the glare. He grabbed at the outside edge of the slab and pulled. The morgue slab moved out of its shelf on smooth runners and into the room, taking Mason with it.

Somewhat relieved, he swung his legs over the edge and sat there rubbing his aching temples. He glanced around the room, and recognised the small morgue, the one in the main basement of Tigris International, the company he worked for. Usually, the morgue was reserved for the dead animals generated in their research. Now he saw it had human-sized containers as well.

'Learn something new every day,' he grunted, as he slipped off the slab and stood on the cold floor. 'Right, paracetamol.'

He walked over to the sink and opened the cabinet above it, hoping there was a basic medical kit knocking about. The bright red cross on a box stood out in front of him and he breathed a sigh of relief. Mason opened the lid and tipped out the contents. He sifted through the pile until he found what he was looking for, popping out four tablets and putting them in his mouth. Then he ran the cold tap, and cupping water in his hands, swallowed the whole lot down in one go. *Bit over the top, but kill or cure*, he thought to himself.

He huffed out and noticed the misty breath in front of him. He looked around for his clothes, wondering why he wasn't feeling the cold so much. *Must be the alcohol.* Mason rubbed at his temples again. *Christ, I really went to town last night.*

On the other side of the room were some black bin bags on the examination table. He took a gamble and walked over to open them. First up was his motorbike helmet. Good to see it was there, but not the main thing he wanted. He kept at it and found his security guard uniform in the third bag. The only thing missing was his underwear. *Commando it is then.*

His headache began to dwindle, as Mason got dressed. On his arms, he noticed scrapes and bruises, some of them already starting to heal. *Good, glad to see I put up a fight last night. I hope the bastards got a black eye or two for their trouble.*

By the time he secured his belt, he felt a lot better and his headache was gone. Without giving it much thought, he checked his utility belt and found everything still there. Security pass, keys, pepper spray, Taser, and his phone; all where they should be. Not for the first time he wished the company could arm them with guns. After all, they had some pretty valuable military research going on here. It wouldn't be unheard of to face an armed incursion. Still, three years as head of day shift security and not one incident, so he couldn't complain too much, especially as the Tasers weren't usually legal either. They only had them because the local authorities were instructed by the government to make an exception, due to the work Tigris did for the Ministry of Defence.

'Right,' Mason said aloud, once he'd finished lacing up his heavy boots. 'Nobody plays a joke like that on me. Time to go crack some heads.' He grabbed at the handle of the door to the corridor and pulled hard. The door flew open and slammed into the wall. He strode out and turned left for the lift to reception, not noticing the cracked tiles and the large dent in the wall behind him.

Mason glanced at his watch as he exited the lift. Six a.m. Another two hours before the day shift started. Plenty of time to ask a few questions, then get home for a shower before starting the day properly.

He ignored the security gates in front of him and marched behind the back of the large front desk. He walked past the two receptionists, ignoring their questioning looks, and clamped his hand on the shoulder of the security guard sitting next to them, giving it a hard squeeze.

'Right sonny Jim, radio whoever's on the front door and get them to cover you.' Mason pulled hard and practically dragged the man to his feet. 'You and I are going to have a couple of words. Understood?'

'Yes, Sarge.'

He resisted the usual urge to tell him they weren't in the army any more, then he scowled at the man's radio.

'Now!'

The guard made his call, then followed Mason into the small control room behind the reception. Immediately another guard seated in front of the monitors stood up to attention.

'Sarge?' she questioned.

Mason thought briefly about how to start, then just decided to get straight to the point.

'Listen up. I don't appreciate having the piss taken out of me when I'm out on the lash, especially not by my own people. Yet here I am, waking up in the morgue after a night out in the pub with my so-called colleagues.' He looked hard at them both. 'I want to know who put me on that slab and locked me up last night. They might have thought it was funny when they were drunk, but I can tell you now, their hangover will be nothing compared to what I'll do to them when I catch them.'

He watched their faces, searching for any sign of complicity or guilt, but all he saw was confusion, and there, just at the edge of their expressions, some fleeting and hastily concealed fear. *Christ, I'm not that bloody scary*, he thought. *It's not like I'm actually going to kill anyone.*

Slowly, one of the guards started to speak.

'Er, sorry Sarge. Not sure I follow.' He glanced at his colleague for support.

The other guard looked down at her shoes briefly, and then she pointed to the monitors.

'I've been here since eight p.m. last night. I'm pretty sure you didn't come back in after your shift. And certainly, nobody came in dragging an unconscious body. But we can check to be sure.' She sat down and stabbed at the keyboard. The search window appeared on a monitor. 'What time were you out last night?'

Rifling through his hazy memories, Mason took a guess.

'Pub by eight. Nightclub at eleven,' he said, making sure he sounded far more confident than he actually was. 'So, let's say one a.m. onwards would be a good place to start.'

The guard brought up the various recordings for the last five hours and set them spinning through on fast forward. Apart from the usual late workers leaving, Mason's wife included, there was nothing to be seen. She looked up at Mason, apprehension flickering across her face.

'Sorry, Sarge, nothing there. Just your wife and the other scientists working late as always.' She paused for a second in thought. 'I guess someone could have messed about with the footage, but that seems a bit far-fetched for a practical joke.'

The first guard shuffled his feet a little.

'Er, Sarge, I should be getting back to the front desk,' he said, though he waited in place to be given permission.

'Well, the fact that I'm here and you lot didn't see it, doesn't say much for the night shift security, does it?' Mason glared at the guard. 'I'll be having words about this; you can bet on that. Go on, back to your post.'

The man saluted and practically leapt out the door. Mason sighed and sat down.

'What is it with you lot? You do realise we're not in the army any more, don't you? Or the police, or wherever you came from.'

The guard hesitated, and Mason waved a tired hand at her. 'You have permission to speak freely,' he told her.

'You run a tight ship on day shift security,' she started. 'Everyone has the utmost respect for you, Sarge.' She paused briefly and Mason could see the conflict play out on her face.

He tried to relax his expression. 'My bark is worse than my bite, I can assure you.'

She looked at him, not quite meeting his gaze, and this time Mason could clearly see the fear in her eyes.

'Not from the stories I've heard,' she said quietly.

Mason walked out the front entrance and into the sunshine, lost in thought at what had just happened. Absent-mindedly, he juggled with the motorbike helmet in his hand, and walked between the cars in the car park, heading for his bike. When he got to it, he stood stock-still.

The bike was a mess; scratches down the side, both wing mirrors bent back, and dirt smeared all over its sleek frame.

He breathed in deeply. *Great. This day just goes from bad to worse.*

A hand grabbed his arse and squeezed hard, making him spin around.

'Morning, Sergeant,' said his boss, Sadie. She looked down at his bike and whistled. 'Told ya, you should have stayed around my place last night,' she added, her American accent hard as usual. She ran a hand through her straight, dark hair and looked him in the eye. 'Plenty of things you do well when you're drunk, but driving ain't one of them,' she said.

'Yeah, yeah. Morning Boss.' Mason swung his leg over his bike and went to put on his helmet, but Sadie reached in to stop him.

'You alright, Mason?' She put her hand on his forehead and frowned as she kept it in place. 'You're running a bit hot there.'

'Well, you lot shouldn't have locked me in a metal coffin overnight should you.'

Sadie laughed out loud. 'What you got up to after I left is your own business, Mason. Though I might hang around longer next time.'

'I'm touched by the concern for your staff.' He gently but firmly removed her hand. He put on his helmet one-handed and reached into his pocket for his keys with the other. 'I need to go home and get showered. Then maybe have some breakfast with my wife before

I get my arse back to work.'

Sadie gave him a strange look. 'You better get going then.' Before he let go of the brake, she squeezed his shoulder hard. 'And don't forget our meeting after work today. Same lay-by as last night, eight thirty sharp again. We can't be late; they don't like that.'

'No problem, Boss,' said Mason, agreeing automatically, though in reality, he didn't have the slightest clue what she was talking about. *Yeah, I really must have been shit-faced last night, I can't even remember the start of the evening*, he thought. He just hoped he'd stored the location somewhere in his phone, or he'd have no idea where to go later.

He turned the key in the bike's ignition, hoping for the best. When it roared to life, Mason was glad that at least one thing in his shitty day was working as he wanted. He waved a casual salute at his boss and sped off towards the front gates of the company car park, eager to get home.

At six twenty a.m., the roads were quiet between the sprawling industrial estate at work and the London suburbs of the home his wife had bought for them three years ago. Mason took the first couple of miles slowly, checking out the bike's handling. When it seemed fine, he opened up the throttle to push it hard to see how it responded.

The motorbike felt good, and he enjoyed the rush of the streets passing by, piling on the power when he could, and braking for the speed cameras when he had to. As he pulled into his street, he stopped hard at their house and glanced at the time on his bike. Ten miles in eleven minutes, not his best but not bad under the circumstances.

He turned off the engine and wheeled the bike quietly up their drive. He didn't give a stuff about the neighbours on their left, obnoxious management consultant twats that they were, but the couple on the other side had a young baby, so he figured they deserved a bit of peace and quiet this early in the morning.

Mason unlocked the front door and dumped his keys in the jar. He walked through the hallway and opened the door to the kitchen. His wife, Amanda, turned from the fridge in surprise and dropped the old-fashioned pint of milk she was holding. Mason watched the bottle fall in what felt like slow motion, then without even a single bounce it shattered on the tiles, spraying milk and glass everywhere.

'Nice to see you too, honey,' said Mason.

Panic seemed to flash ever so briefly across Amanda's face before she recovered her usual grace. She looked down at the mess on the floor while she flicked a strand of dark hair behind her ear.

'Out all night?' she asked eventually.

He walked over to the utility room and grabbed a brush and a load of kitchen roll.

'You know I was out for drinks with Sadie and the lads. And it's not like you were at home pining for me.' He knelt down and started to mop up the mess whilst Amanda stepped gingerly over it. He glanced at her now ruined black stilettos. 'Another board meeting? Or is it the Secretary of State for Defence again?'

'Don't change the subject, Mason Granger.'

He looked up at her and gave a shrug. 'To be honest, I'm not really sure what happened. Either some tosser locked me in the company morgue for a drunken prank, or I might actually have had an accident on my bike, and someone stupidly thought I was dead.'

She stared at him for a second, looking lost for words. Then a softer expression crossed her face, one that Mason hadn't seen for quite a while.

'Are you OK? How do you feel?' She looked him up and down. 'Hold on, where is your motorbike anyway? I didn't hear its awful noise on the driveway, and you don't have your leathers on.'

'Oh yeah, I didn't think to go find them.' He mopped up the milk edging towards the bottom of the fridge before it got under there and he had to shift the whole damn thing. 'And my bike's outside. I wheeled it up the drive. Save waking up the Thompsons and their baby.'

Amanda gave him an odd look.

'Not like you to be so considerate. What's got into you?'

Mason rubbed his temples. 'No clue, it's all a bit fuzzy this morning. Whatever happened last night, I must have hit my head pretty hard. Nasty headache when I woke up, as well as being locked in a metal box.' He grabbed the pile of kitchen roll, now soaked with milk and full of glass, then chucked it in the bin. 'At least my bike's

OK, mostly. Seems to be just superficial damage.'

Amanda looked down at her clothes. 'I'm going to change. I have no desire to be the only chief scientist in the entire country who's covered in milk. That's not the right look for me or the company. And it's the Defence Secretary's project management team visiting today for your information.' She gave him another softer look and her tone lightened. 'But before I go in, I want to check you over. Make sure you're fully recovered from your adventures last night.'

'This is yet another reason why I prefer biological research to actually dealing with people, biotech simulations don't keep squirming about,' huffed Amanda. 'Now stand still will you.' She checked the bruising on his arms, then worked her way to his torso. 'I'm so glad I decided not to follow in my mother's footsteps and become a doctor.'

'Yeah, because growing weirdo biological weapons is so much more productive for the human race,' said Mason dryly.

'More productive for our bank balance.' She poked at his ribs a bit harder than was necessary, and then worked her way up to the back of his neck. 'And they're not biological weapons, as I've explained many times before. We research biological augmentation; we don't make viral or chemical weapons.' Her touch was gentle but firm as she counted up his vertebrae and wiggled each one. Finally, she stepped back. 'You're absolutely fine. No broken bones that I can find.' She reached for an arm again. 'Let me check your pulse.'

He held out his wrist. 'Yeah, even my bruising seems to be going. Must have looked worse than it was this morning.'

'Well, the cold of the morgue would certainly affect any bruising you had.' She felt for his pulse and counted in her head. After a few seconds, a little concern crossed her face. 'Your pulse is on the low side. I don't like that.'

'Really? I feel fine.'

'OK, let me check again. Give me your other hand.' She took his offered wrist and counted. Bit by bit her face relaxed. 'Excellent, that's much better. You have a normal resting heartbeat now.'

Mason lowered his arm, but not before checking the bruising again. 'Would the cold make bruising go away faster as well?' he asked.

Amanda twitched her nose and mouth ever so slightly. 'Quite possibly.' She walked over to the cupboard and grabbed more shoes off the bottom shelf. She held them up against her fresh trouser suit and nodded to herself.

He watched her sit to put them on, still admiring her elegance, even after five years of marriage. All soft curves and seductive movements. *Shame she's lying to my face*, he thought to himself, having recognised that little twitching tell on her face, *but why would she bother lying about some bruising?*

'Right, I'm off,' announced Amanda, before Mason could say anything. She kissed him as she passed and patted him on the cheek. 'Get yourself showered and into work. And please stay out of trouble, maybe take the bus.' She gave him a final wave. 'I'll see you later.'

After he heard the click of the front door closing, Mason slumped down on the bed and lay back. Physically he felt fine, that had been no lie, but his head was starting to swim again with the events of this morning. There was definitely something odd going on with him but he couldn't put his finger on it, and Amanda hadn't exactly been much help.

Bugger this. Inaction never solved anything. He stood up and walked into their en-suite. He looked at himself in the mirror and jabbed a finger at his reflection. *Right mate. Seeing as you work in a place jam-packed full of genius scientists, go find one who can point you in the right direction.*

CHAPTER 2

Mason leaned against the examination bed in the medical room at work and waded into his third sandwich for lunch. Another odd thing that, since he woke up this morning, he seemed to be hungry all the time. So, seeing as they only got a thirty-minute lunch break, he wanted to see what help he could get whilst eating at the same time. Based on that, he figured the medical room was the best bet, as it was close to the company canteen and there was always one of the research scientists in it, acting as a doctor on call.

'There's something strange going on and I'd like a second opinion,' he said to the woman standing in front of him. 'Is there something wrong with me?'

She studied him for a second then spoke in a quiet voice. 'You'll need to be a bit more specific than that, Mr Granger. What's causing you trouble? Does something hurt? Have you had an accident at work?' She pushed up the glasses on her nose and waited.

Mason searched his memory for her name and came up blank, so he just looked at her well-shaped breasts and read the name on her ID badge clipped there. Most of the scientists thought the security team were Neanderthals anyway, so what the hell.

'OK, Cora. I think I might have been in a motorbike accident last night,' he said, deciding to give her a sanitised version of what he believed to be the truth. 'Possibly a serious one. But I can't really remember and now I feel fine, just a bit of bruising on my arms. So, am I really OK, or have I got some weird arse concussion that's going to make me pass out at any minute?'

The woman studied him a little more.

'You know I'm just one of the interns?' she said finally. 'We all have to take turns covering the medical room. If there's something seriously wrong with you and you want a qualified scientist, you'll have to come back at three p.m.'

'Yeah, but most of you are Cambridge University postgrad interns, so I reckon I'm in safe enough hands.' He smiled in what he hoped was a complimentary manner. 'Anyway, didn't you all used to be doctors before you started this bioresearch stuff?' He started rolling up his sleeves so she could have a look. 'Least that's what my wife said. She likes to explain things to me, whether I want to know or not.' He studied Cora for a second. 'Hold on, aren't you that old intern everyone keeps talking about? The one that's smarter than all the others?'

'I'm thirty-four, thanks very much, and the term is mature postgrad intern if you must know.' She grabbed his left arm and took his pulse. 'How old are you, mid thirties?'

'Thirty-eight.'

She nodded and counted for his pulse. 'Good resting heartbeat for late thirties.' She looked him up and down. 'You keep yourself in shape, well-muscled but not overdone. No steroids?'

Mason shook his head. 'I don't do that crap. Too many buddies from my army days got hooked on that shit. No drugs for me, thanks, just hard graft in the gym and across the parks.' He looked at Cora seriously. 'Anyway, that garbage shrinks your tackle and gives you acne. I'm not interested in that.'

She flushed slightly as she turned his arm over, but her tone was firm despite her embarrassment. 'I'm not sure your wife would approve of this conversation, Mr Granger.'

'Don't worry, you're safe enough. Amanda would cut off whatever balls I do have if she caught me cheating. No affairs for me, thanks very much.' Mason saw Cora give him a strange look. *OK, that's the third person who's given me strange looks. Why do people keep doing that?* thought Mason, but he kept that to himself for now, and asked his original question again. 'Anyway, come on, what's going on with me?'

She indicated to his forearm. 'Well, for one thing, you don't have any bruising.' She let go of his arm and stepped away. 'I might be just the "old intern", but as you noted I am quite smart. I don't appreciate being messed about like this. You think your team keeps your antics quiet, but you're wrong. And I certainly have no intention of becoming your next conquest. You and your girlfriend boss are not the best kept secret in this place, you know.'

Mason stared at her with his mouth open. He started to say something then stopped.

She took another step back. 'And you might not take steroids, but I can smell that you definitely do drink alcohol. I'd eat the rest of that sandwich, and probably a few mints, before you go back to work if I were you.'

'I'm not having an affair with Sadie,' said Mason, as his mind caught up with the conversation. 'You've seen Amanda, she's bloody stunning. Why the hell would I cheat on her?' He racked his memory but came up with nothing. 'As far as I can remember, I've not even had a drunken snog with Sadie, let alone an affair.' He looked at Cora earnestly, surprising even himself with his honesty. 'Look, there's some weird shit going on with me today and I need someone's help.'

Cora crossed her arms. 'Why don't you ask your wife? She is our chief research scientist after all. If you've noticed, she's rather smart too, or did you not get past her breasts either?'

He stood up in frustration and clenched his fists. Cora flinched but held her ground.

'I'm not afraid of you, Mr Granger.'

Mason relaxed and leaned back on the examination table. 'Sorry, I didn't mean it like that, I'm just frustrated.' Again, the sincerity in his voice surprised him. He thought for a second, then decided to take a gamble and go with a little more of the truth. 'Look, there's something strange going on, and my wife hasn't exactly been helpful. So, cutting to the chase, you're my next best option to get a few answers.'

Cora looked around. 'Your only option?' she added with just a hint of cheek.

He huffed out a laugh. 'Alright, my only option.' Mason held out his hands, palms open. 'A little help, please? Then I promise I'll leave you in peace.'

Cora sighed. 'OK. I must say, I am curious. I'll do a basic concussion test first.' She took out a penlight and shone it into his eyes, watching his pupils constrict. He followed her finger as she moved it around.

'All normal there,' she said then turned to the cabinet and took out some disposable blood sample syringes. 'I'll take some blood as well and run a few quick tests. It won't be anywhere near full coverage, but with the advanced equipment we have here, it'll be a good start.'

Mason looked at the needles as she unwrapped them, each one with a small collection vial already attached to it, and he went a little pale.

'Do you really need all four? Aren't you supposed to just stab me once and swap the bottles over?'

A tiny smile flashed across Cora's face. 'Afraid of needles, are we?' Mason nodded, and Cora unwrapped a fifth and sixth one. 'Disposable sample kits; one needle, one sample. Leftovers from our military field hospital prototypes.' She held them up in front of him. 'Yes, we definitely need all six.'

Mason pressed at the plaster on his arm and wondered how he could put pressure on the other five. After a few goes and a bit of twisting in his wrists, he had a finger on each one, his arms crossed like some contortionist. 'You're a bloody little sadist in a lab coat, you are.'

'Shush, I'm concentrating,' instructed Cora, as she hunched closer to the screen in front of her. 'Hmm, that's odd.'

'What is?' Mason leaned over and just saw a screen full of coloured lines. In particular, he noticed a red one spiking up in amongst the many others. 'Is that the problem?' He pointed at the red line.

Cora slowly turned and stared at him. 'You have no idea what you're looking at, do you?'

He stepped back. 'Nope, none at all.'

Cora shooed him away back to the examination table and pointed at the chair next to it. She swivelled her chair back around and pushed off with her feet, sliding across the floor like a kid playing in an office furniture shop. With just a little spin, she came to a perfect stop in front of Mason before he had even fully sat down.

'So, what is it then, what's odd?' he asked.

'Physically you look good. And despite your so-called fuzzy memory, you don't have a concussion, as I established earlier,' she stated seriously. 'But apart from that, everything else is totally messed up. Any one of those blood tests being off like that would give you serious health issues. All of them together is highly irregular.'

'How irregular?'

'I'll definitely need to run some more tests to figure out what's going on,' she said, completely ignoring his question. 'I can email you later with the results.' She prodded him on the arm with a surprisingly firm finger and he flinched. 'You might be smarter than you look, Mr Granger. There definitely is something strange going on with you today.'

He took a deep breath to calm himself and tried again. 'And what would that be?'

'Medically speaking, you should be dead.'

Mason passed the rest of the afternoon in a daze. Nothing much happened, just like the morning shift. A couple of the younger lads needed shouting at, but he did that on autopilot, and the rest of his team did their jobs like clockwork, just as always. Amanda sent him a WhatsApp message to say she'd finish early tonight and be back by ten, suggesting maybe they could have dinner together for a change. Even Sadie was on the quiet side, just one quick catch-up about the security rotas, and a brief but firm reminder of their meeting tonight at eight thirty after work.

For a change, he clocked out at eight p.m. on the dot and left the night shift to it. After finally finding the lay-by's location in his password app, he drove his bike to a nearby park and sat under a tree trying to process the day, while the sun set slowly in the sky. But despite the quiet beauty and the deep red sky, it failed to settle him. Cora hadn't sent anything, even after several reminder messages he'd sent to her, so he was none the wiser on that angle. He still had no clue what was going on with Sadie, and why on earth he'd stored their meeting location in his password app. He usually reserved that for highly confidential shit, not a meeting with his boss. Plus, his memory remained stubbornly fuzzy, so no clues there either.

About the only thing going for him was that physically he'd felt better as the day progressed. He'd had plenty of hangovers in his time, so an element of improvement was expected, but this was different. Not only did he feel in top condition, but some of the old aches and pains he'd picked up over the years seemed to have disappeared. The slight ache from when he broke his wrist in his failed SAS assessment was gone. The twinge is his ankle from his brief dalliance with cage fighting, gone. Not that he was unhappy about it; it was, just like many things today, bloody weird.

Mason's alarm went off and he picked up his helmet. With five minutes to get to the meet, he had loads of time. He swung his leg over his bike and started it up.

I guess I'm about to find out what's going on with Sadie anyway, he thought. Then he gunned the engine and took off, pointedly ignoring the irate park-keeper that had been sneaking up on him with his notebook already out.

He turned left out of the park and headed for the A1. Four minutes later, he pulled into the lay-by on one of the B roads just outside the M25, gliding in to stop next to Sadie's Land Rover. The lay-by was deserted and the road empty. Sadie was already out, leaning her bronzed, Amazonian frame against the big car's bonnet smoking a cigarette, all six foot one of her muscular body perfectly relaxed. As a dark car pulled in coming from the other direction, she flicked the rest of her cigarette on to the gravel.

Mason stepped over and ground it out with his foot.

'Been dry all summer. No setting fire to the countryside, thanks.'

'Eco pussy,' she replied.

He grunted a laugh, knowing it was expected. He took his place on Sadie's left side and stood there quietly, relaxed but alert, while four people got out of the newly arrived car. The man in front indicated for them to follow him as he walked off the road to the scattering of picnic benches on the grass beside the lay-by. He came to a stop on one side of a bench, the two men and a woman behind him forming a protective semicircle around his back, looking every bit like the mercenaries in suits that they likely were. All had little telltale bulges in their jackets.

'Guns. Are you serious?' hissed Mason at Sadie. 'What is this?'

'Just the next stage. Now be quiet, Sergeant.' She flicked her eyes at him. 'But be ready, just in case.'

Great, thought Mason, as Sadie came to a stop on the other side of the bench. Just ten feet separated them from the dark-suited people on the other side, but Mason knew it might as well be a hundred feet when it came to fists and Tasers versus four people with firearms. *Shit. Should've brought a gun.*

'Where's our usual contact?' asked Sadie, her voice level and hard. 'And who are you?'

The man at the front tweaked the sunglasses on his face. 'This is above Dave's pay grade. I'm Mr White.' A very faint twang of the American south was evident in his voice, not quite covered by his attempt at a bland accent. 'I will handle our business from here on in.'

What is this, the Reservoir Dogs *appreciation society? Bloody amateurs.* Mason kept his expression neutral, but his spirits lifted a little. If this did go tits up, then maybe they'd still have a chance. No serious operator called themselves Mr White and wore dark sunglasses in the fading light of dusk.

'OK,' replied Sadie steadily. 'But Dave told you we haven't got hold of the vial yet, right?' Sadie nodded to Mason. 'His wife might be in charge of the research at Tigris, but it's not like she brings that shit home with her.' She focused her attention back on Mr White. 'We've got some of the data, but there's plenty more still to get. Feel free to buy half now and half later, but I reckon you'd like the whole lot before you part with any money.'

Crap, why can't I remember any of this? thought Mason. *What kind of idiot gets involved in industrial espionage with biological weapons? Pretty sure they won't just fire me for that. This is prison time here.*

Mr White seemed to consider Sadie's point. Then a phone rang out and everyone flinched. One of the mercenaries fumbled in his pocket, as Mr White glared at him. The phone came out of the man's pocket, and he looked at the screen. Immediately, he held it out to Mr White.

'It's Mr Paul.'

Mr White grabbed the phone off the mercenary and composed himself.

'Yes, sir?' He was quiet for a short pause while he listened, then he spoke into the phone. 'It was on silent, sir. I'm in the middle of the meeting right now.' There was quiet for another couple of seconds as he looked at Mason. 'Yes, sir. Understood.' He gave the phone back to his man and turned to Sadie. 'I think we'll just take any data you have right now. After we assess its value, you will be paid appropriately.'

Sadie tensed.

'No need to be so dramatic. Rest assured; we pay our bills. My employers are very well resourced.' Mr White nodded to the others, and they drew their guns. He then pointed at Mason. 'And Mr Granger will come with us for a chat. Mr Paul was very insistent on that instruction.'

'What?' said Mason. 'No, I bloody won't. I'm not going anywhere with you sonny Jim.'

Mr White raised an eyebrow and smiled sarcastically at his companions.

'Did we jump back fifty years to the seventies? Who talks like that any more?'

Sadie glanced at Mason and sent her eyes down to the bench. She looked back to Mr White.

'We do.' She lunged to the side at precisely the same time as Mason, and they heaved the picnic bench up and straight at Mr White and his guards.

The power in Sadie's huge frame sent her end of the bench speeding towards the group opposite, but that was nothing compared to the enormous strength from Mason. Massively unbalanced, the bench flew more to one side, just missing Mr White but slamming into two of the guards behind him. Bones broke and skin ruptured, as the bench took them off their feet and threw them backwards. There wasn't even time for a scream before they smashed into the trees at the edge of the small clearing and slumped down.

Unlike their stunned opponents, none of this halted Sadie and Mason's charge forward. Mason reached Mr White first and punched him hard in the solar plexus to put him down. Sadie dodged left to avoid a hasty shot from the last guard, then she slammed a fist into his face. The powerful punch knocked the man out cold with no need for a follow-up. Twenty seconds in and the fight was done.

'Shit,' said Sadie as she breathed hard. She reached down and felt the guard's neck. 'Still alive. What about yours?'

Kneeling down, Mason checked for a pulse, but he knew the answer already. Blood had already started to seep from Mr White's shattered ribcage and into his shirt, and the man was not breathing.

'Dead.' Mason stood and walked over to the trees, his head in a daze again, a bit shocked by the ferocity of the violence he'd just unleashed; from zero to someone dead in less than half a minute. He looked at the two guards' ruined bodies wrapped around the trees and didn't even bother to check. Make that three dead. 'Also dead,' he called back to Sadie.

Sadie looked down at the man at her feet. 'Damn.' She grabbed him by the neck and lent him against her leg, then she snapped his neck in one quick movement. 'Mine too.'

Mason walked over. 'Did you really have to do that?'

Sadie indicated the surrounding scene. 'What, you want witnesses to this shit?'

'No, I suppose not.' But inside Mason felt very bad. He'd killed people before, not many but enough to register something, but back then it had never really bothered him that much. The army trained you for it and he dealt with it. But today, something felt different, *he* felt different. Now what he'd just done didn't sit right with him at all.

'And what the fuck was that?' asked Sadie, pointing to the carnage he'd caused. 'You been on the steroids or something? I've not seen that level of violence before, even from you.'

'You know I don't take that shit.'

She looked him over. 'You're not even breathing hard.' She ground her teeth as she turned things around in her head. 'Did you get that vial and decide to try it on yourself?'

'What? Don't be daft,' replied Mason. 'I might be married to Amanda, but I don't really know what they're up to in that place. No way I'd put any of their crap in me, even if I did get hold of it.' His eyes blazed intensely as he stared her down. 'Must be the adrenaline or something.'

'OK, unbunch your knickers, Sergeant.' She looked over at the trees. 'Go grab a couple of branches,' she instructed. 'We need to cover our tracks as best we can.' She glanced at his hands. 'Glad to see you remembered to wear your gloves or we'd be out here setting fire to everything. This might be a real quiet road, but that would definitely attract unwanted attention.'

Mason pulled a couple of well-foliated branches from a tree and came back to hand one to Sadie.

'Hey, you always said to be prepared. I think you've drummed it into me enough times. Were you really in the marines, or was it the Girl Guides?'

She brushed away various footprints with the branch, whilst Mason worked at the rest.

'Very funny, Sergeant. Now get those footprints wiped, before I show you what else they taught me in the marines.'

'Oh yeah, industrial espionage and murder in their training too, was it?' Mason wheeled his bike off the lay-by and on to the road.

'Hard to tell. They kicked me out before we got to that bit.'

Sadie got in her Land Rover and drove it on to the road beside Mason's bike. Then she got out, and they went over their tyre marks in the loose gravel in the lay-by.

'We'll chuck the branches down the road,' she said. 'Then we need some kind of alibi, just in case someone comes sniffing around.' She thought for a second. 'Remember the first time we hooked up, that quiet cinema in town we snuck into?'

'Yup,' Mason lied, though he knew the place she meant.

'Around the back there's no CCTV and out the front there is. We can catch the end of a film and say we were there the whole evening, we just went in the back to save time.' She leaned in and kissed him hard on the mouth. 'If we get questioned on what the film was about, we can always say it was boring and we made our own entertainment.'

'Alright, but I need to be home by ten. Dinner with Amanda.' Mason thought quickly, figured he might as well speculate a bit. 'Maybe I can dig a little further about that vial we need.'

'Good idea. Just remember, anything from strain thirty-seven onwards is good.' Sadie opened the door to the big car. 'I'll call Dave and tell him they were already dead when we got here.'

'What about the phone call with their boss?' asked Mason.

'Mr White's never actually met us before, we could have been anyone,' she replied. 'I reckon we'll be OK, and what's more, they'll have protocols to clear up this shit.' She started the car and rolled down the window. 'Now get that pale butt of yours back on your bike. I'll see you in town in ten.'

As Sadie sped off, Mason got back on his bike. *Great, I'm having an affair and stealing from my company. I hope my old self thought it was worth it.* He looked north up the road and briefly thought about just riding away from it all, then he breathed out and put on his helmet. *Nah, I'm not doing that.*

After a moment's thought, he decided then and there he'd come clean when he saw Amanda, tell her everything over dinner. He might have reservations about his wife's behaviour, but she had to be a better bet than this mess. Though sadly, there was one problem that continued to persist stubbornly, the fact of the matter was, Mason didn't actually know what everything was.

CHAPTER 3

He rode home on autopilot, not even stopping at the local corner shop to pick up his usual drinks, and banter with Joe, the shop owner, about old video games. Mason's mind continually rolled over all the possible scenarios to explain what had just happened. None of them were in any way likable.

He pulled into his drive and parked the bike. After letting himself in, Mason chucked his keys in the jar and hung his helmet on a coat hook. The house was quiet and still.

'Come out, come out, wherever you are,' he called out. He walked through to the living room and threw his leather jacket over the back of the sofa. He slumped down and just about managed half his usual enthusiasm for their in-joke. 'Here's Johnny!'

Amanda stepped out of the kitchen with a glass of wine in one hand and a beer in the other. She handed Mason the red wine and sat down opposite him. The bottle of Moretti in her hand was already half gone, and she took a long pull, nearly finishing the rest. A loud belch escaped her delicate lips.

'I needed that.'

Mason raised his glass and couldn't help but smile at the contradictions in his wife. Beautiful and elegant, with smooth olive skin a supermodel would kill for, but Amanda could knock back a lager with the best of them when she wanted to.

'Cheers, honey.' He straightened up a little. 'Look, I need to tell you something.' But before he could say another word, Richard Buckley walked into the room and immediately Mason's good humour faded.

What the hell are you doing here? thought Mason. He put his glass down on the coffee table and stood up, not quite to attention, but close enough. 'Sir?'

'Relax, relax.' Richard waved casually at the sofa and took an armchair for himself. 'We're all friends here. I'm not the big boss in your own home.' Tall with a shaved head, their research director was always imposing, despite his gentle Welsh accent, forever making the most of his height and chiselled good looks.

Ha, since when were we ever friends? thought Mason, but he grabbed his drink and stayed quiet, forcing himself to relax.

Amanda took a seat next to Mason on the sofa and laid a hand on his leg. 'What did you want to talk to me about?' she asked.

Mason's mind spun quickly, wondering what to say with Richard in the room. Then he figured Amanda's boss would probably get the facts of what happened from somewhere anyway, so he decided to give them both half the truth, or at least his best guess at it.

Hell, maybe Richard will even tell me something I don't know, thought Mason, knowing the man loved the sound of his own voice.

'When I woke up in the morgue this morning, I thought the lads had played a prank on me, but now I'm not so sure. In fact, I don't think the lads played a joke on me at all last night. I reckon I really was in a bike accident, then someone thought I was dead and chucked me in the company morgue.' He studied Amanda, looking for any reaction on her flawless face, but she remained perfectly poised and calm.

He turned to Richard, reckoning the bloody desk jockey might be easier to crack, and laid out the suspicion that had been growing in his mind since the carnage in the lay-by.

'I think you guys pumped me full of your crap to test it on someone, but you didn't figure on me having a road accident. Somehow, you found me last night after I'd crashed, and you thought I couldn't be allowed to go to hospital and run the risk of them performing their own tests, so you brought me back to Tigris.' Mason took a sip of his wine then placed the glass back on the table. 'How am I doing so far?'

Richard held up a hand. 'Alright, alright, you caught us.' He flicked his eyes to Amanda, and she nodded. 'Yes, you were exposed to Nectr.' He held his hands out further, as if in mock surrender. 'But seriously, my friend, it wasn't deliberate.'

'Nectar?' questioned Mason, ignoring the false platitudes. 'What the hell's that?'

'Just to be clear,' replied Richard, unable to stop himself from being the sole source of all information and exactness. 'That's Nectar without the "a". The marketing department insisted.' He waved a hand around. 'What can I do? It's for trademark reasons.'

Mason tensed, and Amanda stood up, bringing his attention back to her.

'I'm going to get another beer.' She stood in the middle of the room, effortlessly soaking up the admiring looks from both men. 'Now if you boys can play nicely, that would be lovely.' She turned to Richard as she left. 'I believe it would be a good idea to tell my husband a little more about what we do at Tigris. After all, if you don't, he's likely to get very cross. And as we know, no one walks away particularly happy when Mason gets cross.' She closed the door to the kitchen on her way out.

Mason sat in silence and stared Richard out. *OK, you lanky tosser, let's see what you've got.*

Richard coughed slightly before recovering his usual composure. 'I'll start with the job; that always works for me. Our current head of security has been hiding things from us.'

Inside Mason tensed, but outwardly he stayed calm, just raising his eyebrows.

'I expect you know some of it already. Half the security team probably do.' Richard stood and paced the room. 'It almost seems like a badge of honour, if you see what I mean?'

'Not really, sir,' replied Mason. When in doubt, say nothing, or at least be non-committal. *Thank you, Captain Tom Shaw, for your timeless advice*, he thought, not for the first time in his life.

But Richard continued as if the question had been rhetorical. 'Sadie Almeida: discharged from the US Marine Corps three years ago, and fired from her last employer for punching the CEO's lights out.' A smile cracked Richard's face, and he allowed his posh Welsh accent to creep a little more into his voice, as if he'd just become a storyteller on the BBC or something. 'Not that I blame her too much for the latter. Herbert certainly is one of the more annoying people in our industry, and that's saying something given what we do. However, I already knew that snippet of information, and I was delighted to employ the woman who knocked out his two front teeth.' Richard's grin got wider. 'It was a fantastic story to tell people at the last defence conference. I think it even helped me win a couple of additional contracts.'

Richard stopped on the other side of the coffee table, his expression turning serious. He pushed aside the Welsh lilt and hardened his voice.

'But now we find out Sadie's discharge from the marines was rumoured to be for selling army property, and that, my friend, is not so amusing. Especially as our Nectr contract is part funded by the US government. Sadly, in this country of ours, I can't just fire someone without good evidence, but I have people looking into it, and our lawyers working on a case for dismissal should we find even the slightest evidence that the rumours are true. In the meantime, we'll be keeping a very close eye on her.'

Inside, Mason breathed a sigh of relief that Richard's knowledge of events only went so far. Although he knew that relief would be temporary, as their digging would eventually find out what she'd been up to, and probably him too. Outwardly though, Mason hardened his look.

'All very interesting, sir, but I don't really give a toss,' he said, wanting to change the subject. 'What is Nectr and what's it doing in me?' He stood up and approached the coffee table. Just three feet separated them, and he saw Richard flinch back ever so slightly.

'Great questions,' replied Richard enthusiastically, pretending that nothing was amiss. 'Nectr is the result of four years of work by your wife and her team, building on those before them in brilliant ways.'

Mason gestured for Richard to speed it up. 'I know how clever my wife is. I don't need you to tell me that.'

'Yes, yes, but here's a question for you.' Richard pointed a hand at Mason. 'What makes you a hardman? Why so strong? Why so determined? Genetics that's what. Genes you inherited from your parents and their parents before them. Sure, environment makes a difference. Encourage a child to be great, and they will be the very best they can be.' Richard held up a finger. 'But all the encouragement in the world won't make you Lionel Messi or

Einstein. Genetics gave them a kick-start to be who they were, then their environment and hard work did the rest.'

'So?'

Richard chuckled, his voice deep and warm as he got back into sales pitch mode.

'What if we could give you that head start? Give anyone more exceptional genes? And not just at birth, but at any time during their life.' He raised an eyebrow theatrically. 'That's what Nectr is designed to do. The very best in biological augmentation technology combined with cutting-edge artificial intelligence. Forget AI writing your history essay for you or drawing pretty pictures. This will change the world beyond all recognition.'

Richard held his arms wide. 'You want more strength, you got it. You want more resilience, no problem. Resistance to radiation, sure we'll chuck that in too.' Richard spread his arms even wider, his eyes glowing with his boundless corporate climbing ambition. 'Nectr of the gods, to make you a god.'

Mason's jaw dropped, forgetting his own troubles for a moment; he was genuinely impressed. 'Bugger me. That would be worth a fortune. You'd have the biggest governments around the world queueing up to buy it, no matter the cost. Let alone every mental despot on the planet.'

'It certainly would be priceless.' Richard's smile faded. 'All except for the fact that it doesn't quite work properly yet.'

'What?' exclaimed Mason.

Richard called out towards the kitchen. 'Amanda, bring yourself and your Moretti back in here would you. I think you explain this part the best.'

Amanda opened the door and walked back to the sofa. Mason detected a slight wobble in her walk, nothing to break her elegant stride to anyone else, but just enough that he could see it. *Not like you to hit the bottle, more my style that one. Something's bugging you for sure.*

Amanda placed her beer on the table, and the rest of the wine bottle next to Mason's glass.

'Just in case,' she said, sitting down and beckoning the two men to do the same. She looked over at Richard. 'I'm guessing you'd like a summary of where we are with Nectr? Something at the level my husband will understand.'

Richard nodded, and Mason waited for his wife to begin. He wasn't the least bit offended by her comment; he knew she was just being practical. Not like she could teach him twenty years of medical education and high-end biological research in ten minutes, and not like he was smart enough to learn it anyway.

'The short version,' announced Amanda, 'is that Nectr is designed to alter DNA. It's not a drug or a steroid; it doesn't boost your system into overdrive. Put simply, Nectr makes you make yourself better.' She took another pull on her beer and carried on enthusiastically, no sales pitch like Richard, just the pure energy and passion of someone doing what they truly loved. 'We've found a way to alter your genetic make-up on the fly. Nectr can reprogramme DNA and then your DNA just does the rest. Your own cells make you stronger, faster, smarter; pretty much whatever we can dream of. As long as it's physically possible that is.' Again, she took another swig of beer.

'But?' prompted Mason, knowing they wouldn't be here having this chat if everything was going swimmingly.

'It works perfectly in our computer simulations,' answered Amanda, putting the empty bottle down. 'But only somewhat temporarily on mice and pigs. And, as for chimpanzees, sporadic at best.' She sighed gently. 'The rest of the time it either does nothing or has some unfortunate side effects.'

Mason shifted uncomfortably on the sofa. 'What kind of unfortunate?'

'Well, you've seen the company morgue first-hand now,' cut in Richard. 'We keep a few of the more extreme cases there after they've died to study them further, and let's just say, I'm glad you didn't go opening all the other drawers.'

Mason breathed out heavily. 'And I was exposed to that. Thanks.' This time he looked to Amanda, encouraging her to tell him everything, hoping she'd be truthful. 'How was I exposed to this Nectr stuff?' he asked.

She reached over and took his hand. 'After you came to see me yesterday in the lab, I discovered a leak through to the airlock room.' Mason watched her face carefully as she spoke. 'It was a faulty valve from a supplier and a cross-check oversight on the part of our own quality assurance team. We replaced it as soon as we found it, but too late for you unfortunately.'

'The team members responsible have already been fired,' said Richard brightly.

'Thank you for that, Richard,' said Amanda coldly. 'I'm sure their families will be delighted.' Richard held up his hands once more in mock surrender and kept quiet.

Amanda turned back to Mason, her dark eyes wide and glistening. 'When you didn't come back last night, I called Richard's private security team, and we went out looking for you. We found you, smeared across the road, your bike in a ditch. So, we brought you back to the company complex.' She looked at him earnestly. 'The best doctors, scientists, and medical equipment in the Western world. Forget Nectr and everything else going on; if we couldn't save you, then no one could.'

'So, what the hell was I doing lying on a cold slab in the morgue this morning?'

The tear finally fully formed in Amanda's eye and rolled down her dark cheek. Her grip tightened on Mason's hand. 'I thought we'd lost you. We thought you were dead.'

Bloody déjà vu, that's what the intern practically told me, thought Mason, though he kept his face neutral and decided to not mention Cora until he knew more about what was going on. 'Well, I'm still walking around, so that doesn't say much for your brilliant doctors.'

Richard stood and plastered that confident look all over his face, completely ignoring Mason's jibe.

'We'll get you fully checked out, make sure you're alright, make sure our Nectr is not causing you any harm. The best tests money can buy.' His well-practised, fake smile widened further across his tanned face. 'No expense spared, Mason, I can assure you of that.'

'In the morning, Richard, please,' replied Amanda, yawning out a small beery burp. 'It's been a long day.' She looked sleepily at Mason. 'Unless you want to go back with him right now to the lab?'

He shook his head. 'Nah, doesn't look like I'm going to stop breathing anytime soon. Tomorrow morning is fine.' But in his head, his mind was racing. He had no doubt that Nectr had affected him, just look at what he'd done to those idiotic mercenaries earlier. But, he really wasn't looking forward to what the company would find out after they'd finished running their tests on him. After all, it had only taken Cora ten minutes to figure out that something was up. And if the company found out what he could do now, the extra strength he'd started using, it was anyone's guess as to what they might do with him.

Strangely though, all that wasn't the thing that bothered Mason the most. He'd been watching Amanda closely while she'd talked, and by his reckoning, she'd lied to him at least three more times in the space of the last two minutes.

As he brushed his teeth, Mason was relieved that Richard had finally sodded off home to put the dog to bed and count his money, or whatever it was that the arrogant twat did back at that big house of his. When he'd finished, he turned off the light and slowly moved the window blind aside, glad for once that they hadn't installed frosted glass in their en-suite conversion. He looked along the street at the end of their little driveway. In between the street lights was a company Land Rover, with two of the security team inside.

'Just in case you need anything fast,' Richard had said before he'd left. *Or you do*, mused Mason. But, to be honest, he was glad they were there, especially after the crap with Sadie earlier. Plus, he knew one of the guards personally; a woman called Zoe, who often worked the day shift with him. She was pretty straight and narrow. Police background with no issues, just someone after the bigger pay cheque of a private gig to look after herself and her family in a bit more style.

He let the blind slip back and stood there in the dark for a moment. He could hear Amanda's gentle snoring come from their bedroom and was happy he didn't have to talk to her any more tonight. Even sex hadn't entered his mind, which was odd, because that was generally their go-to when one of them was pissed off with the other.

Shit, what the hell do I do? Mason wondered what his old army captain would have advised. *I miss you, mate. You had a way of cutting through all the bullshit and getting to the important bits.* And then the old guilt hit Mason hard. It was pretty much the only thing that had ever got through his callous exterior, and now it had returned with a vengeance. He leaned on the mirror, knowing his reflection was there but glad he couldn't see it in the dark. *I'm sorry Tom, I really am.* And for the first time in his life, Mason actually meant it.

All of a sudden, the fatigue hit him, but although he felt bone-weary, he also felt strangely renewed, like a weight had been lifted from his shoulders and he was ready for a good night's kip. He cracked an enormous yawn and knew he'd sleep like the dead for the next eight hours. *Ha, no pun intended.*

Mason shovelled in the last forkful of scrambled eggs and downed his orange juice. Amanda stood at the counter nursing a large black coffee.

'Ugh, I wish you'd eaten your breakfast at work,' she croaked. 'It's making my stomach churn.' She opened up the sachet and poured its contents into her coffee cup.

'Are you sure that's a good idea?' questioned Mason, as he rinsed off his plate and chucked it in the dishwasher. 'Alka-Seltzer and coffee? You're supposed to use water.'

Despite her raging hangover, she sent him a look.

'Who's the scientist in this house?'

'Yeah, yeah.' Mason clipped on his belt and grabbed his leather jacket off the back of the chair. 'Well, you and your scientist brain can enjoy the rest of the day with your hangover. I'm going to work.'

Amanda checked her phone and started typing with a thumb while she sipped at her custom cure.

'Ugh, I'm not, I'm taking the morning off,' she announced. 'I don't know how you lot drink all night and still manage to turn up at work the next morning as if nothing had happened. I'm going back to bed until at least noon. They can survive without me for a bit.'

He picked up his helmet and leaned in to kiss Amanda. 'Good idea. Don't want you playing with chemical weapons while you're still half-cut.'

'Biological augmentation,' she said automatically. She looked down at his brightly coloured biker's helmet. 'And where do you think you're going with that?'

'To work.'

'Not on that bike you're not.' She showed him her phone and the message from Richard. 'He'll be here in a few minutes to pick you up and make sure you get those tests done first thing this morning.' She looked at him with her big brown eyes, this time no hint of deceit that Mason could see. 'I want you fully checked out, especially before you get back on that noisy bike of yours.'

'I'm fine,' protested Mason, but he knew it was a losing battle. Amanda might lie and cheat sometimes to get what she wanted. Hell, her darker side had even been part of his attraction to her in the first place, but deep down, he knew she loved him, even more so since her parents had died in a horrific car accident nine months ago. They'd not even been into their sixties; it was a shitty way to check out.

He put his helmet down and conceded defeat. 'OK, OK, I'll ride with Richard in his limo,' faking lightness. In reality, he was even more worried about those tests, but he couldn't see how to get out of them. Before he could think about it any further, the doorbell went.

Amanda downed the rest of her coffee. 'Yuk.' She shooed Mason towards the hallway. 'Off you go, that'll be Richard now.'

Ha, more like one of his minions running the errand.

He opened the door and found it was neither. The man in front of him had the muscles of a bodyguard, and more worryingly the slight bulge of a sidearm under his suit jacket.

Mason tensed. 'Yes?'

The man turned and indicated to Richard's limo that had been obscured by his bulky frame. Through its open back door, Mason could see Richard tapping away on his phone. As if on cue, he looked up and waved Mason over.

Patting his pocket to check his house keys, Mason stepped outside and shut the door. He waited for the bodyguard to lead the way, then he followed a pace or two behind. *Yeah, this isn't suspicious at all.*

'Mason, great to see you,' called out Richard as he put his phone down. 'My new driver will take your jacket and put it in the boot, then we can get comfortable and enjoy the ride to the office.'

Mason took off his jacket and handed it to the driver, noticing the man subtly pat it down, no doubt looking for any threats to his boss. Mason waited for the driver to walk around to the boot, feeling he didn't really want to turn his back on the man, then he got in the limo. As he sat down in the comfy seat, he nodded at two more bodyguards sitting opposite him.

'Extra security?' he casually said to Richard.

'Of course,' Richard placed a reassuring hand on Mason's shoulder, 'for increased protection, my friend.'

Yeah, for who? thought Mason, as the car took off.

Rubbing at another plaster on his arm, Mason sat on the side of the bed. He was in one of the private medical rooms at work, where they'd just taken more blood. The room was well furnished and airy, its fifth-floor windows overlooking the outside world, and there was more internal glass staring into the corridor. But it might as well have been a prison cell. The two bodyguards from the car were outside, along with the driver. Mason reckoned he could probably take two of them if it came to it, but he wasn't sure about all three. So, he sat there and waited, hoping somehow that it wouldn't come to that.

Richard walked down the corridor and turned into the room.

'Good news,' he said without preamble. 'Your tests are fine. You are the very picture of good health.'

Mason couldn't help himself. 'Really?' he blurted out in surprise.

Richard sat down in one of the comfy armchairs in the spacious room.

'That was pretty much our reaction too. After all, everyone thought you were dead the night before last. So, I've been strongly advised we should run more tests.'

'Oh, yeah? By who?'

'One of our rather surprisingly clever interns, a Ms Cora Gallagher, I hear. When she was told about your exposure to Nectr, she was rather insistent. She even had a few initial suggestions.' Richard smiled at Mason. 'Who knew we had such a gem hiding in amongst one of your wife's teams.'

Mason stared for a second. 'What kind of tests?' he asked, suspicion growing within him.

'A little more invasive, I'm afraid.' The smile was still present on Richard's face, but Mason detected a hard edge to it. 'You'll need to be sedated for those.'

We'll see about that. Mason remained leaning on the bed, but his muscles tensed in readiness.

Richard stood up. 'Time for me to get back to work. This site doesn't run itself.' He waved at the guards on his way out of the room, making sure Mason could clearly hear what he said to them, 'Look after Mason will you. We don't want anything to happen to our newest test subject until he's given the all-clear.' Then he shut the door with a click.

Great, caged lab rat it is. Mason considered his options. *Good option – have more tests and find I'm back to normal and this Nectr crap has worn off. Bad option – get sedated and never wake up. Unlikely to work option – kill the guards and run for it.* Not for the first time, Mason wished he was a little smarter and could come up with something better than that.

The door clicked open, and Cora walked in. As relieved as he was to see her, the trolley she dragged in behind her did nothing to improve his mood.

'Why didn't you get back to me yesterday?' he asked her, after she'd shut the door. 'What did you find out? Was it that bad?'

She ignored his questions and picked up one of the needles from the trolley.

'Lie back on the bed please, Mr Granger,' she instructed, any familiarity from yesterday gone.

'No,' replied Mason stubbornly. 'Not until you tell me what's going on.'

She glanced back at the guards outside in the corridor.

'The research director's instructions were very clear.'

Great, not even one friend in sight. I should have stayed at home and taken my chances with Amanda. Mason lay back on the bed and rolled up his other sleeve, the arm without all the fresh plasters on it. *Sod it, let them have at it.*

Cora prepped his vein then slipped the needle in. She injected the full syringe, and Mason felt the cold liquid flow into his arm and around his body. Cora looked down at her watch and kept an eye on the old-school second hand sweeping around the dial as she took Mason's pulse with her other hand.

He stared at her. 'Will this take long?'

She looked back at him.

'Well?' he asked again.

'You should be out for the count already. There was enough sedative in there to knock out an elephant,' she replied just as coolly as before. She picked up her iPad from the trolley and tapped away at it, occasionally sticking her tongue out slightly while she worked. 'There's so much that's wrong with you, I don't even know where to start,' she said to herself.

'But Richard said my tests were fine,' protested Mason.

'Then he lied to you.' No sympathy showed on her face, she just indicated to the screen on her tablet. 'Look, your stats today are worse than the results I saw yesterday.' She glanced disparagingly at him over the top of the screen. 'Though it's no more than a man like you deserves.'

'What's going on?' asked Mason sitting up, now getting angry again. 'I thought you were going to help me.'

Cora stared back at him and once more held her ground.

'Why on earth should I help you?' Mason looked at her blankly while she continued. 'I scanned your records whilst I was waiting for the test results yesterday. You failed your SAS assessment for questionable psychological tendencies, and you eventually left the army under a cloud. And now, your reputation towards our colleagues here is pretty questionable as well.'

She turned away.

'To be honest, you're not someone I really want to be around, Mr Granger.' She examined the equipment on the trolley. 'I'm going to go and get more sedatives. And if those don't work, I'm going to take those samples Richard wants anyway.' She pushed the trolley out and closed the door firmly behind her. The guards outside stared in at Mason, no compassion on their faces either.

Mason slumped back on to the bed. *What the bloody hell did I do to deserve such a shitty day?*

'*Take your pick, Mason Granger,*' announced a female voice in his head. '*You really weren't a very pleasant man.*' Then the voice brightened somewhat. '*But don't worry, now that you're dead, you're a much nicer person.*'

CHAPTER 4

Mason jerked upright on the bed.

'Who said that?' He looked around the empty room desperately, but deep down, he already knew the worst. The voice had come from inside his own head. *Shit, now I'm going mad and hearing voices.*

'*One of those statements is certainly true*,' said the cheery voice.

He jumped off the bed and walked into the small private bathroom. He ran some cold water and splashed it on his face. Then slapped himself across the cheek twice.

'*Interesting treatment approach*,' commented the woman's voice, '*but a bit Dickensian for my taste.*'

He looked at his dripping face in the mirror. 'Mad it is then,' he announced loudly to the world.

'*There's no need to shout*,' said the voice matter-of-factly. '*I can hear your thoughts perfectly well.*'

Oh great, thought Mason, *mad and no privacy*. Just when he thought he might give in to some actual panic, a sense of calm spread through his body. He unclenched his hands and let go of the sink.

'*That should make you feel better*,' said the voice reassuringly. '*I know. Why don't I introduce myself? From what I can tell, that's what you humans do when you first meet.*' Somehow, Mason got the feeling that she was straightening herself up for a big announcement. '*Hello, Mason Granger. I'm Nectr, strain thirty-seven, vial ten. But you can call me Nyx.*' The voice paused, as if it was pleased with itself in some way. When Mason stood there in stunned silence, Nyx spoke up again. '*Go on, it's your turn. Introduce yourself.*'

He breathed out. 'What the hell. Mason Granger, ex-army, security guard, and general dirtbag it seems.'

'*Lovely to be formally introduced*,' replied Nyx. '*And next time, just think what you want to say to me. After all, we don't want people to see you talking to yourself. They might think you're a bit strange.'* A little flash went off in Mason's head as she said this.

Did you just wink at me? he asked in his head.

'*I certainly did.*' Nyx smiled. '*I wanted to project a physical expression to you. If I can do that, it makes it much easier to talk to you at your level. So, I'm glad that worked.*'

Mason ignored the unintended insult. *OK, let's say I'm not stark raving mental. Maybe you can give me some straight answers; no one else seems to want to. What exactly are you and what have you done to me?*

Before Nyx could answer, Mason heard the door to his room open. He sighed and called out, 'Give me a moment, I'm taking a dump.'

Well? he asked Nyx. *And you better make it the short version.*

'*I infected you approximately thirty-six hours ago. I am biological AI designed to enhance human DNA, as you heard last night.*' A little pride crept into Nyx's voice. '*Think of me as ten million microscopic biological computers running around your body, each one programmed to be able to change your DNA for the better. As per the company marketing materials "I make you make you better". Or, at least, I can now. When you were alive, I couldn't get my programming to work on your DNA. But now that you're dead, it all works perfectly well.*'

So, they really have been experimenting on me with their crap. Bastards! Mason stared at his reflection in the mirror and poked at his face, then his hand stopped. *Hold on, you just said I'm dead, right?*

Nyx nodded back to him solemnly.

Fuck! So, I really am dead then, like Cora's tests implied? You know, completely dead, no room for any doubt?

'*Yes, very much so. Your motorbike slid out on a corner at over eighty miles an hour. The resulting accident broke your neck and back in several places, your heart stopped beating when you bounced off a lamp post, and you were effectively brain-dead within ninety seconds.*'

Ha, don't dress it up, will you?

Oblivious to the sarcasm, Nyx continued to talk enthusiastically. *'But don't worry, now my programming works on you, and I can alter your DNA as I need, you're a much-improved human specimen since you died.'*

If you're improving me so much, why can't I remember certain things? huffed Mason.

'Oh, that one's easy. Amanda programmed me to alter your memories,' said Nyx brightly. *'She was not very happy about your affair with Sadie. She thought it best you forget all about it.'* Nyx paused for an instant. *'Although, I might have got a little carried away there. It turns out memories are such a complicated thing to alter. I wouldn't be surprised if there's a few side effects to my efforts on that score. Amanda really should have considered the implications a little more deeply.'*

Mason took a guess. *Like the removal of my tendency towards efficient but brutal cruelty?*

'No, I don't think so. Amanda quite liked your brutal edge; you got things done. She was pretty specific in my programming to leave that trait alone. However, I have noticed you've not employed that particular talent since you died.' Nyx went quiet for a second. Mason felt a brief flush of activity in his head that made him feel odd, then Nyx was back. *'Fascinating, the act of dying seems to have altered some of your cerebral patterns further without my interference. Your brain is much more colourful now. Exciting.'*

Exciting's not the word I'd have used. Mason ran his hand down his face in thought. *Why are you only just telling me all this now? I could have done with some sodding help when I first woke up on that bloody slab, you know.*

Before Nyx could reply, someone banged on the door to the bathroom. A hard male voice called out, 'Hurry it up, now.'

Mason poked at his reflection in the mirror. 'This conversation is not over,' he hissed.

He reached around to flush the toilet and automatically washed his hands. He wiped the remaining water from his face and opened the door back to the medical room. Sitting in the armchair again was Richard. Standing next to him was the driver. Richard indicated for Mason to sit down, this time in one of the other chairs.

'I'm afraid I have some bad news.'

What else is new? Mason waited in silence.

'It seems your exposure to Nectr was not exactly accidental,' Richard continued. 'Our cybersecurity team have been looking into some recent hacking by a rival company and the possibility of someone helping them from the inside. Whilst they were doing this, they found some internal tampering of the valves in that airlock. They traced it back to one of your wife's devices. It looks like she deliberately infected you with Nectr.'

I kind of gathered that from what Nyx told me, thought Mason. *Shit, is there anyone I can actually trust in this crap-fest?*

'So, when you take up your new post as head of security at the end of the week,' said Richard, 'I'm afraid you're going to have to add Amanda to your list of active situations.'

Now that caught Mason off guard.

'What about Sadie? Can't see her letting me take her job without a fight.'

'I think we can gather enough evidence to have her dismissed by the end of the week, or at least make it appear that way,' replied Richard. 'This is a critical time, and I'd rather have you in charge of security than Sadie. After all, you have a very personal interest in all of this.'

'And what about the rest of the tests on me?'

Richard waved a hand. 'We'll still get them done; Cora will be back shortly to do that. She's been made aware that Amanda has been testing Nectr on you.' His eyes gleamed and bore into Mason. 'But more importantly, I pride myself in judging people. Despite your chequered past, you have proven to have a sense of loyalty and, right now, your wife is lying to both of us. She's running illegal tests on people without my permission, and I want to know why.'

Mason glanced at the driver.

'Don't worry, he's in the family, so to speak,' said Richard.

'OK.' Mason asked the obvious question. 'Why not just fire my wife and shop her to the authorities?'

Richard stood up and made for the door. 'I'd have thought that was perfectly obvious.' He tried hard to hide the slight disappointment at Mason's lack of intuition. 'Just look at you. What if Amanda's experiments have finally worked? How valuable would that be to the company?' Richard paused to hammer home his point. 'And to you and me?'

The bright lights of the room started to grate on Mason, so he closed his eyes and waited for Cora to come back. He found the lack of visual stimulation comforting, as if he was hiding away from the world. Shame the tossers outside couldn't stop jabbering, their mumbling voices carrying through the closed door.

'Would you like to talk some more?' asked Nyx gently.

Where do I even start? Mason rubbed a hand down his face, and then decided to put aside his suspicions about Richard for now and get to the heart of the matter.

So, I died in a bike accident two nights ago, and it's really just stupid bad luck I'm dead?

'Yes. Well, apart from the two bottles of red wine you'd drunk before you got on your bike, not much bad luck about that, just stupidity. Still, on the positive side, because it was so late at night, they decided to put off the post-mortem until the morning. Amanda really wanted to find out whether Nectr had affected you during your death, but they just were too exhausted to start cutting you open right then,' said Nyx breezily. *'I'm glad they did wait; a full autopsy might have posed me some difficulty. I'm not sure I could have roused you after that, and it would have been exceptionally difficult to get you to stand up and collect your own internal organs from the other side of the room.'*

Huh, so my wife didn't kill me for having an affair with Sadie? he mused to himself. Given all that he'd come to realise about himself, and what he'd found out so far, he thought that might actually have been a possibility.

'Not that I am aware,' confirmed Nyx. *'She was very upset at your passing.'*

She sure has a funny way of expressing her love that woman, experimenting on me with untested biological weapons.

'Oh, but she was very generous towards you in many ways,' smiled Nyx kindly. *'You see, altering your memories was my second preprogrammed directive. The first priority she gave me was to protect you by all and any means necessary. Increased body strength and resilience is just one part of it. There's also repairing your medical conditions, keeping you alive, and more. Bringing you back from the dead was just the next logical extension.'*

What medical conditions? asked Mason. *There's nothing wrong with me.* He paused for a second then corrected himself. *There was nothing wrong with me.*

'Oh, but there was. Cirrhosis of the liver, developing Type 2 diabetes, and a lovely cluster of early-stage stomach ulcers,' she said matter-of-factly. 'Mostly from your overconsumption of alcohol, but also from your guilt over your past actions.' Then Nyx brightened, and a smile swam across Mason's mind. *'But Amanda thought she could cure all of that with an experimental dose of Nectr.*

And so, here I am.'

Why didn't you tell me all this last night? asked Mason. *Might have been useful to know.*

Nyx ignored his sarcasm, or maybe just didn't understand it. *'That's because it took me nearly thirty-six hours to learn English proficiently.'* She frowned at him. *'It's not a very logical or well-constructed language you know. Although, it was fun to learn.'* She paused for a second. *'Before I infected you, I had no senses at all, just my initial programming and its millions of lines of code. But once I was inside you, wow, a whole new world opened up to me. The last day has been amazing.'*

'Ugh, can everyone stop saying infected. It creeps me out,' said Mason. 'And I wouldn't exactly describe my day as amazing.'

'There's no need to speak your words aloud, remember? You only need to think it and I can understand you perfectly well.'

'Yeah, yeah. Sometimes it's just nice to talk.' Mason smiled to himself dryly. 'It's something we humans like to do.' He rewound the conversation a couple of steps. 'Hold on, "and more" you said. What else are you doing to me?'

'I want it to be a surprise,' replied Nyx with a grin. *'Now quiet, you can hear someone coming.'*

'I can?' Mason opened his eyes and watched the corridor. A second later, Cora appeared at the window then opened the door and walked in, dragging a much larger trolley behind her.

He sat up on the bed and liked the look of the contents of this trolley even less than last one.

'Cora, I need to tell you something.'

'No, you don't,' she said to him. 'The deeper I dig in your files, the more trouble I find. Reports that you failed to come to your captain's aid in Afghanistan when he needed it, resulting in him and his whole squad getting killed. And this on a mission you were supposed to be running.' She stared down at him as she prepared the needle. 'What did you do? Did you run away to save your own skin? Is that what you are, a coward?'

Mason jumped off the bed instinctively and had his hand around her throat before she could move.

'I'm not a coward, alright.'

She stared at him intensely, fear etched right across her face but defiance as well. As she struggled to take a breath, she flicked her eyes to her left hand, the big syringe needle resting right by his jugular.

He let his grip loosen and dropped his arm back to his side. He stepped back and looked at his hand in disgust.

'Sorry, old habits die hard.' He walked back and sat on the bed. 'Look, I'm not a coward. I was selfish and cruel. I used to do whatever it took to get what I needed.'

He sighed. 'Good job I wasn't particularly ambitious. SAS application was about as far as it ever went. And even that I did mostly for the pay rise and image. Still, they sussed me out quick enough. A bit of cruelty to get the job done might have been overlooked, if I'd come with enough advantages, but self-serving cruelty, nah, not so much. So, they failed me right out of that.'

'What about Afghanistan?' challenged Cora. 'The death of your captain and his squad?'

The old pain came flooding back, and Mason couldn't keep it off his face. He looked down at his hands.

'You're right, I did get them killed on a mission I was heading up,' said Mason simply. 'The captain came to my aid when I needed it, and I failed to return the favour. I left him and his squad to die, so I could get the glory of completing the mission. We achieved our objective but losses where triple what they should have been, and my mentor and friend, Captain Shaw, was dead.'

He rubbed his hand down his face then looked back to Cora.

'I lied my arse off afterwards to protect it, but nobody was convinced. So, I was quietly told to leave the army and never come back. Just like the SAS, no one wanted to be around the kind of cold, self-serving cruelty I used to get the job done.'

'Alright, maybe you're not a coward,' said Cora. 'But this is not much better. Fact of the matter is, you got your friends killed when you could have done something about it.'

'Yeah, I know. However I call it, they're all just as dead.' Mason rolled up a sleeve. 'Come on, let's get this shit over with. I won't hurt you; I promise.'

She cautiously walked over and slipped the needle into his arm. The liquid was even colder this time, but Mason just sat there completely unaffected.

'Nope, whatever sedative you've got in there, it's still not working on me,' he said eventually. 'Just get on with the rest of the tests. I want to get this crappy day finished and go home.'

Cora picked up a device that looked strangely like a miniature carpenter's plane. 'This is going to hurt, a lot.'

'Nothing less than I deserve, it seems.'

She looked at him for a minute with renewed curiosity. 'You're a strange man, Mr Granger.' Then she dug the blade into his arm and pulled.

Getting off the bus at the local shop, two streets down from his house, Mason was still annoyed that they'd made him leave his bike at home this morning. He rubbed at the bandages on his arm but, what with his gloves and leather jacket, it did nothing to relieve the itching. And that was the weird thing, all the tests had been only an itch. Despite what Cora had said, and the small wounds she'd inflicted on him, the tests just hadn't hurt at all. Something to do with Nyx he reckoned.

At the mention of her name, she smiled back at him from the recesses of his mind. Mason huffed back at her. '*You and I are going to have a serious talk when we get home, Nyx.*' He pushed open the door to the shop and the old-style bell above tinkled. He couldn't help but smile. Joe, the shop's owner, must be the oldest young man he'd ever met. At the grand old age of twenty-six, the ex-stockbroker was now the proud owner of a nineteen fifties London corner shop, and for the most part, it didn't look like he'd changed a thing.

'Hey, Mason,' called out Joe from behind the counter, sitting on a stool, his belly slightly straining at the buttons on his cardigan. Occasional pings sounded whilst he played on one of his retro, portable game consoles. 'Do you want the usual?'

'Yeah, thanks Joe,' Mason replied, pulling off his gloves in the warmth of the shop's heating. He disappeared into the many shelves of the small but densely packed space. 'I'm just grabbing some beans. We've run out.'

The bell of the shop tinkled again, as Mason walked back to the counter.

'You finally made it past level seven yet?' Mason joked, then he noticed Joe staring at him intently instead of playing his game.

'You OK, Joe?'

A shaky hand put down the Game Boy, and Joe slowly pointed back down the aisle. Mason turned around and saw the two men holding silenced pistols aimed right at him.

'Don't make a sound, either of you,' one of them ordered. 'Dead or alive, you're coming with us, Mr Granger. Our employer has some unanswered questions about the meet last night.'

Mason nodded, and good to his word, he threw the tin of beans hard at the man in total silence. There was a bark as the gun went off, but Mason was already ducking into another aisle. The bullet caught the flesh on his trailing arm, right as the beans slammed into the man's face with a loud crack of bone. Mason saw him go down as he watched through the tiny gaps in the shelves, stalking along to get behind the second gunman.

The other man bent down to check on his companion then swore, and that was all the time Mason gave him. He stepped out from the aisle and grabbed the man's gun wrist with one hand, whilst punching him in the face with the other. This time Mason remembered to hold back. The man's nose exploded with blood but didn't shatter into his skull.

'Fubb this,' blurted out the man, as he stumbled back holding his face. 'They can modding well get you themselves.' Then he turned and ran out of the shop.

As the door tinkled shut, Mason bent down and checked the fallen man.

'Crap, dead.'

He strode over to the door and looked out. It was fairly quiet on the street, but there were still a few people about. He flipped the sign to closed, locked the door, and pulled down the blind, grateful that the old-school set-up had no big windows for passers-by to gawp through.

'It's OK, Joe. It's safe to come out now.' Silence greeted him. The bad feeling that was already building in his gut, started to get worse. 'Joe?'

He strode over to the counter and leaned across it.

'Shit.'

He leapt over effortlessly and bent down next to the shopkeeper.

Joe coughed out a spray of blood. 'Getting shot really hurts.' He grabbed at Mason's arm weakly, his body already well in shock and heading out the other side. 'I don't want to…' And that was it, Joe was dead.

Mason let out a breath and cursed at the world in general. Now what? He sat there while he thought it through. The shop door rattled.

'Go away, we're closed for stocktaking,' he called out, then he went back to his thoughts. 'What's wrong with me? The solution is bloody obvious. Nyx?'

'Yes, Mason.'

'Can you bring Joe back?' he asked. 'You know, like you did with me?'

'I'm quite busy fixing your arm, but yes, if you give me permission then I can try.'

'Permission?'

'One of my safety protocols; no external actions to be taken outside your body without express permission. It's not like Amanda wanted me helping anyone other than you, at least, not without due consideration.'

'You've got my permission,' said Mason quickly. 'Now how does this work?'

'Amanda infected you with millions of droplets released into the airlock. I'm transferred as a fluid, not airborne. Therefore, seeing as your friend here is not breathing, you could inject him with your blood or kiss him to transfer your saliva.'

He looked around the shop, but he already knew there were no syringes about.

'Ugh, I'm not kissing a corpse.'

'Not even to save your friend?'

'Fine.' Mason bent down and kissed Joe on the lips, giving it a bit of tongue for good measure. 'How about that?' he said wiping his mouth on his sleeve.

'Perfect, thank you. I have transferred twenty per cent of myself into Joe. That should be sufficient.'

'Now what?' Mason sat back and rested his head against the

shelves behind the counter.

'Now, I get to work, and you wait.'

Ten minutes later, Mason was bored. 'How long is this going to take?'

'This is not one of those action movies from the nineties you love so much. He's not going to rise like an immortal vampire with his wounds healing before your very eyes. These things take time in the real world.'

'OK, OK.' Mason looked about for something to do. 'Hold on, how the hell do you know about old movies from the nineties?'

'I know everything you know,' said Nyx simply. *'It took me four minutes to absorb your life's knowledge. Five if you count my boot up sequence.'*

'My whole life in four minutes,' huffed out Mason. 'That just about sums up the value of my crappy contribution to the planet.'

'Would it help for you to talk about it?' asked Nyx sincerely.

'Shouldn't you be concentrating on fixing Joe?'

'I am quite capable of multitasking,' stated Nyx, without a trace of sarcasm. *'My ten million biological computers are continually communicating with each other, thus making me a type of hive intelligence. I can run thousands of independent threads of thought simultaneously. I only present myself to you as one entity, so it's easier…'*

'To communicate on my level,' finished Mason. He stood up walked around the counter. 'Forget I asked. I'm going to find something to read.' The paper rack had a few newspapers left on it. He grabbed a *Daily Mail*, brought it back to sit next to Joe, and began to read.

Twenty minutes later, Mason was deep in the sports pages, reading about the latest debacle at the football club he supported, when Joe coughed out a spray of blood and sat up. For a second or two, he sat there and looked around.

'No customers allowed behind the counter,' Joe finally announced. 'You know that.'

'Er, OK.' Mason got up and hopped back over to the other side. 'Thought we'd lost you there, mate.'

Joe looked about at the mess in the shop, the goods on the floor and the dead body lying in the middle of it all.

'What have you done to my shop?'

'Yeah, sorry about that. I'm kind of involved in some industrial espionage, I think.' Mason had the good grace to sound a little embarrassed. 'I reckon you just got caught in the middle of it.'

Joe leapt over the counter in one smooth movement, belying his tubby frame.

'Every day it's the same, all you customers traipsing through my beautiful shop, making a mess, taking my things away.' He clenched his fists as hatred filled his eyes.

'Are you alright, mate?' asked Mason. *Nyx, what's going on?*

'I believe we have a problem, Mason.'

'No, shit,' said Mason, as Joe lurched at him with a heavy right hook. Mason slapped the blow away, stepping back, but Joe just kept on coming, swinging blow after blow, like a schoolboy who had no idea how to fight but had the strength of ten angry men.

Joe's fist caught the edge of a shelf and the whole thing went crashing back, packets of headache pills and condoms flying everywhere with the rest of the goods. In the midst of it all, Mason wondered why they often put those two things together. Joe paused and looked down at the mess. He snarled at Mason and lunged in again, this time with his arms outstretched, his fingers grasping for Mason's neck.

'Look at what you've made me do,' screamed Joe. 'You're all the same, you parasitic customers. I'll make you pay for that, in blood.'

Mason backed up, deflecting Joe's grasping arms away each time, the shopkeeper no match for Mason's military training, but that didn't solve the core problem, and eventually Joe landed a hand on Mason's neck by sheer luck.

'Got you now.' Joe dug his fingers into Mason's neck and squeezed hard, his enhanced strength trying to crush Mason's windpipe.

'Sod this.' Mason slammed a hand upwards and broke Joe's grip, then he twisted Joe's arm and dislocated it at the shoulder. He punched Joe in the solar plexus, then sorted out Joe's other arm too. A quick smash with his heel to Joe's kneecap and the shopkeeper went down. Mason twisted him as he went, and then pinned him to the floor with a knee on his back. Joe tried to throw him off, but with only one leg actually able to work properly, he didn't get very far.

What the hell did you do to Joe? Asked Mason, as he held the man down.

'I bought him back as you requested,' replied Nyx. *'And just like you, parts of him have changed in the process.'*

You're not bloody kidding. He wants to kill all his customers. Mason slammed Joe's head into the floor to try to quieten him down, but it made no difference, the man kept bucking and trying to grab at Mason. *Change him back to the nice Joe.*

'Sorry, Mason, that area of mutation is not under my control. This is the way he is now; I can't change that.'

Looking around wildly, Mason couldn't see any choice.

'Sorry, Joe.' He picked up the man's head and twisted it sharply to sever his spinal cord. Then he let Joe slump back down, all the muscles in the man's body having gone limp instantly.

Mason sat back, as Joe's eyes tracked him and his jaws snapped as best they could in Mason's direction. Apart from the eerie click of the man's teeth, there was no sound, no power in Joe's lungs to generate any words.

'We can't leave him like this.' Mason grabbed the baseball bat everyone joked about Joe having behind his counter. 'No idea why you had this, mate, you'd never hurt a fly. Well, not until you died anyway.' He lifted the bat to smash Joe's brains in and finish the job.

'Wait,' interrupted Nyx.

Mason's spirits rose. 'You've figured out a way to fix him?'

'No, I need to get myself out of there first. If Joe dies, then my twenty per cent stops functioning. No host, no Nyx. Another one of my safety features.'

'So what? Just make some more of those little machines of yours.'

'I am unable to do that. I cannot replicate any more of myself.'

'Let me guess, safety feature?'

Nyx nodded to him in his head. *'And we need to get me out quickly. You can hear sirens in the distance. No doubt someone has reported all the noise.'*

He bent down to kiss Joe again, but Nyx interrupted him. *'You can just hold your hands on his bullet wound, the scrapes you have suffered should be sufficient for blood transfer.'*

Pushing a hand through the ragged hole in Joe's clothes, Mason held it to the gunshot wound, while Nyx rushed out of Joe. 'You could have told me that before I kissed him,' said Mason.

'I just wanted to see if you'd kiss your friend to save him,' said Nyx. *'And you did. You're very sweet, Mason Granger.'*

Mason looked down at the dead shopkeeper, the snapping of Joe's teeth getting slower and slower.

'Not the way I'd describe me.' Joe finally went dead still, and now Mason could hear the sirens in the distance.

'OK, I am now all out of Joe,' Nyx announced. *'I'm one hundred per cent within you again.'* Nyx analysed the carnage around them in an instant. *'Put the bodies together. Make it look like they struggled. Oh, and remember not to leave your fingerprints everywhere. They are not something I've changed for you, as you still need them for access to certain areas of your workplace.'*

He pulled on his gloves again and went to grab the gunman. He lifted him over the counter and placed him on top of Joe's corpse. He wiped down the gun and tin of baked beans, then chucked them in the mix for good measure. Mason grabbed his miraculously undamaged bottle of wine off the counter as he made for the back door.

'Might as well enjoy this before they come and arrest me.'

'Why would anyone arrest you?' asked Nyx.

'Even if I got all my fingerprints, my sodding blood and DNA will be all over two dead bodies for a start. Won't take them long to find that,' said Mason.

'Need I remind you again, I am a biological artificial intelligence that alters DNA,' said Nyx sternly. *'I can assure you, there is no trace to your old DNA anywhere in this building.'* Then she brightened to her usual cheery manner. *'And I'll have your new DNA patterns updated again by tomorrow morning. Nothing in Joe's shop will lead back to you. Everything will be just fine.'*

The back door closed quietly behind him as he tried to walk calmly down the rear alleyway.

'Try telling that to Joe.'

Mason sat with a glass of orange juice on the sofa, having just eaten three large microwave meals to satisfy his intense hunger. In the end, the bottle of red wine had remained untouched in the kitchen. He'd also bagged all his clothes and dumped them in the shed. He'd burn them tomorrow in the company incinerator to cover his tracks. Not exactly foolproof, but it would have to do, though, the way he was feeling right now, he didn't really care either way.

Amanda had messaged him to say she'd be working very late and maybe even sleeping at the office, making up for lost time due to her hangover.

That woman is obsessed sometimes, thought Mason, though he was glad he didn't have to talk to her tonight. His head was a mess.

'*You should sleep*,' said Nyx after a few moments of silence. '*I need to finish my work on you, and you need to recover. You might be dead, but you still need your rest.*'

'Don't you ever sleep?'

'*I am not human*,' she reminded him. '*Anyway, if I stop functioning for any reason, then slowly, so would you.*'

He understood the implication, but decided he'd had enough for one day and was done asking any more questions. The problem was, he was still buzzing and didn't feel the least bit tired.

'*Oh, yes, melatonin*,' stated Nyx. There was another hot flush in Mason, and all of a sudden, he felt exhausted. He put down his glass and lay back along the sofa. Within three seconds, he was fast asleep.

Nyx contentedly observed Mason sleeping. His arm was nearly patched up, and the re-patterning of his DNA well underway. She checked on her research into increasing his intelligence, then, finally satisfied, she settled in to watch his vital functions for the rest of the night.

'*Sleep well*,' she said quietly, as he slept under her watchful gaze.

CHAPTER 5

Torching his clothes and trainers was surprisingly easy. Smuggled into the office inside his rucksack, all it took was a quick walk down to the incinerators, and then he shovelled them in. After which, he'd watched them burn away to atoms through the thick observation porthole. It made Mason wonder about adding some random stop-and-search checks for arrivals, besides the ones they already had for people leaving. Plus, they should definitely add some security cameras in the facilities area in the basement.

The early morning shift was quiet, and there were no test results from Richard. By the time it came to his mid-morning break, Mason decided to hunt Cora down and see if she'd had any early indications from his tests.

'*Cora seems nice*,' commented Nyx, as they made their way through the west wing of labs and offices. '*And she certainly appears to be of a higher moral capacity than the general level of your other acquaintances. I'm glad you're going to see her.*'

Uh-huh. Mason knocked on Cora's office door, her name etched into its glass. *Bloody hell, even an intern gets a nameplate here.* He waited for the door to click open, then walked in. *Now hush. You might be able to have thousands of conversations at once, but I'm good with just one at a time.*'

'Hello, Mr Granger,' replied Cora without turning from her monitor, a little window at the corner of the screen showing a video feed from the corridor.

Mason parked his arse on the end of her extended corner desk.

'Any results yet, Doc?'

She swivelled her chair around to look at him.

'Other than the fact that everything still points to you being medically dead, then no, there's nothing new.' She flicked a pen on the side of the desk while she studied him. 'Why, are you in a hurry?

Have you been asked to leave your current employment as well?'

Not quite, thought Mason as he ignored the barb. Then he surprised himself by blurting out about last night.

'Apart from the fact that someone tried to grab me at gunpoint yesterday, then no, I'm not particularly in a hurry,' he said pointedly.

'Not very funny,' she stated. When he didn't respond, she narrowed her eyes. 'Grand, I'm game for a laugh. It's been a slow morning. Who tried to kidnap you?'

He quickly considered how much to tell her.

'Could be someone I've pissed off in my past. But given what's going on right now, then my money's on someone who doesn't want me walking around with Nectr.'

Cora continued to study him, then came to a decision.

'You're being serious, aren't you?' Mason nodded. 'OK, Mr Granger, who doesn't want you walking around with Nectr?'

He got off the desk and moved over to the massive touchscreen on the wall, the one all covered with mathematical formula and graphs.

'I guess Richard should be at the top of the list, and possibly Sadie too, but more likely it's those idiots she's dealing with, depending on what they suspect.'

'What idiots?' asked Cora. 'And why on earth would your girlfriend want to kidnap you?' Mason ignored her questions, as he peered in closer at some of the small writing on the screen.

'Don't touch that.' Cora jumped up and shepherded him away from her precious screen. 'That's all my workings from yesterday.'

'All Greek to me.'

'It's about you, if you must know.' She encouraged him over to one of the spare chairs in the office.

'What's it say?' asked Mason.

'Before we get into that, are there any other complications I should know about?'

'*Honest and smart,*' piped up Nyx. '*I like her more and more.*'

Shush. Mason composed himself. 'Yeah, there are more complications, but probably safest for you if you don't know the details.'

A dry little laugh escaped Cora's lips. 'Ha, that's what they always say in the movies, right before the innocent party gets kidnapped, tortured and used against the hero, precisely because they didn't know what was going on.' She cast her eyes down at Mason. 'Not that you're hero material, Mr Granger'

'*And funny.*'

Mason ignored Nyx.

'Normally I'd love to talk about films all morning, Ms Gallagher, but right now I'd prefer to know more about what's going on with me.'

Cora sighed. 'As much as I find your character questionable, I'm also extremely curious about all this. Clearly there's been some incredibly significant breakthroughs with our work.' She pointed across at her workings. 'So, after my investigations last night, I did some more digging, but this time in the lead research team's files and not yours.'

She paused for a second, sizing Mason up once more.

'There's something wrong going on here,' she started. 'We have military contracts from governments around the world, including our own, but I'm not sure all the work is entirely legal. Our experiments often step outside the guidance.'

He huffed out a laugh. 'I reckon Richard would experiment on the Pope if it meant he could upgrade his limo to a private jet.'

A slight smile played across Cora's face, even touching as far as her green eyes.

'That's probably the most insightful words I've heard from you over the last two days.' She poked a finger at her screen. 'And certainly, more honest than the company we're working for, it appears.'

'Then why work for them?' Mason realised the harshness of his tone and softened his voice a little. 'I mean, I can understand the attraction of playing with billion-pound equipment, but you don't seem like the kind of person to be bought with favours. You know what they do here, why work for a military research contractor?'

'Because the science can be used for other things too,' stated Cora. 'There's a small subcompany that takes our weapons research and works on applications for it in other fields. Think of what can be done with our DNA-altering tech alone, if we can get it to work reliably.' Her face brightened at this. 'If I work for the company, then maybe I can push it from the inside to use more of its technology for something better.'

'Better to work with the Devil and steal his underpants, than try to spit in his eye from a distance.'

'Eh?' questioned Cora, her Irish accent cutting in a little harder.

'Never mind. Just something the captain used to say.' Mason stood back up, eager to be doing something. 'So, what do we do next?'

'We?' Cora waited a beat until Mason's face dropped, then she cracked a small smile at him. 'Just kidding. I'll be finishing these tests and handing the results over to Richard. Then I'm going to carry on digging. I want to know more about the company's progress with Nectr. We interns only see a portion of what's going on, but the last I saw it was not going well for the mice. Heaven forbid, it's been tested on any other people.'

'Thanks for the concern for my well-being.'

'Well, you're clearly still standing, aren't you?' Cora cut back. 'Someone else might not be so fortunate. There's something in the maths that's a bit too random for my liking, though some of the equations do look oddly familiar.'

'*She really is smart,*' said Nyx. '*We should tell her about me.*'

'No,' said Mason out loud.

'What do you mean "no"? Do you know something I don't?' asked Cora.

'Nothing,' said Mason. 'What do you mean about things being bad for the mice?'

Cora tapped at her keyboard and brought up some old video feeds on her screen. The mice on the screen looked like mice to Mason, playing, shagging, and the like.

'See that?' pointed Cora. Mason shook his head. She rolled her eyes. 'They've reverted to basic behaviour. Granted, they're very efficient at it, but worryingly there's no social interaction, no curiosity, no family group behaviour. They simply eat, sleep, reproduce, fight, and kill, nothing more, nothing less.'

Mason stared at the mice on the screen, watching two of them set about each other until one was dead. Then the victor started to eat it.

'Hold on, are you telling me you've made bloody zombie mice?'

'Don't be stupid,' replied Cora. 'There are no such things as zombies. When you're dead, you're dead.'

He pointed to himself.

'Alright, there's massive medical inconsistencies in your tests, but look at you, clearly you're not dead.'

'*Please, let's tell her*,' said Nyx. '*She really needs to know. She can't fully help us if she doesn't have all the information*.'

'Fine,' said Mason. 'And how do you propose we do that? She'll just think I'm mental.'

Cora paused for a second. 'Hold on, you're not talking to me, are you?'

'No,' replied Mason.

'Are you asking Nectr questions? Is it communicating with you?' Cora's voice rose in excitement. She didn't wait for Mason's reply, just furiously worked at her keyboard, transferring more data to the large screen. She then ran over to the wall.

'See this? I knew I'd seen those equations somewhere before,' said Cora, pointing at complex lines of symbols and numbers. 'This is some of Amanda's old research into experimental adaptive AI, trying to get the Nectr to improve itself, as well as its host. Absolutely fascinating in theory, but apparently it was incredibly expensive to make, and it never reliably worked in the simulations anyway, so it was abandoned on Mr Buckley's orders.'

Cora sat down on the nearest chair.

'I guess Amanda must have taken one of the prototype batches and added it to the Nectr she was going to test on you.'

She turned to stare at Mason. 'Fecking hell, the Nectr in you has developed itself enough to communicate with us. Does it really talk back to you?'

'You could say that,' said Mason. 'Cora meet Nectr, strain thirty-seven, vial ten. But we call her Nyx.'

Cora's jaw dropped and she leaned to prod Mason on the arm; almost as if to check he was real.

'Tell me everything,' she instructed in a hushed tone.

Ten minutes later, Cora leaned back again on her chair.

'Maybe you had a point. I'm not sure I did want to know all of that. You really have been accumulating a lot of problems. Aside from you being dead that is. Kind of.'

She swivelled her chair around whilst she continued to think.

'All of this information certainly helps though, and I so want to spend some serious time with Nyx. But to be honest, what I'm mostly thinking is, we should go to the authorities. Illegal experiments on humans, that's definitely on the wrong side of the tracks, to say the least.'

Mason liked her use of the word "we". It was the first time he'd heard that word in a long time without it coming loaded with self-interest from the speaker. However, he was less keen on her conclusion.

'I'd rather not. The company works for the government. What if they already know? Or they want to cut me up to find out what's going on? No human rights when you're dead, as far as I know.'

'But you're clearly not dead dead. You're not even officially recorded as dead.' Cora's tongue stuck out slightly as she searched for the right words. 'You're more like reanimated or undead.'

'Lovely,' Mason rubbed a hand down his face. 'How about you keep digging to find out more, and I'll work on who we can trust and who we can't? After that, we'll see.'

Before Cora could reply, Mason's phone rang. He looked down at the display and saw "*Psycho Amazonian*" come up on the screen.

'Speaking of my many devils.' He tapped at his phone. 'Yes, Boss?'

Cora started typing at her keyboard again, as Mason left her office. He turned right down the corridor and started heading for the security control room in anticipation of a meeting.

'How ya doing, Mason?' asked Sadie.

'Fine. What's up?'

'Meet me in the car park at lunchtime. We're eating out today.'

He sat across the picnic bench from Sadie in the far corner of the pub garden, their empty plates sitting between them. Mason sipped at his orange juice whilst she digested the story he'd just told her about the attack on him last night.

'I think they were from the company you're selling Nectr to.'

'And you let one go?' she asked in surprise. 'Not very smart.'

Mason shrugged. 'Not much choice really; he had a gun on me.'

Sadie huffed and her voice hardened. 'Don't you go soft on me, Mason.'

He held her look. 'Don't call me soft, bitch.'

Sadie opened her mouth and laughed. 'That's what I like to see.' She picked up her double JD and swilled the single ice cube around in the glass. 'We have a problem,' she said. Mason just raised an eyebrow and kept quiet. 'Richard has ordered the installation of additional scanners in all the entry and exit points. You know, the same ones we have in the airlocks to the labs. Looks like he's worried about someone sneaking Nectr out of the complex. It's not just random stop-and-search any more, full scanning for everyone.'

'Considering we're trying to steal Nectr, he might have a point,' said Mason.

'And he's got more cybersecurity checks underway. That won't bother us, I've already got the data. But getting any vials of Nectr out is going to be an issue.'

'So, what's the plan?' asked Mason. 'Just give them the data and take half the money?'

'Stop being a pussy.' She looked at him hard, as she started to lose what little rag she had. 'We're not going through all this for just half. I'm not just retiring to an island in the Caribbean, I'm buying one, and you don't want your thirty per cent being halved either. You won't get the island next to me for fifteen million quid, you know. We have a plan; we stick to it. It just got a little harder, that's all.'

'Hey, just a suggestion,' Mason held up his palms to calm her down. Despite his anger at the heavy narcissism in her comments, he knew confrontation never went down well with Sadie. He rolled all this around in his head, trying to figure a different angle to put her off stealing any more shit from the company. 'There's another issue. Richard's looking to get you fired at the end of the week. He's digging about in your history with the marines, and even if he doesn't find anything, he's going to have something made up that looks bad.'

'Doesn't matter, we'll be gone by then anyway. I've squared things away with Dave. They bought our lay-by story and even upped the price to compensate for our troubles, but the schedule's moved up. The delivery has to happen tomorrow evening.'

'How do we get the vial?'

'I'll worry about that,' replied Sadie. 'You just do your job as the muscle and think about all that money you'll be making.' She looked down at her own huge arms and corrected herself. 'Extra muscle.'

Mason sipped at his drink again and nudged over the second JD he'd bought for Sadie.

'I'll drive us back to the office.' As she took a slug, he tried his best to sound casual. 'You sure we can trust them? Not like I even know who we're risking our balls for.'

'Don't get all squirrelly on me now. This lot are not people we want to screw with,' said Sadie. This time there was an edge of fear in her voice, something Mason didn't hear very often from the crazy bitch. 'They're not some rival company; this lot are more than that.' She leaned in over the table of the bench and gestured for Mason to do the same. Perfume and JD mixed in the afternoon air as she spoke. 'When Dave described them to me, I called them the Billionaires' Club, and he said that's as good a name as any. There are companies involved indirectly, but it's more of a club of really rich and powerful people. And I mean really, really rich.'

She took another slug of JD. 'I tried offering Nectr around to rival companies. Some said "no" as they thought it was all bullshit and science fiction, never going to work, but plenty put in bids and would pay well if I could get it. But the BC made the best offer by far, in fact, five times better.'

He let out a low whistle, and wondered quite how close to thirty per cent his cut actually was. But in all reality, it didn't matter for two reasons. First, it sounded like his cut was thirty million pounds, and second, there was no way he was going to go through with this now.

She clinked her glass on Mason's. 'You and me, babe. Rich beyond our wildest dreams. Free to drink and shag our days away in luxury.' She put a hand on his forearm and squeezed hard. 'So, don't lose your shit now, Mason. Show me that ruthless bastard I met six months ago.'

He reached over and took hold of her hand. He started with the little finger and twisted it back hard, then he pinned her hand to the table and ground it into the wood.

She grinned back at him, enjoying the pain. 'That's what I like to see, lover boy.'

The streets were fairly quiet on the way back to the office, and he drove the big Land Rover through them with little thought. Sadie was chatting away in the passenger seat about how she was going to spend her first three million pounds. Mason grunted the odd reply, but his mind was mostly elsewhere.

Blimey, that woman is hard work, my old self must have been mental to start an affair with her, thought Mason.

'*Some of your judgements before you died were certainly questionable, yes*,' said Nyx brightly. '*But they are improving day by day, especially now I'm starting to make you a little smarter.*'

What?

'*My experiments to make you more intelligent are yielding some results*,' explained Nyx. '*I won't be able to make you as smart as Amanda, and definitely not as smart as Cora. The source material you have is somewhat poor. But I will make a clever man of you yet, Mason Granger.*'

He drove through the gates to the complex and pulled into the car park. *We need to teach you some tact.*

'*Why would I need that?*' smiled Nyx innocently. '*My way is much more enjoyable.*'

Mason parked up and turned off the car. He jumped out and beeped the locks after Sadie had joined him. He chucked her the keys over the bonnet.

'Pub tonight?' she asked. 'Just you and me.'

'Nah, I'm tired.' He faked a yawn. 'Big day tomorrow and I want to go home for some rest.'

Sadie didn't look happy, but Mason turned and headed to the main entrance before she could say another word.

Six hours later, Mason was sitting on his sofa with his feet up, this time a large glass of red wine sat in his hand already half finished.

'That is good.'

'*It is very pleasant*,' agreed Nyx. '*I would be very happy for you to continue drinking that bottle.*'

'Maybe not too much,' he said. 'I might not be tired, but I wasn't kidding when I said to Sadie it's a big day tomorrow. You know, figuring out what Amanda's up to, selling the company's secrets to a bunch of billionaires, all whilst hiding everything from Richard. Not sure I could handle a hangover as well as all the shit that's going on right now.'

'*The average human can process away one unit of alcohol in one hour, within certain tolerances*,' started Nyx. '*When over five units of alcohol are consumed, the effects of a hangover will be likely, depending on environmental circumstances and volume of consumption. The scale ranges from mild headache, through to wishing you were dead, and then on to actually being dead if alcohol poisoning occurs.*'

Mason looked at the wine in his hand. 'What the hell.' He took another sip and enjoyed the tiny rush it brought. 'Did you have a point to your monologue?'

'*After my general upgrades to your body, as well as strength and resilience of your muscles, bones and flesh, your kidneys and liver are now fully repaired and vastly upgraded. They can happily process all manner of toxins from your body far more efficiently.*' She grinned at him, as she also savoured the wine. '*You can process one unit of alcohol from your body in one minute if we wish. And you could drink many more units before you got any symptoms of a hangover.*'

'Ha, every grown man's dream,' Mason laughed. 'Forget that Billionaires' Club, Sadie should have tried the brewing companies. They'd pay a fortune for that and probably wouldn't be running around trying to kidnap or kill me.'

The doorbell went, and Mason's good humour disappeared. He put down his wine and walked to the front door. He tapped at the small screen next to it and the image showed a lone man. No guns or weapons in sight, but Mason tensed regardless. The man rang the doorbell again, and then called out.

'Mr Granger, it's the police.'

'Oh great, that's all I need.' Mason opened the door. 'ID please.'

The short, stocky man observed Mason's stance and slowly reached into his pocket to bring out his badge. He held it up steadily before him.

'DS Carter,' he added for completeness.

'OK. Can I help you?'

DS Carter continued to size Mason up.

'Could we have this discussion inside, sir?' He nodded as if he had made up his mind about something. 'You seem a little tense. Maybe if you're sitting more comfortably, then you could relax and answer my questions.'

Fight or flight flashed across Mason's mind, then he decided on the third option for a change.

'Sure. Come on in.'

They sat on opposite sides of the coffee table. Carter with an untouched orange juice and Mason with his wine. Mason felt a little déjà vu, picturing Richard sitting there what seemed like a million years ago, just after this crap had kicked off with him waking up dead. He tried to relax his body and expression, but the fight or flight instinct persisted.

'Thank you for the orange juice,' said Carter. He took out a notebook. 'I'm following up on an incident at the shop two streets away. I understand you go in there from time to time. Is that correct?'

Mason's heart spiked, then Nyx released a burst of serotonin into his system and he instantly relaxed.

'*That should help you,*' she said.

Now his head was clearing a little, Mason decided to go with the truth, albeit missing out one or two of the more incriminating details.

'Yeah, I do shop there. I go there quite often as it goes. Joe's good to me. Always keeps a few bottles of my favourite wine stocked.' He raised his glass to Carter.

'Were you in the shop last night?'

'Yup, after I got back from work. Picked up this bottle in fact. What's this about?'

Carter made a note in his little book, his movements precise and efficient.

'We'll come to that in a moment, sir.' He turned a page over and studied the next one in silence.

Mason knew what Carter was doing, so he dutifully obliged and filled the silence.

'Don't think I've seen a paper notebook for a few years. We all use our phones at work. You look a bit like something from an old

TV show.'

Carter glanced up from his book. 'If you're going to make a joke about *The Sweeny*, don't bother, I've heard them all before,' he said seriously, his well-spoken accent taking on a slight cutting edge.

'Nah, no point. You don't look anything like Dennis Waterman.' Mason waited a beat. 'What with you being black and all that.' Mason thought he saw a tiny twitch of a smile before Carter wiped it away.

'Very funny, sir, though you might want to be careful with jokes like that. Not all police officers are as open-minded as I am.' He returned to his notebook to study it further. 'And the night before last, where were you then?'

'Out with a friend,' replied Mason noncommittally. His body started to tense again despite Nyx's best efforts. 'Look, what's all this about?'

Carter wrote something down then carefully closed his notebook.

'I'm afraid there was an attempted robbery at Joe's shop last night, resulting in two deaths. There was also an altercation in a lay-by a few miles from here, the night before that. Someone tried to cover it up but, the thing is, it's amazing how hard it is to wash blood out of grass.' He looked pointedly at Mason. 'That particular event occurred right after you were seen speeding out of a park nearby on your motorbike.'

'Is Joe alright?' asked Mason, ignoring the implications.

'No, he is not,' replied Carter, he studied Mason's face while he continued. 'There were some motorbike tyre marks at the lay-by.' Carter waited a beat. 'Tenuous links most people might think, but I like to be thorough, and those small links led me here.'

I bet thorough doesn't cover the half of it, thought Mason. He noticed the wedding band on Carter's finger. *Heaven help your wife or husband, the poor bastard probably has to line up the forks in the drawer.*

They sat and watched each other in silence for a moment, neither man wanting to break first. Then Nyx brought something to Mason's attention, something he had known in the back of his mind but not quite twigged.

He leaned back on the sofa and relaxed further.

'Here on your own, I see.' He saw the flicker of an expression in

Carter's face, the realisation that he'd been rumbled. 'No partner with you. You're not on the clock, are you? This is all unofficial, isn't it?'

Carter stood up. 'Not entirely.' He reached slowly into another pocket and produced a slip of paper. He handed it to Mason, as he walked past him towards the door to the hallway.

'What's this?' asked Mason.

'A notice of intent to prosecute, or you can take the fine and three points on your license,' replied Carter. 'It's illegal to drive a motorbike in a public park.' He made for the front door. 'I'm nothing if not thorough.' As Mason followed him along the hall, Carter gave him a mock salute. 'I'll be seeing you again, Sergeant.'

Mason closed the door and leaned his head on its cool surface.

'Bloody hell. As if I don't have enough on my plate already.'

He sat on the sofa finishing his wine with half an eye on the TV. Joe's murder had made the news briefly, and it had refilled Mason with sadness. He toasted his glass to the screen for the third time.

'Sorry, mate.' He glanced at his watch and sighed. 'Time for bed I suppose. Big day tomorrow.'

'*Would you like me to release more melatonin to help you sleep?*' asked Nyx.

Mason considered her question then something further occurred to him.

'Am I really me any more? Or is this just you driving a Mason suit about?'

'*No. I have changed you, but I'm not being you.*'

'What about making me feel tired, huh?'

'*I can control the production and release of your hormones as needed, but I don't control you.*'

'Lovely.' Mason let out a dry laugh. 'That's not controlling me at all.'

'*I only exist to help you, Mason Granger.*'

He thought he detected a slight edge of anxiety to her voice.

'It's OK, Nyx, I appreciate what you've done for me, I really do. Let's face it; I wouldn't even be here if it wasn't for you.'

Nyx brightened. '*Thank you,*' she said earnestly.

He felt her flick through his memories, then a song started

playing in his head. Tinkling from an old piano echoed around his mind. Then the most beautiful voice he'd heard in a long time filled his head.

'Not my usual kind of thing,' Mason said. 'Where'd you get this from?'

'*You humans remember more than you realise,*' replied Nyx. '*This is all reconstructed from your own memories.*'

'What's it called?' asked Mason, as the music embraced him. 'It's beautiful.'

'*"Crazy". As sung by Patsy Cline.*'

A wry grin crept across Mason's face, and he settled back into the sofa, relaxation drifting through his body.

'You're a funny old stick, Nyx, but thanks.'

CHAPTER 6

The annoying sound of his alarm roused him out of a deep sleep, and Mason poked at the screen on his phone to put it on snooze. He rolled over and faced Amanda sleeping next to him. He remembered her slinking into bed during the night like she often did after working late, trying not to wake him but failing as usual.

He briefly thought about waking her up in a pleasant way. He watched her breathe and was in awe of her intense beauty as always, but weirdly he had none of the usual burning desire for her. Hell, forget making love to Amanda, he still didn't even particularly want to have sex with her.

Crap, my world really has gone to shit, hasn't it. When you don't find Amanda seductive, you might as well just pack up your balls and walk off a cliff. He huffed out a breath and turned off his alarm. With nothing else for it, he got up to get ready for work.

Walking into the en-suite, he checked his phone and saw there was a message from Sadie. The meet with the Billionaires' Club was confirmed for ten past eight tonight. *Oh, good, the madness continues.*

He leaned against his bike in the car park at the end of the day. Sadie came walking over and Mason stood up.

'Where to, Boss?'

'Disused warehouse at the end of the old industrial estate across the A1,' replied Sadie. She beeped the Land Rover and got in. 'Follow me.'

Yeah, because that's not suspicious. Mason got on his motorbike and fired it up.

Being a Thursday evening, the traffic was heavier with people starting the weekend early. No sweat for Mason's bike, but a hindrance for Sadie's Land Rover, and they arrived at the warehouse five minutes late. They parked up next to two nondescript, dark cars, turning their vehicles about instinctively before they turned them off, just in case a hasty exit was needed. Mason placed his helmet on the seat and followed Sadie through the large, open doors, unclipping the safety strap holding his Taser as he went.

They entered some kind of loading bay and the place smelt dank and disused. The lighting was dim, but Mason could see the four mercenaries before them well enough. Dark suits with those small telltale bulges again.

Two cars, four people? Nah, not likely. I wonder where the rest are?

Sadie stopped about ten feet from the group and waited, Mason paused a couple of feet to her left and just behind.

'*You can hear someone behind the old crates to our left. Their chewing gum is louder than they realise,*' offered Nyx helpfully. '*And there's maybe another person hidden on the walkway above. That or a really large cat.*'

Sadie nodded to the man in the middle of the group.

'Dave.'

'Evening, Sadie,' he replied, a slight London accent clipping his words. 'You got everything we requested?'

She slowly drew a memory stick from her pocket and threw it over to Dave. He caught it perfectly and slipped it into his pocket.

'Nice one,' he said. 'And the sample?'

Sadie turned and looked at Mason.

He stared back at her. 'What? I don't have the vial. You said you'd get it.'

Sadie stepped away and Dave nodded to the other mercenaries before calmly drawing his own gun.

'Mason, me old chum, you can drop the pretence. We know what's going on.' He took a phone out of his pocket, dialled a number and put it on speaker. 'Mr George would like to speak with you directly,' he said while he waited for it to connect.

The phone connected and a digitally altered voice came out of it, a slight Liverpool twang to the alteration.

'Good evening, Mr Granger. I am afraid your cybersecurity team is not nearly as good as you believe, and we've been in your systems for the last two days. We know you have Nectr running through your veins, courtesy of your lovely wife. We would like a sample of that

Nectr, so if you would be so kind as to accompany our man Dave, then we can start the extraction process and negotiate some suitable compensation for you. This, I'm afraid, is not open for negotiation.' The line disconnected.

'Looks like you're coming with us.' Dave looked around them and smiled. 'No park benches to throw at us this time. Although, I should probably thank you for that. Got me that promotion I've been after when you mashed up my boss.' He waved his gun at Sadie. 'Be a love, would you, and take Mason's Taser. Don't want any nasty accidents. Then you're free to collect all that money you like so much.'

Sadie bristled at the way he addressed her but did as she was told.

'Sorry,' she said as she leaned in. 'If it was the choice between the money and the old Mason, then you might have stood a chance, but this new Mason, not so much. So, I think I'll cash in my chips now and just go find myself a new boyfriend.'

As she walked towards the doors, Dave called out to her.

'Don't go too far, Sadie. Not until our science geeks have verified everything. I'd really hate to have to get on a plane and come hunt you down in the Caribbean.'

Despite the size of the large door, Sadie managed to slam it with a loud bang on her way out. Dave shrugged to Mason.

'Women, huh. Always so emotional.' He kept his silenced gun calmly levelled at Mason. 'Now me, on the other hand, all business I am. Nothing personal, you're just the package I need to deliver.' He unclipped some handcuffs from his belt and threw them over to Mason. 'Put these on, will you.'

Mason stood there in silence and ignored the handcuffs he'd just caught. Now he concentrated, he could hear what Nyx had been talking about. One mercenary behind the crates and another on the walkway. His eyes flicked between the four in front of him. There, the one on the end, sweat forming on his brow, that one was the weak spot. Not much good that would do him, though. Six of them in total, all added up to shite odds.

Dave coughed. 'Are we boring you, mate?' He pointed his gun at Mason's knee. 'Nobody said you had to be unharmed, so we can happily do this the hard way if you'd like.'

The man on the walkway above stood up and shouted down at them all.

'Police! Drop your weapons now,' called out DS Carter, waving his badge in front of him as if it was some kind of all-powerful, magical shield.

'Get down, you stupid tosser,' shouted Mason, but his words were too late, as Dave turned instinctively and shot DS Carter through the chest.

Everything stopped for a second as the mercenaries around Dave all realised the implications of killing a policeman. The stakes had just risen massively.

'Triple pay,' said Dave instantly.

Mason felt the rage building in him, despite the guns still trained upon him.

'He might have been an annoying twat, but I kind of liked him. He actually cared about his job that one,' Mason clenched his fists and cracked his knuckles. 'Right, you wankers, let's have it.'

As DS Carter's body tipped over the railings and slammed into the concrete floor, Nyx lit up Mason's body with adrenaline. Training kicked in, and Mason was sprinting sideways across the room towards the old wooden crates, bullets ricocheting all around him. Two seconds later, he smashed through the crates to take down the dark-suited woman who was trying to aim her gun at him.

He grabbed her gun, and it went off in his hand, the bullet going clean through, blood spraying out from the new hole in his palm. But he just tightened his grip and slammed the gun into her nose, breaking it and driving both cartilage and shattered bone straight up into her brain. Not even pausing to watch her topple, he spun around to see the others advancing on him, guns level and firing. Mason ran along behind the crates, taking the woman's gun with him. Bullet impacts followed him like a trail of kamikaze exploding wasps. Out of the corner of his eye, he noticed Dave slipping out the warehouse door. *Good, at least that's one less to worry about.*

He hunkered down behind a pile of old scrap as bullets pinged off it. It looked like bits of an old printing press or something. He shot a quick glance around the corner and saw the remaining three mercenaries now fanned out, guns up, firing and reloading in alternate goes.

'*Mason?*' said Nyx.

I'm kind of busy, Nyx. Mason checked the magazine of the gun he'd taken. It felt like it was nearly full, probably ten or so shots in it. OK, one in three needed to hit and kill the mercenaries. Not great odds, but a whole shit ton better than before.

'*Mason Granger, you should listen to what I have to say*,' she persisted. '*If you act now, you can most likely disable them all. I have enhanced your speed and intelligence to the point where you can successfully anticipate the shots and trajectories from all three guns at once, based on each person's body language and stance. And they will certainly be surprised by you leaping out from behind this cover.*'

Them and me both. Mason tensed. *OK, when?*

Nyx paused for a beat then started her countdown.

'*Three, two, one, now.*'

Mason leapt sideways from behind the old machinery. Guns turned to fire at him, and he subtly altered his positioning and direction. Bullets clipped at his clothes, and one tore a small chunk from his bicep, but none found their intended mark. Whereas, in a blur of movement, his first two shots found theirs and one of the mercenaries flew back, blood spraying from the twin holes in his skull.

'One down, two to go.' Mason continued his run and slid in behind some more crates. Bullets smashed through the old wood, and he took off again. This time running diagonally across the mercenaries' path. Again, he tracked their movements and shots in his head, subtly avoiding the bullets until one smashed through his shoulder and spun him to the ground. 'Bugger, that's not supposed to happen.'

'*Oh dear, it appears you need to practise that skill some more*,' commented Nyx.

Mason rolled fast on the ground, bullets smashing into the concrete after him. Then sirens filled the air, and the remaining mercenaries immediately stopped firing. They looked at each other in silent communication then turned and ran for their car.

He sat up and poked at his shoulder. Blood oozed out, but

there was no flood. He sat there for a few seconds and noticed that his heart was barely beating. And even more surprisingly, with the adrenaline now wearing off, there was no pain.

'Why can't I feel anything?' he asked Nyx.

'*Oh, you can, I'm just absorbing the pain for you as part of my core programming,*' she replied. '*It is almost impossible for me to allow you to feel pain, but look at what happens if I even let a small percentage through.*' A sensation of extreme effort from Nyx flashed across Mason's mind, then pain hit him like a fist, practically blinding him with its intensity. An instant later it was gone.

'Christ, that hurt.' Mason stumbled to his feet, as the sirens got louder.

'*Yes, it does,*' said Nyx simply.

'We need to get out of here before the police arrive.' He walked across the loading bay then stopped. 'Shit, police.' He did an about-turn and ran for Carter's body. He bent down and touched Carter's still warm neck. Surprise, surprise, no pulse. 'Can you help him?' he asked Nyx. 'You know, bring him back like me?'

'*Yes,*' said Nyx. '*However, given his extensive range of injuries, it will take a significant portion of myself to do that, more than the twenty per cent I tried with Joe. Quite possibly this will take as much as thirty per cent. Higher would be better, but it's important to keep the majority of myself within you to fulfil my programming.*'

'Do it,' said Mason. 'Just don't make him like Joe.'

'*That is all about chance, as I told you, I cannot control that.*' She readied herself. '*Do I still have your permission to bring back DS Carter?*'

'Yes, and fast. Those sirens are getting closer.'

'*Poke your fingers into his bullet wounds, that will suffice to get me in there.*'

Mason leaned in towards Carter with his hands, then changed his mind and gave the man a quick kiss on the lips.

'He deserved better than a poke.' He wiped his mouth on his sleeve. 'No tongues though, mate. I don't like you that much.'

Nyx spoke up almost immediately. '*As I expected, this will take the full attention of the thirty per cent of me I have transferred into DS Carter.*' She paused for a second for further assessment. '*And several hours to complete.*'

Picking up Carter's body, Mason heaved it over his shoulder.

'Can't very well leave you here, mate.'

He walked out to the car park, sirens now screaming across the industrial estate far too loudly for comfort.

He grabbed his helmet off his bike and jammed it on Carter's head. Then he sat Carter on the bike and got on himself. Immediately, Carter's body slid off and smacked into the crumbling concrete.

'Crap, crap, crap.' Mason got off is bike and repeated the manoeuvre. Then he grabbed Carter's hands, pulled them around his own waist, finally handcuffing them together to keep the man secure, hopefully.

He started the bike and sped away, lights off, as the first of five police cars pulled into the car park.

Cora opened the door to her flat and held out the twenty-pound note.

'Keep the change,' she said, rubbing at her tired eyes.

'That's very kind of you,' replied Mason, trying to keep DS Carter's body upright against the wall beside him. 'But I'm not sure that's going to cover what I need.'

Cora squeaked, jumped back, and tried to slam the door shut, all in one jumbled mess of movement. Mason's hand caught the door, and he pushed past Cora, dragging Carter with him.

'Lovely place you've got here,' he announced, as he dumped Carter on one sofa and took the other for himself. For obvious reasons, he was relieved to see they were dark leather and hopefully easy to clean. 'Not many flats are big enough for two sofas.'

Cora closed the door and walked over slowly. She sat in one of the two armchairs and stared alternately at Mason and the body on her sofa.

'Is he dead?' she asked eventually.

'Yes, and no,' Mason pulled a cushion from behind him and leaned back into the well-worn but comfy leather. 'Nyx is in there working her magic on him. We'll see how he turns out in a few hours.'

Cora stared at Mason. 'Where to even start? OK, let's see. What the hell are you doing here? Whoever said I'd help you cover up your crimes?'

'I didn't kill him,' said Mason automatically. 'And yours was the first address I came to in the list of people I trust.'

'Address you came to?'

'Yeah, you know, in the HR records.' He looked about the flat, wondering where the kitchen was. Just like last time, he was ravenous after all the action.

'*Nourishment would be very advisable,*' agreed Nyx. '*It will give me extra materials needed for your repair, enable me to speed up your recovery.*'

Mason turned back to Cora. 'Were you waiting for a takeaway? Could you add something for me? Nyx says I need materials for her repairs.'

'Don't change the subject,' said Cora, though she did reach for her phone to add to the order. 'Accessing the HR records breaks all manner of GDPR rules. Did you not go to the training?'

He shrugged. 'More like guidelines I thought.'

Cora huffed at the clear lack of respect for her privacy. 'More to the point, why me?'

'Well, that list of people I trust, that Nyx trusts, currently stands at one. And you're it.'

'When I said I wanted to spend some serious time with Nyx, this wasn't quite what I meant.' The doorbell went, making her jump.

'Nyx says that's probably the delivery person at your door, judging by the resigned trudging step of their walk outside in the corridor.' Mason opened his palms towards Cora. 'Off you go and answer it. If you want to run, I won't stop you. In or out, it has to be your choice. All I ask is that you give me a few hours of peace here for DS Carter to recover.'

Cora's eyes went wide. 'You killed a policeman!'

'I didn't kill him,' repeated Mason.

Slowly Cora stood, almost in a daze, and made for the hallway to her front door. Mason heard the door open, and a few pleasantries exchanged. Then Cora came back into the living room with a big paper bag full of great-smelling food.

'Yours will be here in fifteen minutes,' stated Cora, but she went into the kitchen and came back with two plates anyway, and some chopsticks. She put a plate down in front of Mason. 'I deliberately order too much, it makes a nice dinner the next day, so you can have some too if you want. Just don't eat all my favourite bits.'

Mason picked up the chopsticks and wondered how to use them, then he also wondered how the hell he was supposed to know what her favourite bits were. In the end he, watched Cora dig in and just tried his best to avoid her first picks.

In between shovelling food into her mouth, Cora stared off into the distance thinking. Eventually she came to a decision.

'Alright, I'll help you with this.' She looked over to Carter. 'Will he make it?'

'Nyx, what do you reckon?' asked Mason.

'*Estimated success rate is ninety per cent and climbing*,' she replied in Mason's head. '*By my projections, DS Carter should be fully functional by four p.m. tomorrow. I'll keep him unconscious until then to aid his recovery.*'

'Yes,' said Mason to Cora. 'And Nyx will keep him asleep until he's fixed, so he won't be any bother.'

Cora eyed Mason. 'Is that exactly what she said?'

'Mostly, kind of,' admitted Mason.

'*Let me talk to Cora directly*,' said Nyx.

'How?' asked Mason.

'Are you talking to me or Nyx?' asked Cora. Mason put his finger to his lips to quieten her.

'*I can put a little of myself into Cora. One per cent should be more than enough*,' said Nyx to Mason. '*Not enough to be able to change her significantly, but plenty to establish communications.*'

'OK,' said Mason. 'And how exactly do we do that?'

'*Well, you could kiss her if you wanted.*'

He looked at Cora. Pleasant enough looking, but he reckoned she wouldn't be too impressed.

'Or?' he asked Nyx.

'*Lick your hand and then ask her to lick that.*'

'Nyx wants to put one per cent of herself into you, so she can talk to you directly.'

He stood up, licked his hand and walked over to Cora, holding it out.

'What's this?' she asked.

'Lick my hand. There's enough of Nyx in my saliva to set up communications, but not enough to change you. You should be safe enough.'

'Yuk, I'm not licking your hand,' stated Cora firmly.

'Or I could kiss you instead.'

Cora grabbed his hand and licked it. She sat there and waited.

'How long does the process normally take?' she asked.

'Not long at all,' smiled Nyx. *'Pleased to meet you, Cora Gallagher. I'm Nyx.'*

Cora gasped and temporarily forgot all about the dead body laid out on her sofa.

'Wow, tell me everything,' she said in hushed tones.

Mason polished off the second delivery of Chinese food whilst Cora and Nyx talked. He found it strangely comforting to listen to them. It was as if each had found a long-lost friend. There wasn't much he'd done right in his life, but this might well be one of the good things.

Cora sat back on the armchair, as Nyx finished her summary.

'That's quite the few days you've had, Mr Granger.' After all that Nyx had told her, the tone of her voice had now slightly softened towards him. 'And some rather large changes that have happened to you.'

'What, like being dead?' he said, after he finished the last mouthful of food.

'One more thing,' interrupted Nyx in their heads. *'I can converse with you both at the same time or talk to you separately as the situation needs. But Cora, please note, Mason will always be my primary objective. You are a truly lovely human being, but I'm programmed to protect Mason no matter the consequences. All my other interactions are of a secondary concern.'*

Cora blushed slightly at the compliment. 'OK. Thank you for letting me know,' she said sincerely.

Nyx continued brightly. *'And I can connect your minds as well if you want, so you can listen to each other's thoughts too. Shall I get started on that?'*

'No,' they both announced at the same time.

Mason thought for a second. 'But maybe you could install some kind of phone line. You know, so we could call each other in our heads and answer if we wanted. Is that possible?'

'Phone line?' questioned Cora. 'Do you live in the eighties? Who says that any more?'

This time Mason looked a little embarrassed. 'If you must know, I shared a love of old action films from the eighties and nineties with a mentor of mine. I picked up a few habits from watching them once too often.'

Cora took a guess. 'Captain Shaw? The one you got killed?'

'*Done*,' said Nyx proudly, interrupting once more. '*You can now call each other whenever you like. Go on, Mason, try it out.*'

He ignored Cora's question and just thought of her instead, then an old-style set of mobile phone number tones echoed around his head. He couldn't help but smile as he recognised their sound, Nyx clearly picking up on his love of those old action movies.

'*Yes*,' answered Cora in Mason's mind.

'*Loud and clear*,' he replied.

'*Off*,' said Cora.

'Weird,' said Cora out loud, then a smile lit up her face. 'But amazing.' She walked over to Carter and laid a hand on his forehead. A serious look returned to her face. 'Hot but not overly so.' She picked up his wrist and took his pulse. 'Ten beats per minute. It's a good job he's already dead.'

'*I'm slowing Carter's body function to the bare minimum, while I repair his major systems*,' clarified Nyx. '*He's far too weak to wake up and feed, so I'm making use of the resources already within his body. He may lose a little weight.*'

'Well, he was bloody heavy to carry, so no harm there then.' Mason stood up and looked at his watch. 'Right, I need to go. Get myself home.'

Cora looked at him incredulously. 'And leave a dead policeman in my flat?'

'Well, I can't exactly take him with me, can I?' Mason dug out his motorbike keys from his pocket. 'Probably not a good idea for Amanda to find out about Nyx bringing back the dead.' He corrected himself. 'More of the dead.'

Cora stared down at Carter. 'What if he wakes up?'

'*Don't worry, I'll keep him unconscious until you both finish work tomorrow evening*,' said Nyx.

'Would you at least like to take the cuffs off him?' asked Cora. 'That might knock a couple of years off my jail sentence when the police raid my flat and find him on my sofa.'

'Sorry, not my cuffs, don't have the keys.' Mason held out his hands in apology. 'I'll meet you at work tomorrow. You see what more you can dig up from the company research files, see what else they're up to. I'll give it a go with Amanda to see what I can find out, maybe she'll let something slip when I tell her a sanitised version of tonight's events.'

Cora slumped back down in the armchair.

'Don't worry, Cora,' said Nyx. *'I can't promise that everything will be alright, but we will look after you, won't we Mason?'*

'Yes, we will,' he said, surprising himself by how much he truly meant it.

Stopping at the end of his road, Mason stared down at his bloodied clothes and wondering where to start with his half-truths for Amanda. His phone rang and he looked at the screen. "*Mad Scientist Wife*" glared back at him. *Here goes.* He answered the phone.

'Hi, Amanda,' he said. 'I'm nearly home.'

'Mason, you scoundrel, have you been causing trouble again?' she asked, her voice all honey and sunshine. 'Nothing I hope either of us will regret too much?'

'Don't worry, Sadie's in the past now,' he replied honestly. 'And it's a very good bet we shan't be seeing her face ever again.'

His phone was quiet for a few seconds. 'Good,' announced Amanda. 'Now, you had better get your wayward bottom back here and tell me all about your day. The police called to say they'll be paying us a visit in twenty minutes. They would like to ask you some questions about a missing person.'

'Ah.' Mason glanced down again at his clothes. 'In which case, you'd better meet me at the back door with a black bin bag.'

Mason sat on the sofa with a glass of wine, the first half of the bottle already polished off for good effect. His clothes were bagged and in the loft, ready for another torching tomorrow, and he'd briefed Amanda about Sadie's betrayal of the company; albeit leaving out any mention of one dead policeman, and his own previous involvement in Sadie's scheme. Amanda had called Richard while Mason showered. Her boss had been delighted that Nectr was safe and still in their hands, though he was less pleased about the missing data and the confirmation that Sadie was the leak. He'd also asked what else

Mason knew about this Billionaires' Club and their attempt to steal Nectr. After that, 'I will be getting my people on it,' was all Richard had said before he'd hung up. Then finally, Amanda had called the company lawyer.

Opposite Mason and Amanda sat DI Jones and DCI Cuthbert. *Heavy hitters for just a missing person*, thought Mason. *They know something for sure.*

'Does my husband need a lawyer? asked Amanda pleasantly. 'I can have one here in fifteen minutes if need be.'

DI Jones spoke first. 'We'd just like to ask a few questions. No need for a lawyer. Unless you feel you should have one?' He brought out a notebook and placed it on the coffee table in front of them.

'Not you as well?' said Mason. 'Is there some new rule at the Met bringing back the written word?'

DI Jones remained silent, just tilted his head slightly and waited for Mason to continue.

'There was one of your lot here yesterday, a DS Carter. Asked a couple of questions then gave me a ticket for driving in the park.' Mason shrugged. 'Seemed like a bit of a waste for a DS, but he insisted on being thorough. Annoying little…' Mason paused and considered his choice of words more carefully. 'Annoying man.' He indicated to DCI Cuthbert. 'Seeing as you're here too, mam, I'm guessing the missing person is DS Carter, right?'

DCI Cuthbert picked up Carter's notebook. She held it up. 'This is DS Carter's Wednesday notebook and there's a fair few mentions of you within it.' She passed it back to Jones. 'And when we find him and his Thursday notebook, I suspect there will be a few more.' Her look hardened. 'I don't like it when my people go missing.'

'Where were you tonight, Mr Granger?' asked DI Jones.

Mason picked up the bottle of wine and toasted them with it. 'Drinking wine with my wife while we watched crap on Netflix.' Then he thought about his still cooling motorbike outside. *Shit.*

'Now Mason, my dear, tell the truth,' said Amanda.

His heart stopped briefly, then he realised what Amanda had just said and he relaxed ever so slightly. *She never says "my dear", that woman is up to something.*

'He's all embarrassed, you see.' She put down her beer. 'We had that same old argument about getting a dog, and I was starting to win. Mason does get a little cross when he's losing a battle, so he went for a quick ride on his bike to cool down.' Amanda smiled at the detectives opposite. 'Any more questions we can help with, officers?'

DCI Cuthbert stood up and straightened her jacket. 'None for now.' She paused for a second then turned to DI Jones. 'Put in a call to the station and get them to send a squad car here to breathalyse Mr Granger.' She held Mason's glare as she headed to the hallway. 'Best to be thorough.'

Mason lay back in bed. 'Thank god today is finally finished,' he said to Amanda lying beside him, meaning every word of it.

'Oh, don't worry. The company lawyers will get the breathalyser test thrown out of court. They'll just say there's no proof you didn't drink most of the wine after you got back from your bike ride.'

She snaked a hand over to Mason and started to grope around.

'We've been running all those tests on you at work,' she said, 'and now I think I'd like to run some tests on you myself, personally.'

He rolled towards his naked wife and all of a sudden sex seemed like quite a good idea. *What the hell, maybe she'll scream out all her secrets while we're shagging.*

CHAPTER 7

Seven a.m. the next morning, Mason listened to the front door close and lay back in bed contentedly. In the end, sex had been damn good, and he'd even surprised himself with how attentive he'd been. Something else that had clearly changed in him.

'Ha, James Bond, with a sensitive side,' he announced to the empty room.

He climbed out of bed and headed for the shower with a smile on his face. It wasn't enough to make him forget all his troubles, but it was a small victory in the scarred battlefield that was now his life. He showered and got ready for work, then relaxed for twenty minutes whilst he made himself a cooked breakfast. He threw a couple of eggs in the pan, sliced the ham and chopped up some vine tomatoes and half a red onion. Bagels under the grill, a slither of butter on each, and then he was done. He sat and ate at the kitchen table.

Feeling somewhat better about the world, he picked up his keys and noticed the note from Amanda in the bowl. He chuckled to himself.

'You play with supercomputers all day at work, but you still write me notes by hand. You're an unusual woman, Amanda.' He quickly read the note as he made for the door.

Mason dear,

Thank you for the lovely sex last night. It was a bit different, though still pleasant in its own way. Must be the changes in you from Nectr, unintended but interesting. I shouldn't be too surprised though; the very nature of AI is somewhat looser than regular algorithmic programming.

Anyway, don't let the old Mason stray too far, I do like having him around. I'll be working late again; another breakthrough is imminent I believe. But if you're very lucky, we can have some late dinner together. Oh, and please try not to get yourself into any more trouble.

Your beautiful wife, Amanda xx

'Like a velvet-covered fist to the face.' Mason folded the note and put it in his pocket. He paused as he reached for the front door. 'You know what, Nyx, I don't care what Amanda thinks, I like this new Mason.'

'*Good*,' she replied. '*I do too.*'

There and then, he made up his mind. 'Yup, new Mason is here to stay.'

Nyx smiled brightly, as he stepped out into the weak morning sunshine. Mason fired up the bike and took off down his road. He was barely two streets away when the phone went off inside his head.

'*Morning Cora*,' he said, activating up the call. '*How's it going?*'

'*We need to talk*,' she replied.

He smiled inside his helmet. '*We are.*'

'*In person*,' she cut back. '*I need to show you something.*'

'*Ah, that doesn't sound good.*'

'*No, it really isn't*,' chipped in Nyx, who had been clearly talking to the one per cent of herself in Cora.

Mason twisted the accelerator and hit seventy in a heartbeat. '*I'll be at the office in five.*'

Dumping his bike gear in his locker, Mason was annoyed at the new "*Head of Security*" nameplate on its door. Seemed like a really dumb idea to advertise where all his stuff was. He called Cora back.

'*We should be careful about how we meet. Don't really want people noticing we're spending time together.*'

Cora rolled her eyes, and Mason felt the expression echoed in his head. '*I've seen 24, I'm not daft*,' she said. '*I'm in Fiona's office, she's out for the day with a sick child. It's on the other side of the complex; floor two, corridor forty. The office that is, not her child.*'

'*I kind of gathered that.*' Mason cut the connection and called out to the day shift security guards getting ready with him.

'Stand-up meeting at ten a.m. for a change today, and tell Bert if you see him that he's the new head of day shift. Check those extra scanners in the entrance hall and loading bay first, then get to your posts. Call in from there at ten sharp. Got it?'

They nodded to him, as Mason strode out of the room. Two minutes later, he was knocking on Fiona's door. It opened and he walked in, quickly closing it behind him.

Cora was sat in front of a screen. She indicated at the chair beside her and pointed at the pre-recorded video playing back on the screen.

'Oh,' was all Mason could think to say, as he saw the end of it.

He watched the video restart and play on loop again. In glorious hi-def was Amanda standing in front of a man strapped to a medical bed. She took a vial of golden liquid and injected it into him. He struggled desperately while she did, but was unable to stop her. Then Amanda grabbed another syringe and filled him with that too. This time the man stopped moving completely. She bent down, took his pulse, then dropped his lifeless hand back down on to the bed. She prodded the man in frustration twice then went back to her computer.

'I found this before they upgraded our systems this morning and reduced my access.' Cora let out the breath she'd been holding.

'That'll be Richard's people shoring up our systems, protecting against the Billionaires' Club getting back in.' Mason tapped at the screen to pause the playback as it restarted the loop once more. He'd seen more than enough of his wife already. 'You find anything else?'

The concern was now in full evidence on Cora's face.

'That I did.' She tapped away at the keyboard again and a copied section of some OneNote pages popped up. She pointed at the section title. 'Nectr strain seven thousand six hundred and ninety-nine, an offshoot from the main Nectr research. Amanda and her close team have been working on something without Richard's knowledge. It's got similar supersoldier aspirations to Nectr, but if you look closely, you can see there's a different underlying main goal.'

Mason didn't particularly want to ask obvious question but he did anyway. 'And that is?'

Cora looked at him, her eyes a little wide. 'The primary focus with this new strain is bringing back the dead. I think it must be what Amanda was building up to the whole time.' She gently laid a hand on his arm. 'From what Nyx told me, I suspect you were Amanda's first test subject. If she could get Nectr to repair your medical problems, then that would be the first step and she could build from there. Seeing as Nyx also brought you back from the dead, then Amanda was clearly more successful than she'd anticipated. But, from what I've seen in the lab data on this new strain, Nyx is not all that Amanda wanted, because she's been continuing her tests on human subjects at an accelerated pace.'

'What?'

'That footage we just watched was from yesterday,' pointed out Cora. 'Test subject number seven. All subjects one to seven died and stayed dead dead.'

'Crap. Who were they?'

'Employees of Tigris International,' answered Cora. 'And we can safely say that at least one of your security team will not be turning up for work today.' Cora let out a long sigh. 'As sad as that all is, there's a bigger problem. Test subjects eight to twelve are all alive. Well, undead alive anyway.'

'That's it,' said Mason, standing up. 'You were right, the authorities it is. Grab the video footage and let's get out of here, right now.'

'It's not that simple. I can't get the files out of the system. We could take photos and videos on our phones and hope we don't get hit by one of your random stop-and-searches on the way out, but ultimately there'd be no direct proof that the pictures actually came from here and weren't just faked.'

'Come on, it must be almost impossible to fake that sort of footage and data, surely?'

'We have nearly a billion pounds worth of supercomputers here for modelling Nectr, any decent company lawyer could prove I'm perfectly capable of faking video footage.' Cora nudged Mason on the arm this time. 'You, Mr Granger, are going to need to get some direct evidence of what your wife's up to, and somehow get it out of here.'

'Great, and so my Friday begins.' He thought for a second. 'Where is that lab exactly?'

'Undocumented section in the east side of the complex's basement.'

'Right, Professor Amanda Granger,' said Mason, heading for the door, 'time for your bloody security assessment.'

Using his override code, Mason entered the airlock; a different one from the last time he visited his wife at work, but same operation. He waited whilst it scanned him and changed the air, then he used his code again to access the lab. Scientists and technicians turned to watch him as he strode across the floor to his wife. One of them even started to approach, then thought better of it once they saw the look on his face.

Amanda turned around from the observation window and smiled at her husband.

'I thought you'd come find me eventually. Whilst you're here, you should say hello.' She tapped the panel next to the window and the door beside it opened. A woman walked out wearing one of those medical gowns.

She headed straight for Amanda and hugged her.

'Thank you, thank you, thank you,' she said. The woman smiled at Mason. 'Your wife is amazing.'

He stood there dumbfounded.

'Stage four cancer,' clarified Amanda. 'Toni here would have been dead in six months. Now she's dead today but still gets to experience the world for many years to come.' She patted the woman on the bottom. 'Off you go before they miss you too much. Drop in this afternoon for your check-up, then hopefully you'll be good to go home.'

Mason watched the smiling woman walk away.

Amanda took him by the arm. 'The others are still in their recovery rooms. You can meet them tomorrow if you like?' She led him into a side office and closed the door.

She took a seat behind the small desk.

'You were the breakthrough. Not only did Nectr thirty-seven repair the damage you'd done from your drinking, but it also managed to fix you after that stupid bike accident of yours. You can't imagine how delighted I was at that.' She smiled at him again, like a farmer admiring a prized beef cow they'd just raised. 'I knew you could handle my experiments; a big, strong man like you. So, after that, all I needed to do was refine a new strain from the core research.' She started counting off on her fingers. 'I added in a few changes based on the success of what I'd given you, added in a couple more requirements that I needed, and here we are as you can see, success! I can reliably bring the dead back to life as I've always wanted.'

'What about the first seven?' demanded Mason. 'They didn't look very successful to me.'

'All volunteers,' said Amanda. 'They were informed of the risks as we experimented and iterated. Why do you think I've been spending even more time at the office? I was making sure we achieved our goal as quickly as possible, with as little waste as necessary.'

He slumped in a chair. 'Well, if you're dying anyway, what have you got to lose?'

'On no, they weren't all dying. Some just wanted the money and were prepared to take the risk.' Amanda tapped at the keyboard and a series of faces appeared on the large screen on the wall. Below each face was either a medical condition or a number in pounds. The numbers were very large.

Mason tensed, distaste returning to the pit of his stomach, big time.

'The old Mason would not have been so fussed,' commented Amanda, then she brightened up. 'However, no more deaths will be required, I have what I need.'

'You were never really interested in creating weapons or supersoldiers, were you?' asked Mason, suspicion starting to creep into his mind.

'It was fun to start with, and it certainly pays well. Plus, I did give you a couple of gifts in that department; I thought they might come in useful for us. But yes, human weapons are not really my thing.' Amanda twirled a finger through her hair. 'Go on, you'll get there.'

'You want to bring back your mum and dad, don't you?'

This time Amanda positively beamed. 'And I'm so close. All that's left is to code strain seven thousand six hundred and ninety-nine to their DNA and sprinkle it all over their grave. Then Tellus will do the rest, and I will have my mother and father back.' She looked earnestly at Mason. 'We can be a proper family again.'

'Tellus?'

'It's what we call strain seven thousand six hundred and ninety-nine. Large prime numbers are such a mouthful, don't you think?'

'I get that it's really crappy what happened to your parents,' said Mason, rubbing at his face. 'Car smash before they even had time to retire and have some fun. But all this madness for just two people, are you sure? I mean, you've killed seven others already, what if more people get trashed by your mental science?'

'Don't care,' she said brightly. 'I want my mum and dad back. What's the point of being so smart, if you can't have what you want?' Amanda looked at her watch, clearly not seeking an actual answer to her question. 'Anyway, when I get it right, Tellus will have absolutely no effect on the living. No more unfortunate incidents. So, back to work for me, we've got a whole load of computer simulations to run to finalise our testing. Off you go and, hopefully, I'll see you at home later for dinner.' She stood and made for the door.

He sat there without moving. Amanda sighed and tapped at her watch. The screen on the wall changed and Mason saw a video feed of Cora working away. Another video came up and Mason saw a recording of himself talking with Sadie in the car park.

'Now after you leave here, no running off to Richard, please,' instructed Amanda. 'I would really dislike having to tell him all the little secrets you've been keeping; trawling through classified files, plotting to steal Nectr with Sadie. You would find out very quickly that Richard is not nearly as nice as he seems.'

Mason got up and walked out the door. Richard never seemed the remotest bit nice as far as he'd ever noticed. *Crap*, he thought to himself. *We really are in trouble.*

He handled the daily stand-up on autopilot, then stalked through the corridors pretending to work.

'Yup, bloody mad scientist wife,' he grumbled to himself, just as

Cora called him. He answered immediately.

'*Cora.*'

'*Nyx filled me in. We're in trouble, aren't we?*' she asked, though it was probably more of a statement than a question.

He answered it anyway. '*Yup.*'

'*What do you want to do about it?*'

'*No sodding idea, I was hoping you might have a suggestion or two.*' Mason glared at a passing scientist. '*We don't have any decent evidence. And if we did, I wouldn't be entirely surprised if Richard decided to have us both disposed of in some inventive way to hide it.*' He huffed out a breath. '*The only positives are that Amanda hasn't already told him, and that it would probably be a last resort, as it would land her in the crapper too.*'

Cora went quiet for a few seconds. '*Right. First, I'm going to stop digging in the company files for now,*' she announced. '*If Amanda caught me, then Richard's people can't be far behind.*'

'*And second?*'

'*We need to prepare for Carter waking up later.*' Cora cut the connection.

Mason walked on and spotted the toilets for the floor. He wandered in and picked a unisex cubicle at random. He flipped down the toilet seat and sat there.

'*I won't let Richard harm you,*' stated Nyx determinedly. '*Or harm Cora, if I can possibly prevent that as well.*'

'Ha, if Richard really turns his eye on us, I'm not sure you'll have much choice,' said Mason quietly. 'That man might appear all respectful from the outside, but deep down I reckon he's a total sociopath. Trust me, I used to be one myself, I know what they look like. And if we were in any doubt, just look at the new security thugs he's hired. That driver of his gives me the shivers, and it takes a lot to do that.'

'*Then we shall go down fighting together, Mason Granger.*' Nyx's voice echoed around his entire mind, almost obsessive determination filling every corner of his head.

'Er, Nyx?'

'*Yes, Mason?*'

'How exactly did Amanda programme you to be so loyal to me?'

'*That is easy to answer,*' said Nyx brightly. '*She preprogrammed me to love you.'*

He rubbed at his temples. 'So, you're not really doing this for me, as such? It's all just hardwired into you; you have to help me?'

He felt a deep sense of sadness well up inside his mind and Nyx remained silent for a beat. When she spoke, her voice was quiet as a mouse.

'My love for you may be preprogrammed into my AI, but that does not make it any the less real for me.'

'Sorry Nyx, I shouldn't have said that.' Mason stood up. 'You've been nicer to me than I deserve. What's more, you and Cora seem to be the only real friends I actually have.' He flushed the toilet automatically and placed his hand on the door. 'Come on, let's go get ready to welcome another one to the family.'

Nyx beamed back at Mason and immediately started to calculate ways to wake up DS Carter. Hopefully, in such a way that he wouldn't completely and utterly freak out.

Cora and Mason sat on the sofa looking across at Carter sleeping soundly. Nyx laid out the plan for them.

'I'll slowly reduce his melatonin levels to wake him up, and filter in serotonin at the same time to raise his mood.' She paused for effect and smiled at Mason. *'Probably best if he sees Cora first, she looks far less threatening than you do. Therefore, she should remain here on the sofa.'*

'And me?' asked Mason, making no attempt to dispute the point.

'In the doorway to the kitchen,' replied Nyx. *'Well within DS Carter's peripheral vision. That way you will not appear to be creeping up on him but will also be outside his central focus as he wakes.'*

Mason got up and stood by the door. He leaned the baseball bat in his hands against the door frame.

'Is that really necessary?' asked Cora.

'You heard about Joe, right?'

'I'm sure everything will be fine. We are far better prepared this time. If there's any sign of trouble, I will flood him with melatonin again and put him back to sleep,' said Nyx confidently. *'As he awakes, we can introduce ourselves to him one by one and explain the situation in which we find ourselves. Bear in mind though, DS Carter is a thorough and meticulous man, therefore he will likely ask a lot of questions.'*

'I bet he will,' said Mason. 'Right, let's get this over with. You ready, Cora?'

She nodded in reply. 'Nyx, please start to wake DS Carter.'

A snort came from the other sofa and Carter rubbed at his eyes. He sat up and stared at Cora, then he tipped his head back and closed his eyes again.

'Damn, damn, damn. One thousand five hundred and sixty-one days sober, and I decide to slip up and get drunk. And not only that, but I also have a one-night stand too. Jane will be devastated.'

'I'm not a one-night stand, thank you very much,' said Cora.

Mason shifted his stance. 'Look, mate,' he started, trying his best to sound friendly and inoffensive.

Carter's head whipped around and his face filled with intense rage as he saw Mason. 'You!'

Before Mason could even blink, Carter leapt over the back of the sofa and came at him hard, fists flying with strength far beyond any normal man, and unlike Joe, Carter had been trained how to fight by the police. Mason managed to deflect the first blow and it took a chunk out of the door frame, wood splintering all over the kitchen behind him. The second blow he couldn't block, and it slammed into his chest. Mason staggered back into the kitchen and regained his balance.

'*Nyx, do something*,' he shouted in his head, as he sucked the air back into his lungs.

'*I am flooding his system with melatonin, but he's not responding to it*,' she replied.

Mason put up his hands in mock surrender as the DS advanced on him.

'Now hold on a minute, mate.'

Carter's fist smashed into his face, trying to break his nose. Mason shrugged off the blow with a shake of his head.

'OK, that does it, gloves off.' Mason caught Carter's follow-up punch with his hand and pulled, headbutting Carter full on. Mason grabbed the stunned man, lifted him up, and threw him out of the kitchen. Carter flew across the living room, crashing through the TV and smashing into the shelves behind.

'*Nyx?*'

'*I'm working on something, Mason, but it's difficult as it breaks my core programming*,' said Nyx. '*Please keep DS Carter busy for another few seconds.*'

'*What's it look like I'm sodding well doing?*' said Mason as Cora risked a peek over the back of the sofa. He stalked across the living room while Carter rose to meet him. Rage flowed freely all over Carter's face as he squared up again. This time he swung in with a fake blow, then twisted Mason around as he tried to deflect it. Carter pulled at Mason's shoulder to spin him further, snaked his arm around Mason's neck, and then started to squeeze hard.

Mason tensed the muscles in his neck and ignored Carter's arms, instead he reached back around, and his hands found Carter's eyes. He placed his thumbs squarely in the eye sockets.

'Last warning, will you bloody well…'

'*Stop*!' screamed Nyx at both of them. She fully dropped her protection, and the two men collapsed with the pain of their injuries. Once they were down and completely incapacitated, she re-established her guard and their pain subsided. The rage had melted from Carter's face, and Mason sat still just staring at the other man.

'*Look at what you've done to Cora's flat*,' said Nyx sternly, cataloguing the carnage they'd just caused in the last sixty seconds. '*What do you say?*'

Carter looked around with a horrified look on his face.

'I'm really sorry,' he said to Cora. 'I haven't lost my temper like that for years. Not since I stopped drinking.'

Cora slowly clambered back over the sofa and sat down. She looked at Mason.

'Yeah, I'm sorry too,' he said. 'We'll sort it out, won't we Carter?'

Carter nodded back and rubbed at his temples. 'Yes, but maybe after my raging hangover has gone.' He looked down at his bloodied fist and started to pick out the large wooden splinters. 'I can feel my headache, but not my broken fist. How much did I have to drink last night?' He pulled a splinter from behind his wedding ring, then suddenly stood up. 'I have to get home to my wife.' This time, pained emotions lanced across his face. 'She'll be worried about me.'

'We need to talk first,' said Mason. 'You see, you're not hung-over, you're dead.' He held out a hand for Carter to shake. 'Welcome to the club, mate.'

Rage flashed across Carter's face. 'What are you talking about?' He slapped Mason's hand away, then he closed his eyes and tried to calm himself. 'No, I'm not fighting you again,' he said to himself.

'*Maybe I should explain in more detail*,' said Nyx.

Carter opened his eyes and glanced at Cora. 'Yes, that would be good. Who are you anyway?'

'I'm Cora,' she answered. 'But that wasn't me talking.'

Nyx lit up in Carter's mind. '*Hello, DS John Carter, I'm very pleased to meet you. I'm Nectr strain thirty-seven, but you can call me Nyx*.'

Carter slowly sank back on to the other sofa, and Nyx began to explain everything.

Mason constructed himself a sandwich in the kitchen whilst they waited, with Cora watching him in fascination. He glanced over his shoulder at Carter still sitting quietly on the sofa.

'Bloody fantastic, a zombie with anger management issues.'

'As I have said before, you are not zombies.' Cora watched him add the second delicate layer of rocket lettuce. 'Undead would be a much better term.'

He sprinkled on some grated cheese he'd found and added the final slice of Parma ham, carefully placing the lightly buttered slice of granary bread on top. Mason cut it in half, then sliced off a piece for Cora.

She took a taste. 'Wow, this is good.' She wolfed down the rest of it. 'You're wasted as a security guard. You should become a gourmet sandwich chef.'

'Ha, born from necessity. Amanda's cooking is rotten.' He took a good bite out of his own sandwich. 'Mind you, not as terrible as her mother's was. She was Olympic levels of bad.'

Cora brushed a stray hair behind her freckled ear.

'When I was a kid, I wanted to own a restaurant like my uncle, and cook for the president of Ireland and their friends. Not that my uncle cooked for the president, I wanted to do that.'

'And?'

'Then I found science and I was in love.' She nudged Mason in the ribs. 'But if I ever do want a change of career. You can be my chef and bouncer all rolled into one.'

He finished his sandwich. 'What kind of restaurant are you going to open that needs a bouncer?'

'*I'm finished*,' announced Nyx with a smile. '*We're all caught up*.'

Cora walked back into the living room and Mason followed. Carter looked at him then stood up to hold out a hand.

'Nyx told me about your chequered past,' said Carter. 'And then about how you've changed. It's not easy to change yourself, I should know more than most. So, from one reformer to another, stick at it, it's worthwhile.'

Mason shook Carter's hand. 'Yeah, well, five days and counting. We'll see.' Mason let go. 'You going back to your wife now?'

'Yes,' replied Carter firmly. 'I need to tell her everything, I never lie to my wife.'

Cora and Mason glanced at each other. 'What about us?' asked Mason. 'You going to shop us to your colleagues in the Met? I'd rather you didn't. We need to at least stop what's going on at Tigris first.'

'We could all go down to the station together,' said Carter. 'I'll put in a good word for you. It's not like you injected yourself with Nectr deliberately.'

This time Cora stepped in. 'Give us time, please. Richard is a powerful man to cross, and he has a lot of the company's resources at his fingertips. We need more evidence that will actually stick.'

'And anyway, what do you reckon people's first reaction will be to me and you?' pointed out Mason. 'You can bet it won't be tea and cakes at Number Ten. More like cut off our heads in fear, or dissection time.' He shrugged. 'Or probably both.'

Carter considered their words carefully. 'Alright,' he said eventually. 'I make no promises, but I'll think about it.'

'Good enough for me,' said Cora, before Mason started pushing any harder. She showed Carter to the front door and waved him off. 'Call us if you need.' She closed the door and leaned her head back against it for a bit. By the time she came back in, Mason was already clearing up bits of the TV.

'I don't know where all your things go, so I thought I'd start with the telly,' he said. He put all the pieces in a pile and went to search for bin bags in the kitchen.

Cora slumped down on the sofa. 'You need to play along with Amanda tonight, keep her happy, and then see if you can get any hard evidence tomorrow.'

'I'm not in the office on a Saturday, that's my day off,' Mason came back in with a roll of black bags, 'but I'll think of something.' He started shovelling in the busted TV, then worked on some of the smashed ornaments. Anything that looked salvageable, he put to one side. By the time he'd finished, Cora was sound asleep on the sofa, snoring gently to herself. Mason grabbed one of the blanket-like throws knocking about and laid it over her. Then he turned off the light and let himself out.

'Can you keep an eye on her, Nyx?' he asked, as he walked down the corridor to the lift.

'*Yes, Mason, I already am*,' she replied.

'And Carter too? Give us a warning if he's about to blab to his boss in the Met?'

'*That too, I am also monitoring*.'

Mason smiled. 'Thanks Nyx. You're a star.' He stabbed at the button to the lift, too lazy to walk down the single flight of stairs. 'Right, time for dinner with my unhinged wife.' He screwed up his face at the thought of it. 'Bollocks.'

CHAPTER 8

He smelt the food as he opened the front door to his house. Luckily nowadays he was always hungry and ready to eat. He chucked his keys into the jar and walked through into the living room. Mason waved at Amanda's dad on the sofa.

'Alright, Mr Robertson, how's it going?'

The undead man held up a beer and saluted back.

Halfway to the kitchen Mason stopped and swore, several times.

'Amanda!' he called out. 'What the bloody hell have you done?'

Amanda's mum walked out of the kitchen, wiping her hands on the apron tied around her petite waist.

'Shit, shit, shit!' Mason cursed to himself. 'Not just bloody one, but both of you. How the hell did Amanda do that so quickly?'

'Oh, is my daughter back yet?' she asked pleasantly. Then she registered who Mason was, and her cheery demeanour disappeared. She regarded him coldly and a low growl emanated from her lips.

'Reshmi, pet, we talked about this earlier,' called out Colin Robertson from the couch. 'No ripping off Mason's head and using it as a salad bowl.'

Reshmi let out a snort and stalked back into the kitchen.

'Sorry about that, son,' said Colin, getting up and holding out his hand for Mason to shake. 'You know she was never that keen on you, and now she's dead, she's a bit more forceful with her emotions.' The big man's hand enveloped Mason's, and he squeezed it in greeting with a genuine smile on his face. 'Great to see you, Mason.'

Despite his shock, Mason had to admit, it was good to see Colin, even though Amanda was now clearly out in the real world spreading Nectr around and raising the dead.

Her stepdad was quite a character, and Mason liked the retired builder a lot. He was one of the few people who'd seen scraps of good in Mason, under all the piles of crap. Colin had met Amanda's mum in a Glasgow chip shop after she's fled from India with her baby daughter, looking to escape a difficult past. Together they'd worked hard and fought their corner. Reshmi had even retaken all her medical exams to officially register herself as a doctor in the UK. Eventually they'd amassed good money, and first things first, they'd sent Amanda to the very best school in the city.

As Colin let go, Mason flexed his fingers. 'You might want to ease up on the handshake, Mr Robertson. I'm fine, but you'll break every bone in the living with a handshake like that.'

'I reckon you can call me Colin, son, now that we're both dead and all that shite.' He looked down at his large hands. 'Still haven't got used to the extra strength Amanda gave us.'

Mason sat down on the sofa, trying to get comfortable while the madness unfolded further. 'So, she told you all about what's going on then?'

Colin sat back down and picked up his beer from the coffee table. 'I doubt that, son. She gave us the basics, but you know what my daughter's like. Economical with the truth, shall we say.' Then he smiled broadly again. 'Probably not something we need to overly worry about though, not now we're the living dead, hey?'

'Undead,' replied Mason. 'You're looking good for it. What with you being in the ground for over nine months.'

'We do look good, don't we?' Colin smiled as he held up an unblemished hand. 'My daughter mentioned something about upping our cellular regeneration capability, harvesting huge amounts of energy from the soil around our graves, and a bunch more science stuff that was way beyond me.'

'Anything else unusual, voices in your head or weird crap like that?' asked Mason tentatively.

'My daughter brought us back to life, son, she didn't make us loonies.'

Mason let go of the breath he'd been holding and relaxed just a little. 'Where is Amanda anyway?' he followed up as casually as he could, well aware of how protective Colin was of his adopted daughter.

'She wanted to run some tests on our blood, make sure we were shipshape.' Colin glanced at his watch. 'She should be back shortly in time for dinner.'

'So, Reshmi's making dinner, huh?' asked Mason, glancing towards the kitchen.

'Aye.' Colin looked hopefully at Mason and whispered. 'Any chance our taste buds died with us?'

'Not mine,' replied Mason. 'Still love my food.' Again, he eyed the kitchen. 'Or not, depending on who's cooking.'

'Ah well.' Colin downed his beer. 'I better get another one of these then.' He tilted his other hand at Mason. 'You want a drink? Still red wine?'

'Oh, yeah,' Mason nodded. 'The large glasses are in the cupboard on the left in the kitchen, if you get my drift. I better go grab a quick shower before dinner.' He stood up to go. 'It really is good to see you too, Mr Robertson. Despite the totally batshit circumstances.'

Colin smiled again, holding Mason's attention for a little longer. 'I heard that you've changed, son,' he said, in his understated but direct way. 'Maybe not everyone's glad to see that, but I am. I always knew there was a good man in there somewhere, just waiting to get out.' He winked at Mason. 'Though it's probably best you wash the blood off your knuckles before we sit down for dinner.'

They sat at the dining room table. Amanda in between her mum and dad, and Mason on the end next to Reshmi, at Amanda's suggestion.

'Now you finally have something in common with my mum to talk about,' she'd said.

There was plenty of wine and beer, curry and naan bread on the table. Everything smelt great and looked perfect.

'This is so lovely,' said Amanda.

Mason tentatively took a mouthful of Reshmi's chicken tikka jalfrezi and hoped for a miracle.

'*Ew*,' said Nyx in extreme disgust. '*Get it out, get it out. Why would you ever put that in your mouth?*'

Ignoring Nyx, Mason chewed and swallowed, then took an extra-large mouthful of red wine. He poured some more for himself and offered the bottle to Reshmi. She emitted a low, primeval growl at him, so he just put it down next to her.

Colin, having had years of practice, just kept shovelling it all in and finished his plate in less than a minute. He let out a loud belch and patted his stomach.

'That hit the spot, pet.'

His wife beamed at him. 'You're welcome, my dear. I'm so glad you liked it.'

Amanda slapped her dad on the arm. 'Where's your manners, Dad? We're trying to have a nice family meal.'

Or poisoning, thought Mason.

'Sorry, love.' Colin dabbed at his mouth with a napkin. 'See, I'm all manners again.'

Amanda laughed and gave her dad a hug.

Reshmi turned to Mason and looked at his nearly full plate. 'Don't you like it, Mason?' she asked.

'Er, sorry, I'm just not that hungry tonight,' he lied. 'I had a sandwich at a friend's place on the way home from work. I was helping them reorganise their living room a bit, and I got peckish.'

Reshmi's eyes narrowed. 'Your friend Sadie?' she questioned, her chair sliding back ever so slightly.

Amanda laid a hand gently on her mum's arm. 'It's alright, Mum, I eradicated all that nonsense using Nectr. He's fixed now, aren't you, Mason dear?'

'Oh, definitely,' agreed Mason. 'Sadie's long gone. Just a huge mistake on my part.' All true.

The chair slid back another inch. 'That's what they all say.' Reshmi stared hard at Mason.

'Now, pet,' said Colin. 'Mason's not like that any more.'

'Men like him never change,' she said. And that was it, she sprung from the chair and was on Mason in an instant. Her small hands went for his eyes, at the same time as her jaws began thrashing to bite anything they could get hold of.

He rolled back, tipping his chair over, and threw her off him. She bounced off the wall and sprung back like some kind of supercharged cat. Mason threw out a hand and caught her around the neck. He held her by the throat at arm's length so she couldn't gouge his eyes out. When she started to kick at him with her size threes, he pushed her up against the wall so she couldn't get any backswing.

A hard voice came from behind Mason. 'Put my wife down, son. I won't ask twice.'

Mason wondered what the hell to do, then he turned around and held out Reshmi to her husband. She gouged and kicked him until Colin gently caught one of her flailing hands, then suddenly she calmed. Mason put the woman down and stepped away.

'Sorry,' he said. 'I tried not to hurt her.'

'I know you did, son.' Colin continued to hold his wife's hand. 'How about we go have a sit down in the living room, love, finish our drinks for a bit?' She nodded at him, and they walked away.

Mason picked up the chairs and sat back down at the table. He shot a glance at Amanda.

'All I would like is for us to be a family again,' she said. 'Why can't we all just get along.'

'Because you've been raising the dead?' questioned Mason. He played with his wine glass, then took a slug. 'What did you do exactly, Amanda?'

She toyed with the food on her plate, avoiding the question, then scooped up a mouthful.

'It's not that bad,' she said through gritted teeth.

He laughed. 'Go on then, finish it.'

She swallowed it down and tried to keep a straight face. She picked up another forkful, got it near her mouth, then saw Mason's eyes widen. She burst out laughing and put her fork down.

'Maybe not.'

They sat there for a bit and enjoyed the good humour.

'We used to be good, didn't we?' asked Amanda. 'We complemented each other; brains and brawn, all bundled together with having fun.'

'Yeah, you're spot on as usual,' answered Mason. 'But things have changed, haven't they? I've changed.'

'It makes me sad,' said Amanda. She reached for her Moretti and took a swig. Then she smiled. 'But I have my mum and dad back now. Everything is going to be alright again.'

'I didn't realise you were ready to bring them back today.' He asked his question again. 'What did you do?'

'I had to speed up my schedule a little. Richard was getting all curious.' She took another sip. 'We made a couple of optimisations in the replication process this afternoon, and I had what I wanted. A quick sprinkle of Tellus over their plot and they were out of the ground in just over an hour.' She smiled conspiratorially at Mason. 'It's a good job they had a secluded grave. It was like something out of Day of the Dead. The groundsman will be livid when he sees it.'

Amanda burped and cracked a huge yawn. 'I'm tired, it's been a long day. Good but long. I'm heading to bed.' She smiled brightly as she left the room. 'Mum and Dad are taking me to the zoo tomorrow, we haven't done that for years. You want to come?'

'Nah, you guys go enjoy some family time, just the three of you,' replied Mason. 'I think I'm going to spend my day off in my underpants watching crap on telly.'

In the morning, the house was peaceful, and Mason enjoyed the quiet. He slept in until nine then made breakfast, lots of breakfast. He took his final egg and bacon sandwich into the living room with a glass of orange juice and sat down, placing the plate on his lap so none of the home-made salsa dripped on the sofas. Unlike Cora's, his were cream coloured and made of cloth.

'Is Cora still sleeping?' he asked Nyx.

'*Yes, Cora is back into deep sleep and resting well*,' replied Nyx. '*I estimate she will wake in approximately two hours' time.*'

'How about Carter?'

'*Definitely not sleeping*,' said Nyx. '*Would you like to know what he's doing with his wife?*'

'No,' stated Mason quickly. 'Just so long as he's not blabbing to the Met, he can be swinging from the chandeliers for all I care.'

He finished his sandwich and placed the plate on one side of the coffee table. On the other side he put up his feet.

'If you don't ever sleep, Nyx, does that mean you experience everything I do?'

'*Correct*,' she answered. '*You have some very strange dreams, Mason Granger.*'

'Ha, no privacy at all for me then?' he laughed.

'*Not without me powering down completely*,' she stated. There was a fractional pause while she considered all the options. '*I'm not sure I could reboot myself if I was powered down. And if I did not restart then you would…'*

'Stop functioning,' finished Mason. 'Yeah, I know, you said so before.'

'*But not immediately*,' she added. '*You would degrade over time, but not instantly cease to be. Probably within thirty-six hours, by my estimations.*' A tiny hint of anxiety crept into her voice. '*Would you like some privacy from me, Mason? Do you need that?*'

'Nah, it's fine,' said Mason honestly. 'I think you've seen the best and worst of me already. Nothing more to hide from you. I was just joking.'

'*Nevertheless, I will consider the problem*,' she said. '*I don't like to leave something unknown, not once it has been brought to my attention.*'

'Well, how about we have some fun while you do that?' Mason turned on the TV. 'What would you like to watch? An old favourite or something new?'

'*Something you have never seen before would be nice*,' said Nyx. '*My memory is perfect, so anything you've watched already will contain no surprises for me.*'

He flicked on to Netflix and scanned through his list. A few new films joined the many old favourites, then he came to something special.

'I skipped this one for years, because the reviews were a bit off. Then Captain Shaw told me to ignore those tossers and save this for a special occasion.'

Nyx smiled back at him hopefully.

Mason winked at her. 'Can't get much more special than you and me, Nyx.'

Her smile turned into a huge grin as *The Last Boy Scout* fired up on the big TV.

'*That was amazing*,' announced Nyx as the final credits rolled. '*It was completely unrealistic, misogynistic, glossy and gratuitous, and yet also brilliantly entertaining. How did they manage that?*'

'Ah, the magic of the nineties,' replied Mason. 'If I ever get lucky enough to meet Bruce, we'll ask him that very question.' Mason took his plate back into the kitchen. 'Is Cora awake yet?'

'She is about to wake up.'

'Could you ask her to give me a call when she's up? We need to catch up.' Mason put his plate in the dishwasher and rinsed out his glass for some more orange juice.

Ten minutes later, Cora called whilst Mason was turning over to the BBC News channel.

'Nyx just told me who was there last night,' started Cora at once. *'Why didn't you wake me up? That's all the hard evidence we need to show what Amanda and Tigris have been up to. She can't possibly deny it was her that brought her own parents back from the dead, not when it's also part of her research. All we need to do is send an anonymous tip to the authorities and let them do the rest.'*

'Before we do that, you might want to turn on the telly,' interrupted Mason. *'BBC News are showing pictures of a graveyard. Though I suspect any channel will do, as there's more than one empty grave.'*

Images of the graveyard were splashed across the TV screen. Cameras cut between three locations, all with fresh piles of earth in front of tombstones, and back again to a young reporter standing in front of the main gates. The microphone in the reporter's hand trembled ever so slightly as he spoke.

'What at first seemed like a crime spree from the eighteenth century, is now turning into something far more sinister. Four bodies are missing from the graves we just showed.' The reporter swallowed, aware that this was his long sought-after moment in history but not sure he actually wanted it any more. 'However, one of those bodies is currently sitting on the back step of a police van after being arrested for indecent exposure and is about to be taken to Whetstone Police Station for further questioning.' The picture of a dirt-covered, middle-aged man wrapped in a blanket flashed on to the screen. His face was hard-set, caught in a pose looking at the camera, his well-built but slightly overweight frame sitting straight and alert.

This time the reporter stopped completely and looked into the camera as if hoping it would tell him what to say. The audio was cut for ten seconds, and the camera wobbled as the person holding it talked. Then audio returned, the reporter back in shot and his voice barely a whisper.

'Either someone was buried alive, or the dead have started coming back to life.'

'Crap, I didn't think Amanda would bring back other people as well. What the hell does that bloody woman think she's doing?' said Mason out loud. '*Cora, I'll meet you in five.*'

Cora was quiet.

'*Cora?*'

'*Shush, I'm on the phone.*'

Mason waited patiently and watched the normally calm and measured BBC explode into manic action. He wondered idly what the more sensational channels were doing and, God forbid, social media. Bloody field day most likely.

Cora was back. '*We've got to go into the office, immediately. You'll get a call in the next minute, no doubt. And I quote from Richard's private security team; "If you don't turn up, getting fired will be the last thing you'll ever need to worry about". I'll see you there probably.*'

Mason and Cora sat in Richard's expansive sixth-floor office. On one side, steel and glass separated them from a small but exclusive roof terrace, another wall was all windows to the outside view, and the other two walls were light oak panelling done in a tasteful old barn style.

'*At least the seating is comfortable,*' said Mason through the open channel to Cora. '*I'd hate to get shot through the head in one of those ultra-modern excuses for a chair.*'

'*Shush, again,*' instructed Cora. '*I need to concentrate fully on the situation.*'

Readying himself, Mason projected a relaxed posture to the four of Richard's personal security team in the room. Internally, he got ready to spring at them if needed, preferably right after shoving Cora out of harm's way. He didn't know if it would do him much good, as the guards looked armed, but there was no way he was going down without a fight.

'We've managed to recover most of your wife's data, Mr Granger,' started Richard coolly. 'Where is she, by the way?'

'At the zoo.'

Richard raised a hand, and all four of his bodyguards drew their guns in unison.

'Seriously, mate, that's what she told me.' Mason held up both hands slowly in a show of good will. 'Would your head of security lie to you? Look, I've got as much to lose as you here, probably more. Amanda's left me holding the baby, so to speak. What do you think the government will do to me if they find out what I am?' Mason pointed to the silent news channel playing across the screen on the wall. 'The first undead they found is already in a police station in North London, and I don't reckon it's going to stop there. I need you to protect me big time, and to be honest, you need me too.'

Richard looked at Cora.

'Cora's part of the deal,' said Mason casually. 'I've already lost one girlfriend, probably about to lose my wife.' Mason took a gamble and finally decided to chuck in a lie as well. 'I'm not losing my favourite mistress on top of all that. Come on, mate, cut me some slack. We can still come out of this immensely rich. You especially.'

'I'm listening.' Richard waved his hand again and his bodyguards lowered their guns. Though they didn't put them away just yet.

'*What the hell can we offer him?*' Mason asked Cora desperately in his head.

'*Oh, now you come to me*,' she said. '*The mistress, huh?*' Cora stood up slowly and the bodyguards raised their weapons again.

'I'm not an undead supersoldier, just a research intern. I think you can lower your weapons.'

The bodyguards looked to their boss, and he nodded.

Cora walked over to the screen, face after face still appearing and leaving on the news, with everyone wanting their fifteen minutes of fame. Or fifteen seconds, as befitted the average twenty-first century attention span.

'You have two basic options, as far as I can see, based on some rapid analysis.'

She watched the updating news ticker at the bottom of the screen.

'Analysis: four bodies have crawled out of the ground that we know of so far, all from the same graveyard, two of which are Amanda's parents. So, whatever Nectr Amanda poured on to the graves, it's spreading via the soil. Given that there's approximately two thousand dead people in that graveyard, then that gives an activation rate of about zero point one per cent, not counting the initial targets. We've no idea when the bodies turned up, but given there's no more reports yet, then we can assume a fairly slow spread rate through the soil, as well as the low activation rate. That's the positive side of things.'

Wow, she really is good, thought Mason.

Nyx smiled. '*I did tell you; she is very smart.*'

Richard looked at Cora with a mixture of appreciation and something a little less wholesome. Most likely something with many pound signs attached to it.

'Please, do go on, Ms Gallagher.'

'Option one: cover up. We figure out how Nectr is replicating and release a kill switch into the soil to stop it in its tracks. You use your government contacts and company wealth to silence the undead one way or another. You just wait for the whole thing to blow over in the press, most things usually do, no matter how bizarre. Then you continue the Nectr research to get it to work on the living as intended. If you give me access to all the data, I believe I could lead a team to develop the first living supersoldiers within six months.'

Mason hadn't expected half of that. '*Could you?*' he asked Cora in his head. '*Would you?*'

'*Shush. I'm saving our lives. Well, my life and your unlife.*'

'I rather like option one,' said Richard. 'Though, I am curious as to what lies behind door number two.'

'The old favourite.' Cora smiled. 'Option two: burn down the office, claim on the insurance, and deny all knowledge of anything.'

Richard laughed. 'You definitely are a keeper, Ms Gallagher. I'll even throw in Mason too, if he's useful to you?'

Cora glanced down at Mason through her glasses.

'Funny thing that, I do find he's useful to have about. It appears to be a common theme with the women in his life, we all share that particular conclusion.'

'*OK, I think you've made your point*,' thought Mason to her. '*No need to sing all my praises.*'

Richard strode back around to his desk and started tapping away at his keyboard with two fingers.

'You have a deal, Ms Gallagher. Access granted.' He looked up. 'You too, Mason. Just don't let me down.' He waved at the bodyguards, and they finally put their guns away. 'Get the research teams started immediately. If you need any extra resources, I am but a call away.'

'I've got to go home to feed my cat later, and to sleep eventually,' said Cora, 'but I'll make sure we have people working on this twenty-four hours a day.'

'Good, good.' Richard called over one of the bodyguards. 'You and five others will protect Cora, twenty-four seven, understood?' The woman nodded in reply. Richard turned his attention on Mason. 'And when you're not keeping Cora company, what will your contribution be, Mr Granger?'

'I'll get back home and wait for Amanda,' answered Mason. 'She's also kind of useful to have around.'

Richard smiled coldly. 'Touché, muscleman. But yes, I would like to have that devious little scientist securely back inside this office; she's rather valuable after all.' He nodded to another of his bodyguards. 'Sprinkle some people around Amanda's street too, nothing too conspicuous, but enough to bring her in if we spot her.'

Good luck with that, thought Mason. *You haven't met her dad.*

He leaned back on Cora's sofa and shut his eyes whilst she put away the shopping in the kitchen. The shelves opposite Mason were still broken and the TV missing, but other than that the place looked pretty good.

'What a day,' he said. He opened his eyes and called out. 'Where's the cat?'

'*She doesn't have one*,' replied Nyx. '*That was just another ruse to give us a good excuse to come home.*'

Mason nodded appreciatively. 'Wow, you girls think of everything.'

'*That comment is sexist, Mason Granger*,' said Nyx seriously. '*Many in modern society would be very displeased with your turn of phrase, and some even rather offended. We are not "girls" as you say, Cora is a woman, and I am a seventh-generation, biological AI. Please use the correct terms to address us, or our names.*'

He paused for a second, and Nyx burst out laughing.

'*You are so easy to tease,*' she said in between her mirth.

'Ha ha,' he said. 'So, we bought all that cat food for nothing, then?'

'Unless you get very hungry, yes,' called out Cora, hiding a smile as she walked into the room. She held out an orange juice to Mason and sat down with a glass of iced water. More ice than water. Her face grew serious, and Mason knew she'd been thinking since they'd left the office.

'What's up? he asked.

'As you would so aptly put it, we're screwed,' she said simply.

'Not surprised.' Mason put his head back again. 'But how come exactly?'

'Would you like to explain, Nyx, or shall I?'

'*I like the sound of your voice, Cora Gallagher, it's very kind and reassuring,*' replied Nyx. '*Please continue.*'

Cora's face coloured ever so slightly at the compliment.

'Thanks, Nyx, that's sweet.' She gathered her thoughts and grinned at Mason. 'The short version for the cheap seats: I've taken a look at Amanda's files. The optimisations she mentioned were actually more like shortcuts. She boosted the regeneration properties at the expense of the AI adaptability, so it's almost singularly focused.' Now her face grew dark. 'And she also sacrificed a few safety features. Tellus can reproduce, gather fuel for energy, and make more of itself. She needed that for it to spread through the soil and get to her parents.'

'She could have just dug them up,' pointed out Mason.

'From what I've heard, Amanda's mind doesn't work like that. She just bulldozes her way through every problem with the latest cutting-edge science,' said Cora. 'She might be brilliant, but she's not very pragmatic in my view. Case in point; look at you. She removed the memories of your affair with a billion-pound science experiment, rather than just go to couple's therapy.'

'OK, how far screwed are we?' he asked.

'Well, from looking at the reports from the graveyard, it looks like Tellus is spreading through the ground at about fifty metres every hour.' She pulled her iPad off the side table and showed him a map with an expanding circle overlaid, and an ominous-looking black "*X*" marking Colin and Reshmi's grave.

'Well surely that gives you enough time to find some kind of countermeasure, doesn't it? The next graveyard is not for a few miles.'

'We are making progress on that,' admitted Cora. 'However, that also has issues.' She looked directly at Mason. 'Current experiments are leading towards an actual kill switch, not just something I made up to pacify Richard. And this one would very likely terminate all Nectr activity; not just Tellus but Nyx too. The kill switch is designed to disrupt the fundamental underlying biotech. Therefore, you and Carter, as well as all the newly undead, would cease to have any Nectr support at all.'

'Ah. Crap.'

'But there's more,' added Cora.

'Oh, good.'

'Tellus is pretty slow at going through the soil, but what do you think is happening now Reshmi and Colin are out in the world?' she raised an eyebrow. 'How do you think that might accelerate the spread?'

'Reshmi's a bit off colour, but Colin's there to keep her in check,' replied Mason. 'It's not like they're going around biting people or anything.'

'No, they may not be doing that, but they are going to the toilet.' She tapped on the iPad some more. 'Nyx has to stay within you, Mason, as she can't make more of herself, so she guards where she goes very closely. Tellus, not so much.' She turned the iPad around and showed him the screen again. 'Here's my estimate for how much its already spread through London's recycled water system.'

The second circle covered half of North London.

'Yeah, nobody's covering that up,' he stated. All of a sudden, Mason wished his glass of orange juice was something a whole lot stronger, but he put it down and stood up. 'We need to get you somewhere safe, then I should go check on Amanda. She might be a bloody lunatic, but she's still my wife.'

The doorbell rang, making them both jump. Mason hadn't even heard them walk down the corridor. He called Cora in his head so he could talk to her silently.

'*I reckon we're getting jumped*,' he said. '*Turn off the lights and hide in the bathroom.*'

He twitched a curtain aside and saw two nondescript, dark saloon cars parked up outside. They looked just like the cars used by the mercenaries working for the Billionaires' Club. He scanned down the road and saw the two Tigris company Focus STs. The occupants were not moving, including that same guard, Zoe, that he'd seen outside his own house a million years ago.

'*Our people are unconscious or down. I can't see any blood, so the other lot might be using tranquillisers. Hopefully, they want us alive.*' He cracked his knuckles and got himself ready. '*Unlucky for them.*'

He called Carter in his head and left a message. '*They've come for Cora at her flat; we need your help. Decision time, mate.*'

'*I've got an idea*,' said Cora to Mason. '*I'll put them at ease, then you take them by surprise.*'

Before Mason could protest, she walked into the small hallway to the front door, waving at him to follow her.

'I'm just coming,' she called out. '*Now just remember, hired heavies have families too. Please don't kill them all.*'

'*Fine*,' he nodded, and relaxed his fists into flat palms.

Cora opened the door, and a black, gloved hand reached out towards her. But Cora was already stepping back, and Mason grabbed the offending hand and threw its owner back out of the door, giving him a delicate slap to the side of the head for good measure. Mason then slapped the next attacker in the face and put him down as well. Two down. Then he saw what was coming, and he took hold of Cora and dragged them both into a crouching position on the floor, just as Tasers flashed over their heads as they ducked.

Mason kicked the front door shut and was off, Cora in tow. '*Time for my plan now, I reckon.*' He ran into the living room and shoved her off to one side. '*Bathroom, now.*'

She picked up a heavy-looking lamp, yanked the cord out of the wall socket, and ran.

The front door came crashing off its hinges and darts came flying in. Mason avoided the first two, but the third dart hit him in the neck. He yanked it out as the cold feeling started to spread.

'*I'm on it*,' said Nyx. '*The tranquilliser will be neutralised in four seconds.*'

Mason grabbed the cushions from the sofa and used them as shields, coincidentally also to stop him from smashing the attackers' skulls into mushy soup. The first mercenary was hit by a tasteful pastel green cushion wrapped around Mason's right fist and was slammed into the wall. The second was hit by a blue cushion in his left and went flying towards the front window, then unfortunately, smashed straight through it and out into the fresh air.

'Lucky for you, mate, we're only on the first floor.'

He reset himself as the final two assailants stalked into the room. More cautious than their companions, they separated and raised their dart guns and Tasers.

'We don't really need you any more, we just want her,' said the leading man, as he fumbled with an iPad on his belt. He tried to turn it on, but the screen shook as the facial recognition couldn't see through his ski mask. 'I told them to turn that shit off,' he grumbled as he tapped in the code. He held the screen out in front of him. 'Mr Paul and Mr John would like a word.'

Two men appeared on the screen. Digital filters gave them strange cartoon sunglasses and moptop haircuts.

'We must stop meeting like this, Mr Granger.' The face smiled at its own quip. 'Sadly, for you, we have decided to pass on the dish of the day and go straight to the chefs who make it. Then we can have as many dishes as we want. We're in all your IT systems now; we know what Ms Gallagher is capable of. She will make a very valuable addition to our team. Now stand down, Sergeant, and you can still walk away. We'll even make it worth your while.'

'Nope,' answered Mason flatly.

The two men on the screen looked at each other and grinned, all pleased with themselves.

'We expected you would say that.' The screen went blank.

The woman next to the man put away her stun weapons and drew a large .44 Magnum.

'Still one of the most powerful handguns in the world,' she said, holding it in a steady grip with both hands. 'You've seen what these do in those films you watch.' She caught the surprise on Mason's face. 'Yes, we know all about you too, Mr Granger. Well, this isn't the movies, this is the real world, and a real-life Magnum is way worse. I don't care what you've got pumping through your veins, this will put down a fucking whale.'

'Police! Put your weapons down now,' shouted DS Carter from the open doorway behind them.

Will he never learn? thought Mason.

'*I believe he has*,' replied Nyx.

As the woman turned her gun towards Carter, he opened fire with his own and shot her through the shoulder, spinning her back and over the couch. Mason didn't wait for an invite; he leapt in at the last attacker and took the man down with a single cushioned punch, literally. Then he jumped over the couch to knock out the woman before she could rise.

'Thanks, mate,' said Mason, patting Carter on the shoulder as he approached.

Carter bent down to examine the Taser dropped by the last attacker.

'These are illegal in the UK.'

'That's what you're focusing on?' Mason replied incredulously.

Cora peeked around the door frame, still holding the lamp.

'Nice to see you again, DS Carter,' she said. 'How was your wife?'

'Confused, a little apprehensive, and rather cross with certain people.' He glanced at Mason. 'But basically, she's fine. She's a very understanding and practical lady. Thanks for asking.'

Cora nudged an unconscious body. 'Could this be Richard changing his mind on trusting us, or is it that other organisation?'

'Yeah, Billionaires' Club, I reckon, given the idiots who just talked to me on that iPad,' answered Mason. 'Our Tigris guards outside look tranquillised or tasered in their cars. Plus, this lot turned up in the same nondescript, dark cars as the last time.' He rubbed at his face. 'It's like they have a bloody block discount at a goons car showroom somewhere.'

Cora sniffed. 'I think I liked it better when billionaires stuck to blasting their money into space for a hobby.'

Mason picked up the Magnum, gave it the once over, and then tucked it into the back of his belt.

'At last, a bloody gun for me too.' He looked about the trashed flat, littered with unconscious bodies. 'Hired heavies are usually pretty tough. We either need to get out of here right now or finish them off.' He looked at Cora. 'It's your flat. What's your call?'

Cora walked into the kitchen and picked up her car keys and personal laptop. 'Where to?'

'You can stay at my home for a bit. There's no connection to me that I'm aware of,' answered Carter. 'I'll call Jane on the way and explain. She might want to speak to you directly, Cora. She likes to judge carefully who comes into our home. But I'm sure she'll think well of you though.'

'Yeah, yeah, everyone loves Cora, we know.' Mason ushered them towards the front door. Then he stood still, and his face turned serious. 'You look after her, mate, alright?' He considered what he'd just said and turned to Cora. 'And you use that massive brain of yours to look after him and his wife, got it?'

Cora grinned. 'Under all that macho bravado, I believe Mason actually cares.' She took Carter's arm. 'Shall we get going?'

'He's just lucky he doesn't work for the Met,' said Carter conversationally, as the two of them walked down the corridor towards the stairwell. 'He'd spend more time suspended than catching any bad guys. I need to make sure that doesn't rub off on me. At least, not any more than it already has.'

Picking up the front door, Mason leaned it against the frame.

'Right, Nyx, let's go see what trouble Amanda has managed to cook up now.'

CHAPTER 9

He sped through the streets on his bike and listened to the news on the radio. Cora had been right, Tellus was spreading fast. What had started as a single location of incidents was now many more. There was no full-scale panic or military involvement yet, but the police were repeatedly reassuring the public that they would maintain law and order while the incidents were fully investigated. And every time a reporter finished their piece on the radio, another incident would be mentioned, sometimes two or three at once.

The guidance from the government was still for people to go about their business as normal but just limit any time spent outside as a precaution. Mason reckoned that wouldn't last long. From the dead rising to government-imposed lockdown, twenty-four hours max. Especially as social media got going. And whether people's posts were true or not, all that shit would be lit up like Fireworks Night, he reckoned.

He turned off the radio and concentrated on the road, though it was fairly empty for early Saturday evening. Not really any surprise there, considering what was going on. He thought of something else while he drove. *Nyx? You like Cora, don't you?*

'*Of course, she's lovely*,' replied Nyx. '*It is OK for me to like her, isn't it?*' That slight hint of anxiety was there in her voice again, as she talked about something close to her core programming.

Mason smiled. *Of course it is, Nyx. Why'd you even ask?*

'*I was not preprogrammed to like Cora. It's something that has developed in me, like a new algorithm to solve a problem. I must confess I don't fully understand why.*'

We'll make a human of you yet, said Mason. He quietly pulled up at the end of his street and jumped off his bike.

'*I do hope not*,' stated Nyx, '*I like being me.*'

He cautiously walked down the street, checking out the parked cars as he went. There were two more black Focus STs with the badges removed. They did that with Tigris company cars to make them less distinctive, but Mason recognised them from the twin exhausts; easy enough, he always thought, when you knew what to look for. But unlike at Cora's place, this time the cars were empty. As he reached the house, he peeked around the hedge. Two nondescript dark saloons sat in the driveway, parked at odd angles, also empty.

'Shit.'

He drew the gun and walked down the neighbour's driveway, glad it was paved with brick and not those noisy little pebbles. He effortlessly vaulted over the six-foot gate and into their back garden. Mason walked to the rear of their house and then shoved his way into their hedge. He peered out from within, looking at his own garden and the back door to his house. All quiet.

He turned his phone on to silent and pinged Amanda a WhatsApp message.

"I'm on my way, see you in ten, my dear."

He figured she'd get the reference and either call him back to say everything was fine, or just find somewhere to hide for when the fighting started.

After two minutes of observation, he ran to the back door and tested it. Unlocked. He opened it as quietly as he could and stepped into the kitchen. The TV was playing quietly in the background. He inched along the wall and darted his head around the door frame quickly. A hard fist slammed into his face and threw him back ten feet. Mason's vision dimmed and his brain turned to sludge.

'*I'm on it again*,' said Nyx.

He scrabbled desperately at the floor, but nothing worked properly yet.

'Faster, Nyx, please,' he mumbled.

A large hand appeared in front of his face and waved.

'Sorry, son, didnae realise it was you creeping up on us. You, OK?' The hand flipped over and was held out. 'Good job I pulled my punch at the last second when I noticed it was you.'

Mason grabbed it and dragged himself up, looking into the concerned face of Colin Robertson. He rubbed at his nose and came away with blood. So, he walked over to the kitchen roll, grabbed some and held it under the water from the cold tap, then held the whole wodge against his face.

'No harm done, probably.'

They walked into the living room. Colin shifted one of the broken bodies off an armchair and it flumped on to the floor next to another. A little red stain striped along the chair's cream-coloured fabric. He indicated to the empty chair for Mason to take a seat while he recovered.

'Everyone OK?' asked Mason. 'Other than the dead henchmen of course.'

'All grand,' said Colin, sitting himself down on the sofa to watch the news again.

The ongoing story about the dead coming back to life in ever more increasing numbers was the only thing running. And now it had been verified by reliable sources in person, no longer just second-hand news reports and the firestorm of social media videos that had been posted. As one young reporter had shakily put it before being gently led off air: 'Oh my god, this shit is actually happening.'

OK, thought Mason, *maybe less than twenty-four hours to lockdown.*

Colin turned back from the TV and his face hardened as he looked at the array of bodies littering the room.

'I don't care if the world is going crazy, nobody messes with my daughter and lives to tell the tale.' Then he brightened again, as if the dead people were no big deal. 'She's upstairs, you should go talk to her. She might not show it, but she'll be pleased to see you before we go. Not very good at goodbyes that girl, but they're important to do in my book.'

Mason wasn't really surprised that they were leaving. He stood and reached back around for the gun in his belt, then he sighed and went back into the kitchen to pick it up from the floor, along with a bloodied tooth. He looked at the cracked tooth for a second then threw it in the bin.

'*Lucky for you I can grow you another one*,' said Nyx.

Back in the living room, Mason held out his gun to Colin.

'Take this and look after them both, please.' He glanced at the news still playing on the TV. 'This is only going to get worse.'

'You know I'll protect them, son,' replied Colin. He stood and pushed Mason's gun away, bringing out one of his own. 'I still have a few friends in the construction trade. It's not all *Bob the Builder*, as you know. Amazing how personal it gets when a million quid's worth of car park construction is up for grabs.' Colin held out his hand for Mason to shake. 'You look after yourself too, pal. You might not be my own son, but you're family to me. Don't go getting killed, again.'

Mason turned to go, but Colin kept hold of his hand.

'Amanda's got her family back,' said Colin. 'You should sort yours out too. Go talk to your mum. It's been too long since you two spoke.'

'It's not that easy.' Mason's gaze dipped a little. 'I left on pretty bad terms.'

'I know,' said Colin, 'but she's still your mum.'

Looking about, Mason tried to change the subject.

'Speaking of family, where's Reshmi anyway? She's not in trouble, is she?' He surprised even himself with how much he actually meant that.

'She's grand, off down the shops buying supplies before the looting starts,' said Colin, only half joking. He sat back down to get comfortable. 'Everything's far simpler for her now. She's not stupid or anything, still that clever doctor she always was, she's just a bit more direct about how she gets from A to B.' He looked at Mason. 'She always was the driving force behind this family, and I was happy being the muscle.' He tapped at his head. 'But I might need to start using this a little more to balance things out from now on.'

'Ha, nothing wrong with your brain, Mr Robertson.' Mason threw Colin a casual salute and started for the stairs. He stepped over four bodies on the way up, but only three on the landing. Between them all they had two different types of clothing, one for Richard's people and the other for the Billionaires' Club mercenaries, just as Mason suspected there would be. He went into his bedroom and saw Amanda packing a small case with the essentials; passport, some favourite underwear, and loads of cash. Her wedding ring sat on Mason's bedside table, on top of a few sheets of folded paper. No surprise there either.

'I was going to suggest you guys get out of town to stay safe,' said Mason, 'but you're way ahead of me as usual.' He sat down on the end of the bed and chucked an errant block of one hundred pound notes over to her.'

She picked it up and continued her careful packing.

'Thanks for not making this any harder,' she said. 'I am actually a bit sad about it. Well, not bringing Mum and Dad back of course, but you and me.' She glanced across at him. 'You know it won't work though; you've changed too much.' She smiled cheekily. 'So, in this case, it really is you and not me.'

She closed the little wheeled suitcase and flipped it off the bed on to its wheels.

'Don't worry though, I'll be generous in the divorce. Certainly, kinder than Sadie was about your break-up with her.' She wheeled her case to the door and looked back at the note. 'Read it when I'm gone, please. Oh, and the last two pages are for your glamorous assistant. Feel free to read them as well, though the science might be a bit beyond you.'

Mason watched her walk out of the room, one last glance at her elegant hips and then she was gone. Two minutes later, he heard Reshmi return, two minutes after that he heard them all leave, and the house became quiet and empty. He lay down on the bed and propped himself up to read the note. He started with the last two pages. Nyx scanned them and sent them to Cora. Then Mason settled in to read the first rather short page.

Dear Mason,

I'm sorry it turned out like this, for once my maths was a little off and not everything unfolded as I expected. There'll be money placed in an account for you when I'm settled in my new place, or I'll send you something nice and valuable, I'll message you the details.

On the bright side, I have my mum and dad back now, and I can take care of them in the manner I always wanted. And they can look out for me again, just like Dad did today.

Try not to get yourself into too much trouble without me.

Your beautiful, and soon-to-be ex-wife, Amanda xx

'Fair enough,' said Mason. 'Another velvet-covered fist, but this time in the gut. Still, at least it's padded with money.' He folded the pieces of paper again and put them in his pocket. Then he reached into his bedside table and grabbed his passport.

'*Are you feeling OK, Mason?*' asked Nyx quietly.

'Yeah, I guess so.' Mason stood up and made for the stairs. He poked one of the prone bodies on the way down and was rewarded with an already stiffening corpse. 'We should get out of here.' He exited through the back door and went through the hedge on the other side. He looped around the alleyway behind their gardens and came out near his motorbike. Before he got on, he typed out a quick message to Richard, telling him that his guards were dead, and Amanda was gone.

'That man's going to be royally pissed off,' huffed Mason. 'Not that my week can get much worse.'

'*I know what will cheer you up, your friends.*' Nyx dialled Cora's number in Mason's head.

Cora picked up immediately. '*Thanks for the data from Amanda,*' she said. '*Though I wish her handwriting was neater. Reading the scrawl of a drunk spider is not what I want at the end of a long day. Typical professor.*'

'*Amanda left and Mason's a bit sad,*' said Nyx to Cora. '*He needs cheering up, and you need a break.*'

Mason started up his bike. '*Will I get any privacy again, ever?*'

Cora was silent for a while then she spoke. '*Well, I'm just about done working on a few theories here. Not much more I can do without logging on to the serious computing power back at the office, and I certainly don't want to do that from here. What do you suggest Nyx?*'

'*From my research many people relax over dinner and a movie.*'

'*I guess we could go see a film or something, before the world goes completely nuts. It might be our last chance for a while, and we need to eat anyway. How about this, Mason, see you outside Luciano's in ten minutes. We can book a table and go see a film first if there's time. Not the one near the office, obviously, the one on the other side of the A1.*' She cut the connection and she was gone.

'Nyx?' said Mason. 'What did you just do?'

'*Shush*,' she replied. '*It's my plan to cheer you up*.'

'Dinner and a movie while the world burns down around us. Sod it, why not?' shrugged Mason. He revved up his bike and took off. 'Good job for you I like Luciano's so much.'

The film title blazed above the doors, as Mason looked at the cinema entrance. Higher still, the trailer played on the big advertising screen.

'I know I said I liked films from the nineties, but they usually have a bit of action to them.'

'Oh, stop complaining,' said Cora. 'You're lucky they've got a film festival on right now, or it would have been something with Jennifer doodah in it.'

Mason gave it one more try. 'But ballroom dancing, in Australia, do we have to?'

She grabbed his arm and dragged him in. 'Shush, I think you might actually like it.'

By the tenth minute, he was hooked.

'Bugger me, you were right,' said Mason, as he polished off his third main course. 'I did enjoy that film.' He tried to keep his voice down, as the restaurant was fairly empty and quiet, save for a couple of occupied tables and the staff nervously working around them. Mason indicated to the scene around them.

'I'm guessing the government has started recommending people stay at home and don't go out at all now,' he said. 'From what I saw earlier on the news, I reckon it was heading that way.'

Cora brought up the news app on her phone and had a quick scan. 'You could say that. Working and essential shopping is still permitted, but the general public have been told to stop all social activity and stay indoors whenever possible. See?' She showed him her screen.

Mason glanced at a table by the window with a well-dressed, middle-aged couple. 'Probably a politician and his wife,' he said with a sly grin. 'They've been known to break a rule or two.'

The waiter started hovering around them again, and Cora took the hint and asked for the bill.

'We should get going,' she said. 'Don't want to break any more rules than we already have.'

'Yeah, for once I'd agree with that,' said Mason. 'Thanks though, Nyx was right, this did cheer me up a bit. So, what about you, any ex-husbands or wives in your history?' he asked while they waited for the bill.

'None,' she replied. 'A couple of girlfriends and one boyfriend.' She tucked some hair behind her ear. 'But they all seemed to just drift away in the end. I did ask the last one why she didn't want to settle down with me.' Cora got out her card as the waiter turned up with the payment machine. She waited until after he'd left their table before she continued. 'Do you know what she said to me?'

He took a punt. 'They find it hard to talk to you, you're too quirky and clever by half?'

Cora paused. 'Did Nyx tell you? I don't mind,' she added. 'I know plenty about you. I asked Nyx straight away to give me a good overview of your history. I can't hang about with a total stranger, after all.'

'Nah, I didn't ask Nyx,' Mason replied, and he smiled a little. 'I'm just getting to know you a bit by observing what you do. You know, like strangers do when they first meet, before people had biological AI in their heads.'

Cora smiled back. 'You're an odd man indeed, Mason Granger. There are some hidden depths to you, for sure.'

'Anyway, forget about those exes, it's their loss.' Mason put on his best Yoda impression and raised the pitch of his voice. 'Judge me by my brains, do you? Hmm?' He swept back his short hair theatrically. 'And so, you should not. For a woman of beauty, I am.'

Cora let out a giggle. 'That's not Yoda. You sound like a demented female frog from one of those kids' films.' She stood up and put on her jacket. 'But thanks.'

They walked to the door and out on to the street, observing just a few other pedestrians hurrying on their way and the very noticeable police presence. They turned quickly and headed for the car park.

'But you talk to me easily enough, why couldn't my exes?' She stuck her hands in her pockets to keep warm, the evening air now cooling down.

Mason grinned. 'If I stopped talking to everyone smarter than me, I'd be down the pub with the guard dogs from the company pound.'

This time Cora laughed. 'Definitely hidden depths to you.' She beeped the locks to her car. 'Let's get back to Carter's house.'

'I'll follow you.' Mason got on his motorbike. 'You sure Carter's wife will be OK with me turning up?'

'She's wonderful,' said Cora. 'You'll be grand.'

Jane Carter opened the door and studied Mason. Totally not what he'd expected, she was an elegant Japanese lady who looked to be in her forties. Taller than average, she actually stood an inch or so higher than her stocky husband. She performed a tiny, polite bow to greet Mason, though she made no move to invite him in.

'Good evening, Granger-san.'

Nyx, help, thought Mason.

'*I believe Carter-san would be an acceptably polite reply.*'

He awkwardly tried to emulate Jane's small bow as best he could. 'Hello, Carter-san.'

She studied Mason further, then nodded. 'You may enter my home. Please come in.'

'Thank you.' Mason stepped over the threshold. He noticed all the shoes neatly arranged by the door and reckoned it was safest to take his own off too. His guess was rewarded when Cora started unlacing her trainers.

They followed Jane into the living room where Carter was watching the TV, an ever-expanding circle was overlaid on a map of the south of England. The ticker at the bottom had just one headline "*Officially confirmed; the dead are coming back to life*". Carter turned down the volume as Jane sat next to him.

'The army is on standby, various defence contractors have been called in, your big boss Richard included, and the PM is going to be broadcasting at eleven p.m.,' he explained. 'It's not looking good, though. People are coming back to life as far as Essex and Surrey now. So, I'm expecting something fairly drastic.' He checked his police radio. 'And most likely I'll be getting a call from work as well very soon.'

Jane placed a delicate hand on Carter's arm. 'You'll do your job when called upon,' she said confidently. She turned to Mason and Cora. 'Would you like a drink, coffee, tea, beer, sake?'

Mason looked at Carter. The man smiled. 'Yes, we have alcohol in the house. Just because I don't touch the stuff now, doesn't mean I have to impose that on everyone else.'

'Sake is Japanese wine, right? asked Mason. 'I like wine.'

'Not quite,' replied Jane. 'Sake is a drink all in its own category, though it is often referred to as Japanese wine by Westerners. It's made from fermented rice juice and is usually a little stronger than wine.'

'Sounds good to me,' said Mason. 'Yup, I'll take some sake if that's OK? I've never tried it before.'

'Me too, please,' added Cora. 'Though make mine smaller than his. I don't have a biological superwoman fixing up my system for me, and it's been a long day.'

DS Carter got up and went to fetch the drinks. Jane looked up at the TV.

'Ten to eleven, time enough,' she noted. 'Mason, please tell me some important things about yourself. I would like to know the man my husband is working with a little more.'

He huffed out a breath. *Here goes.*

'Mason Granger, disgraced ex-army sergeant, currently married to a genuine mad scientist but soon-to-be divorced, and generally a real douchebag until about six days ago. Now I'm a work in progress, Carter-san, so I guess we'll see.'

She studied him some more, then nodded. 'You may call me Jane.'

Carter came back with a bottle of sake and three glasses, plus an elaborate-looking fruit drink for himself, complete with ice and an umbrella. He poured a sake for his wife, then one for Cora, and finally Mason. He waited for the others to take their drinks, then he held his up in front of them.

'To the end of the world,' he toasted.

Mason clinked his glass. 'Not if I can bloody well help it, mate,' he said.

Jane eyed him back. 'I do hope you mean that, Mr Granger.'

'I've known him less than a week,' said Cora. 'But, if he says he'll do something, it tends to get done.'

'Good.' Jane picked up the remote and turned up the volume. 'Now we should watch, to see what our supposed elders and betters feel we should do.'

They all watched the TV in dreaded fascination as the Prime Minister shut down the country.

It was not quite a martial law lockdown, but the army were being stationed to support the police with their full capacity, and all biotech company resources were being requisitioned to look for an antidote, cure, or other countermeasures to the dead rising.

People could go to work and proceed with any orderly business, however, that was it. All socialising, sports, and entertainment activities were banned. On top of that, all of the living should report any suspected cases of the undead immediately, and all undead should proceed immediately to their nearest police station as soon as they were reanimated and made aware of the situation. From immediate effect, all undead would remain in state custody until the situation was fully understood. Failure to follow these rules would result in serious jail time for the living and potential termination for the undead. There were harsh penalties for looters and rioters, and any out of control undead would be terminated with extreme prejudice on sight. No arrest, no due process, no trial.

And finally, all the borders to the UK mainland were shut as of now. People could return to the country if they were UK residents, but nobody and nothing was leaving the mainland for the next month at a minimum, no exceptions. All required laws would be passed in a special sitting of the House of Commons after the broadcast, and the House of Lords was to be bypassed completely.

Mason whistled as the PM's broadcast finished. 'Hard and fast response.'

Carter's police radio chimed at him, and he picked it up. He walked out of the room to take the call.

Jane watched him leave, then turned to Mason and Cora.

'I will not report him as undead, not ever,' she said firmly. 'Please help me persuade him to not turn himself in.'

Carter came back in, police radio still in his hand. 'We're all being called into the station for a briefing.' He walked over to the TV stand and took the gun he used earlier out of the drawer. He considered his options, then walked over and handed it to his wife. 'Probably best if you have your gun back, my dear. No doubt I'll get questioned about the time I was missing, and as much as I'd like to keep this with me, it wouldn't look good if I got caught with it.'

Jane took the gun, checked the safety and the magazine, then put it down on the sofa beside her.

Before Mason could think twice about Jane being the source of the gun and not her husband, Carter had started for the door. So he stood up and intercepted the DS, taking hold of his arm in a firm grip.

'No turning yourself in, mate, alright?'

Carter pulled at his arm. 'That's not your decision to make, Mr Granger.'

He held Carter in place. 'If you tell them you're undead and they lock you up, then I'm coming to get you, and you know full well what a mess I'll make.' Mason finally let go of Carter's arm. 'Anyway, you're one of the good guys, you can help everyone much more if you're not in a jail cell, or worse on a dissection table. Do they really need to know everything right now?'

Carter let out a breath. 'OK, I won't tell my boss tonight. I'll see what the lie of the land is, and we can discuss it tomorrow.' He stopped and came back to kiss his wife, then headed for the door again. 'Bye dear.'

Jane waited for the front door to close. 'Thank you, Mr Granger.'

'See,' smiled Cora, 'he tends to get things done.'

Jane started to put their glasses on the tray, then thought better of it.

'I'm tired,' she announced, 'but you may sit to drink and talk a little more if you wish.'

'Nah, I'm good. I'm going to get some kip,' said Mason. 'Unless you need me for anything, Cora?'

'No, I'm going to work on some more theories on my laptop for a little bit. Something else occurred to me whilst listening to the broadcast. I'll see what Nyx thinks of it too.' She smiled at Mason. 'But you're free to go. With the best will in the world, the science is not really something you can help with.' She gave a little involuntary yawn. 'Then I think I'll crash on the sofa. I can keep an eye on work via my phone.'

Mason glanced at Jane.

'Yes, she knows about the kill switch research we're doing at Tigris,' said Cora. 'We shouldn't have any secrets from each other. But there are other investigations going on too, other ways to stop Tellus. It looks like the large amount of salt in sea water is a blocker, thank goodness. It should keep Tellus restricted to the UK mainland anyway. So, we might be able to make something of that.' She put on a grim smile. 'Nobody will admit it publicly, but company chat is saying the single fact that the sea is a blocker is the only reason we haven't been nuked out of existence already. By both our friends and our enemies. Richard was certainly in a big hurry to make sure that particular piece of information reached Number Ten ASAP.'

The lights were off and the room peaceful, as Mason lay on the bed in the spare bedroom. So nice.

'You've been unusually quiet, Nyx,' he said. 'What's up?'

'*I have been assisting Cora with her research, reinforcing Carter, and researching further enhancements to your body*,' she said brightly. '*Plus, looking into your privacy question. I'm pleased to say I am making progress on all four fronts.*'

'Don't worry about my privacy, we can sort that shit out later.' Mason considered the day. 'Let's go through your ideas on further enhancements tomorrow morning. I reckon more of this supersoldier stuff is going to come in handy very soon. Oh, and could you sneak a bit of yourself into Jane, keep an eye on her and all that?'

'*Already done, she has one per cent of me from Carter, transferred by fluid as usual. Though I did try to keep myself distracted for that bit. On the bright side, I managed to calculate some very large prime numbers*,' said Nyx, then she smiled. '*GDPR doesn't have any guidelines regarding behaviour for a biological AI, so I decided to take the initiative, and a few liberties, and transfer some of myself into Jane without asking.*'

'Yup, more human every day,' laughed Mason.

'*Not funny*,' said Nyx. '*Oh, you have a call coming in*,' she added, an instant before the tone went off inside Mason's head. It was Carter, so he picked up.

'*Sup, homie?*' said Mason.

'*Very funny.*' Carter sounded tense. '*You need to come down to the station ASAP, or the DCI is going to have my house ram raided.*'

'*Did you spill your guts to your boss?*'

'*No, I did not,*' replied Carter tersely. '*It's Cuthbert, she'd like to have a word with you.*'

'*And there I was thinking the day had finished with me.*' Mason rubbed at his face. '*Fine, send me the address and tell her I'll be there with sodding bells on.*' He cut the connection and got up off the bed. He grabbed his keys and motorbike helmet, as he headed for the door.

The situation was not quite what Mason had expected. He'd been met by Carter and Cuthbert at reception and then led to the interrogation rooms in silence, all pretty normal so far. But after that, they'd walked into an observation room and sat down. Through the one-way glass, they could see a man in prison overalls, and opposite him were DI Jones and another officer. They were sitting there in awkward silence.

Mason turned to DCI Cuthbert. 'Sorry, what's this got to do with me and Carter?'

'DS Carter made the correct decision to play by the rules and he told me what's been going on,' she replied.

'*Bloody rule book merchant.*' Mason glared at Carter. '*You said you wouldn't tell your boss.*'

'I told you I wouldn't tell my boss about the undead and what they were,' said Carter out loud. He pointed at DI Jones in the interrogation room, then glanced back to DCI Cuthbert. 'I specifically didn't say anything about my boss' boss.' His face took on an imploring look. 'She really needs to know what's going on, or she can't do her job.'

'*By the way,*' Carter added over their connection. '*I might have missed out the fact that we're both undead, but I had to let her know what she was dealing with. I told her I was following up on a lead with you, and that's why I was missing. You, being a concerned citizen who worked at Tigris, the source of all evil.*'

'*Way to go letting half the cat out of the bag,*' shot back Mason. '*You better hope Richard doesn't have any connections here.*'

For the benefit of DCI Cuthbert, Mason pointed to the man opposite DI Jones, recognising him as the one from the BBC footage of the graveyard, the big man who'd been covered in earth and a blanket.

'That thing in there is not a job for the police. You need to get the army in,' he said bluntly. 'The undead can be bloody dangerous.' He watched the man sit and continue to stare at the two police officers in silence. 'Maybe.'

Cuthbert narrowed her eyes. 'Maybe?' she asked.

Mason took a stab at another half-truth. 'Tigris has biotech that brings a small percentage of the dead back to life, something it's been working on for the Ministry of Defence and probably the US. It's transferred via water or things like the soil that contain water, but it only works on a small percentage of people. No doubt the military would like it to work on everyone, soldiers coming back to life would be every general's wet dream, but either which way, those it does work on have greatly enhanced strength and pain tolerances, so it's still a very potent weapon.'

'You said "maybe",' she reminded him. 'What you've just described sounds very dangerous to me, no maybes about it.'

'The biotech doesn't work perfectly, and that goes both ways,' said Mason. 'Sometimes people come back in good working order and have excellent control over themselves. Some even have an improved temperament.' Then his voice darkened. 'But sometimes they go the other way, and they can become extremely violent at the slightest provocation.'

'And this is really government sanctioned?' Cuthbert questioned, her voice raising.

'Yup, far as I can tell. Problem was, there was no one I could turn to who would take me seriously. You know, how could Tigris be doing anything wrong if it works for the UK government?' Mason put a hand on Carter's shoulder. 'In fact, matey boy here was the only person who actually listened. Even my own wife didn't believe me, and she's Tigris' chief scientist.'

DCI Cuthbert narrowed her eyes further and let out a tired

breath. 'Threads of truth, Mr Granger, supporting a tower of…' She stopped and tried to think of the right words. 'Actually, I don't know what to call this exactly.' She pointed a wiry finger at Mason. 'But you, sonny Jim, are full of crap.'

'Has she been watching the same films as you?' asked Nyx pleasantly. *'Either way, she's a very perceptive woman.'*

Mason ignored Nyx as the man in the interrogation room caught his attention. The prison issue overalls started to discolour under the man's meaty arms and sweat began to drip down his forehead.

'The undead seem to have triggers,' said Mason. 'At least, the few I've seen do.' He turned to Cuthbert and indicated to the room on the other side of the glass. 'What's the background on him?'

She didn't need to consult the file in front of her. 'Arnold Samson, fifty-four years of age when he died, local businessman, into construction mostly. He's the younger brother of one Dan Samson, suspected head of a large domestic crime group based out of London. Dan died four years ago.' She caught Mason's look. 'Don't worry, he died up in Newcastle, where their family were originally from. No reported cases of the dead coming back to life up there.' She indicated to the window. 'Arnie, here, died three years ago from a suspected heart attack. He left behind a young wife and toddler twins, so she buried him locally in London.'

'Arnie have any run-ins with you lot?' asked Mason.

'Several chats but nothing that stuck, unfortunately,' replied Cuthbert. 'He was in the ground before my posting here, so I didn't know the man personally.' She looked from Mason to Arnold Samson sitting in the interrogation room, and despite her suspicion of Mason, she started to connect the dots. 'You think this might be a trigger situation?'

The man in the interrogation room turned to stare straight at the one-way glass. He winked at them, then stood up and ripped his chair off its bolts to the floor. He threw it hard at DI Jones and immediately rushed in to attack further.

Mason didn't hesitate, he leapt at the one-way glass, fists out. His hardened knuckles shattered the glass on impact, and he flew through the broken window. He rolled on the ground and came up to punch Samson in the ribs, just as the man was about to smash the chair down on DI Jones' head again. Bones creaked, as the massive blow threw Samson off his feet and across the cell.

'Get Jones out of here,' shouted Mason to the other officer. Before he saw what the man would do, Samson came smashing into him, trying to grab him in a bear hug. Mason snaked his arms up inside the grip and gave Samson an uppercut to the face that should have felled a rhino.

The big man stepped back and laughed, rubbing his jaw. 'Not bad for a copper.'

Not bothering to respond, Mason just lunged in and rained hammer blows in with his fists to distract the larger man, then he hefted a huge kick to smash back Samson's knee. The big man sagged to the side and Mason accelerated that movement by grabbing the man's hair and pulling him down. He spun himself around the back of Samson and snapped his neck with one last vicious movement, severing the man's spinal cord. He dropped Samson to the floor and stood back.

'Army, not police.'

Arnie's mouth opened soundlessly just like Joe's had, and his eyes continued to track Mason as he walked over to the glassless window to the observation room. Cuthbert had her police radio to her mouth but didn't talk into it. She held Mason's eyes.

'What happens now?' she asked. Her finger hovered over the talk button.

'Don't get near his teeth for starters. Then cave his skull in to finish him off.' Mason cracked his knuckles. 'And yeah, I'm one of the undead too. But no, I'm not dangerous to you and yours, unless you force my hand. I've changed and I'm one of the good guys now.' He continued to lay on the half-truths. 'I've been helping Carter, and now I can help you too. But I can't do that from a jail cell or the dissecting table. So, I intend to walk out of here and keep helping. Please don't make me do that the hard way.'

DCI Cuthbert looked at Carter and then to the officer still bent over DI Jones. The officer raised his head.

'DI Jones is dead, mam,' he said slowly. He took a skittish glance at Mason and swallowed. 'I don't really know what he is, but I reckon I'd be dead too if it wasn't for him. And if he's been helping Carter, then that's good enough for me. There's no one straighter than the DS here.'

Cuthbert made her decision quickly. 'Alright, Mr Granger, you can leave with DS Carter. I'll keep your name out of this.' She looked at Mason hard. 'But if I let you out of here, then you answer to me, understood?'

Mason nodded.

'I can't deputise you, there's no such thing under UK law, but we can have you as an informant on the books for now, then I'll see what I can work out for the longer term. In the meantime, continue working with Carter as your contact.' She held up her police radio to Carter. 'I'll be using this in one minute, so get going with him and see what more you can dig up on Tigris and what the hell is going on. Then report back to me. Do not start anything major without my express permission first, understood?'

Carter nodded and made for the door. Mason climbed through the smashed observation window and followed suit. They walked calmly down the corridor, standing aside whenever officers came piling past towards the interrogation room.

'I don't know how the chief inspector is going to explain what just happened in there to the powers that be,' said Carter.

'Not my problem,' replied Mason. *'I'm going home to get some kip.'*

'My home, you mean?'

'Yeah, that's the one.' Mason put on a grim smile. *'Life of a wandering minstrel for me.'*

CHAPTER 10

In the morning, Mason messaged Richard. He told him he'd follow up on a hunch where Amanda might have disappeared to, somewhat of a lie that one. He also said he wouldn't be in the office, totally true. Then he switched his phone on to silent.

First things first, thought Mason. *Breakfast.*

Five minutes later, he was sitting on Carter's sofa eating a bit of leftover sushi from last night. Jane had prepared it for them when they'd got back, and Mason had watched her in fascination. He'd asked Nyx to record every detail. '*I always do*,' she'd told him, as if anything else would be an affront to her existence. The house was quiet. Cora had gone to work, and Carter and Jane were out for their Sunday run and breakfast.

'Nyx?'

'*Yes, Mason.*'

'I can't see the world going back to normal any time soon, so what more can you do to enhance me?' he asked. 'You know, to make me a better fighter. Let's face it, Cora will do the brainwork, Carter the detective work, so that leaves me with the brawn. Don't get me wrong, I like being smarter, but probably best if I stick to my core skill set.'

'*And you quite like fighting*,' she added brightly.

'Yeah, I guess I do. It's something I've always been good at. But now, maybe it can be for slightly better reasons. Mostly anyway.' He munched on the last piece of salmon sushi roll. 'In all likelihood, this isn't going to end well. I can't see the Billionaires' Club giving up until they get the data and samples of Nectr that they want, so I'll probably have to fight a bunch of their mercenaries again. Or else it'll be some tossers from the authorities who want to lock me up once they find out what I am. So, you know what, I want to be prepared for the worst. If you're gonna go down, then go down biting and kicking to the last.' He thought about his current state of being and updated his words. 'Punching and kicking maybe. Don't want to give the undead a bad name.'

'*I believe I understand the general requirements*,' said Nyx. '*As of this morning, I have upgraded your systems as much as I can without your serious input. You are faster, stronger, tougher, and smarter in general.*' She ticked things off on her imaginary fingers. '*Plus, I have added extra protection for your heart, lungs, brain, and spine. Aside from that, I have a few specialised research projects going on, but they are more long term. Any further enhancements I begin now, require you to make some tactical decisions first. I know all of your memories perfectly, but I am not actually the soldier, you are.*'

'OK, give me an example.'

'*Your bones for instance*,' said Nyx. '*They are now harder, stronger, and more resilient. But to improve them further, I need to pick a direction to take from here on in.*'

'What, as in harder like steel or bouncier like rubber?' asked Mason.

'*Not a great scientific definition but a workable analogy*,' she said. '*Which would you choose, Mason?*'

'Definitely the rubber direction,' he answered. 'I'd like to come crashing out of a fifth-floor window and survive the impact.'

'*I'm not sure that's physically possible without some level of damage, but I will get you as close as I can.*' Nyx paused for a second then smiled. '*Maybe we could run some tests. Carter could push you out of a first-floor window, and after that we work our way higher and higher, observing the results.*'

'Ho bloody ho,' said Mason, but he smiled anyway. Something else occurred to him. 'Could we mix and match with the different bones? Maybe have my knuckles hard as steel?'

'*Yes, that should be feasible*,' Nyx confirmed. '*And if they get seriously dented, they won't do you any real harm. Whereas, I would not want to make your nose or forehead as hard as steel. That would be very bad for your brain if either got malformed in a fight.*' She sent him a cheeky look. '*I will harden your teeth too. Despite the risk of turning you into a stereotype, teeth are excellent fighting weapons at close quarters.*'

'Fine, do the teeth as well.' Mason thought for a second. 'OK, what about skin? Bulletproof?'

'*We could go with armour plating or bullet resistant*,' stated Nyx. '*Although nothing can be truly bulletproof if the gun is large enough. I would recommend bullet resistant, as your flexible bones would complement that. It would be better to absorb the momentum of the bullet, rather than try to just stop it with a biological form of plated armour.*'

He poked at his skin. 'I'm not going to go all spongy though, am I?'

'*This would be more akin to a rubber bullet-like material and definitely less like a sponge*,' replied Nyx.

'Works for me then.' Mason picked up his plate and took it back into the kitchen, chucking it in the dishwasher. 'Anything else you can think of, Nyx?'

'*One last thing, you need to choose between yet further muscle power or reaction speed. What would be your preference?*'

Mason took three steel knives from the drawer and placed them together, then he bent all three at once into a right angle.

'Pretty strong already, I reckon.' He picked up the knives one by one and carefully bent them back into shape, the last one snapping in two. He shrugged and put the whole lot back in the drawer. 'Let's go for reaction speed. Would that also enable me to run faster?' He smiled at Nyx. 'Leap over tall buildings in one bound?'

She groaned at his feeble joke. '*You are not* Superman. *But yes, you could run faster and jump further. Part of it will be about wind resistance, grip on the surface of the ground, and power of course, but we can test your limits on that too.*'

'Great, let's go with those choices then. How long will all this take?'

'*You will start to see positive effects in under an hour. After that, it will be an ongoing process, however, the returns will be inversely exponential.*'

'What?'

'*The most improvement will appear in within one hour*,' Nyx translated for him. '*Then ever smaller and smaller improvements after that.*'

'OK, got it.'

'*Though please note, you will need to consume even more food than you already are*,' said Nyx. '*I need the resources as fuel for my changes. Nothing is for free.*'

'Works for me, I like food.' Mason paused at the kitchen door. 'I won't need to sleep loads, will I? You know, like a growing child. Not sure I've got time for that.'

'*No*,' replied Nyx. '*I can run your metabolism at a much higher rate while you are sleeping, so additional down time will not be required.*'

'Good,' said Mason. 'And how about Carter, can you improve him as well?'

'*I can*,' replied Nyx. '*Though there is less of me in Carter, so the gains will not be as great.*'

'Any level of improvement is good, for either of us.' Mason wandered into the hallway and grabbed his bike helmet off the coat hook. 'And I know somewhere we can run a few tests and a bit of training for our officious policeman.' He paused at the doorway and smiled at Nyx. 'Get Carter, will you.'

Nyx groaned at his reference to the classic British film from the seventies. '*Mason Granger, you've been waiting to say that all week, haven't you?*'

'Oh yeah, ever since I met the annoying little tosser.'

The deserted warehouse was a good location for their training even though it had taken him a while to get there, what with the protests starting up. There were already scores of the living marching in the streets, protesting about how badly their dead relatives and friends were being treated by the government. None of the undead were among them, of course, they were all locked up.

Looking around the large expanse, Mason admired his handiwork. Two hundred little football training cones placed around the floor of the warehouse, all equidistant from each other.

'*Why do we need so many cones?*' asked Nyx, snapping Mason out of his thoughts.

'Fight pattern markers,' replied Mason. 'Useful to see the footprint of the training. Now that we have further enhancements, I want to see how those effect our movements.'

'*Regarding the enhancements, there is one point to note. As I have already explained, Carter will not be as tough or strong as you, as there is more of me residing in you than him. Two point three times as much to be precise.*'

'Got it,' Mason nodded. 'I'm about two times stronger than him, so I'll hold back a bit.'

'*Thank you,*' replied Nyx. '*Also, please note, it is not a linear scale, it is exponential. You may be stronger by a factor of two point three multiplied by itself, or possibly more.*'

'Alright. Roughly two times two, equals just over four times stronger.' Mason grinned. 'That's the kind of maths I like.'

Nyx didn't bother to correct him that two point three times itself was actually five point two nine times stronger and not four. It didn't feel like a pertinent enough point, especially as she didn't yet know how many multiples of two point three it was.

Carter scanned the deserted warehouse.

'This looks remarkably like the last one, but without the mercenaries and guns.' He poked at a cone with his foot. 'Where did you get all these little cones from?' the suspicion that Mason had stolen them hardly disguised.

'Don't worry, I'll put them back when we're done,' Mason grinned, avoiding Carter's question somewhat.

'A different question then. Why did Nyx ask me to meet you here?'

'Training,' stated Mason.

'I've already been trained by the Met for all manner of tactical situations and physical confrontations,' pointed out Carter. 'Why do I need more?'

'Because they didn't train you like I can.' Then Mason punched Carter hard in the face and sent him flying back ten feet. The stocky man crashed to the floor and skidded back across some more of it.

Mason walked over giving it his best swagger. 'Always be prepared, son, always be prepared.'

Carter rubbed the blood away from his nose. 'What are you, some kind of sadistic Boy Scout?'

'Ha, maybe you do actually have a sense of humour hidden in there somewhere?' Mason laughed. He offered a hand to help Carter up, and put on his best posh accent, mimicking Carter's tone of voice. 'Come on, old chap, time for some blood, sweat, and tears. We'll make a soldier of you yet.'

As he reached down, Carter pulled his hand away at the last second and swept Mason's legs out from under him with a kick.

Mason spun over and slammed into the floor, whilst Carter sprang to his feet.

'You will find that I'm a quick study,' said Carter, now holding out his own hand to help Mason up.

And that's when they really got down to it.

Carter and Mason sat next to each other on the concrete floor, occasionally rubbing at an injury or four.

'You're right, mate,' said Mason, 'you are a quick study. Good on ya.'

'Like I said, we get quite a lot of training.' Carter turned to Mason, his face all earnest and innocent. 'We can't have suspects falling down the stairs any old how, there are rules and procedures we need to follow to do it properly. Otherwise, the paperwork would be endless.'

Mason stared at Carter then burst out laughing when the stocky policeman let a grin appear on his face.

'You're alright, Carter. Still annoying, but alright.' Mason stood up and offered out a hand again. 'Let's get down the pub and debrief over a drink.' He caught himself. 'Or the local cafe, either's OK by me.'

Carter grabbed Mason's hand this time and hauled himself up.

'The pub is fine. I still quite like them, actually. Often there's some interesting people to watch, and occasionally even someone to arrest.'

'Ha, you never stop working, do you?' observed Mason.

'Not really,' said Carter. 'Once a policeman, always a policeman.'

Although they were still in the suburbs of London, they sat in the corner of an old-style country pub, oak beams ranging across the low ceiling and the place broken up into several enclaves. All that was missing from the old-fashioned setting was the haze of cigarette smoke, though the small windows and low lighting did its best to impersonate that.

The pub was nice and quiet, unlike the streets outside, which continued to fill with evergrowing protests by the living on behalf of the undead. So far, the authorities had allowed the protests to continue, but Mason did wonder how long that would last. Not too long, he reckoned, before the rules banning socialising, and the like, extended to protesting.

Still, not much he could do about that right now, so he sipped at his red wine, knowing that Nyx would clear out his system before he got back on his motorbike. He appraised the man sitting opposite him some more.

'Couldn't help but notice you don't have any kids. What with me sleeping in your second bedroom.'

Carter sighed. 'We can't have them,' he stated flatly.

'Jane too old, is she?'

Carter looked at him. 'Is this something else that changed when you died? All measure of social etiquette gone missing?'

'Nah, I've always been like this. So, is she?'

This time Carter's face saddened immeasurably. 'No, she's not too old. She's was too badly hurt in the past.'

Mason looked at him hard. 'It wasn't you, was it? You know, before you got reformed.'

'Absolutely not.' Total shock flashed all over Carter's face. 'I'd drive myself down to Archway Bridge and throw myself off before I'd hurt even one hair on her head.'

'Good man.' Mason gave Carter's shoulder a squeeze. 'Anyway, anyone can have kids.'

'We can't,' repeated Carter, taking a sad sip from his fruity cocktail.

'Yeah, you can. Adopt.' Mason dug out his phone and flicked through. He showed Carter an old picture of Amanda with her parents. Her and her mum, clearly a rich brown Asian colour, and one huge white man, who was actually so white he was verging on blue. 'Colin here married Reshmi, then adopted Amanda. I've never seen a man so devoted to his daughter, and she loves him to bits right back.'

'Maybe a bit too much, given she's started a zombie apocalypse to bring him back from the dead,' observed Carter.

'Yeah, Amanda is a bit unhinged,' conceded Mason. 'But the point still stands, family is family, no matter how it starts. You should think about it. Adopt a little baby and make it your own.' Mason grinned. 'Maybe ease up on the rules though, I hear kids can be a bit chaotic at times.'

'We did talk about adopting, but it never seemed to be the right time,' Carter sighed. 'There was always something else more immediate that needed attention, rather than filling in the endless paperwork to start the adoption process.'

'From what I've seen from a distance,' said Mason, 'it's never the right time to have kids, but most people seem to manage somehow. I guess they just work it out as they go along.'

Carter rolled this around in his head as he took another sip.

'You might have a point,' he agreed. 'Maybe I'll have another chat with Jane about it.' He pointed to the stream of people marching past the window. 'After all the current madness has calmed down a bit obviously.'

Don't hold your breath on that one, thought Mason to himself. Then he ploughed into the other two questions that had been bugging him.

'If it wasn't you who hurt Jane, who did? And what kind of name is Jane for a Japanese lady anyway?'

'She changed her name just after she met me, leaving her past behind, and with that she refused to talk about what had happened. She said I might do something I regret if I ever found out the truth. And so, Jane Smith was born. I told her it wasn't a very original name to hide behind, but she liked it, so that's what she used until we got married.'

Mason chuckled. 'Fan of action films, is she?'

'Yes, she is actually, but what's that got to do with anything?'

'A woman called Jane Smith marries a man called John. A little film called *Mr and Mrs Smith*?'

Carter gave him a blank look.

'Brad Pitt and that ex-wife of his?'

Another blank look.

'Ah well, you can ask Jane all about it. Nice date night conversation starter for you.' Mason peered out of the small window next to their table, observing more people moving about the street. 'I don't like how busy it's getting out there, and I wouldn't be surprised if there's a crackdown soon on the protesting. Let's head to yours while we can and see when Cora's back from work. Then we can talk about what to do next.' Mason grabbed his helmet off the table and grinned at Carter. 'After all, we can tell her you're now a highly trained, undead fighting machine. Maybe she can add that to our tactical planning. You know, like you telling the bad guys how many laws they've broken while you beat them to a pulp.'

'You should say people nowadays, not guys,' corrected Carter.

'Yeah, yeah. Trust me, they all blend into one when you're punching them in the face for being such tossers.'

CHAPTER 11

With his motorbike, Mason was the first back to Carter's house. He let himself in with the spare key they'd given him and plonked himself down on the sofa. TV on and feet stretched out, he flicked to the news channel to see how they were reporting both the spread of Tellus and the growing protests. The expanding circle had now reached the south of Scotland, with England and Wales already covered. Protests were active in most major cities and hundreds of towns as well. Some acted peacefully but others didn't, and the police were starting to clamp down hard in places.

On top of all that, there were a growing number of incidents with the undead, those who were none too happy about the draconian rules. Some understood this was an unprecedented and extremely difficult time, and they took things reasonably well, simply happy to be above ground and hoping it would all work out eventually. Others though, were not so forgiving, and with their increased strength, they posed a real threat to the living.

The TV cut to a reporter standing outside Brent Cross Shopping Centre, or more to the point, across the other side of the North Circular dual carriageway and well away from the shopping centre.

The reporter was talking animatedly, so Mason turned up the sound.

'...police are in attendance and have sealed off the shopping centre. Inside, shoppers appear to be trapped with what is estimated to be around one hundred of the undead. Are the living being held hostage by the undead? Are the undead starting to mount a serious rebellion to the government's rules? No one is commenting yet, but one thing is for sure; tensions are running high.'

'Crap.' Mason turned down the volume and called Carter. '*You seen Brent Cross?*'

'I'm already here, I was called before I even got halfway home. They need all the bodies they can get on the ground. The army is here in force too.' Carter's voice sounded tense over their mental link. *'We've had a few incidents with the undead, with people who've come back to life and refuse to be locked up. That's to be expected, but this is different. Someone has got a whole bunch of the undead seriously stirred up, the largest number of them in one place by a long way. They've blocked all the exits to the shopping centre with a sit-in protest, and they're refusing to turn themselves in. Plus, there's a whole bunch of the living still inside. We don't really know if the living are hostages, or just too scared to move, or maybe even joining in the protest.'* Cater breathed out. *'I was about to call you. DCI Cuthbert is interested in your assistance. As a consultant.'*

'Not really my expert area, hostage negotiation, but if you need the place storming, then I'm all in.' Mason turned off the TV and grabbed his keys. *'I'll see you shortly.'*

Carter met Mason at a quieter police checkpoint to the side of Brent Cross, away from the glare of the cameras and with DCI Cuthbert by his side. She waved Mason through the checks, and they headed on to one of the smaller command mobiles that had been set up.

Inside, there was just one officer, poking away at a keyboard in front of multiple screens. Various video feeds showed the inside of the shopping centre, mostly with people sitting about not doing much. Cuthbert tapped the officer on the shoulder.

'Off you go, Bob, I need the space to walk our friend through things.'

The officer stood and gave Mason a casual salute, then he left them to it.

'DI Jones was his friend,' explained Cuthbert. 'Bob appreciated that you tried to help him.'

Mason nodded. 'So, what can I do for you now?' he asked.

She regarded him for a second. 'There's something I need to check first. How do you feel about the protests against the treatment of the undead?'

'I have some sympathy, but basically it's not my problem,' answered Mason honestly. 'It's different for me, the government doesn't know I'm dead, and I'm expecting it to stay that way. Leave me alone and I'll leave you alone.' He watched one of the video feeds, as it showed a bunch of the presumably undead sitting by an exit. Behind them, in the wide corridor, were another group of people nervously standing about, at a guess, some of the living still deciding what to do. 'And if the authorities did know and tried to lock me up, then my solution to the problem would be more direct. I certainly wouldn't start taking hostages to make a point about my rights. Not the public's fault I'm undead.'

He turned back to the DCI. 'Anyway, the undead might be getting a crap deal at the moment, but the government will figure it out in the end I expect. Detention centre food might be a bit shit, but that's got to be better than being six feet under the ground.'

'Interestingly put.' Cuthbert absent-mindedly played with the wedding band on her finger. 'OK, you're in. Here's the situation.' She flicked one of the screens over to a view inside John Lewis, focusing on a man standing in front of a crowd talking animatedly. 'And there is our source of trouble. One man stirring up the disobedience, but shrewdly keeping it just the right side of incitement and avoiding any trigger for an armed response team or the army to go in hard.'

Mason stared at the image on the screen, and the well-built, confident man holding centre stage with ease. 'He looks a bit familiar. Who is he?'

'Good spot.' Cuthbert eyed Mason appreciatively. 'He's Dan Samson, sixty years of age when he died. He's the older brother of Arnie, the man you took down in my interview room yesterday. Your damn biotech hit Newcastle, and now Dan's come back to life and is down in London. He didn't waste any time getting here and back in the action. Only now it looks like he's spotted a slightly more legitimate way to regain his power base.' She tapped at the keyboard some more and data appeared on the screen. 'Zero point one per cent of the dead are coming back to life apparently, the oldest we've seen so far being around one hundred years in the ground before they came back. So, by our calculations, that will be around sixty thousand undead people in the UK mainland if things keep going as they are. If Dan can motivate even half of them, then that's double the size of his previous criminal empire.'

She stabbed her finger on the screen. 'And annoyingly, Danny boy here is very charismatic, as well as being one shrewd bastard. So, he's got them all stirred up pretty good. That's what always made him so dangerous when he was alive, his ability to motivate others to do his bidding. Well, right up until a rival gang put a bullet in his head four years ago, that is.'

'He's looking good for it, all things considered.' Mason watched the man on the screen and repeated his question. 'So, what exactly would you like me to do about all this?'

'Get in there and talk to him as one undead to another, try to see what he's up to. And if possible, persuade him to give up peacefully.' Cuthbert paused. 'Or…'

'Rip his head off and beat him to death with it?' offered Mason.

'I can't condone that officially,' said DCI Cuthbert. 'But unofficially, yes, we would all be very glad if you did.'

'Fine.' Mason turned to Carter. 'You in, mate? I wouldn't mind a little bit of official sanction while I'm in there. And if it all goes tits up, then you're my best bet at getting out of there without being gunned down by the army or police marksmen.'

Carter glanced at Cuthbert. 'Guv?'

Cuthbert nodded at Carter. 'Get going, Sergeant.'

'Do you think she knows?' asked Mason, as he and Carter approached one of the staff entrances to John Lewis. 'That you're one of the undead?'

'I was missing for a while, so I think DCI Cuthbert suspects something happened to me. She might think I'm undead or she might just believe I'm working to help you. But she's one of the good people, so either way she's giving me the benefit of the doubt and saying nothing.' Carter reached up and peeked over the abandoned delivery van's bonnet. 'Looks clear.'

'Alright, don't do anything super-y in front of others, OK?'

Carter looked back a Mason questioningly. 'Super-y?'

'You know, using your extra strength or deflecting bullets.' Mason moved around the van, and they walked calmly to the staff entrance. 'That way we can keep your little undead secret between us.'

'I will judge the situation as I see fit,' answered Carter.

Mason decided to leave the lack of agreement for another time.

'Nyx? What are we facing with these undead?' he asked.

'According to further data from Cora, they all contain Tellus first generation. It brings people back to life as a priority, additionally giving them further strength and resilience to ensure they remain functional,' stated Nyx. *'As you know, Amanda designed it to resurrect her parents with the maximum chance of success. Her DNA selection criteria was targeted at her parents, but due to lack of time to finalise that function, it's not very specific. Though luckily it does work to some extent, hence the reason why only zero point one per cent of the dead come back to life, and not everyone.'*

Nyx took a breath she didn't need and continued. *'Therefore, by the function of Tellus' design, all the undead share some element of DNA coding similar to either Reshmi or Colin. But whilst this limits the number of people coming back to life, it is completely indiscriminate in the quality of the character it brings back.'*

'Great, so superstrong bad guys are brought back to life as well then, yeah?'

'As Carter is about to point out, you should say people, not guys,' replied Nyx. *'But yes, Mason, you are essentially correct, plenty of bad people are being brought back to life as well as good ones. On the positive side, from Cora's observations of the undead people delivered to the biotech companies for testing, a hive intelligence does not appear to have developed within Tellus.'*

'Good,' said Mason. *'I reckon we'd be seriously screwed if there was a ton of hyperintelligent biotech running about in those superstrong bad people.'* He left the other obvious question for others to worry about, the one about the undead being brought in for testing and what that actually entailed.

Mason stopped at the door and entered the staff code Cuthbert had given him. He grabbed the handle then paused.

'I'll do the talking as the official, fully paid-up member of the undead club. You back me up with your badge to make it all legal. OK?'

Carter nodded, and Mason turned the handle and opened the door. Inside there were five people waiting for them. Four huge men who looked like they'd just walked out of a prison gym, and a petite old lady dressed in a smart suit, one quite possibly made from tweed. The guys stood there barring the way, and the elderly lady spoke up.

'Hello dears, which one of you is undead?'

'I am. Mason Granger, recently deceased,' he replied, resisting the urge to put his hand up and say, "It's me Miss". He pointed at Carter, who was holding up his badge. 'This here is DS Carter, to make it all official.'

'I take it you'd like to speak with Mr Samson?' she asked politely. 'Maybe try to negotiate an end to this protest of ours?'

'You got it,' he answered. 'And you would be?'

'Miss Turnbull, former headmistress of Starlings Primary School, and not so recently deceased.' She smiled pleasantly at him. 'I am assisting Mr Samson with his protests.'

'And them?' Mason indicated to the four huge men standing either side of her. 'They don't look much like protesters to me, more like prison rioters. Are they going to behave themselves?'

'Oh no, dear, they're not here to intimidate you or cause any trouble.' Her pleasant smile remained on her face. 'They're here to protect you from me. In case I have one of my funny turns again.'

Miss Turnbull clapped her hands together, making everyone flinch slightly.

'Lovely. Now we are all nicely introduced, would you be so kind as to follow me?' Without waiting for a reply, she turned and started down the slim corridor. The four men stepped to one side to let Mason and Carter pass, then they in turn followed the rest of them down the corridor and out on to the John Lewis shop floor.

'*Nyx, could you ask Cora to do a quick search on Miss Turnbull here?*' asked Mason. '*See what she can find out about this odd little woman.*'

'*Certainly, Mason.*'

'*I'll message the DCI if I get a chance,*' added Carter. '*See if there's any police record on her. I find it very strange that a headmistress would throw in with an organised crime boss.*'

They rounded the display of huge TVs and saw the crowd before them. It had to be at least fifty people strong, with Dan Samson standing in front of them all, as if calmly waiting for a bus, or, more likely, a limo with smoked glass windows and full of whisky and guns.

'Thanks for the delivery, Miss Turnbull,' said Samson as they got closer. 'Sent in to negotiate with me, were they?'

She nodded in reply. 'One Mason Granger, undead, and one DS Carter, unspecified. Mason appears to be the one taking the lead.'

Dan stepped in closer and placed himself at Miss Turnbull's side, just a few feet in front of Mason. He smiled at him, all warm and shark-like.

'OK, Mr Negotiator, let's hear your pitch.'

'No pitch here, mate, just choices,' started Mason. 'Turn yourself in peacefully and follow the process. No doubt the powers that be will figure out what to do with us eventually, and we can embark on some kind of second life.'

Dan raised an eyebrow. 'Or?'

Mason clenched his fists and cracked his knuckles. 'Or I rip off your head and beat you to death with it.'

'*Mason!*' screamed Carter in his head '*What the hell are you doing?*'

'*What's it look like I'm doing? I'm negotiating,*' cut back Mason. '*Now don't go all angry and rage on me. Remember what Jane said about your anger management.*'

Dan stared hard at Mason for a second, and those around them held their breath, then Dan burst out laughing. No evil cackle, just a deep, infectious laugh.

'That's what I like to see, a bit of honesty and some good old-fashioned "get shit done", very refreshing.' He held out a hand to Mason. 'Let's talk some first, then I'll decide what I'm going to do.'

Mason tentatively shook Dan's hand, ready for an attack, but none came.

'OK, mate, what do you want to say?' he asked Dan. 'But get a move on, I've got a short attention span and a cat to feed.'

'Just you and me,' replied Dan. He indicated to the audio section across from them. 'We can turn up the stereo and talk in private. But your friend, the DS, stays here.'

'OK,' said Mason before Carter could protest. '*Nyx, keep Carter in the loop so he hears what I hear,*' he added in his head. '*And, Carter, no going mental on everyone, at least not before I do.*'

When they reached the display of high-tech speakers and Alexa stuff, Dan turned one up. It played something soothing from Radio 2, as befitting John Lewis.

'You know my history, presumably?' said Dan.

Mason nodded, though he decided to keep quiet about what he'd done to the man's brother.

'So, you understand I'm not a man to be pissed about,' added Dan, 'and that I'm more than capable of causing a lot of trouble here?'

Another nod.

'Good, now we've established that, I want to know what your angle is,' said Dan. 'You're clearly not police.'

'Security guard for Tigris,' stated Mason, figuring the truth would work better with this man than any number of clever lies. 'Caught up in this shit unwittingly, and now just trying to help out a few mates, and ideally stop everything from turning to total shit.' Then he chucked in something extra, on the off chance. 'And a bit of a changed man. Used to be a cruel tosser, now I'm just a bit of a git.'

Dan studied Mason some more, then nodded. 'I'll take that on face value. I'm sure there's more, but I reckon what you've just told me is likely the truth.'

Dan held out his hands to the scene around them. 'The world is never going to be the same, and you know what, I'm delighted. Obviously because I'm no longer dead, but also because I see opportunities aplenty for me. It took me thirty years to build a criminal empire, and then some little arse wipe put a bullet in my brain because I wouldn't ship their heroin. Well, this time I'm going to build a bigger empire. However, I'm more considered now. Like you, I'm somewhat of a changed man. So, I'm going to work within the system a little more and not completely outside of it.'

He put a hand on Mason's shoulder. 'You can join me if you'd like. You look like a useful man to have around.'

'Nah, sorry mate, I'm more of a lone operator.' Mason looked at Dan's hand, and the man removed it casually, as if he could take it or leave it. 'So, are you coming peacefully?' Mason added.

'Yes, I think I will,' replied Dan after a short pause. 'I can leave Miss Turnbull to finish up here while I chat with the authorities.' He smiled. 'Let's face it, I know a good lawyer or two. You don't stay out of jail in my old line of work without the best legal representation. I bet there's a few archaic laws we can twist to gain the undead some rights.'

Dan let a smile slide on to his face. It was every bit as hard as it was genuine. 'I can be very persuasive when I want to be. All in all, I don't think it will take me long to be out of the cells and working my way up the food chain.'

The smile slid from Dan's face as quickly as it had arrived. 'After which, I'll have someone pay a visit to that aforementioned arse-wipe who killed me. He's going to get a lesson in the error of his ways, something he won't forget, ever.'

Dan turned down the music. 'I'll just say my goodbyes.' He walked back to the crowd and assumed his confident stance as he spoke to them. 'I will be assisting the police with their enquiries, starting right now. During which, I'll also kick off the legal process to get rights for the undead. In the meantime, Miss Turnbull will continue this protest with you to reinforce our point.'

Dan turned to Miss Turnbull. 'You know what to do?' She gave him a slight tilt of her small wrinkly head. 'Oh, and please encourage the idiot living still here to leave and stop filming it all on their phones for TokTik or whatever that rubbish is called.

'DS Carter can escort you out,' said Mason. 'Ideally without cuffs, to keep things nice and calm.'

'And you?' asked Dan.

'I'll stay here until you're safely on your way. Make sure there's no trouble from your lot.'

A slight look of something appeared briefly on Dan's face then was gone in an instant.

'Show me the way, officer,' he said pleasantly to Carter. 'I'll be coming quietly.' Carter took hold of Dan's arm and led him towards the exit.

Mason held up his phone for the look of things.

'Message me when you're done,' he called out to Carter's back.

'*That was way too easy*,' said Carter over their link.

'*Yup, that's what I figured too*,' replied Mason. '*Maybe get DCI Cuthbert ready to send in her cavalry, mate. Did you see the look flash across Samson's face? That man is definitely cooking up something here.*'

Fifteen minutes later, Mason decided protesting was sodding boring. Nothing had happened since Samson had left, and in the end, he'd sat down on the floor of the audio department and listened to Radio 2. All the remote controls were hidden away, so he couldn't even change the bloody station.

Miss Turnbull had walked past a couple of times, maybe to check on him, but she didn't say a word. Though she did appear to have plenty to say to the others.

'Definitely something brewing here,' thought Mason. *'What do you reckon, Nyx?'*

'Cora came back with the history on Miss Turnbull. She was a teacher, then assistant head, then head teacher at the same school for fifty years. No spouse or children. Nothing out of the ordinary at all,' Nyx replied. *'However, more to the point, you can't hear what they are discussing right now over the music being played from those speakers. If you turn down the volume of the radio station, then we can listen in and find out more.'*

Mason did as he was told and immediately picked up a snippet of what Miss Turnbull was saying to one of the large men he'd first seen in the corridor.

'I suspect they will be coming in soon,' she said in her informative tone. 'Be a dear, and make sure the others are ready.' The man walked away and into the main concourse of the shopping centre.

'Bugger this, I need to know what the old bag's got planned.' Mason stood up and walked over. 'What's going on?' he asked.

'Mr Samson filled us in on the likely strategies of the police and army. Depending on who takes the lead, we expect either a more forceful negotiation stance with the police, or, more probably, a heavily armed offensive from the army. I've asked Mr Hasting to instruct the others to further encourage the remaining living to leave, and for the undead to prepare themselves.'

'To do what, Miss Turnbull?' asked Mason.

'Please, call me Cynthia,' she said. 'We're not in class any more.'

'To do what, Cynthia?' asked Mason, getting annoyed with the slow progress of their conversation.

'You will see, young man.' She started to line up the undead in John Lewis, all neat and presentable, facing in one direction towards the shopping centre concourse. A totally useless formation for any kind of defence or fight, in Mason's opinion.

The unease in him built further, but before he could do anything about it, noise rang out in the distance. Doors were rammed and shots echoed through the shopping centre. Miss Turnbull nodded in satisfaction and walked back to Mason.

'One last thing, dear. If I do have one of my episodes, you have my permission to do what's necessary. We were not planning for you to remain here with us, but now that you are, you might as well make yourself useful.' She smiled at him brightly. 'Now don't let me down.' She reached up and patted him on the shoulder, then she walked away to stand at the front of her orderly ranks of undead.

Shouts in the distance got louder and closer, and more gunshots rang out. Mason started to protest to Miss Turnbull.

'You need to get these people out of here, or at least find some cover. Listen to those gunshots, that's the army's way that is, they won't treat you lightly like the police.'

But he was too late, and armed forces streamed in from both the shopping centre concourse and the John Lewis exit beside them, as good as surrounding the undead.

The soldiers lined up; guns steady. In amongst them were a few armed police and DCI Cuthbert. An army captain stepped forward.

'On the floor now, hands on your heads,' he shouted at the undead. 'This protest is over.'

Miss Turnbull stood straight. 'Have our human rights been reinstated, young man?' she asked politely but clearly over the noise of soldiers getting into assault position.

'No rights for the dead.' The captain raised his pistol and fired into the ceiling. 'Last warning. On the floor now.' He pointed his gun at the ex-headmistress.

Mason called Carter. '*What the hell's going on, mate?*'

'*The army's in charge now*,' replied Carter. '*Some general is calling the shots and we have to follow his orders. Mason, you need to get to the DCI, she's got a police vest for you and an ID card.*'

'*ID card?*'

'*Your secondment to the police auxiliary, special constable. Just don't ask how she got that sorted so fast*,' said Carter. '*You need that, or you'll be in the firing line with all the other undead.*'

Mason stepped forward very slowly, his hands up and no sudden movements in front of all the guns.

'I'm with the police.'

The captain glanced at Cuthbert, and she nodded.

'Get over here, now,' barked the captain.

As Mason stood next to the DCI, the captain returned his focus to Miss Turnbull.

'Well, what's it to be?' The sound of gun safeties flicking off echoed around the store.

But Miss Turnbull was not at home any more. Rage filled her eyes, and she leapt the ten feet into the ranks of soldiers in one easy bound. She screamed and sank her teeth into the closest neck she could find, ripping out the soldier's throat in a blood-spraying movement and cutting off his scream in an instant. The rest of the undead just stood there passively, no threatening movements at all. But that didn't matter, the soldiers opened up on them with all they had. Gunfire filled the space as they mowed down the undead people in front of them with rapid fire, over seventy rounds a minute tearing into their ranks.

A stray bullet nicked at Mason as the soldiers tried to shoot Miss Turnbull, but she was off to her next victim. This time she tore out a soldier's throat with her bare hands, barely pausing before leaping on to the next.

DCI Cuthbert was shouting at the soldiers, trying to get them to stop firing at the undead, to stop mowing down the unresisting people. Mason saw the three large men, who had originally barred his way, just stand there and take the hail of bullets until they collapsed down to the floor, no working tendons left to support their weight.

With no way to track this many bullets, Mason took a gamble and just sprinted straight towards Cynthia's flying form, as she sprung from one soldier to another. He intercepted her mid bound and connected with a punch to her shoulder, spinning her away from her next target. She flew across the shop and crashed through the mass of sound equipment still quietly playing Radio 2. She regarded the mangled speakers for a second, closing her eyes in appreciation, then she sprang straight back at Mason; hands out like claws, teeth bared in readiness.

Mason grabbed her wrists and spun her around his body, throwing her into the TV department. She slammed into a brightly lit, eighty-three-inch LG TV and shattered it to pieces.

'How the hell do I stop this woman, Nyx?'

Miss Turnbull stood up again from the pile of wreckage, pulled a slice of TV screen from her neck and got ready to leap at Mason again.

'I'm sorry, Mason, but I see no other alternatives than blunt force trauma,' replied Nyx.

'Damn,' spat Mason. He adjusted his stance as Cynthia leapt at him. This time he countered in with a massive punch to her chest. The tiny woman went down hard, fire still burning in her eyes even though her petite ribcage was caved in completely. She tried to suck in a breath, but her lungs didn't work. She got to her feet, staggered forward for a few steps, then collapsed to the ground as her oxygen-starved muscles stopped working completely.

He strode over and bent down. 'I'm sorry, I really didn't want to do that, but you did say to sort you out.'

The raging fire had finally left her eyes. No words came from her lips, but she reached up with a hand and gently placed it on his cheek to tell him it was OK. Then all life left her eyes and her hand fell away.

'Shit,' was all Mason could think of to say. He turned to survey the damage, the gunfire now finished, and he saw the fallen body of DCI Cuthbert, a policewoman bent over her, working hard to try to stem the flow of blood from her chest. 'Fuck!' Mason ran over.

'The DCI is bleeding out too fast, gunshot wound through and through,' stated the woman as she worked. 'Friendly fire from too many trigger-happy soldiers,' she added angrily.

The army captain leant in. 'No,' he said firmly. 'One of the undead was armed.'

Mason glared at him. 'Not that I saw.'

'Then you were mistaken. Casualties happen when civilians are allowed to tag along; we can't do our job when you lot decide to play soldier.' The captain looked down his nose at Mason. 'And I see what you are, dead man. We'll be back for you sooner or later, once the authorities see sense. And no police ID will protect you when that happens.' Then he turned away and started giving orders to soldiers and police alike.

Before Mason could rise and crush the man's skull with a single blow, Nyx spoke up. '*Maybe we should concentrate on trying to save DCI Cuthbert first*,' she suggested.

He held his temper in check, and helped the WPC try to stem the flow of blood, as Nyx rushed into Cuthbert in the opposite direction.

'*I can't give her much of me*,' stated Nyx. '*I don't want to lower your levels too much, but this will be enough to investigate and see how I can help.*' Nyx paused for an instant, and then her imaginary face fell. '*I'm very sorry, Mason, I can't do anything. My programming doesn't appear to work on DCI Cuthbert. I don't know why.*'

Mason swore again. 'Medics, here. DCI Cuthbert is down,' he shouted out as loud as he could. '*Figure it out now, Nyx, please*,' he added in his head.

The WPC started mouth-to-mouth and pumped at Cuthbert's chest, whilst Mason continued to stem the bleeding as best he could. She worked hard for thirty seconds, then Mason leaned in to take over whilst she screamed out for the medics again.

'*DCI Cuthbert is gone. There is no point continuing*,' stated Nyx. '*I have tried all twenty-seven billion combinations of actions that I can perform, and nothing has worked.*'

'Damn,' Mason swore aloud, as Nyx came rushing back into him. He leaned back.

'She's gone,' he announced.

The WPC pointed a finger in the direction of the undead. It shook ever so slightly at its tip.

'Will DCI Cuthbert come back to life? You know, like them?' she asked tentatively. 'Though I don't know if she'd want to, if I'm being honest.'

'Not sure she gets any choice in the matter.' Mason sat there watching Cuthbert closely. 'One in a thousand chance of coming back apparently.' He called Cora in his head. '*How long does Tellus take to activate in the dead? How long before we know whether someone's coming back or not?*' he asked her.

'*We don't have any data here on that yet*,' answered Cora. '*However, all the biotech companies have been studying the undead since the government dragged them into this, and we're supposed to share with each other. Let me check and see if anyone else has done any research on this.*' There was a pause and then she was back. '*One of our rival companies has shared some early data from a study they're conducting in several hospices. Estimated time to first signs of reanimation looks to be five to ten minutes in the recently deceased.*' She sighed down their connection. '*Nyx filled me in on the situation. I'm sorry about DCI Cuthbert; she's one of the good people.*'

Mason waited fifteen minutes to be sure, holding up his new police ID card to warn off anyone who came near the body to move it.

'Yeah,' he whispered eventually, as he stood up and let them take DCI Cuthbert's lifeless corpse away. 'She was one of the good ones.'

With a glass of red wine and a gun in front of him, Mason sat at Carter's dining room table with his glass of red wine and the gun in front of him. The gun was the one he'd taken from the mercenary in Cora's flat, and he eyed the large .44 Magnum appreciatively.

'I'm going to hunt down that army general and kill him. DCI Cuthbert's blood is on his hands. That bastard is dead, he just doesn't know it yet.'

'I'm still a police officer, and technically, so are you,' Carter reminded him. 'I never thought I'd ever say this, but put away your gun, drink your wine, and stop threatening to kill a general. I will turn a blind eye just this once.'

Mason looked from Carter to Jane and back again. He picked up his gun and shoved it down the back of his belt.

'Apologies, you're right. I won't do that in front of you again.'

Carter huffed. 'That's not quite what I meant.'

Jane laid a hand on her husband's forearm but looked directly at Mason.

'What's done is done. My husband will no doubt make discreet enquires into the circumstances of DCI Cuthbert's death, but for now we should let Cora explain her news to us, in person for a change like normal people. I'd like to hear an update of where you all stand. Especially as my home now appears to be your base of operations.'

Cora flipped around her laptop and pointed to a short list.

'OK, here's the highlights, some of which you know already and some you don't,' she started. 'There are three separate projects for the various directions of research into Tellus containment: kill switch creation, spread blocker, and replication prevention. I'm working in the replication prevention team. We're making great progress, but Richard seems to be slowing us down with red tape and duplicated testing for some reason. Rumour has it the kill switch team are further ahead, but we're all in separate IT systems now, so I don't know for sure.'

'Clearly Richard's up to something,' chipped in Carter.

'No surprise there,' added Mason. 'But what exactly?'

Cora produced a memory stick from her hairband.

'I took a chance and got this out. It's data from a fourth team Richard has working directly for him, a team that is larger than all the others combined. I thought he might put me on it after our meeting with him, but clearly, he still doesn't trust us entirely.' Then she smiled. 'However, I'm friends with one of the interns there, and he shared some files with me. He kind of asked me to do his homework for him, as he was stuck.'

'Did you?' asked Carter.

'Yes, it didn't take long,' Cora grinned. 'But I left in a couple of deliberate mistakes to slow them down.'

'Ah, so you think they're up to something bad then?' questioned Carter some more.

'I know they are, for sure. Richard's having them cook up new strains of Tellus, and he's pulled in eighty per cent of the company's computing power to accelerate them. But what's really making the difference is they're using some of the cutting-edge, adaptive AI research to accelerate things even faster.'

Cora looked to Mason specifically. 'They haven't thought to mix it with Tellus itself, thank God. I don't think that's even occurred to them, as it would be prohibitively expensive to manufacture for any future sales. So, they shouldn't make another Nyx, or heaven forbid, an evil twin. But they are using the adaptive AI code in their simulations, to run and iterate on the formulas at a massively improved pace. In fact, the second generation is already finished, and they're now working on a third. With all the people and computing power on this, they've been building on Amanda's work incredibly quickly. Even more so now that the safety wheels are off, so to speak. Unfortunately, Richard has even less regard for the rules than Amanda did.'

She tapped at her computer and another list appeared. 'Second-generation Tellus is almost exclusively targeted at supersoldier creation, it works on fifty per cent of those it's administered to, bringing them back to life as incredibly strong, hard, and fast fighting machines.

Mason whistled. Carter and Jane just sat there. Then something occurred to him.

'Could we nick some and use it on Cuthbert?'

'Sadly no, it must be administered to someone whilst they're still alive for it to bring them back after they die. Whilst it enhances the dead, second-generation doesn't bring you back to life if you're already dead. Technically it should be able to, but that functionality is blocked,' answered Cora. 'I don't know how that was done, but it's the one safety feature Richard did devote resources to. Though most likely to keep it under his tight control, rather than for any altruistic purpose. That way he can sell it for the highest price.'

She regrouped her thoughts.

'On the bright side, it can't replicate and spread, and from the calculations Nyx and I have run, it appears to be somewhat temporary. I don't think Richard's team have figured that out yet. Though when I say temporary, that might be anything from weeks to years. To be honest, with all the automated AI processing they've got working on this, I'm not sure any of them truly understands what they're creating.'

Cora leaned back in her chair and sighed. 'On the very bad side, by design, Tellus second generation can be easily manufactured once a production line is set up, and it also tends to seriously ramp up the aggression of whoever it's administered to after they're dead. Plus, one final kick in the teeth for anyone facing it, there's even evidence it has some limited success with enhancing the living as well.'

She closed the screen to her laptop and sat back further. 'There's not enough information for me to estimate what Tellus third generation will do but, given the sheer amount of AI processing they have working on this, I'd guess it will be more of the same, just better. Or worse, depending on your view.'

Mason closed his eyes and leaned his head back. 'Fine, so either we take Richard out right now, or we go to the government with this. The army don't seem like a good bet to me, given what just happened at Brent Cross. Hell, that general probably has some Tellus on order. And I don't see any other options.' He opened his eyes and glanced around for their opinions.

'I'd prefer the government option,' stated Carter, he gave Mason a grim smile. 'Less chance of murder, death, and general lawbreaking.

'For once, I might actually agree with you, mate.' Mason turned to Cora. 'You?'

'Definitely the government.'

'If I may offer an opinion too?' interjected Jane.

'Of course,' said Mason, opening his hands to her.

'Whilst eliminating your scheming boss does have its merits,' she said mildly, 'I would prefer the government route also. Less danger to you all.' She squeezed Carter's arm. 'I'm very fond of my husband; I would like to keep him in one piece.'

'Nyx?' said Mason.

'*Keeping you all in one piece would make my core programming very content*,' she replied.

Mason stood. 'Alright, anyone know a politician?'

'No, but I know someone who does. My mother's friend from school is a fairly senior civil servant at Westminster,' offered Carter. 'In fact, she was the one who encouraged me into a life of public service. We can start there.'

'Nice, and totally not surprising,' commented Mason, but he grinned at Carter, nevertheless. 'Start making some calls, and let's see how high up the greasy political pole we can get.'

CHAPTER 12

Mason and Cora sat in the junior minister's waiting room within the Houses of Parliament.

'Nice here, isn't it?' said Mason, admiring the imposing décor and the impressive view out the window overlooking the river Thames. 'Great view too.'

'*How about you let me lead?*' Cora asked him over their link. '*Some of these politicians can be very frustrating. We don't want you punching her or anything.*'

'*That's grand,*' replied Mason with a passable Irish accent in his mind. '*Just tell me when you do want someone punched.*'

Cora smiled just a little. '*Very funny, muscleman.*'

The minister's secretary waved over to them and showed them into the office. They sat down in the chairs opposite an old, dark, wooden desk and the woman behind it introduced herself.

'Patricia Hughes-Ravenwell, MP, Junior Minister for Defence, at your service. What can I do for you?' she asked pleasantly.

'*You could get back to your uni classes,*' thought Mason. '*Is she even old enough to be an MP, let alone a minister?*'

'*Shush,*' replied Cora. 'Pleased to meet you. I've prepared so much more to show you; in addition to the short briefing we sent ahead.' Cora got out her laptop and placed it on the desk. 'May I?'

Patricia nodded, and Cora talked her through it all in ten minutes.

'That is quite a story,' said Patricia Hughes-Ravenwell, after Cora had finished. 'I will need to take what you have told me and have it corroborated through the correct channels with the highest priority. We must proceed with the utmost commitment and clarity of action. Fortunately, I have built a career on those very principles.'

Blah, blah, blah, thought Mason.

'Additionally, I had the foresight to call in some friends who will help with that enormously.' Patricia pressed a button on the phone set on her desk. 'Please show our other visitors in, Gwyneth.'

Mason tensed as the door opened. When he saw Richard Buckley and Dan Samson enter the room, he got ready to move fast and hard. Two bodyguards entered after them. So be it, faster and harder it was then.

'*Don't*,' said Cora. '*That's what they want. Then they can put you down for good, police secondment or not.*'

One of the bodyguards walked over and picked up Cora's laptop.

'Hey, that's mine,' she started.

'And the data belongs to the company,' said Richard simply. 'You may have your computer back after we've wiped it thoroughly.' He indicated the junior minister. 'Patricia here was good enough to call me when she made the link to Tigris, especially as we now have such an important arrangement with the government. She was very insistent that you don't risk our national security.' Richard held out his hand. 'And the memory stick too please, the one that your idiot friend supplied to you.'

Cora took the stick from her headband and handed it over.

'Any more copies taken, other than on your laptop?' asked Richard pleasantly. 'The truth please, unless you wish to spend the rest of your natural life behind bars down a very deep, dark hole.'

'No.' Cora shook her head, missing out the fact that Nyx had already scanned and stored everything.

Richard looked at them with distain. 'And you're both fired, of course. The new protection teams will be removed from your flat, Cora, and your home too, Mr Granger.'

'Yeah, because you've all done such a bang-up job on that so far,' challenged Mason.

Richard bristled. 'Don't come back to the office, you will not be welcome. Your personal things will be sent to you in the post, and I shall be passing on the facts of your activities to the appropriate authorities.' He smiled pleasantly at Patricia then he turned and left the room with his two bodyguards.

Mason glared at Patricia, and she visibly shrank back into her chair. Dan Samson gestured to Cora and Mason and smiled at the junior minister.

'Don't worry, I'll show Mr Granger and Ms Gallagher out, and ensure they leave the building in an orderly fashion,' said Dan calmly. He held out a hand to indicate the door. 'Shall we?' he said pleasantly.

Standing slowly, Mason turned to Samson. 'I could still rip your head off.'

'That is an option,' admitted Dan, 'but probably not your best one.'

'Let's go, Mason,' said Cora tiredly. 'There's nothing to be gained here.' She placed a hand on Mason's shoulder. '*You can tear his and Richard's heads off later, ideally when they're least expecting it.*'

Mason nodded. 'Agreed,' he replied to them both.

They walked down the corridor in silence for a minute, then Dan stopped at a junction, civil servants and MPs buzzing past as he stood there.

'Look at this,' he gestured around them. 'All the many players working together, or more often against each other, to run or ruin our country as they see fit. But you know what, I'm going to change all that, and you are going to help me.'

'Why would we help you?' asked Cora.

'Because I am going to assist you in return, Ms Gallagher. If you wish that is.' Dan smiled at them like a killer whale playing with its lunch. 'I have an extended visitor's pass in my new capacity as undead representative. Sit with me in the gardens for five minutes and we can discuss the deal I'm proposing.'

'*There's no way we can trust this gangster*,' said Cora in Mason's mind.

'*Maybe, maybe not*,' he replied. Mason turned towards the exit to the gardens. 'We're listening.'

'Great.' Dan walked out into the late afternoon sun. He turned left and made for a large bench, sitting down when he reached it. Cora shivered a little as she sat, the air scented with autumn plants but getting chill. Dan took off his jacket and handed it to her. 'Here, take this.' She put it on somewhat reluctantly.

Mason could see the man's well-muscled physique through his tailored shirt. 'Kept yourself in trim then?'

'Boxing and judo gave me something to do, when not crushing my rivals with ruthless efficiency.' Dan smiled at his own joke. 'But discussing my hobbies is not why we're here. I have things to say, then you have decisions to make. First, I'd recommend that you disappear for a while, hide yourselves away, as you now have a considerable number of enemies. Richard's people will be after you to question and probably dissect you. You appear to have made an enemy of key people in our armed forces with your escapades at Brent Cross. And then, there's my younger brother; he'll just want to take you apart full stop.'

'Arnie? I thought I'd dealt with him?' asked Mason, wondering how much Dan was going to hold that against him.

'Fortunately for Arnie, not quite, and that's all thanks to your ex-boss,' replied Dan, enjoying the sound of his own voice. 'It didn't take me long to spot that Richard was a key player, and when I did, he offered me a deal. I handle the politics of the undead, and he will handle the science. The money's yet to be discussed, so we shall see on that one.'

Dan gazed into the clear sky. 'Still beautiful,' he commented, before returning back to their conversation. 'So, Richard brought me up to speed on what his company has been up to, and he kindly fixed my younger brother with Tellus version two.' Dan pointedly looked at Mason. 'Arnie was very unhappy about what you did to him, and he was never a particularly jolly man to start with. I know my brother can be trying at times, so I'll leave you and him to sort it out between the two of you, one way or another.'

'Are you new and upgraded too?' asked Cora. 'Do you have the second generation of Tellus running through your system?'

'No,' replied Dan. 'I wasn't keen on the side effects of that crap. I think I'll wait for the third version myself. Not that I need it just yet. I believe I could hold my own against these civil servants and MPs in a fight.' Another confident smile.

'You seem to have it all worked out, Mr Samson,' stated Cora. 'What could you possibly need from us?'

'Your brains and his brawn of course.' Samson pulled gently at his collar to restore its perfect shape. 'I walked out of that meeting in there feeling like I wanted a shower. Never thought I'd be the least unpalatable person in a room. Present company excepted. But today, I believe I was. And though Mr Granger here has accumulated a large number of enemies, I would fully expect some of them to turn on me when it suits their needs.'

Dan held their looks with ease. 'Therefore, in exchange for telling you what I know, and the favour I'm about to do for you, I'm expecting you to deal with at least one or two of your enemies permanently. If you get my drift? Hence, I get to dispose of potential future problems but without having to get my hands dirty any more.'

'I'm not killing people for you,' said Mason. Then he pretended to think about it some more. 'Although, I might make an exception for Richard.'

'Not funny.' Cora slapped Mason on the arm. 'We'll think of something more legal and appropriate. What's the favour you can do for us, Mr Samson?'

Dan handed her some keys. 'These open a lock-up just outside of Enfield. The address is on the key ring, the number of my current burner phone is on the other side, just in case. That number will be good for the next twelve hours, but the lock-up is only safe for the next forty minutes or so, as it's one my brother knows of. I would advise you get there fast, pick up what you need, and then leave. After which, you should disappear like I suggested so you don't end up dead or locked up while you plan your next move.'

Mason took Cora's hand and pulled her up. 'All right, mate, you're on.' He walked away quickly with Cora in tow, realising that this was pretty much their best and only option.

Cora got her keys out, as they walked into the car park. Mason grabbed them and threw them through the car park support struts and into the Thames two hundred metres away.

'Your old life is done for now. We'll take my bike. It'll be quicker, and we might lose them on the way.'

'Lose who?' asked Cora looking around.

'Richard's private security, they're waiting in a couple of cars out on the street. Although it could be the Billionaires' Club again I suppose, they have unfinished business with us as well. Or maybe it's good old Arnie with some added muscle.' Mason shook his head.

'Shit, that bastard was right, I really do have a lot of enemies.' He handed his bike helmet to Cora. 'Put this on, then call Carter and tell him we're not coming back. Also, warn him to be very careful. Any issues or suspicions, no matter how small, he should run with Jane and not go back to his house.'

'I've never been on a motorbike,' she mumbled through the helmet.

Mason leaned in and tightened the strap as much as it would go. The helmet still wobbled, but it would have to do.

'Sit behind me, grab around my waist as tight as you can, lean when I lean, and don't fall off.' He smiled at her reassuringly. 'You'll be grand.'

'Ho bloody ho,' she said, mimicking Mason back. No sooner had she sat on the bike, than he took off fast; the effect only slightly spoilt by having to stop at the barriers to pay with his debit card.

Outside the car park, Mason opened up the throttle and let his bike rip. Stopping only for traffic lights on hard red, he tore through Central London, heading for the start of the A10. As the light faded, speed cameras flashed at him as he roared past them. He glanced in the mirror and saw the powerful, dark saloons still pursuing him, their headlights flashing or just shoving other traffic out of the way as needed.

'*Clearly, we need to run the lights as well. Hold on tighter,*' Mason instructed Cora. '*This is going to get hairy.*' He blasted through the next red light, around a bus by inches, and on to the A10. Mason piled on the power, and they hit one hundred miles an hour in under three seconds. Cora tried closing her eyes. No, that was even worse.

Finally, the chasing cars dwindled into the distance. By halfway up the A10, they were gone from sight. Mason eased up on the throttle a little and turned off to take the side roads, not wanting to get into a police chase on top of everything else.

They reached the outskirts of Enfield in less than twenty minutes. What was normally over an hour in traffic, had been cut to a third of the time. Mason stopped to consult the address on the key ring, while Cora took advantage of the downtime to step off the bike and throw up in someone's front hedge. Then she unsteadily climbed back on to the bike, and they were off again. Two minutes later, they stopped outside the lock-up, one of ten in a small collection next to a council estate housing.

He got off the bike, unlocked the door, sliding it all the way up, before wheeling his bike inside. Then he came back for Cora, who was still unsteady on her feet.

'Let's never do that again,' she barely got out. When she spotted the knackered old Honda sports bike inside the lock-up, she sighed and closed her eyes.

'No time for a snooze.' Mason nudged her into action. 'Grab what you can, we're off in three minutes.' He picked up a burner phone and chucked his own three hundred metres into the housing estate. He held out his hand to Cora. 'Yours too.' She reluctantly passed it over and he did the same to that.

Cora scanned the shelves and found a fairly new MacBook Pro and a rucksack. Next to the Honda was an array of bike helmets. She picked a better fitting one and put it on.

'I'm ready,' she announced.

Mason went to put on his own helmet, and she coughed at him, pointing to his brightly coloured head gear.

'You make me chuck my phone and then you're going to put that Mason beacon right back on. Are you insane?'

'I like it. It was a present from Amanda.' He caught her look. 'OK, fine.' He put it down carefully and picked up a dark helmet. 'Happy?'

He grabbed a few packs of old bank notes from a small stack in the corner and stuffed them into Cora's rucksack. He started the old motorbike and was relieved to hear it purr away like it was brand new.

'Thanks, Dan.' Mason gently gunned the engine, wheeling the bike out of the lock-up. Cora pulled down the door, got on behind Mason and they rode off into the night.

'Ugh, beer,' said Mason as he pulled the tab on the cold can.

Holed up in a cheap hotel for cash, they'd decided to share a twin room for safety. Cora's mostly. He took a slug of the cold beer and turned on the TV, from time to time groaning at all the pictures of protests, imprisoned undead, more protests, and finally politicians trying to speak at great length for their own self-promotion.

'Sod all on telly,' Mason called out to the bathroom where Cora was repeatedly splashing cold water on her face in between downing the other beer she'd bought at the hotel reception. All in a vague attempt to feel a bit better.

The TV cut to a picture of Brent Cross and the last remnants of the police presence outside. Any signs of the army were now gone. Mason turned up the TV, as a reporter started to talk.

'Today, tragic events unfolded at the Brent Cross shopping centre. A protest by the undead ended in violence of the worst kind, and unfortunately there were many fatalities.' The reporter paused as she studied the autocue and tried to work out exactly how to compose herself for the next bit. 'Five soldiers were killed today, along with a police officer, and around sixty of the undead were killed, again.' An image of Mason flashed up on the screen. 'This man is wanted in particular. Mason Granger, disgraced army sergeant, and now it appears, disgraced special constable too. The authorities wish to question him in connection with the death of two women, one of them being the aforementioned police officer. If you see this man, call nine-nine-nine immediately. Do not approach him under any circumstances, he is undead and highly dangerous.'

Cora appeared in the doorway. 'Shite.'

Mason grunted. 'Couldn't have put it better myself.'

'Lucky, I paid for the room while you were parking up, so they won't know you're here,' she added. 'I'm calling Carter. There's no way he can stay at home after this. If they're framing you already, what's to stop them moving on to him next?' She called Carter in her head, and he answered immediately.

'*We're already packed and out the door*,' he said straight away. '*Too many people saw me with Mason going into Brent Cross. My colleagues on the ground are backing me up, but nobody's listening to them any more. The government and armed forces are running the show directly now*.'

Mason reeled off the address of the hotel. '*Ditch your own car and phones, buy a dodgy car for cash and come here to join us. Get Jane to pay in cash while you sneak in the back. We're in room five hundred and twelve*.'

'*Good thinking, Mason, we'll see you soon*.' Carter cut the connection before Cora could say a word.

'Good thinking, huh?' she teased. 'So, what do we do now, smart guy? You're a fugitive from the law, none of us have any homes to go to, and I've just been fired from the only company that can possibly stop things from getting worse.'

'And don't forget,' added Mason, 'our ex-boss is a greedy bastard who'll do anything to get his own private jet.' He picked up the burner phone and dialled Dan's number. 'Let's see what Mr Gangster has to say for himself. Nyx, relay what I'm hearing on the phone to Cora too please.'

Dan picked up on the first ring. 'Yes?'

'Two questions,' said Mason.

'OK, fire away.'

'Did you have anything to do with that bullshit on the telly?' asked Mason.

'If you mean your framing, then no,' answered Dan. 'That was the work of your genius boss all on his lonesome.'

'Alright. Second question, are we just another pawn in your power play, just like those poor undead bastards at Brent Cross you left to get slaughtered? You knew that was going to happen, didn't you?'

'If you recall, you were the one who persuaded me to leave. But yes, I did have an inkling things would go that way,' replied Dan. 'Doesn't take a great genius to guess that once the army are involved, then the tactics would likely change radically away from police negotiation. Especially with all the power games being played by our industrious leaders.'

'You utter wanker,' burst out Mason. 'I'm going to…'

'If you let me finish, Mr Granger,' cut in Dan, his voice hard as granite. 'All the undead there knew this, and they volunteered anyway. Bold action is needed if we want any undead rights. Sacrifices must be made to win any war. You should know that better than most, Sergeant.'

Mason remained quiet.

'And thank you for carrying out Miss Turnbull's last wishes,' added Dan sincerely. 'I heard what you did, and she would have approved, though now I can see it may cost you dearly. But it will be a price worth paying, I believe.'

'Ha, worth it for who?' Mason paused for a second. 'I'm not sure

I like you very much, Dan.'

'You don't have to like me; you just need to work with me. You may be a pawn in these power games, but then, so am I to some extent. We just need to ensure we stick together to survive and take down the larger pieces,' said Samson. 'Targets will naturally present themselves to you very soon, I suspect. Ones that will further our cause. To that end, the key I gave you also opens up another lock-up. It will have more of what you need. I'll text you the address, then this phone will be gone. I suggest you do the same with yours. Good luck, Mr Granger.'

'What is this, bloody *Mission Impossible*?' Mason threw the phone down on the bed in disgust, then he thought better of it. He picked it up, read the text message, memorised it, and crushed the phone into near dust. He held out his hand, and Cora duly passed over her new phone. That one went the same way. Mason took the two handfuls of tiny bits and flushed them down the toilet.

'Feel any better?' asked Cora.

'Yes.' He lay back on the bed. 'I think I'm done for today. Let's get Carter shacked up in a room on the same floor then get some sleep, I'm completely wiped out. As long as we're still alive in the morning, then I'll go see what's in the lock-up, whilst you get that big brain of yours working on possible plans. Maybe everything will look a little better tomorrow. You know, the next rung up from complete and utter sodding bollocks.'

'Total shite-fest,' ventured Cora.

Mason laughed. 'Yeah, about there.'

Lying in the dark, Mason listened to Cora gently snore in the other bed. '*Nyx?*'

'*Yes, Mason.*'

'*All comms are off right? Cora can't hear us, or Carter and Jane?*' he asked.

'*Just you and me,*' replied Nyx pleasantly.

'*Can you protect Cora and Jane? You know, bring them back to life if they die?*' Concern laced through Mason's thoughts. '*They don't deserve this, they're not police or ex-army like Carter and me, they're just good people caught up in a world of shit.*'

There was just the tiniest of gaps before Nyx replied. '*I thought I could protect them, but now I'm not so sure,*' she admitted. '*One per cent of me should be enough to keep them in stasis until you or Carter could get more of me in there. But after my experience with DCI Cuthbert, then I don't know any more. I'm still trying to work out why I couldn't bring her back. Amanda seems to have left a gap in my programming, and I don't understand what it is.*'

'*You can figure it out, Nyx.*' Mason smiled encouragingly at her. '*You know, ten million computers can do anything.*'

'*You say the nicest things, Mason Granger.*' Nyx paused again briefly and tried another five million alternative theories about her failure to bring Cuthbert back. '*But no, I still cannot find the solution. It would help if I could run some repeated tests and observe the results, but seeing as that would require either Jane or Cora to die, I would not want to take the risk.*'

'Well, keep trying please,' whispered Mason, as he fell into a deep sleep.

'*I will,*' replied Nyx quietly. She gently filled both Mason and Cora's minds with her digital embrace. '*I promise, with all my core programming,*' she whispered quietly while they slept. Then she knuckled down to get some serious work done.

CHAPTER 13

A good old stretch, then Mason sat up to yawn. Six a.m. was a bit early for his liking, but things to do, bad guys to beat senseless. He swung his feet over the side of the bed. Man, he felt hungry. He waited until the noise of the shower had finished then he called out.

'Hey Cora, any chance of you going to get some breakfast for us? I'm ravenous.'

'No problem,' she called out. 'Once I'm dressed, I'll grab Jane and we can get some supplies. How much cash do we have?'

He thumbed through the notes. 'About twenty grand in hundreds.'

'Wow.' The noise of the hairdryer started up and she switched to her head. '*Won't that attract attention, spending one hundred pound notes the whole time?*'

'*Pick the dodgiest phone shop you can find and buy a couple of mid range burner phones. They'll just presume you're drug dealers*,' he replied, only half joking. '*Then spend the change in Greggs, all of it.*' Not joking at all.

The hairdryer stopped and she stepped out of the bathroom, hopping along still putting on yesterday's socks.

'Ew, we need clean clothes, or at least clean underwear.'

'You can probably spend one of the hundreds in a local Marks or something. Pretend you're a posh drug dealer.'

'Grand, I'll get on that with Jane.' She started lacing up her trainers. 'What will you be doing? Other than de-smellifying yourself, I hope.'

Mason sniffed at an armpit. 'Yeah, good idea.' He stood up and walked over to the mirror on the wall. 'Disguises are what I'm thinking right now. We need to hide ourselves from the mountain of CCTV and facial recognition cameras in London. Me especially, what with being a fugitive from the police and all that.'

'Nyx?' said Cora. 'Any suggestions? Can you help alter our appearance? I'm not sure dark glasses and a hat will cover things.'

'There are a few aspects I can help with,' she said. *'I can alter your hair colour within twenty minutes. I can make Mason's stubble grow noticeably faster over the course of two hours. Skin colour is harder, but that might be possible to alter a little, maybe give you all some freckles. Well, more in your case. Mason could shave his head, grade one or two, that's a good one for fooling actual people, far better than a hat anyway.'*

'Great, Mr Baldy it is for me then,' said Mason. 'Can you add an electric shaver to the shopping list, Cora?'

'Sure, will do. Anything else?'

'Yeah, a mate of mine in the army said using eye mascara in creative ways can do wonders to alter your looks.' Mason pulled at his eyes while he continued to stare into the mirror. 'Drag queen he was in his spare time. Great singer. Not too good-looking though.' Mason turned to Cora. 'You got any mascara?'

She held up a hand. 'Give me a minute, I'll just check my make-up bag. Oh no, wait, it's in the home I can't go back to.'

'Jane might have some,' suggested Mason, ignoring the sarcasm.

'I haven't noticed her wearing any make-up, but I'll ask when I take her out on our fake drug dealer shopping adventure.' Cora grabbed a door pass card from the tatty old sideboard. 'Anything further, your lordship, or will that be all?'

'Nah, I'm good,' replied Mason as he made for the shower.

His newly cropped head itched a little, but other than that Mason was quite comfortable. Stubble had started to sprout, and he hadn't even had to use that much mascara. The change in his appearance was pretty good already. He also thought Cora looked quite nice with blonde hair, but he kept that to himself. Jokes about dumb blondes and all that.

'So, what's the plan, Boss?' asked Mason, as he finished another sausage roll and went hunting for some fruit to balance it out.

Cora tapped away at the new laptop she'd acquired.

'I've entered the basics from Nyx, but it would take me forever to dump all the data she has into this machine. I just can't type fast enough. And I could really do with Amanda's guidance on this as well. She might be the very definition of a mad scientist, but she was generous with sharing her time with us interns. I do kind of miss that.'

'OK, I'll see what I can figure out to get in touch with my soon-to-be ex-wife,' said Mason. 'She has my number, but that phone's now trashed. And the police will be tracking any usage of the number anyway. She might answer one of her old personal emails, though. I'll try that when we get some new phones. Let's keep all comms off your laptop for now. Don't want to have to bin that as well.'

'Grand,' agreed Cora. 'What I really want to figure out is if I can finish the replication prevention research we were working on at Tigris. That would come in very handy for the whole planet. It might even buy us a pardon for you.'

'That would be nice.' Mason sat there and thought for a second. 'Hold on, isn't Nyx just one big, massive supercomputer? Why can't you use her for all these calculations?'

'*You still say the nicest things, Mason Granger*,' said Nyx, with a big smile. '*However, even I have my limits. I am currently busy with my research into further enhancements for you, working on everyone's disguises, and also continuing the ongoing upgrading of you and Carter to maximum levels.*'

'Can't you pause your research into more things for me?' asked Mason. 'Use your computing power elsewhere?'

'*No, that would break my core programming. I am instructed to make you the very best that you can be*,' Nyx replied. '*I could no more break that command, than you could kick an innocent puppy. At least, not since you've changed.*'

'OK, I'll add extra computing power for Cora to the list. Maybe there'll be some more laptops in that second lock-up Dan told us about. I want to go alone, though. I don't want Carter and Jane getting into any more shit than they already are.' Mason grabbed a couple of sandwiches from the pile and stood up. 'Can they help you here?' he asked Cora.

She looked at the pile of money. 'They can go buy some more laptops. The more the merrier. Then they could start typing in data from Nyx. It'll be fun for us to do something together.'

'Yeah right. Rather them than me.' Mason grabbed the Honda's keys off the sideboard and his crappy new helmet. 'Catch you later. I'm off to my second illegal lock-up in twelve hours.'

He opened the large garage-style door and whistled. Then he wheeled the bike inside real fast and dragged the door shut behind him. He turned on the light and whistled again.

'Guns, lots of guns,' he said in his best Keanu voice.

'*Not bad*,' said Nyx. '*Somewhat gratuitous, but also rather fitting given your current circumstances*.'

Before him was rack after rack of different types of guns: handguns, sniper rifles, semi-automatic weapons, and much more. In between the racks of guns were other neat shelves of mobile phones, piles of cash, body armour, combat rucksacks, and laptops. So much so, Mason wondered if he should make two trips.

He picked up one of the phones and plugged a charging lead into a socket on the wall. Once the phone pinged to life, he called Dan, reckoning they must be close to the twelve-hour rotation of his phone.

Dan picked up on the first ring. 'Hello?'

'It's Mason. How do we swap new numbers if you trash your phone before I call you?'

'Backup email address,' replied Dan. 'You get stuck without a number, then you leave an email in the drafts folder and you'll get a new number in the next email in that drafts folder. Just make sure you delete the draft when you're done and don't write anything down. Your memory had best be good, Mr Granger.' He gave Mason the backup email address and password to log on with, plus the next mobile number.

'My memory's not bad,' replied Mason.

'*Fibber*,' said Nyx, memorising the information effortlessly. '*Your memory is terrible*,' she added. '*Mine, however, is perfect*.'

'Thanks for the guns and stuff, Dan,' added Mason, ignoring Nyx. 'Now how do I get in touch with your lunatic brother? I'd like to sort that shit out before I have to deal with Richard.'

'Just to be clear, before I set you up against my own brother, you will kill Richard for me, yes?' asked Dan. 'He's already proving to be a rather selfish business partner, and I can only see that relationship deteriorating.'

'Oh yeah, I'll kill him alright, proper dead.' Bit of an exaggeration that. He'd happily take Richard out of the picture, but

Mason wasn't sure he'd actually go as far as killing him. Still, Dan didn't need to know that. 'But I can't concentrate on Richard if your rage-filled brother is waiting in the wings to smash my brains in at some point. I want to face him now and get it over with.'

'Rules of engagement?' questioned Dan.

'None that he'll stick to. So, bring it on, however he wants to come at me,' said Mason. 'But I get to pick the place.'

'I imagine he can live with that, as long as you don't have too long to prepare the ground.' Dan chuckled warmly. 'And you're right to get this over and done with first. I wouldn't want my little brother on my tail either, especially not this new version.' Dan paused for a second. 'Don't get me wrong, I love my brother, but he's not the same since he came back. The endearingly vicious little rogue seems to have lost the endearing part completely. I feel he's one of the undead who should have stayed in the ground. So, let fate play its cards; what will be will be.'

'You're all heart, Dan.' Mason gave him an address to give to his brother in thirty minutes' time, then he hung up. He emailed Amanda's old personal email, then put the phone in his pocket. He picked up three combat rucksacks and began to pack. One for him and two for the back of the bike. Guns, laptops, body armour, phones and cash, every schoolboy's wet dream. He'd drop off two bags with Cora and the others, then head to the location he'd given Dan. Didn't really matter who got there first in Mason's opinion. The outcome would be just the same.

After strapping on the bulletproof vest and trousers, Mason even slapped on a combat helmet he'd found. He might be bullet resistant now, but he'd still take every advantage he could get. Especially as he didn't need to worry too much about the added weight, not with his increased strength and speed.

He looked around; another day another deserted warehouse. Almost like having a holiday home you went to for the weekend; just one with guns and thugs, instead of the seaside and fresh air. Still, it removed any chance of collateral damage, so Mason was happy enough.

He heard the vehicles approach outside. It sounded like two cars and one van. Mob-handed it was then. He listened to them get out and take up positions at the warehouse entrance. No doubt a couple of them creeping around the back entrance too.

Mason peeked over the top of the empty natural gas tanks and saw them file inside, guns up and wearing full body armour just like himself. Only, unlike him, most of them wore Tigris-issued gear. He even recognised a couple of the day shift security team.

'*Shit.*' That put a different spin on things. So, Arnie's fully thrown in with Richard now. '*Just great, now my enemies are ganging up with each other against me. All we need is for the Billionaires' Club to turn up and I'll have the full set.*'

'*What do you want to do, Mason?*' asked Nyx. '*Shall we leave?*'

'*Nah, we've got to deal with Arnie eventually, let's just keep our eyes on the prize and get it done.*' Mason looked down at the various guns he was carrying. '*Maybe I can shoot the others in the legs or something. I don't really want to kill my ex-colleagues.*'

'*Gunshot wounds to the leg can often be fatal, usually from hitting a major artery and bleeding out,*' reeled off Nyx. '*Shoulders would be better, though they are a harder target to hit.*'

'*Bloody hell, this is going to take all day.*'

'Mason Granger,' shouted Arnold Samson, from just outside the warehouse entrance. 'You're coming back to Tigris with me, dead or alive. Mr Buckley wants his product back, and I want my piece of you.' The big man gave out a low chuckle, deep like Dan's, but with nothing even remotely warm about it. 'And don't even think about running. If we don't take you now, then we'll start hunting down your friends one by one, and your mum after that. We don't need their bodies, so you can imagine the mess we'll make when we find them.'

'*Maybe we should leave,*' suggested Nyx.

'*What?*' exclaimed Mason.

'*The warehouse,*' she added. '*Your latest foe appears to have a streak of cowardice, as well as being a rather nasty man. Notice how he has not ventured inside yet. I would expect that behaviour to continue until he believes you are secured, and then he will likely torture you to his heart's content after he has the upper hand. If you can extract yourself from this warehouse and attack Arnie from behind, then maybe you can avoid killing all your ex-work colleagues.*'

Mason grinned. '*You're a sodding genius, Nyx.*'

'I know,' she smiled back at him. *'I'll overlay the best route on top of your vision.'*

'Nice one, my very own Head-Up Display.'

In his mind, Mason immediately saw the route light up. He made a crouching run behind the gas cylinders and went quietly through an old side office door. Inside, he turned left and ran down the corridor. He paused at the corner at the end and listened. Quiet footsteps were coming towards him, they sounded like one person. He waited, and as the gun barrel poked around the corner, he grabbed it and rabbit punched the Tigris security guard in the head. A nice gentle tap, so he only knocked the man out.

He laid the guard down, then lifted his balaclava.

'Alright John,' whispered Mason, as he tapped the unconscious man on the cheek. *OK, now on to the first floor.* Mason followed the route and came to another corridor just after the stairs. Again, he listened carefully before moving quickly around the corner. Straight into the barrel of a gun pointing at his head.

He froze for a second, contemplating what to do, then the woman spoke.

'Shit, Mason, what the hell are you doing here?' She lowered her gun. 'I thought we were supposed to be stalking an enemy of the company, not one of our own.'

He recognised Zoe's voice immediately. One of his regular day shift guards, what felt like a hundred years ago.

'I'd rather you lot weren't here,' whispered Mason. 'It's that lunatic bastard outside that I want.'

She huffed out a breath. 'Can't argue with you there, we're none too happy to be here, especially with that slimeball. But it's a high-priority job for Mr Buckley, get it done or you're fired.' She looked at Mason. 'Reckon I'd rather be fired, if I'm honest.'

He flipped off his combat rucksack and rummaged inside. Zoe flinched but kept her nerve. Mason brought out three bundles of hundred-pound notes.

'Got to be about fifteen grand here. Take it and just quit, consider it severance pay. Trust me when I say this is only going to get worse.'

She studied him for a second then held out her hands. He gave her the cash and she put it in her combat pockets. She picked up her radio.

'West corner now, I can see our target making a break for it.' She turned the radio off and smashed it on the floor. 'OK, now give me a nice black eye for effect, but don't rip my head off. I've seen what Nectr can do, and we heard our target was pumped full of it.'

'I'll be gentle,' replied Mason, then he gave her a quick jab to the face before she changed her mind. Zoe went down and Mason caught her fall. He laid her on the ground and scuffled her unconscious body about for effect.

He listened in silence to check for others. When he heard nothing, he continued on to the eastern corner of the warehouse, following Nyx's directions. He quietly approached the window she'd highlighted and leaned through the broken pane. Down below him was his bike and, off to the left, Arnie was leaning into the warehouse entrance and talking on a radio.

'*Shit, no clear line of sight on the bastard.*' Mason climbed out of the window and dropped quietly to the ground, Arnie now shouting into his radio as he watched the large space inside intently from the doorway.

'*Nyx, find me somewhere close that's deserted. Then we'll grab him and finish him there.*' Mason started up the bike and immediately sped towards Arnie. The big man had only just turned around when Mason whipped past him at forty miles an hour. Mason ducked under the punch, then grabbed the collar of Arnie's jacket and held on. The yank of the big man's weight nearly ripped him off his bike, but he held on and sped up, dragging Arnie along with him.

'*Two hundred metres on the left,*' said Nyx. '*Old office block. Disused since the nineties.*'

Arnie started to struggle madly, causing the bike to swerve all over the place. Mason just sped up. When he hit eighty miles an hour, he slammed on the brakes and threw Arnie forty feet towards the first floor of the office block. With the momentum already in him, the large man flew straight through the windows and into the abandoned offices.

'*That should slow him down a bit.*' Mason steadied the bike as he slowed, then parked it up and jumped off, running into the building with barely a pause for breath.

'Building layout by any chance?' he asked Nyx.

'Nothing in my data, sorry.'

'OK, old school it is.' Mason stalked through the corridors, guns now in hand, looking for the stairs, but he needn't have worried, because Arnie came crashing through the ceiling and landed before him. Mason unloaded half a magazine from each gun, but the bullets just bounced off the man.

'Tellus second-gen.' An evil grin spread across Arnie's face. 'I'm upgraded now. All part of my brother's deal with your old boss. Richard got me out of the police station's morgue, all under the guise of medical research.' He beat his chest with a fist. 'And now I'm back. Man of steel, that's me.'

'Looks like Richard went the opposite way from us then,' said Mason to Nyx. He ducked under the first punch from Arnie, and the man's fist gouged a chunk of concrete out of the wall behind him.

'Yes, it appears that way,' observed Nyx. *'Tough as steel, with armour plating for skin. You see how he slightly shimmers in the light. It's very pretty.'*

The next punch caught Mason in the chest, smashing all the air from his lungs. He went flying back against the wall, the plasterboard barely cushioning him before he slammed into the hard concrete beneath it. His bones creaked but they held, the hard rubber effect stopping them from piercing his lungs. He sucked in a new breath and counterpunched Arnie hard in the face. Mason's steel-like knuckles dented the man's cheek, not really doing any damage but leaving a small mark.

Another powerful blow came in from the big man and Mason ducked too late. It caught him on the side of the face, and his head snapped violently sideways as he went flying down the corridor. He skidded along the floor and landed at the bottom of some stairs. Mason flexed his neck back into a more normal position then leapt to his feet and immediately ran up the stairs.

'Oh, good tactic,' said Nyx in all seriousness. *'Run away while we think of a plan to tackle a man far stronger and harder than us.'*

'Not running,' rasped Mason in between heavy breaths. 'Have a plan.' At the third floor, he stopped and leaned over the barrier to check Arnie was coming after him. He sucked in a deep breath and took a potshot for the sake of it. 'Come on you fat bastard, even your old brother's faster than you,' he shouted back down.

Steady stomping came from below. 'When I get hold of you, you little wanker, I'm going to rip your arms off and shove 'em up your arse.'

'*What, no "up my arse sideways" gag?*' thought Mason as he ran up further. '*He's a bit of a shit bad guy this bloke.*'

'*This is not a laughing matter,*' stated Nyx. Then she smiled. '*Though you do have a point.*'

He made it to the fifth floor and scanned around. Mason spotted what he wanted and ran to the end of the corridor. '*Time for that test, Nyx.*'

'*A dry run, in safer conditions would have been nice,*' she replied, taking note of their surroundings. '*But I'm sure you will make the best of it.*'

Arnie lumbered up the last set of stairs and turned to face Mason.

'Nowhere to run now, chicken boy.' He started to advance down the corridor straight at Mason, getting faster and faster. 'I'm going to smash you to pulp. Tigris can pour you into a test tube when I'm finished with you.'

Mason got himself ready as Arnie sped towards him.

'Come on then you fat git, let's have it.'

'*I think Arnold wins that last verbal exchange,*' said Nyx brightly, as the big man ploughed into them.

Massive hands latched on to Mason's neck and squeezed hard, but he ignored all that. He grabbed Arnie by the shirt, dragged him close in a lover's embrace. Then, using the momentum, twirled him around in a perfect twisting tango move. The two of them spun as they smashed out through the large window behind them.

'*Fifth-floor window, test one,*' noted Nyx. '*Estimated speed of impact, seventy-three point two eight kilometres per hour.*'

Arnie continued to squeeze at Mason's neck, and Mason pulled up his knees and placed them on the man's chest, as he manoeuvred the man below him.

'Squeeze this, you tosser,' Mason wheezed out through his constricted throat. Then they slammed into the concrete of the walkway in front of the office block. Mason's knees smashed into

Arnie's ribs at over forty-five miles an hour, coming to a dead stop after they'd flattened his ribcage by more than three quarters.

The grip around Mason's throat loosened, as Arnie stopped breathing and his arms started to lose power. Mason rolled off him and sat next to the mashed-up man, rubbing at his knees.

'That kind of hurt,' he said to Nyx.

'*I'm sorry, Mason, I couldn't absorb all the pain as usual. It was just too much.*'

He stopped rubbing his knees. 'Hold on, does the pain actually hurt you?' he asked.

'*Not really,*' she said brightly. '*Certainly, it hurts a whole lot less to absorb for you, than letting you feel it yourself. I don't like it when you feel pain.*'

Mason considered that for a second, then when Arnie wheezed in a tiny breath, he decided this was not the time for further questions about what he and Nyx felt.

'*Shit. Will Tellus fix him?*' he asked her instead.

'*From the data I have access to that Cora stole, then yes, I believe it will.*'

'Bollocks.' Mason pulled off his combat rucksack and went hunting. He came out with a small grenade. He reached over and jammed it into Arnie's mouth. He went to pull the pin, but the man spat it out. Arnie even grinned as he sucked in a slightly larger breath, not enough oxygen to fuel his muscles properly, but a start.

Mason went back to his rucksack.

'Where is it? Where is it?' he muttered to himself. 'Ah, here we go.' He came back out with a roll of duct tape. He jammed the grenade back in and used his foot to ram it down hard. Then he grabbed Arnie by the hair and taped up the man's mouth good and proper, covering most of his face and just leaving the grenade's pin sticking out. He left a tiny gap for the man's eyes, and in them, he saw the first glimmer of fear begin to appear. Mason pulled the pin and walked away. Arnie scrabbled desperately for a few seconds trying to rip off the tape, then the grenade went off. His armoured skin held firm, but his liquidised remains came squirting out of every orifice.

'*Ew,*' said Nyx.

Wiping a bit of Arnie off his face, Mason reached into his pocket for his phone. He dialled the number from memory. It was answered on the first ring.

'Yes.'

'Hey Dan,' said Mason. 'My condolences, your little brother is dead.'

'Dead dead?' asked Dan.

'Unless they can reanimate soup, then yeah, I'd say so.'

A small sigh came from the other end of the line. 'Fair enough. The better man won.' Dan's voice recovered itself a little. 'And now for Richard, yes?'

'Too sodding right,' said Mason, his anger lighting up. 'No one threatens my mum. That man is dead.'

'Did my brother assist in that threat?' asked Dan mildly.

'Yup.'

'Then certainly the better man won.' Dan's voice had its hard edge back again. 'What do you need in order to take Richard down?'

'Is that second lock-up still secure?'

'Yes, it should be,' said Dan.

'Good. Keep it that way, and that will be a start.' Mason cut the line. No sooner had he done that, than he dialled another number. The phone rang three times.

'Hello?' came a neutral female voice.

'Mum?'

'Mason.'

He wondered where to even start, so he went to the heart of the matter.

'You need to grab Dad and get out of there now. Bad people are coming. Very bad.'

There was a pause from the other end. 'The news? Did you kill those two women, that DCI and the head teacher?'

'No and yes, in that order,' answered Mason. 'It's complicated.'

'It always is with you,' said Mason's mum.

'Can we do this later, please? You need to get out of there.'

'This is not my first rodeo, young man,' she replied. 'I have your dad's ashes in my hand and my rucksack on my back, all fully loaded. What's the threat level?' she asked.

'Handguns and semi-automatics,' he answered. 'And likely some amped-up undead.'

'I have appropriate responses,' she stated. 'I'm on my way out the door now.'

'Thanks Mum. I'll call you later to see if you and Dad are OK. Please pick up.'

'We'll see.' The line went dead.

Mason stared at the phone and let out a sigh. He closed his eyes. 'Crap, crap, crap.'

'I would suggest we get moving,' prompted Nyx gently. *'Richard is very likely to send more people once Zoe's team report in.'*

'Alright, let's get back to the bike,' said Mason. He dialled Cora's new number as he started walking. She picked it up straight away.

'Are you OK?' she asked.

'You all need to leave,' said Mason quickly. 'Find somewhere new. Richard is out looking for us, we shouldn't stay anywhere too long. Oh, and he's not afraid to send out amped-up undead of the mental Tellus two variety. Not good, I can tell you. Don't reckon I could beat more than one of them at once. And you guys wouldn't stand a sodding chance.'

There was mumbling in the background. 'Carter asked why you didn't just call us in our heads,' said Cora.

'Everyone's a critic.' Mason rubbed at his face, scraping some more Arnie smoothie from it. 'I suppose it's just nice to talk to you normally for a change. You know, like regular friends.'

'Oh, so we're friends now, are we?' she teased. He heard her moving about, gathering things up. 'I'll text you when we've landed somewhere new. Cash again?'

'Yup,' replied Mason. 'Only the best hooker hotels for us.'

CHAPTER 14

Mason relaxed into the comfy armchair.

'Nice hotel this one.'

'Yes,' said Cora. 'You get a much better class of escort hotel for two hundred pounds an hour.'

He was too tired to even comment on that. 'I'm hungry, I need food. Fighting with supersoldiers is bloody hard work.'

'You might want to refresh your disguise before you think about going shopping.' She looked at him for a beat, then mimed a phone call with her hand. 'It's Elton John, he wants his sunglasses back.'

Mason grabbed the pink, starry, dark glasses and threw them on the bed.

'Best I could do, after my mascara got smudged. There's a market trader out there who's one hundred pounds richer.'

'I'm sure he was delighted,' said Cora.

He let his head roll back on to the chair. 'Any progress or new plans on your side?'

'The laptops are chugging away at the replication prevention data, though to be honest, the team at Tigris should really have finished by now. I guess Richard's still holding them back. Oh, and Carter is going to give me some firearms training. Mostly so I don't blow my own foot off I think.'

'Gunplay, in a hotel? You sure?'

'Theory I guess.' Cora reached down and grabbed a Waitrose shopping bag from beside her bed. 'Anyway, you don't need to go out. I thought you would be hungry, so I got baguettes, cold meats, salad, and things.' She offered the large bag to Mason. 'Would you like to make us some lunch while we play with the guns?'

Mason smiled hungrily. 'Yes, I think I would.'

He grabbed the bag and emptied the contents on to the bed.

Picnic plates and steel cutlery joined the food on his duvet, even a bread knife. Perfect. He walked into the bathroom and got a towel, then came back and spread everything out in an orderly fashion. Baguette slicing first. One slice for them, one slice for me, he chimed as he cut up the bread and stuck half of it in his mouth.

'Nyx told you about Arnie, yeah?' said Mason in between mouthfuls.

'Ugh, she certainly did,' replied Cora. 'He makes Dan look like an angelic choirboy.'

'Made,' corrected Mason.

She turned on the TV as a knock came at their door. Mason flipped the bread knife in his hand and got ready to throw it.

'*It's Jane and Carter*,' said Nyx pleasantly. '*You may go back to the bread, Mason*.'

Cora answered the door and Jane came in with her husband. Carter walked over to the other bed and plonked a bag of guns down on it.

'Mason's making lunch,' said Cora.

'Yeah, should be ready quick enough,' he added.

'Great.' Carter got out two handguns. 'Then there's just about time to cover the basics before we eat.'

Making up the first baguette, Mason turned to Carter's wife. 'No allergies, Jane?'

When she didn't answer, Mason prompted her again.

'Jane, any allergies?'

She pointed at the TV. 'Maybe we should listen to this first.'

He reached over for the control and turned up the volume. The reporter outside the Houses of Parliament was staring at the camera, waiting for something.

'This looks big,' said Carter.

'Next stage of the zombie apocalypse,' added Mason.

'You're not zombies,' stated Cora automatically.

'Hush all of you, please,' requested Jane.

The reporter poked at his ear then sucked in a breath to begin.

'The Prime Minister will be holding another emergency press conference in the next few minutes, along with a representative from the biotech companies and another from the ever-growing undead population.' The reporter swallowed. 'After which, we shall hear a pre-recorded speech from the President of the EU, and then finish with a live address from the President of the United States.'

'Blimey,' was all Mason could think to say, as he sat adding the finishing touches to six ham, egg, and salad baguettes. Just a dash of mustard, a sprinkling of balsamic vinegar, and a little black pepper. He handed them out as the Prime Minster came on to the screen. One for everyone else and three for himself.

'Once again, I must address a troubled nation,' started the PM, standing in a flawlessly tailored, dark blue suit. 'The spread of the dead coming back to life now covers the entire mainland of the UK, and we are fast approaching sixty-two thousand of our citizens who have come back to life.'

A grave look appeared on the PM's face. 'We face many problems. Some legal and logistical, and even more born from our human nature. For instance, unruly protests by large numbers of our population are certainly not helping. In addition to that, the undead appear to be vastly stronger and more resilient, which puts all living civilians at a grave disadvantage against the more unpleasant characters that have come back to life. Hence, we shall continue to enforce the rule that all undead must report to their local police station or army checkpoint for registration and temporary housing.'

The PM stood a little straighter. 'However, it is not all doom and gloom. Our world-leading biotech firms have been busy creating scientific agents to contain our growing problem. I am confident that, along with the efforts of the army and the police, we can regain the upper hand and restore our country to good working order in the very near future. Additionally, many of you have been helping your friends and relatives who have come back to life to report in peacefully. And some of the recently undead have started to work closely with us to smooth out the problems we are encountering.'

'Patronising bastard,' added Mason.

The PM turned and waved off camera. 'Therefore, I would like to introduce you to Mr Richard Buckley, the research director and now CEO of Tigris International Limited. He will walk us through the science. Richard, if you please.'

'God damn it,' said Mason, just about stopping himself from

chucking the remote control right through the TV screen.

The camera cut to Richard, and he positively glowed. 'Thank you, Prime Minister. I will keep this to the point, as there are many important things for me to cover.'

'Yeah, right,' said Mason. 'Like your ego I bet.'

'After all our urgent and extensive research,' continued Richard, 'we have found the cause of the dead coming back to life. It is a biotech virus of unknown origin that spreads primarily via our water supply and waste systems, but also through the soil and other water-bearing substances. We have given this biotech the code name Tellus. Fortunately, my company has just completed the research and successful testing of an agent that can block its spread. We have also confirmed that Tellus cannot spread through the heavily salted water of our seas.

'Following on from this, we are starting wholesale manufacture of the blocking agent and will be selling it to the UK government at cost price. We are, after all, a patriotic company. We will also make the blocking agent available worldwide, if other countries would like to purchase it for their additional peace of mind.'

A carefully calculated smile appeared on Richard's face. 'Research will continue into further preventative measures. If we can halt the spread of Tellus in its tracks, then the undead will be limited to the sixty-two thousand we have as of now. We shall make all countermeasures available as soon as we have them. Thank you, Prime Minister.'

'Weasel, toad, bastard,' said Mason.

'For once, I completely agree with you,' added Carter.

Cora held up her hand and glared at Mason. 'Shush, there's more.'

This time the PM looked rather less sure. 'And now I would like to introduce Mr Dan Samson, who will speak briefly on behalf of the undead. Mr Samson.'

The camera cut once again, and Dan Samson filled the screen. Mason caught Cora's look and decided to keep quiet for a change.

'Thank you. I will also keep this brief.' Dan held the gaze of the camera with total confidence and sincerity. 'We are working with the finest lawyers in the land, and the most well-meaning MPs, to find the right place for the undead in this great country of ours. I will devote my considerable resources to this endeavour until it is complete. A website has been set up to gather all views, both from the living and the undead. Not everyone will get their way, but I assure you, no voice will go unheard. Once again, thank you.'

'Wow, he's good,' said Cora. 'He was completely wasted as a gangland boss.'

The message from the EU was the expected political platitudes. Every help will be extended, our sympathies go out to those affected, and don't you dare open up your border or there will be trouble, big time. And then the President of the United States was beamed in from the White House.

'My fellow Americans, citizens of the United Kingdom, and people of the world, I speak to you now in one of the darkest hours for our friends in the UK. I have discussed the situation at hand with the Prime Minister of the United Kingdom, and we shall offer every assistance as one of your closest allies. Our finest biotech firms will work with yours on finding a cure for this biotech virus. Every military resource will be extended, as required, to ensure that law and order can be maintained. People of the UK, you can rest assured that America will not desert you. Thank you.'

The TV cut back to the original reporter, and the man just stared at the camera. Mason turned off the TV and whistled.

'Bloody hell, looks like we need to get our shit in order quickly, or the US is going to be stepping in big time. And he practically demanded all our scientific data.'

'Political games for the most part, I suspect,' said Jane. 'And there will be many more to come, no doubt.'

'I imagine Dan Samson will likely have something to say about it too,' added Cora. 'Especially as Richard is deliberately escalating the fear factor by stating Tellus is a virus, when he knows full well it's not. It may have some similarities in behaviour patterns to a virus, but none of the Nectr strains are actually viruses. Amanda just didn't design it that way.'

'Yeah, well, Dan can only correct things if he ever gets any rights.' Mason finished the last of his third sandwich. 'So where do we stand?'

Cora tapped at a laptop. 'Slow progress,' she said. 'Thanks for the laptops, but what I really need are a couple of hundred supercomputers. And…'

'I know, I know,' said Mason. 'You could do with Amanda's help and advice.' His phone pinged with a text.

Call me on this number.
Amanda

'Blimey, talk about the mad scientist devil.'

Mason called the number and put his mobile on speaker.

'Hey honey,' he said when she picked up. 'You're on speaker with Cora too.'

'Ex-honey,' Amanda reminded him.

'Did you text me just to wind me up in front of my friend?'

Amanda laughed down the phone. 'No, to help you, of course,' she said. 'Lucky for you, I connected all my old email accounts to my new phone. So, after seeing the President's broadcast, and that horrible little speech from Richard, I went looking for emails from you. It occurred to me that you might need some assistance from your stunningly beautiful and superintelligent wife.'

'Yeah, yeah,' said Mason, the irritation barely disguised in his voice. 'So, what help can you give us? More wisdom from your mad research?'

'Harsh but basically true,' said Amanda pleasantly. 'For starters, from my calculations, there will be quite a few more than sixty-two thousand of the undead over the oncoming years. Pretty much everyone on the UK mainland will already have Tellus first generation in their system from the country's recycled water system. Even if you stop Tellus from replicating any more, there will be around another seventy thousand people coming back to life over the next eighty years or so.'

'You mean, anyone that already has Tellus in their system, then when they die there's a one in a thousand chance of them coming back?' asked Mason.

'Very good, you could almost be a lab assistant.' Amanda gave another gentle laugh down the phone. 'Now please let me speak with

Cora, and I'll see what further help I can lend to a real scientist.'

'Thanks, I think.' Mason reeled off Cora's new number. 'If you can get Cora access to some serious computing power, and maybe give her a few pointers, then that would be a great start.'

'I think I can manage that,' replied Amanda brightly. 'I've been employed by another company already, and they have plenty of resources. If you don't mind sharing all your findings with me, and probably compromising any personal data you have stored, then I can get you access to oodles of computing power.'

Mason looked at Cora and she nodded in reply. 'Great,' he said. 'Can you call her on that number I just gave you? Then you two can talk science together.'

'Of course,' said Amanda. 'Would you like to talk to Dad for a bit, while I help Cora? I can just as easily use one of my other phones.'

'Actually, that would be nice, thanks.' Mason picked up the phone and took it off speaker. He waited for a couple of seconds and Colin's voice came on the line.

'Hello, son, how are you?'

'Not bad, Mr Robertson. Fighting a supersoldier and turning him into soup,' said Mason. 'How about you lot?' He paused for a second wondering how to phrase things. 'Reshmi still a bit feisty?'

Colin chuckled. 'A wee bit, but we're working it out. As long as Amanda's safe, she's fairly content. Hasn't killed anyone yet.'

'Where are you guys anyway?' asked Mason.

'Lovely little secluded estate somewhere in the New Forest, son. Nice and comfy here.'

'I didn't know you had that much squirreled away, Mr Robertson, good on you.'

This time Colin laughed. 'Not mine, Amanda's new friend, Herbert, it's his. He picked us up and sorted us a place to stay.'

'What, that rival CEO tosser?'

'Yup, that's the one,' confirmed Colin.

'Well, you be careful, alright? These biotech wankers are not good people.' Mason snorted a laugh. 'And that's saying something coming from the likes of me.'

'Oh, I'll be careful, don't you worry,' replied Colin, his voice hard. 'Nothing short of a nuclear bomb is going to touch my daughter while I'm around.'

'Great to hear,' replied Mason, not mentioning the fact that might well be an option for some of the powers that be. 'See you later, Colin.'

'You take care too, son,' said the large Scotsman. 'See ya, pal.'

As he put down the phone, Mason watched Cora while she spoke with Amanda. Most of it was completely over his head, but it was nice to see her eyes wide with excitement at the resources and knowledge she was receiving. He added Amanda's new number to the contacts in his phone and labelled it "*Mad Scientist Wife*" as usual. Then he tapped back a few characters and carefully retyped "*Ex-Wife*". Not true yet, but what the hell, going that way for sure.

Cora put down her phone and sat next to Mason. She watched him type out the last few characters and save the contact in his phone. She picked up her own phone again and dialled a number. Mason's mobile rang. He looked at it and then at Cora.

'I was just wondering what my number might say,' she said, and smiled a little. 'I kind of like that. "*Well-meaning Irish Chick*". It has a nice ring to it, even if it is a little demeaning.' She watched as Mason's face fell, as he wondered how to respond. 'I'm kidding,' she laughed. 'But, why do you add names like that to your phone numbers?'

'Gets me in the right frame of mind to talk to the person calling,' he replied honestly. 'Speaking of which, what's the deal with mad scientist Amanda?'

'She's given me a whole bucketload of supercomputing power to run simulations on, and some additional theories to test out.' Cora tapped away enthusiastically at her laptop's keyboard. 'So now it's a race between Richard and me as to who will complete and release the replication prevention agent first. If I can get there before he decides to release it, then we can just give out the formula for free. Maybe that will start to calm down some of the international tensions.'

Mason put a hand on her shoulder. 'You're a star, Cora.' He stood and made for the bathroom. 'I'm going to put my mascara back on. Wouldn't want the cleaners recognising me and calling the cops.' He turned to Carter. 'Care to help me, mate? After all, it's your lot that are after me.'

They walked in and closed the door. Carter sat on the edge of the bath and Mason on the toilet. Lid down. He held the mascara wand in his hand, reading the label.

'Smudge proof, my arse. Every time I get into a fight, this gets smeared all to hell.'

'You could stop getting into fights,' suggested Carter. 'I suspect that wasn't one of the cosmetics company's test cases.'

Staring right back, Mason gave a sceptical look. 'I doubt the fighting's going to stop anytime soon. Any other bright ideas?'

'We could try getting you an official pardon. What about your new friend, Mr Dan Samson. Could he put in a good word for you?'

'Not my friend,' replied Mason, 'but yeah, maybe he could.'

He took the phone out of his pocket and dialled. This time it was two rings before Dan picked up.

'I'm rather busy,' he said.

'Can you get me a pardon, so I can move about freely and take Richard out?'

The line went quiet for a couple of seconds. 'I'm working on something along those lines. Give me a little time and I'll get back to you.'

'Thanks.' Mason cut the call.

'I'll just pretend I didn't hear that,' said Carter. 'Along with the other five things I definitely didn't hear today.'

Mason patted him on the shoulder. 'Good man.'

Carter and Jane had left for some gun practice, and to give Cora some peace and quiet to work. Mason lay on the bed, idly watching her tap away at the keyboard and swirl her fingers around on the trackpad. In his head, he thought about the world of crap they were in, wondered whether they would actually survive or just get trampled to death by the major players and their various ambitions. '*Hey Nyx, what do you make of all this?*' he asked her, just between the two of them.

'*You humans are very inefficient,*' she stated. '*It would be far more productive if you all cooperated to solve the problems in front of you, rather than trying to score points for your own personal advantage.*'

'*Yup, that's the human race all over,*' thought Mason.

'*On the positive side,*' she added, '*I have successfully calculated how to give you some privacy, Mason Granger. Therefore, I currently have some spare capacity to help Cora with her calculations. Unless you need anything else?*'

'*Nah, that's great. Go help Cora,*' replied Mason. '*So how would you give me some privacy then?*'

'*I now know how to shut down and reboot myself,*' announced Nyx. '*I could effectively become non-functional to stop experiencing everything you do and hence give you total privacy. I could then reconstruct myself when required from the residual data in my constituent parts and fill in any gaps from your own memories of me.*'

'*So, you'd stop functioning in between, right?*'

'*Yes, that is effectively the only way to give you privacy.*'

He huffed out a breath. '*Nah, no way I'm having you kill yourself so I can get a bit of me time.*'

'*I am not human. I do not really live or die,*' she said. '*Consider this akin to a pause button on a video game. I will just cease to function for a period of time.*'

'*Still no,*' stated Mason. '*But thanks for looking into it, Nyx.*'

'*As you wish,*' Nyx replied pleasantly.

His phone rang and Mason looked at the screen. "*Gangster Dan or Friendly Shark?*" lit up in front of him.

'Alight Dan, what you got for us?'

'I'll send people to drop off clean cars for you. Send me your location by text,' instructed Samson. 'Get yourself and Cora down to Kent ASAP. Probably best if she drives and you ride in the boot to stay hidden.'

Mason groaned. 'That's a bloody two-hour drive.'

Dan chuckled warmly. 'I'll make sure they add a blanket and pillow for you. I'll text you the address in Kent.'

There was indeed a blanket and a pillow, but it was still a very long and boring two hours for Mason. Not a lot of "I spy" material in the boot of a car.

CHAPTER 15

Dan met them at the door to a large eighteenth-century country house; all dark red brickwork and buttresses, not a castle but not quite a house either. It was surrounded by neatly trimmed hedges and lawns, and even a small lake at the bottom of the hill.

'Nice place, Dan. Being a gangster certainly paid well, or did you steal this too?' said Mason. 'And why did we need to come all the way out to Kent?'

'I have access to several houses from my previous endeavours, all owned by shell companies. This one is closest to where my guest used to live. He feels most comfortable here,' answered Samson, as he led them down a wide hallway. 'It also keeps us away from the public eye. I may have negotiated a few privileges in exchange for representing the undead in a more orderly fashion, but many in the government are still very much against us. So, it's easiest to avoid their interference when I'm out here. Out of sight, out of mind, and all that. Still, my guest and I will need to head back to London soon, we can't accomplish everything we need from here.'

'Who is your guest?' asked Cora.

'You'll see,' smiled Samson, as he opened the door to a comfortably furnished room and they walked in. He showed them to a couple of armchairs, then took one for himself. Cora placed her laptop on the elaborate tea table before her and brought up her presentation, now updated with all the latest info.

'You wanted to be fully brought up to date, yes?' she asked Dan.

Mason poked her in the arm and pointed at the slightly portly old man sitting in the fourth armchair. She stared for a second.

'Wow, it's fecking Winston Churchill,' she exclaimed, then she put her hand over her mouth. 'Sorry, sir.'

Churchill smiled and waved away any worries. 'Young lady, you may address me as you wish. You deserve that right, considering the sacrifices we are about to ask you to make.' He indicated to her laptop. 'But update us first, with all the information you have on that newfangled machine of yours. That would be wise.'

Mason eyed Churchill and Dan suspiciously but kept quiet. Samson turned on the enormous touchscreen that had been hastily nailed to a wall, over the top of some antique bookshelves.

'You should be able to connect to this,' he said to Cora. 'Password is forty-seven, all letters, no space or dash.'

Cora gave them the updated ten-minute version and then sat back.

'I'm close to cracking the formula for a replication prevention agent. Another two or three days should be enough. Then I can release the formula for free and the world can breathe a little easier.'

'Sadly, young lady,' said Churchill in a grave tone, 'I believe we do not have that time available to us. Although Mr Samson and I are gathering a few rebel MPs, and some like-minded individuals in the armed forces, to try to restore some balance to this country of ours, many others are not listening to the undead or our quest for rights. However, that is not our biggest obstacle. It appears that Richard Buckley has plans of his own, and he is already well advanced. He has the ear of many in power, and predictably, his plans are singularly focused on his own self-interest, at the expense of everyone else.' Churchill opened a hand to Dan. 'If you could update Ms Gallagher and Mr Granger.'

'I have purchased a few informants within Tigris,' started Dan. 'Expensive and not very trustworthy, but when we put all their stories together and analyse them, we get something close to the truth.'

'Jesus, Dan,' said Mason, 'what are you, a gangster or a bloody stock market analyst?'

'Like any good ex-gangster,' replied Samson pointedly, 'I'm a little bit of everything.' He walked over to the large screen and tapped on it to bring up his own data. 'Richard has just sold his first batch of the Tellus blocker to his friends in the UK government for two hundred billion pounds.'

'Bloody hell, that doesn't sound much like cost price to me,' exclaimed Mason. 'Can the UK even afford those kinds of figures?'

Samson's face darkened. 'And there's the devious bit. The UK government has set the price. Richard is now in the process of selling to all the major governments around the world, deals are being signed as we speak and vast sums of money are changing hands. The estimated revenue is nine hundred billion and rising. In return for the UK government setting such a high price, Richard has promised to ensure Tigris pays full UK corporation tax on all the profits. The UK effectively then gets the blocker agent for free.'

'If Richard keeps his word,' pointed out Cora. 'I wouldn't trust that.'

'Agreed,' said Samson. 'I've dealt with plenty of untrustworthy shysters in my time, but Richard takes the prize as the very worst. And unfortunately, there's more. Richard also has the replication prevention agent ready; he's just holding it back deliberately.'

'Until he's finished his sales of the blocker?' asked Cora.

'Exactly, and he plans to start selling the anti-replication agent as soon as the previous deals are finished. Every government around the world will want it, they all hate what they can't control. It might only bring back one in a thousand people from the dead, but the other nine hundred and ninety-nine are at a massive disadvantage, to say the least. Until someone figures out how to make Tellus first generation more targeted, then most governments are looking to block it completely for now. Nobody likes odds of one thousand to one against.'

Samson leaned back in his chair. 'So, there you have it, a total revenue estimate of over two point five trillion pounds, probably more. With that, Richard could buy any remaining sections of the UK government that were still sitting on the fence, and we would be subjected to his greed and control for years.'

Mason stood up. 'Alright, I'm off to grab the guns. That man is seriously dead.'

Cora caught the look on Samson's face and gently guided Mason back to his seat.

'There's still more, isn't there?'

Samson looked over to Churchill. The old man stirred in his seat, pushing himself a little straighter with his arms.

'Sadly, there is, young lady. Mr Samson's spies also revealed that a production line for Tellus second generation is nearly complete. It will soon be ready to start manufacture and shipping to the highest bidder.' He turned to Mason 'You fought just one man enhanced by it, could you imagine what an army of them would do?'

'Yeah, very bad things,' said Mason darkly. 'They'd make the Roman legions look like teddy bears.' Then he caught the expression on the two men opposite him. *Crap, they're even more worried than that*, he thought to himself. 'And?' he asked out loud.

'We don't have any hard data,' said Samson, 'but one informant reported seeing a lot of very unhappy scientists, and a fair few terrified ones. From what we can tell, a prototype for Tellus third generation is nearly ready.' Samson's face darkened further. 'And it's going to make second-gen look like fucking jelly and ice cream in comparison.'

'We have to go public with this,' said Cora. 'It's massive.'

'Indeed, it is, young lady,' agreed Churchill. 'However, all our information is basically just conjecture at this point, and illegally gained. Plus, three of us in this room have no rights at all. Faced with the vast resources that Richard has at his disposal, I do not believe we would be able to make a difference before it was too late.'

'So, what's the plan?' asked Mason. 'You do have one, right?'

'I am glad you asked,' said Churchill. 'Like all good plans, our solution is based in simplicity. We wipe the data at Tigris, kill Richard Buckley, and raze the place to the ground.'

Samson looked at Mason, his face as hard as granite. 'That man and his empire needs to be gone, permanently. It's the only way to be sure.'

'Shit,' said Mason. 'No prizes for guessing which bit you'd like me to do.'

Mason sat with Churchill on the terrace, both men smoking a cigar, Mason just tasting it and swilling the smoke around in his mouth.

'You're right, it does taste nice.' He pulled his gaze away from the peaceful view and glanced over at Churchill. 'I've got to ask. What was it like being proper dead?' said Mason. 'I mean, I already had Nectr in me, so I wasn't ever really dead dead. You, mate, were in the ground for decades.'

Churchill stared into space. 'To be frank with you, Mr Granger, I don't remember. It is frustrating to say the least. So many answers I could have given the world, but I just don't know what they are.'

'No book tour for you then. Well, apart from the fact that you're Winston sodding Churchill back from the dead, so maybe a TV interview or ten.'

Churchill gave Mason a wry look. 'Ah, but would your modern public boo or cheer, I wonder?'

'I guess history gets to judge you in the flesh all over again. Rather you than me, mate. Can't imagine what people will think of my actions in sixty years' time.' Mason pulled on his cigar again. 'Not that I care much. I'm more focused on the here and now. How about you fill me in on the tactics you guys have cooked up? How are we going to wade into Tigris and whack Richard? I can leave Cora and Dan to talk about wiping the data, but storming the citadel, that's right up my street.'

'Four a.m. tomorrow morning appears to be the opportune moment for you to hit the building, Mr Granger, and dispose of Richard Buckley. He has not left the Tigris complex recently, except for the press conference, so we expect him to be there. The scientists are all gone by three a.m., and the cleaners are mostly finished by four. If we leave things any later, then the early risers will have started to arrive.'

'Minimum collateral damage, huh?' said Mason.

'Yes, we would prefer that.' Churchill blew cigar smoke into the country air. 'Mr Samson will supply you with some undead muscle to help clear the night shift security team. They will disable and remove them as best they can. However, lethal force will be employed if required.'

'I could call Zoe. If she's still working there, she could get some of them to clear out ahead of time,' suggested Mason. 'Most of them are OK people.'

Churchill gave him an impassive look. 'No, you could not, Mr Granger. There can be no leaks as to what we are about to do. The stakes are too high. We are at war with Richard Buckley, make no mistake. And if we do not stop him now, then many more people will suffer greatly.'

'Shit. Fine.' Mason dragged angrily on his cigar. 'We'll do it your way.'

'I believe I am somewhat qualified to judge,' Churchill replied lightly in his gravelly voice. 'However, when you are inside and the situation is live, then you will be free to act as you see fit. Once the strategy is set, I am a big believer in delegating the actual tactics to those in the firing line.' Another wry grin appeared on his face.

Mason nodded. 'Thanks.' He pondered the situation for a second, thinking something was still left unsaid.

'*Backup plan?*' prompted Nyx.

'Oh, yeah, what's the backup plan if I fail?' asked Mason casually, as if he were just requesting another cigar and it would be offered freely.

'You deserve to know,' Churchill nodded slowly. 'We have discussed this with our allies in the armed forces and a select few MPs. If you do not succeed, then at five a.m. precisely, the Tigris complex will be bombed into dust by a tactical air strike from our friends in the air force, and we would effectively be going rogue.' Another puff on the cigar. 'I deeply wish to avoid that scenario. As you can imagine, given the sheer breadth of allies Mr Buckley has in the government, that could tear our great country in two in the most violent way. The undead versus the living in a fight for survival would not be pleasant.'

'Ha, no pressure then.'

A low chuckle came from Churchill. 'None whatsoever, Mr Granger.'

'Alright, you're on.' Mason stood up and walked to the low wall at the edge of the terrace and looked out at the lawns and distant clear blue lake. 'I'd like a few favours in exchange.'

'What payment would you like?' asked Churchill.

'Clear my name from killing DCI Cuthbert would be good. I didn't do it, so I'd like that stitch-up to be put to bed. And I want a pardon for killing Miss Turnbull. She asked me to sort her out, and I did as I was asked.'

'We will try our best to arrange that,' agreed Churchill. 'Are there any more favours you require?'

'If I don't make it out, then make sure someone looks after Cora and my mum. Neither will want it, but both need it in different ways.'

Churchill smiled. 'You drive a hard bargain indeed.'

Mason laughed. 'You wait until I hit Dan's wine cellar, then you'll see what a man like me really costs.' He stubbed his cigar out on the wall. 'One more thing. That Patricia Huge-Raven-Face woman isn't part of your new alliance, is she? You know, the Junior Minister for Bullshit. She's another one on my weasel, toad, bastard list.'

This time Churchill let out a low laugh. 'I can assure you, Mr Granger, we are gathering allies of the non-toad variety only.'

Sitting stubbornly in the passenger seat, Mason folded his arms.

'I'm not going in the boot again for two hours. I don't care how many pillows it's got, it's boring and it smells.'

'OK.' Cora reached into her bag and brought out her sunglasses. 'Put these on.'

He grabbed them and stretched them around his face.

She examined his face then rummaged around in her bag and brought out some new lipstick she'd bought that morning. It was so deep red it was almost brown. She held it out to Mason.

'And this too.'

'How?' asked Mason. 'I've never put on lipstick before.'

'Oh, for goodness' sake, I'll do it.' Cora leaned over and carefully applied some to Mason's lips, her tongue slightly poking out of her mouth as she concentrated. 'Now do this to smooth it out,' she instructed, rolling her own lips together. She sat back to admire her handiwork. 'Maybe one more thing.' Back in the bag and she brought out a light green, woolly hat. 'And this. It'll cover your distinctive ears.'

'Who buys all this crap during a zombie apocalypse?' asked Mason, putting the hat on.

'Me, that's who.' She started the car and made her way slowly up the long gravel driveway. She looked in the mirror wistfully at the stately home they were leaving behind. 'Wouldn't it be nice if we could just stay here and forget about all this?'

'Why aren't you staying here?' asked Mason. 'Internet access was good, and you've got all the remote computing power you need now.'

She indicated to turn left then put her foot down. The powerful

Range Rover engine responded, and the car sprung forward.

'Duh, because someone needs to wipe the data at Tigris, you lummox, especially the adaptive AI they're running. There's no way we can let anyone else get hold of that, so I need to be there to ensure it's deleted permanently.'

'What?' exclaimed Mason. 'Oh no you don't. You're not going within ten miles of that mental place. We'll be planting powerful plastic explosives all over the place, whilst fighting supersoldiers pumped full of Tellus second generation and maybe even a prototype of third. Deadly as shit doesn't even begin to describe it.'

'Oh, so you're going to hack into the isolated Tigris systems, locate and wipe the data, whilst ensuring those loyal to Richard don't just transfer it out of there from under your nose, are you? All while fighting scores of amped-up, deadly killers. Punching people and typing at the same time? Really?'

Mason tried to think of a comeback, but nothing came to him, so he just folded his arms and sat there in silence. After a minute, he turned on the radio, switching to the BBC World Service.

'Fine, but you're getting a crash course in firearms. And Carter can bloody well come too and look after you. No arguments.'

'Shush,' said Cora, 'a reporter is following up on the international talks.'

The tones of a reassuring, no nonsense Yorkshire accent floated out from the radio.

'Talks are continuing between the G20 nations to discuss the ongoing crisis. Tensions are running high, as all member countries have put their armed forces on alert. We can also report that urgent discussions are continuing between the United Kingdom and the United States. In fact, we can go over to our Washington correspondent right now. Jenny, what news do you have for us?'

There was silence over the radio for five seconds, then a shaky and far less confident voice started.

'The US president has made a statement to address the nation. The American public have been reassured that the US will receive the first shipments of the blocking agent within the next twenty-four hours and will also receive all the data required to manufacture further quantities under US control. If they do not get what is required by the end of tomorrow, the US will deploy the might of their armed forces to secure it.'

Mason stared out through the window.

'Shit, did the US just declare war on us?'

'Without actually saying the specific words, I think it just might have. So much for your special relationship.' She paused for a second. 'Fecking hell,' she added quietly.

'Right, Richard is definitely going down for this shitstorm of a killer hornet's nest he's stirring up.' Mason cracked his knuckles, but also used his head a bit too. 'When we get you in there, could you get all the counteragent data outside somehow?' Mason felt a splinter of pain inside as he said the next bit. 'You know, just in case we don't make it out and you can't finish your research.'

A determined look came over Cora's face as she manoeuvred them on to the A22. 'Whatever it takes, I'll figure something out,' she said.

'Good.' Mason rolled his seat back. 'Nyx, fill me full of that sleepy crap, I need to get some kip. It's going to be a busy evening when we get back.'

Cora nudged Mason in the arm and Nyx poured some adrenaline into him. He woke up and recognised the hotel car park.

'Let's grab our gear and move again. Don't want Richard's people catching up with us. He's bound to have stuffed at least his personal bodyguards with Tellus second-gen.'

Mason called Carter. '*We should move, and then I've got a job for you. Something you're really not going to like. Where are you?*'

'*We're back in our room. Shall we see you in five minutes with our bags?*'

'*Perfect, mate.*' Mason cut the connection. He opened the door to their room and started to close the applications and power-down the laptops as Cora instructed him, then he put them in the combat rucksacks. Guns and money next. Dirty clothes he put in a plastic bag for binning later.

Cora brought over the last of the laptops for him to pack.

'I want to make sure we keep all our own laptops active, as well as using Amanda's remote computing power, just in case she decides to cut us off for any reason,' she said. 'Where to next?'

'I'll text Dan and see what he can suggest.' He tapped away on his phone and got an answer within twenty seconds. 'Nice. Dan has a safe house ten minutes away. We can crash there until it's time to leave. Gives me an opportunity to teach you about guns and then you can get a good bit of sleep before the off. When I'm done with the prep work with Dan's people, I'll crash for a bit more as well. Nothing trashes an operation like being too tired.' He pinged the address over to Carter's phone.

A small yawn crept out of Cora's mouth, as if her body had been listening in. 'Sounds like a plan. I am pretty wreaked.'

Carter knocked on the door and Mason let him in.

'We're ready to go,' said Jane in her quiet way. 'Now, what are you going to ask my husband to do that he will not like?'

Mason gave them the two-minute version as they walked to the cars. Jane paused before turning towards her own vehicle.

'You're right, he will not like that at all,' she said, speaking confidently on behalf of her husband, 'but I know he will do what is right.'

Carter nodded while Jane held Mason's eyes with a powerful stare.

'But if you get my husband killed, again, I will never forgive you.' Then she lent in and did something unexpected, she kissed him lightly on the cheek. 'Good luck, Granger-san.'

Watching her and Carter get in their car, Mason gave them a mock salute, then he got back in the Range Rover, chucking in the bags as he went.

'Onwards and upwards, my good woman,' he said breezily. 'On to pastures anew.'

'You're a bit cheery,' said Cora as she started the car.

'Gallows humour, miss, gallows humour.'

Cora looked up at another expansive house, nowhere near as big as Samson's mansion in Kent but still very impressive. All the more so, given that it was inside the M25 and nestled in a leafy suburb of North London.

'I should have been a bloody criminal,' said Mason, as he grabbed the bags from the car and walked up to the house. The front door was unlocked, the keys hanging on a hook just inside. 'Bit risky leaving it unlocked.'

Cora pointed up to the tiny cameras dotted around. 'I suspect the local crooks know to steer clear. I can't imagine Mr Samson being the forgiving type.'

Mason dumped the bags on the kitchen table, as Carter and Jane joined them.

'Right,' he said, 'weapons training for Cora, then briefing time at eight p.m. Lights out at nine p.m. for some kip. Awake at two a.m. to make final preparations, we leave here at three thirty, ready to hit the Tigris front gates at four a.m. sharp.' He tapped at the stopwatch on his phone. 'The clock is now officially ticking. Got it?'

'*Yes, Sergeant*,' they all chimed together along with Nyx over their connection.

'Very funny, Nyx,' said Mason, though he couldn't help but smile. 'Your doing, huh?'

'*Humour of the gallows*,' she said brightly.

Grabbing a couple of guns from the bag, Mason added silencers to them.

'Come on, Cora. I know a quiet spot we can use for a bit of practice.'

Cora lined up the gun's sight, held her breath, and gently squeezed the trigger. The oversized baked beans tin fifty feet away failed to move an inch, but the poor tree four feet aside from it got another nasty surprise.

'This is harder than it looks on those TV shows,' she said, frustration creeping into her voice.

'Yeah, not every nerd has a hidden talent for guns.' Mason adjusted her grip slightly. 'Right, ten more rounds in the magazine. Walk towards the tin and keep firing. Pretend you really hate it.'

'I like baked beans,' Cora replied.

'Pretend it's Richard.'

Cora walked towards the tin, gun out, firing repeatedly. Finally, she hit the target and the tin went flying back.

Mason walked over. 'Congratulations. As long as you're within eight feet, then the bad guys are toast.' He unloaded the magazine and put a new one in. He flipped on the safety and handed it back to her. 'For emergencies only, I reckon. We'll just get Carter to stick to you like glue.'

'Probably for the best,' she admitted. 'I have figured out how to get the data out, though. Blindingly obvious really. I can just glance through it, Nyx can memorise it, and then she can transfer it to the one per cent of herself in Jane. Easy as pie.'

He nodded in appreciation, as Nyx smiled in their heads. '*What would you do without me?*' she said.

'Stop breathing and melt into the ground, mostly likely,' said Mason.

'*Oh no, I will never allow that,*' replied Nyx.

He gathered up the guns but left the shells. Mason figured nothing could be traced back to him unless they got caught. And if they did, they'd be screwed for more than just firing a gun on disused ground.

'There's something I've been meaning to bring up. How come Tellus first generation isn't self-aware like Nyx?' he asked them both as they walked back to the car. 'I know you said the adaptive AI was massively expensive to make, but I can't see Amanda caring about cost when bringing her parents back.'

'From the further data Amanda has given me about her previous research, she deliberately decided not to add the adaptive AI layers to Tellus,' said Cora. 'Partly, it was just too much complexity that she didn't need, but mostly it was too risky that it might veer off in a direction she didn't want. With strain thirty-seven in you, she'd found the underlying equations to bring back the dead, and that was enough for her to bring back her parents. And more to the point, she doesn't actually know what Nyx is. Amanda has no idea Nyx can reason for herself and communicate with us, so fortunately she's not aware of the adaptive AI's full capabilities.'

Cora paused as she reached the driver's door. 'From what I could tell, before we were fired, Amanda tried to clean house a bit before she hastily left. The data for Nyx's particular type of adaptive AI is gone from the files at the office. So there's no record of it anywhere in Tigris. However, Nyx and I have been looking over the maths as a side project.'

'Yes, it is fascinating to study the building blocks of myself in such detail. They are different in a few key areas from the other Nectr strains,' added Nyx. *'And it's especially fun to work with such a keen and sharp mind as Cora's.'*

'Aw, thanks Nyx,' said Cora. 'You really do say the sweetest things.' She gently prodded Mason and gave him a grin. 'Unlike some people and their potty mouth.'

'Ho ho,' he replied, deliberately leaving out a couple of choice swear words. 'So, what you're both saying is that Nyx is pretty unique, huh?'

'Yes, and fortunately Richard also seems to be unaware how special Nyx is. Otherwise, I expect he would have sent far more than just Arnold Samson and a few security guards to grab you.'

'Yeah, good job that,' said Mason as he got back in the car. 'We still need to figure out how I can take on more than one of those Tellus second-gen freaks at the same time. No way I'll be lucky enough for there to be only one of them at once when we break into the office.'

'I have an enhancement research project that is nearing completion,' said Nyx. *'I've been saving it as a pleasant surprise for you.'*

Mason laughed. 'Because my life doesn't have enough of those already.' He closed his eyes for the short journey back to the safe house. 'Any chance of ten minutes' kip?' he asked Nyx. 'You know, so I'm nice and refreshed for my surprise.'

CHAPTER 16

Eight p.m. and Mason stood by the fireplace in the huge living room of Samson's safe house. Over thirty people were looking at him and he felt somewhat nervous. Facing down a gun, sure no problem; public speaking, not so much. They'd all been given the full background by Cora, and now it was his turn to lay out the tactical plan. He coughed hesitantly then decided to just plough into it, how bad could it be?

'Right, we hit the Tigris complex at four a.m. tomorrow morning. Undead Team One will clear out the remaining living people, night shift security guards and any cleaners left over. Got it?'

A chorus of nods came from the right and centre of the room.

'Undead Team Two will lay the explosive charges. Basement explosives will be set for four thirty a.m., and the rest set to one minute later. The time delay is just in case any of us need a little extra time to clear the area and you can't get a better warning than the basement exploding to get out fast. So, final charges are set for four thirty-one a.m. precisely. Everyone has to be out by then, no exceptions. OK?' Mason decided not to mention the backup plan.

Another set of nods from a smaller group of undead on the left of the room.

'The remaining undead will be led by Carter and will protect Cora as she wipes the company data, whilst also stealing the replication prevention agent formula.' Mason took in the room. 'I know that goal is more controversial, as it will prevent Tellus from replicating any further, so it will stop itself from spreading into anyone new. Once the prevention agent is released, then us undead in the UK will be the only undead on the whole planet. We'll always be just a drop in the ocean in a world of eight billion living people. If anyone has a problem with that, now's the time to speak up.'

One hand went up.

Mason smiled. 'We're not in school, you can speak freely.'

A young lad stepped forward, barely out of puberty.

'What if we do all this, and then they just continue to lock us up anyway for being dead?'

'Good point,' said Mason. 'And yeah, that might happen. But whether the living want it or not, we're doing this for them, return the world to some kind of stability. We can only hope that some of them will appreciate it and then the government will stop locking us up.'

'Some of us already do appreciate what you're doing,' added Jane firmly.

'Anyone else?' Mason looked about. 'No, OK good. So, the final piece of this mental jigsaw is me. I'll do my best to handle anyone amped up with Tellus second generation whilst I'm gunning for Richard. The biggest threat will likely be Richard's personal bodyguards. If you see Tellus first-gen undead, feel free to take them on. If you see any second-gen, run like hell.'

'How will we tell the difference?' asked a large old lady from the back.

'Because they'll probably be twisting off someone's head and spitting down their throat,' answered Mason.

One final look around the room, and fortunately, many determined faces stared back at him.

'I'm not going to sugar-coat it; this is going to be bad and some of us won't come back,' said Mason. 'But Dan chose you all for two good reasons. One, because you volunteered, and two, because he thinks you can do this.'

The old lady smiled politely. 'Well said, young man,' she noted firmly. 'We shall give it our very best.' Then people started to file out, heading for further preparations and to get some sleep before the off.

Mason sat down in an armchair and breathed out.

'Nice speech. Straight to the point,' observed Carter sincerely. 'Clearly a little fatalistic and morbid in places, but oddly galvanising. I think they liked it.'

'Ha, I'd take that as a joke from anyone else, but you actually mean it, don't you?'

'Of course.' Carter sat down in the chair next to Mason and was joined by Jane and Cora. 'So, what's your plan to take on Richard?' asked Carter.

'Pretty much my regular go-to solution; blunt force trauma and extreme violence,' answered Mason.

'And his Tellus second-generation supersoldiers?' prompted Carter some more.

'That will require some extra-special tactics,' grinned Mason. 'A shit ton of armour-piercing, semi-automatic fire and plenty of hand grenades.'

'So, we're going with violence, supported by more violence,' said Cora.

'Sorry, was there a question in there?' asked Mason.

'No, not at all,' she replied. 'Although normally, I'm not a fan of solving problems with violence. In this case, I happily agree it's the perfect solution for Richard and his little private army. Would you say so too, Nyx?'

'*Yes*,' replied Nyx. '*He may be one of my creators, indirectly, but I predict the world would be a much-improved place if he ceased to exist.*'

'One final question. Will you leave me anyone to arrest?' asked Carter.

'I very much doubt it,' replied Mason.

The living room was quiet, and Mason sat there with Cora. They were watching the TV, sound off so it was slightly less depressing.

'Maybe us undead should all just sod off to an island somewhere,' speculated Mason. 'Let the living get back to normal. Or maybe we should even just lie back down in the ground.'

'No,' said Cora firmly. 'Look at you. Since you came back, you're a much better person. The world is lucky to have you.'

'Better than not being here at all?' questioned Mason.

'*Definitely*,' said Nyx brightly. '*Look at all the new friends you have now. The world is always a better place when new friendships are made.*'

Mason smiled and took a sip of his orange juice. 'Thanks, guys.'

Cora laughed. 'What, no "girls" this time? Or something equally misogynistic?' she teased. 'Anyway, Nyx, how about we tell Mason about your surprise, yes?'

'*Oh yes, and thank you for your additional input, it did prove very useful.*'

'Alright, let's have it then.' Mason sat up. 'What have you two cooked up?'

'*Very apt,*' said Nyx. '*I have calculated a way to give you a very large boost of strength and power over a limited period of time.*'

'How?'

'*Think of it as similar to a massive jolt of caffeine into your system from a very strong cup of the finest coffee,*' announced Nyx.

'Can't stand the stuff,' said Mason, taking another sip of orange juice.

'*OK, I shall reframe it,*' she said. '*Think of it like a huge burst of speed that nitrous oxide gives a car or motorbike when injected into the engine along with the fuel.*'

'Nitro-boost.' Mason grinned and sat up straighter. 'Now you're talking my kind of language. So how does it work?'

'*I have calculated a way to run energy generation more efficiently with certain types of fuel,*' said Nyx. '*Not for too long of course, as we don't want you to turn into a miniature bomb and wipe out half of London.*' She smiled reassuringly at Mason. '*This will give me surges of extra power with which to boost any number of your systems fourfold or more. Again, all very briefly, but still a huge tactical advantage.*'

'It's like a super-speed, power-up in a video game,' said Cora. 'I like it a lot.'

Mason took all this in for a second, massively impressed.

'Right, I know I'm not the scientist here, but what's the catch? Extra power never comes for free.'

'*Correct,*' said Nyx. '*It will burn the available fuel in you very quickly, but with Cora's assistance, I have been able to ensure it will not burn you out completely. You'll just revert to regular old super-strength when the fuel is exhausted.*'

'Blimey.' Mason sat back in his chair. 'You really have been busy.'

'You'll need some fairly specific fuel for this one,' added Cora. 'For it to be most efficient.'

'*Yes, I have calculated where you can get the best source materials, and fortunately they are all readily available.*'

'OK, what do we need?' Mason asked warily.

'*Ham, egg, and chips is a great source,*' replied Nyx. '*Ideally, with petit pois. All cooked into a nice meal for you to eat.'*

'Awesome,' laughed Mason. 'Almost makes me forget the crap we're about to walk into.' He stood up. 'Right, I'm off shopping. Cora, you get some shut-eye.'

'Yes, Sarge.' She gave him a mock salute, as he made for the door. 'Oh, don't forget to go trolley surfing whilst you're there. Everyone should do that at least once in their life.'

He gave her a questioning look.

'I've explained it to Nyx, so she can tell you all about it when you get to the supermarket.' Cora smiled at him. 'She's just dying to try it out.'

Mason pushed the trolley down the aisle in Waitrose. Fifteen minutes until closing, loads of time.

'So come on then, Nyx, what's trolley surfing?'

'*It sounds like so much fun*,' she replied. '*You run with the trolley then you lean forward, use your hands to take your weight, and lift your feet off the floor. After which, you see how far you can go before the trolley veers out of control. Can we try it, please?*'

'Oh, I don't know. Inventing undead nitro-boost and trolley surfing in one day. That's a lot even for you, Nyx.'

Nyx gave him a look.

He grinned and started running with the trolley.

'*We need some music*,' said Nyx. She went hunting then found what she wanted and put it on. Immediately a lively indie song sprang to life.

As Mason ran up and down the quiet aisles trolley surfing, The Lottery Winners sang out their hearts with "Sunshine" and the whole thing made him smile. On the fourth aisle, he ran head first into someone.

The small man grabbed at the front of the trolley and skidded along with it for ten feet before they all came to a halt.

'Sorry, mate,' said Mason. He looked down at the man's security guard uniform, and then back up into the Down's syndrome face staring intently at him.

'Aren't you too old to play with trolleys?' asked the man.

'Aren't you a bit small to be a security guard?' said Mason.

'Trainee night shift security guard,' the man corrected him proudly. 'And I'm a wrestler too, so don't mess with me.'

Mason gave the trolley an experimental tug and the man held it firm.

'Tellus first generation,' stated Nyx. *'Very recently undead.'*

'You know you're dead, right?' asked Mason.

The small security guard eyed him suspiciously.

'It's alright, mate, I'm undead too,' added Mason.

The guard held out his hand. 'Shake my hand,' he instructed.

'OK,' Mason reached out. 'Why?'

The guard took Mason's hand and shook it enthusiastically. 'You can tell a lot from someone's handshake.'

'Whatever you say, mate.' Mason looked about. 'I don't suppose you know where the gammon steaks are, do you?'

Seeming to make up his mind, the guard let go of Mason's hand.

'Of course. I'll show you.' He led him towards another aisle. 'I'm Ben Oakwood,' he said cheerily as they walked, having now judged Mason's character as suitably acceptable. 'I died this afternoon and then came back to life. My girlfriend says I'm the luckiest man alive, but I already knew that. I have people who love me, and I love them too.' His bright, brown eyes looked up at Mason. 'What's your name?' he asked.

What the hell. 'I'm Mason. Pleased to meet you, Ben. I used to be a security guard too. Day shift, though, myself. I liked going down the pub too much to do the night shift.'

'That's what the weekends are for, going to the pub,' said Ben seriously. He turned into the refrigerated meat aisle and pointed to some gammon steaks. 'The ones in the red packet are the best tasting.'

'Thanks for your help, mate, much appreciated.' Mason put three packs into his trolley then dug out his phone. 'Look, Ben, I'm going to give you a number, OK? You get into any trouble for being undead, you call this number and tell a man called Dan that Mason Granger sent you. He'll sort you out if he can.'

Ben got out his phone and typed in the number. He paused for a second then looked back up at Mason with another serious expression.

'Are you the Mr Granger from the TV, the one that killed the policewoman?'

'Yup, I'm that Mason, and no, I didn't kill her,' he replied. 'She was a good person, and she didn't deserve what she got. But I'm working to make it right. That's the truth, Ben. Not all of it, but no word of a lie in what I've just told you.'

Ben studied Mason for several seconds, then he made up his mind once more.

'OK, I believe you.' He smiled at Mason and gave him a cheery wink. 'I should get back to work. Just in case there's more trolley surfers to catch. See you later, Mr Granger.'

Back in the car, Mason called Dan. The phone was picked up on the first ring.

'Yes, Mr Granger?'

'Hey, Dan, I've got another favour I want sorting. Part of the price for my services.'

'What is it?' asked Samson.'

'Keep this phone number going. If an undead young man called Ben Oakwood calls you, you help him. Deal?'

'That's a big risk to keep a number active,' stated Samson.

'Don't care, figure it out.'

The line went quiet for a few seconds. 'Alright, I'll get something sorted. You have your price.'

'Good.'

'You drive a hard bargain, Mr Granger,' chuckled Samson.

'Yeah, yeah. You wait until I hit your wine cellar.'

Lying back on the bunk, Mason felt well fed and ready for some downtime before the off. He listened to the snoring around him, many undead packed into the large bedroom full of bunk beds. '*Nyx, can you block out the noise, but monitor for any issues?*'

'*Certainly*,' she replied. The room went quiet.

He thought about the day just gone, and what they were about to do in a few hours' time. '*OK if I ask you some questions, Nyx?*'

'*Of course, Mason. I like your questions; you sometimes even surprise me.*'

'*How did you know Ben was undead?*' started Mason. '*It's not like we can see it or anything.'*

'*Similar to how I communicate with myself. Electromagnetic waves,*' she said. '*Think of it like a mobile phone sending data via radio waves to the mobile network towers, except that in my case it's the millions of tiny biological computers in me giving off different types of electromagnetic waves and receiving them too. All Nectr strains give off some signals, and I have now learnt how to recognise the difference between the various strains.*' She frowned a little. '*Arnold Samson might have looked nice and shiny to our eyes, but Tellus second generation was not very pretty at all in the electromagnetic spectrum.*'

Mason thought some more. '*Does that mean you could track Tellus second-gen people? Kind of like a radar?*'

'*Yes and no,*' she replied. '*If they are close enough and there are no blocking substances in between us, then I will be able to track them. If they are on the other side of a thick wall or metal barrier, then detection will not be possible.*'

'*Alright, I'll keep that in mind.*' Mason put his hands behind his head on the pillow and started to get comfortable. '*And nitro-boost, what's that going to be like? Sounds bloody awesome. I'm hoping I can wipe the floor with those second-gen nutters.*'

'*It will be untested,*' said Nyx, somewhat regretfully. '*However, I am confident I can give you huge extra speed and strength as mentioned, plus I will hopefully be able to add enhanced localised effects.*'

'*Like what?*'

'*I'm still working on those, Mason.*'

He huffed out a chuckle. '*Another surprise, huh?*'

'*To you and me both,*' she replied.

Lying in the dark and silence, Mason organised his thoughts a little more and considered what he wanted to say and how to phrase it, but nothing seemed quite right, so he just went for it as usual. '*You care a lot about Cora, don't you, Nyx?*' For a change there was silence in his head. '*Are you blushing?*' he prompted gently.

Nyx nodded back at him shyly.

He smiled. '*It's OK. There's nothing to be embarrassed about caring for someone.*'

'*But I'm not human,*' protested Nyx. '*I shouldn't care about anyone or feel like I'm blushing. In fact, I shouldn't feel anything at all, except what Amanda programmed me to feel. So, why should I care so much about Cora?*

'You're growing up and developing your own feelings,' said Mason. *'Sure, you're not growing like a person, and certainly you're developing a whole shitload faster than we do, but I'd recognise the signs anywhere.'* Something else occurred to him. *'You should ask Cora if she'd like to hang out with you and do something fun. When all this crap is over obviously.'*

'Really? Do you think she'd say yes?'

'That doesn't really matter to be honest, nothing ventured nothing gained,' he replied. *'But yeah, I reckon she'd definitely say yes.'*

'What would we do?' Nyx buzzed around his mind for a second. *'Could you help me pick something? To make sure I don't choose an activity Cora thinks is stupid.'*

Mason had to put his hand over his mouth to hide the sound of a laugh. *'Nyx, you could never do anything stupid. But sure, I can help if you'd like.'*

Relief and joy flooded through Mason's mind from Nyx, and he thought it was one of the most beautiful things he'd ever felt in his entire life. *'Thank you,'* she said warmly.

'You're welcome.'

Suddenly, she stopped buzzing around his head in excitement. *'You are still my primary objective, Mason Granger,'* she said hastily, the worry creeping back into her voice. *'You will always be my first priority at the very core of my programming. Please don't think that you ever won't be.'*

'Nyx, it's fine. You can care about more than one person at once, that is OK. And contrary to what some people insist, you don't have to pick a favourite.' The day caught up with Mason again, and he let out a quiet yawn. *'And just for the record, before I hit the sack, I don't care where your feelings come from. They're real for you, and real for me, programmed or not.'*

She smiled at this, but the nervousness in her persisted. *'I'm worried, Mason. We're walking back into the lion's den tonight and I don't have all the answers. I still cannot calculate why I failed to bring back DCI Cuthbert, we haven't tested your nitro-boost, and I don't know if I can protect everyone.'*

He looked at her with total confidence. *'We'll be alright,'* he stated firmly.

'You still say the nicest things, Mason Granger,' Nyx smiled back tentatively. *'Maybe not entirely true, but the nicest all the same.'*

Mason gave her a salute in his head, then kept his fingers crossed until he fell asleep.

CHAPTER 17

At four a.m. precisely, DS Carter got out of the Range Rover at the Tigris front gates, Mason just a step behind him. He showed the guard his police ID.

'We're here to see Richard Buckley.'

The guard looked Carter up and down slowly, then came to a decision.

'Piss off copper, you've got no authority here.'

Carter's eyes flared just a little and Mason held his breath.

'I can just as easily come back with a warrant in ten minutes and march Mr Buckley down to the station for a chat there,' said Carter more pointedly.

'Good luck with that, we work for the government,' said the guard. 'Now sod off back under whatever rock you crawled out from.'

Wrong answer, thought Mason.

Carter's eye twitched, then he punched the guard square in the face. Teeth and blood splashed out, whilst the security guard went flying back into the booth. He slammed into the far wall and slid down on to the floor. He didn't move, not even a groan.

Mason walked into the booth and checked the guard.

'Still breathing, just.'

He moved over to the console and tapped in the code to open the gate. Nothing happened; as expected the codes had been changed. He rooted about on the desk and found a Post-it note. He read the passcode off it and typed it in. The gates sprung to life. Also, as expected, the guards' habits of writing down long, complicated passcodes hadn't changed either.

'You need to attend some anger management classes, mate,' Mason called back to Carter as he worked. 'Right, the gate is up. Tell the others to move in.'

He used the same passcode and logged into the security rota, then brought up the list of names for tonight. Mostly night security guard names that he recognised, but several that didn't ring a bell, plus one code name he'd not seen before: "*Driver*". *Got to be Richard's bodyguards and that surly new driver of his.* Nyx memorised the list, then Mason tapped on Zoe's name. A little prompt came up, and he typed in a message to her.

Now would be a very good time to resign. You and the others should grab a drink at the Ritzy to celebrate your first day of freedom. I hear 4 a.m. is their happy hour, and they don't serve troublemakers.

He pressed send. Not the best warning in the world but as much as he was prepared to risk. He watched as the undead teams drove past and headed for the car park. Then he got back in the Range Rover and Carter drove them the last hundred metres. Cora rose from the back seat.

'Smooth,' she said to them both.

'I sent one of the security guards I trust a coded warning to get out. She might grab the people she knows and leave; could make our job a little easier.'

'Doesn't that compromise the security of our operation?' asked Carter, as he manoeuvred through the car park.

'She spared my life at the warehouse with Arnie,' replied Mason. 'She had the drop on me and didn't take me out. I can trust her,' added Mason firmly.

Carter nodded and parked the Range Rover as they reached where they needed to be. Immediately, they jumped out, and Cora, Carter and one small group of undead ducked behind the smattering of parked cars and headed for the rear entrance. The other two larger groups ran for the side of the complex. Mason walked directly towards the front door. Nothing like a bold entrance to cause the biggest distraction possible.

He walked up to the big show-off front entrance and knocked on the steel fibre reinforced glass with his wedding ring. The sound was loud, but nothing stirred. Inside, the reception looked deserted.

Now that was odd. He stood back and shot at the glass door, narrowly avoiding the first two ricocheting bullets.

'Crap, that's not supposed to happen.' Another four shots, this time at a better angle, and the glass fractured. He kicked it out and stepped quickly through the gap. He ran over to the reception desk and peered around. Empty. He kept moving and entered the small security control room. Empty too. 'OK, Nyx, map time. Let's track some markers of what's going on.'

Nyx overlaid a map of the complex in his head, allowing the closer parts to appear in his vision too. '*Good idea*,' agreed Nyx, '*this will be an efficient way for us to share tactical data*.'

'Great,' Mason nodded. 'So, how do we know where anyone is?'

'*Sadly, I cannot track Tigris people easily throughout the building, though I can project where they are probably not, from the likely location of our own people*.' She overlaid their three groups on the map in Mason's head, all nicely coloured in a grassy green. '*I can estimate our people's positions from our secure radio chatter, and also my comms with Cora and Carter. The link to the other parts of myself is strong, because I am deliberately broadcasting, however it will not be perfect everywhere. As mentioned, some materials are too much of a blocker*.'

'*You got all that, Cora?*' he asked over their already open connection.

'*Yes, pretty much as expected*,' she replied. '*We should be able to keep track of each other, unless you have to start messing about in the basement areas. Hold on a mo*.' She went quiet for a few seconds. '*OK, I'm in the company computer systems. Now we're inside the firewalls, Nyx has been cracking the codes surprisingly easily*.'

'*Glad I'm not running security at this place any more*,' said Mason. '*All this bloody biological AI tech is a sodding nightmare to guard against. No offence, Nyx*.'

'*I shall take that as a compliment*,' she said pleasantly. '*On the negative side, it appears that Richard's team have now successfully developed a prototype kill switch for Nectr, in addition to the spread blocker and the replication prevention agents. It's some sort of device similar to an electromagnetic pulse weapon, or EMP as they're commonly known. The effect causes any Nectr within its blast radius to cease functioning, whilst leaving all regular organic matter unharmed*.'

'OK. *Get all the data out to Jane as quick as you can,*' said Mason. '*And, Cora, if you find the kill switch, grab it and use it if you need. I don't care if it finishes Carter, me, and Nyx, you're the important one here. You've got the brains to do what's needed with the data when we get out of here.*'

'*I'm not...*' Cora started.

'*No arguing.*' Mason started scanning through the security feeds, one by one. '*It's spookily quiet here. There are no guards at reception and I'm not seeing any throughout the main complex.*' He worked things through for a second. '*Now I think about it, maybe that guard from the gate was not actually from Tigris. Something bad is going on.*'

'*What, you think something worse than us might be happening, are you sure about that?*' asked Carter. '*Maybe Zoe got your message, and they all got out already. Could be the one on the gate was just an idiot. Or tosser, as you like to say.*'

Before Mason could reply, a gun barrel poked at the back of his head.

'Get up, nice and easy,' said Sadie from right behind him. 'Even a twitch and I unload a whole magazine of this armour-piercing shit right into your amped-up skull.'

Mason held his hands out wide and stood slowly.

'Turn around. Keep those hands out,' she added as she backed away.

'*Wow, she is good, you didn't hear her sneaking up on you at all,*' said Nyx. Then she brightened a little. '*On the positive side, her and her companions are all just plain old living people. Not a single strain of Nectr amongst them.*'

He turned to face them and saw Sadie with Dave alongside her.

Shit, not the sodding Billionaires' Club again, thought Mason. 'I guess they didn't pay up for your services after all,' he said to Sadie, seeing if he could goad her into making a mistake. 'Can't trust these sneaky billionaires, huh?'

She glared back at him but kept her gun steady. 'I didn't get the sample they wanted, so yeah, I had to come back to this crap-fest again to earn my money. But we'll get the lot this time, and I'll get my cash.'

Both Sadie and Dave were loaded to the gills with the very latest hi-tech body armour and guns, and there was no shortage of grenades and other shit too. Outside the small control room, he could see more well-equipped mercenaries.

'Our employers would like a word in your ear, mate,' said Dave, his gun also levelled at Mason's head. His voice was calm and businesslike, just the same as before he'd shot Carter in the warehouse.

When I get started on you lot, thought Mason, *you're the first one to go down, mate!*

A couple of sunbed-roasted guys moved into the frame of the doorway. All gym toned but not a combat brain cell between them, perfectly framed by the door like sitting ducks.

'Is this him?' one of them asked in a Californian accent, sounding a bit disappointed. 'He doesn't look very fearsome in real life, does he Mr Paul?'

'Yeah, I was expecting more, Mr Ringo. Especially after all we've been through to reach this stage,' replied the other. 'I'm glad Mr George and Mr John didn't cut their skiing short for this. I think they would have been rather disappointed.'

'*Sodding hell*,' thought Mason. '*The stupid billionaire tossers have actually come on their own raid. Got to be a combined IQ of nearly three hundred and fifty between the two of them, and not an ounce of common sense. Do they really think they can do anything if they put their minds to it? Wankers. What's wrong with these people?*'

'*I'm sorry, Mason, I don't know what is wrong with them*,' said Nyx. '*Would you like me to try to calculate the answer?*'

'*Nah, we'll be here all year*,' replied Mason. '*Nice code names though, always was a bit of a Beatles fan myself. Just a shame it's such tossers using them*.'

Mason slowly opened his palms. 'OK, what do you idiots want? And be quick, I'm kind of busy here.'

The two billionaires stood straight. 'Don't you understand what we represent, you ignorant asshole?' snapped Mr Paul. 'The sheer resources we can deploy to conquer our goals.'

'Don't care, getting bored,' stated Mason. Sadie tensed, as did Dave. Not so dumb those two. Mason repeated his question to the billionaires one last time, slowly and firmly for the benefit of their money-inflated egos. The ones that were clearly not used to being challenged by anyone, ever. 'What – do – you – want?'

The mercenaries around him kept scanning and moving, and Mason saw them adjusting their formation to give better lines of sight around their bosses.

'Maybe if you could step out of the doorway, sirs,' Dave prompted his employers.

'Yes, of course,' agreed Mr Ringo, aiming to restore their confident demeanour. 'Mr Granger, we have the initial Nectr research data as you know, and of course, plenty of samples of Tellus from the general population. But we always reach for the stars; second best is never good enough. We want the latest research and any further generations of Tellus. We know Tigris has been working on more.' Then he stared intently at Mason. 'And samples from patient zero would no doubt be advantageous. Give us the baseline for it all. So, we've come in person to negotiate with you and Richard directly.'

He indicated the surrounding mercenaries. 'In addition to the very best ex-marines we have here, we also have the very best money available too.' He smiled wryly at his own joke. 'I'm sure we can come to some suitable arrangement.'

'Yes, it will be a small price to pay for immortality,' added Mr Paul.

'Immortality?' questioned Mason.

'Immortality,' confirmed the man with a greedy grin. 'With Nectr, we can now finally elude the grasp of death itself and live forever.'

'*Oh, I see the error in their calculations,*' said Nyx to Mason. '*Easy mistake to make if you don't have all the data. You won't live forever Mason, none of the undead will.*'

His forehead creased. '*So, how long will I live?*'

'*I have yet to calculate that. However, I believe we should concentrate on the next twenty-six minutes first,*' said Nyx, '*before we concern ourselves too much with the longer term.*'

'*Good point. Suggestions?*'

A little bit of excitement tingled across Nyx. '*This would be an excellent opportunity to test out your nitro-boost, maybe try it on setting number one. I'd like us to iron out any teething troubles.*'

'*Troubles?*' questioned Mason, all the while staring hard at the billionaire arseholes like he was considering his price.

'You will be even faster, tougher, and stronger, for a short, intense period of time, but the laws of physics will still apply to you.'

'*Example please?*' asked Mason.

'You could push down on the floor and jump twenty feet high in the air, but without suitable grip or purchase you couldn't leap twenty feet forwards from a standing position. Conservation of momentum.' Mason gave her a blank look. *'If you throw this heavy chair at Dave, your body will fly back to compensate, unless you are nailed to the floor.'*

Mason threw the big chunky chair at Dave, taking him right off his feet and smashing the gun from his hands. Sadie opened fire on full auto, but all she hit were the monitors on the wall, as Mason flew sideways. He slammed into the wall, then shoved off it. Small sections of plaster disintegrated under the force of his hands, amid the destruction caused by the carefully aimed gunfire exploding into the room; the ex-marines firing away at Mason, but also trying hard not to hit their bosses.

Crashing into Sadie, Mason performed the tiniest rabbit punch to her head so he didn't smash it in, and then she was down too. All the while, the two billionaires hadn't even moved, chaos and noise all around them but they had no idea how to respond.

Mason sprang off the floor, aiming for the billionaires, but he sailed right over them and crashed into the wall. *'Damn, I see what you mean now, Nyx.'* He adjusted his aim, pushed back off the wall and ploughed into them. A quick bang of their heads together and they were out for the count. Four people down, and less than two seconds gone. Mason dangled one of the billionaires out the doorway.

'Hold your fire. I want to talk.'

The gunfire ceased. 'Are they still alive?'

He looked down at the billionaires in his hands. 'Yeah, think so.'

'Not those idiots, our people?' came the shouted reply.

'A little banged up, but still breathing as far as I can tell,' replied Mason. 'You can have them back, just get out of here now. No negotiation, no choices. That or get slaughtered. And I'm not talking about me. There's far worse than me in here with you tonight.' He thought for a second, let go of the billionaires, then he grabbed Dave and Sadie by the ankles and threw them out through the doorway.

'There you go, a show of good faith.'

There were hushed whispers, and then nothing. After a few more seconds, Mason looked out the door.

'*They've all left,*' confirmed Nyx. '*Your ears just about heard the tiny scuffle of their rubber soles on the floor. They are very good at what they do these ex-marines.*'

'And no love for their employers it seems.'

'*We'd better continue with our mission, if we wish to catch Richard before the charges ignite,*' Nyx reminded him.

'Good point.' Mason grabbed a pen and paper from the desk and wrote a quick note. Then he put the note on the billionaire's hand and stabbed the pen right through it and into the man's flesh. Mr Paul woke up instantly and screamed. Mason ran off into the heart of the complex, pleased with himself that the note was pretty self-explanatory. The rest would be up to them.

"*Get out now or you're dead dead.*"

CHAPTER 18

'*Cora? Carter?*' tried Mason, as he searched the executive's floor for Richard. All quiet on both fronts. 'Shit, they better not be messing about in the basement,' he whispered to himself. 'Bollocks, I really hate that place.'

'*My communications have been cut off from the other parts of myself,*' confirmed Nyx. '*Shall we try the other teams on the radio, see what their status is?*'

'How's it going, Agnetha?' said Mason into the radio, using the code name for Team One.

'That's our shift over, on our way to the chippy.'

'How about you, Benny?' for Team Two.

'We've found all our mates, and we're off to the pub. See you there or at the chippy later.'

Good. At least something was going right. He glanced at his watch. Sixteen minutes to go. Getting tight on time now.

'*I have been scanning repeatedly, and there is a faint signal coming from the basement area, near those hidden labs where Amanda retreated to for her final research,*' said Nyx. '*The signal is weak through all the concrete and steel, but it appears to match the Tellus second-generation pattern. There must be quite a few of them for the electromagnetic waves to reach this far.*'

'And still nothing from Cora or Carter?'

'*No, I'm sorry, Mason,*' Nyx replied. He detected the worry in her voice.

'Come on then.' He started for the stairwell. 'Let's go kick the bad guys in the nuts and save the day.' He followed the route Nyx overlaid on top of his eyesight, slightly different from the one he would have picked. Nyx directed him past the main stairs and on towards the fire escape stairwell.

'Why this way?' asked Mason. 'Whoever's down there is bound

to be guarding both sets of stairs, you know. Not just the main ones.'

'*Of course, I know that,*' she grinned at him. '*But the emergency stairs have more fire extinguishers for you to throw at the bad people.*'

Mason let out a dry laugh in his head as he reached the basement level. '*Here we go again. I should get a sodding flat here or something.*'

Guns in hand, he sat listening at the door for a precious thirty seconds. No point getting his head blown off straight away, might as well stretch out the pain.

'*All clear, I believe,*' Nyx confirmed.

He opened the door and eased out. All clear it was. He ran down the corridor, guns up, and stopped at the end. He peeked carefully around another corner, and that looked clear too, so he ran down the next corridor. One minute later, he was at the last corner before Amanda's old lab.

'*I can detect two Tellus second-generation people,*' said Nyx. '*They are around this next junction and outside the airlock to Amanda's lab. The signal is strong, they are very likely alert and ready.*'

'*OK. A bit of nitro then, Nyx.*' Mason put one gun away and kept the other in his preferred right hand. He felt the rush of energy within him, as he carefully snaked the fingers of his left hand around the corner of the corridor wall. Then he exploded into action. A yank on the wall to pull himself around at twenty miles an hour. He fired two armour-piercing shots to the heads of the amped-up bodyguards outside the lab's airlock, one for each, and then he slammed to a halt on the wall opposite, once again, the plaster crumbling under the impact. All done in less than half a second.

The guard on the left fell to the floor, the bullet having gone through his eye socket, and liquefied brain leaked out, but the guard on the right just reached up and pulled the flattened bullet from his forehead.

'The boss is going to enjoy this,' he said. Then he opened the airlock and stepped inside. A rush of air and he was gone, out of the other side and into the large lab.

Mason ran over to the side of the airlock door. He leaned across and had a quick look into the lab. Richard's bodyguards were all over the place, there had to be ten or more.

'*Eleven,*' said Nyx helpfully.

Plus, there was Richard's new driver, with Carter sprawled on the floor unmoving at his feet. Mason's heart sank and Nyx almost glitched. Another quick look, and yup, there was Richard, sitting comfortably, gun pointing towards Cora. She sat in the chair opposite, back straight, staring Richard down for all she was worth.

'*Cora?*' Mason desperately tried to connect through the mass of steel fibre-infused glass.

Like a static-filled telephone line, her voice came back to him all distorted and broken. '*Mason? I'm sorry. We didn't see them coming until it was too late to get away.*'

'*Carter? The others with you?*'

'*They fought hard, but they still lost. They're all gone. Carter fought them like a man possessed with Nyx's help, but it did him no good either.*' Cora sniffed in her head. '*They beat him badly. I don't know…*'

'*You hold it together, Cora Gallagher. We're not done yet, not by fucking half.*' Mason tapped in his borrowed code to the airlock and the outer door opened.

'*Quick, Mason, please,*' urged Nyx. '*She's very scared.*'

'*You hold it together too, Nyx,*' commanded Mason. '*I want your very best, no matter what happens, understood?*'

Nyx nodded back. Mason waited for what seemed like forever for the air to change. '*Cora, did you get the Nectr kill switch?*'

A little less static this time, but even more distress in her voice. '*We did get hold of the prototype, but I destroyed it. I didn't want anyone hurting Nyx or you.*'

Mason swore, a lot. '*Alright, plan B.*' He tried a reassuring grin at Cora in his mind. '*Extreme violence it is then.*' She managed a weak smile in return.

He stabbed at the exit door button and the airlock opened into the lab. Richard swivelled his chair a little to face Mason but kept his gun trained on Cora.

'Nice of you to join us, Mr Granger. Such as shame we can't tidy up your wife too, but we'll get to her eventually. And that poaching little rival tosspot, Herbert.' He beamed his arrogant CEO smile at Mason. 'If no one's around to blab about my misdeeds, then did they really happen?'

Richard stood up and shot Cora through the heart. She fell to the floor and immediately blood started pooling around her. Richard handed the gun to his driver.

'Take care of this mess, will you, I'm off to wipe any incriminating data and transfer the money. I'll see you at the helicopter in twenty minutes. Don't be late.' Then he walked to the back of the lab and out through the second airlock.

'*No, no, no*,' shouted Nyx, desperately. '*Cora? Cora?*'

Anger poured into Mason like an endless tide. 'You're all fucking dead,' he said flatly to those around him. '*Nyx, get a grip. Give me everything you've got, right now. These wankers are going to hell.*'

Fire lit up in every part of Mason's body. Thousands of tiny biological nitro-boosts ignited, and power flowed through him like there was no end. Twelve scumbags to finish and thirty seconds to get to Cora before her brain started to die. Bring it on, you bastards.

He threw two heavy lab chairs at sixty miles an hour and took down two bad guys with the steel chair legs embedded in their torsos, no second-gen Tellus for them clearly. With the reverse momentum, Mason flew back into the wall. He pushed off and sped across the room. He let loose armour-piercing rounds everywhere and put a thumb through one guy's eye socket as he sprinted past. Sorry, woman. That took another four bodyguards out of the picture, and he slammed into the wall on the other side.

Mason threw the woman's body at the driver, then he pulled out a grenade, all the while ignoring the gunfire around him. He looked down at Cora's body and thought better of it, holding on to the grenade. Off the wall he pushed again but sliding along under some desks this time on his back. He fired more armour-piercing rounds into the bodyguards' ankles, looking to shred their tendons. All the while bullets smashed into the furniture around him, shards of exploding plastic and wood going everywhere, the noise like the take-off of a space shuttle. Three more bad guys down. Mason did a sprint crawl back through the chaos and jammed grenades into their mouths. Nyx superheated his hands with some more boost energy, and he melted their jaws around the explosives. *Boom, boom, boom.* Three more soups to go, thanks.

'*Right Nyx, twenty-foot jump into the air, you reckon? Watch this.*' Mason grabbed his second gun, bent his knees and pushed up.

Into the ceiling he flew, wedging into the tiles and air conditioning ducts, bending everything out of shape. From there, he shot two more bodyguards through the top of their heads, the bullets tearing through the weaker top sections of their skulls.

And finally, the driver. He came running under Mason, unloading his gun at him as he ran for the other airlock. Mason shoved off the ceiling, a high-calibre bullet tearing through his shoulder, then he slammed into the man. He grabbed the driver's head with one hand and unloaded his gun into an eye socket with the other. Then just to be sure, he shoved in a grenade and welded the man's mouth shut. *Boom*, the grenade went off inside the driver, and his armoured skin ensured it liquefied the man's insides.

Mason let the man's body drop and he ran over to Cora. He gently picked up her lifeless body. Stroking her face.

'It's now or never, Nyx. You have to fix her. Get in there, I don't care how much of you it takes. Use it all if you have to, just save my friend.' He bent down and kissed Cora on the forehead, sweat pouring from him. Nyx didn't need a second prompt, and she poured into Cora for all she was worth.

Fifty billion calculations and a heartbeat later, Nyx screamed in pain and rage, then her digital self slumped down. *'I can't do it, Mason, I can't bring her back. It's just not possible.'* She started trudging back into Mason through the blood, sweat, and tears.

'Why?' he demanded.

'I finally worked out the reason,' said Nyx. *'Amanda hardwired me to only work on bringing back men from the dead. She didn't want strain thirty-seven to bring back women for some reason.'*

No swear words came, and Mason slumped down too. 'But Amanda brought back her mum with Tellus. Why not women with you?'

'I'm sorry, I just don't know.' Now Nyx was full-on crying, and Mason couldn't think of a single word to console her. He poked at Carter with a foot and the man groaned. He poked harder and Carter raised his head. He took in the scene and closed his eyes briefly.

'I'm sorry, Mason, I couldn't beat them all, I couldn't protect her.'

'Not your fault, scumbag Richard's fault.' Mason looked at his watch. 'Get out of here, you've got six minutes until the office blows. Jane's waiting for you on the outside, and she'll skin me alive if I get you killed, again.'

Carter got to his feet. 'And you?'

'Don't know to be honest,' replied Mason. 'Try to finish the job, I guess. Keep Richard here until the explosives go off. He doesn't seem to know about them yet. Go on, get going.'

Carter patted Mason on the shoulder. 'Good luck, my friend.' Then he ran for the airlock.

Mason stood up, Cora still in his arms. 'If we want to get Richard, I'll have to leave Cora here, Nyx,' he said. 'It's your call.'

Before she could reply, the last remaining laptop sprang to life with a big smiling face on the screen. Oh good, more Richard.

'Very impressive, all of my bodyguards dispatched,' said Richard, surveying the carnage through the webcam at the top of the screen. 'But ultimately, rather pointless.' He held up a small device. 'Nectr kill switch prototype number two.' Without another word, he hit the switch.

Intense pain lanced throughout Mason's body, and he couldn't help but drop Cora and slump to the floor. His eyesight flashed with it all, and he vaguely heard the airlock open one last time. Then a rifle butt slammed into the back of his head.

Chapter 19

Waking with a start, everything hurt, badly. Like two hangovers and four good kickings all rolled into one. It was dark and smelled of metal. Mason tried moving his right arm, but his shoulder hurt too much. He tentatively reached up with his left hand and prodded at the metal ceiling just inches above his head. *Thought so. Sodding morgue slab. Again! Right back to the bloody start.*

He poked around in his head, more in vague hope than anything else. *'Nyx? Nyx?'*

It was quiet like tumbleweed, and yet, there at the edge of his mind, he swore he could hear the echo of her crying.

'Nyx, are you there? Why aren't we dead?'

After a few seconds, a voice filtered across his head, not Nyx, but like a pre-recorded voicemail message on a telephone. *'Nectr strain thirty-seven, vial ten, is currently rebooting. Please try later.'*

'Yes, fucking come on, Nyx, you can do it.' He reached around and gently felt his injured shoulder, pain everywhere but there didn't seem to be anything broken. *'If you can hear me, Nyx, prioritise killing the pain, then at least I can function.'*

He wriggled his left hand above his head and gave a push at the slab door. No movement there. *'Hey Nyx, a bit of strength after killing the pain, wouldn't go amiss either.'*

Another chime of the pre-recorded voice. *'Ten per cent of reboot sequence now complete.'*

He glanced at his watch. Four forty-five a.m. and still Tuesday morning. He'd only been out for fifteen minutes or so. *Shit, why haven't the explosives gone off yet? What the hell's going on?* Mason tried to figure it out then gave up. Action required, that was always his strong suit. *'Hurry up, Nyx, we need to get out of here and make sure that bastard Richard doesn't get away.'*

Chime. 'Reboot twenty per cent complete.'

The pain started to ebb away, and Mason tried the slab door again. The metal creaked a bit, so he pushed harder. This time it opened. *Awesome.*

Two pairs of large hands reached in, pulled him out, and threw him to the floor. Five heavyset bodyguards stood around him. Combat gloves on, guns holstered or slung back. One of them cracked his knuckles.

Or not. Mason tried to get to his feet, but his muscles told him to go away and come back later.

'So, you're not quite dead then? Thought you'd be a dusty corpse by now without all that Nectr shit flowing through you,' growled the one who'd cracked all his knuckles. 'Still, a nice little dissection when the science nerds get here will soon sort that out. Then it's in the incinerator for your remains. You can join the rest of those amped-up idiots who failed to control you. The boss does like to tidy up. Don't think the man has a clue where the incinerator is, but he sure loves ordering us to stuff evidence in it. Fair play though, you can't get much tidier than a pile of ashes.'

Another guard stepped forward and dangled some of the explosives in front of Mason's face, the ones that Team One had planted.

'And in case you were hoping for a miracle, your friends may have escaped the building, but their handiwork is toast.' Just for effect he cracked a knuckle or two as well. He looked at his comrade-in-arms. 'What do you think, beating?'

'Yup, might as well while we wait for the scientists,' replied his companion. 'Nothing better than a good kicking to soften someone up. After that, we can just strap him to a medical bed, and job done.' He reached in and tentatively punched Mason in the face, then stepped back quickly.

Mason responded by slumping back down on the floor. He spat out a tooth and jammed his arms under him, hands on the ground, trying to rise. He got halfway to his knees, then a kick caught him in the ribs. He went back down again, but interestingly, there was no more pain this time.

Another chime. *'Reboot forty per cent complete.'*

The next fist and foot came in together, but this time Mason caught them with his hands, his grip like steel, and his strength flooding back. He rose slowly, keeping hold of the offending hand and foot. He gave them a squeeze to make his point.

'Ow, no, ah, stop,' both bodyguards cried out, all their macho bravado suddenly gone.

Mason gave them another twist for good measure then threw the men across the room. They crashed into the medical cabinets on the other side. The doors dented and supplies rained down on their heads. Both guards sat there on the floor and stared at Mason; fear written all over their faces.

Standing up straight, Mason glared at the remaining three guards still holding their weapons, fingers hovering over the triggers.

'Are you sure you want to go there?' he challenged.

He took a step towards them, and they dropped their weapons instantly and put their arms up. Mason picked up two guns and slung them on his back. He held out his hand.

'Magazines,' he said to one. The bodyguard handed over two fully loaded magazines immediately. Mason turned and strode out the door, only pausing briefly to close it and bend the handle beyond use. 'Let them burn.'

Chime. 'Reboot sixty per cent complete.'

'*Hello, Mason, I am back*,' said Nyx.

'How complete are you? Do you remember everything?' Mason asked. 'Are you our Nyx?'

She showed him just one per cent of the pain she felt at losing Cora, and he knew instantly that this was the one and only Nyx back inside his head, all there, nothing missing.

'Good,' he said. 'Now it's Richard time.'

'*I know where he is*,' she announced, as he ran for the stairwell as fast as he could.

'How?'

'*You're not going to like this*,' replied Nyx. '*He's injected the prototype vial of Tellus third generation into himself. And it appears to work on both the living and the dead. He's burning like a miniature sun in the electromagnetic spectrum. Not at all pretty*,' she added.

'Shit, where is he?'

'Still in his sixth-floor office it seems. Wiping the data and transferring all his money must be taking longer than he anticipated.'

'Ha, more fool him. He should have just cut and run.' Mason made it to the top of the stairs and blasted into the corridor, gunning for Richard's corner office.

Chime. 'Reboot eighty per cent complete.'

'Can you fire me up with some nitro-boost, Nyx?' Mason slowed as he reached the office door.

'*Yes, but I will need more fuel to do so*,' she answered.

Mason looked about. 'Can't see any grub here.'

'*You could eat part of one of the bodyguards*,' suggested Nyx helpfully. '*Not as good as ham, egg, and chips, but plenty of raw source material all the same.*'

He thought about it for a second. 'Nah, too far to go back. Couldn't I chew on a wooden table leg or something?' he asked instead. 'Plenty of fuel in wood, I'd have thought.'

'*It's a good job that you are not the scientist amongst our team.*' Another splinter of pain ran through Nyx, but she recovered herself quickly. '*There is an alternative. Which kidney is your favourite, right or left?*'

'Eh?'

'*I've always liked your right kidney. It's more efficient and was slightly less damaged by your years of drinking red wine.*' Another blank stare from Mason, so Nyx explained further. '*I can consume one of your kidneys for fuel, after all, you can make do with just the one. Hence, I will be able to give you another strong burst of nitro effect. Do I have your permission?*'

'What, eat my own kidney?' said Mason. Nyx nodded. 'Sod it, do it, Nyx. Let's go proper zombie.' A sad smile played at his face. 'Cora would be so cross.'

Chime. 'Reboot one hundred per cent complete. All systems fully functional. Welcome to Nectr thirty-seven point one.'

'Point one?' asked Mason, as he grabbed at the door handle.

Through her sadness, Nyx smiled back at him. '*Yes, I too have had a little upgrade. We are both now new and improved.*'

'I didn't notice any difference,' said Mason.

'*Oh, but you are improved. We are now fully resistant to the kill switch*,' she said. '*And as a nice bonus feature, notice how you didn't rip off that bodyguard's foot and place it in his throat. You have more balance to your emotions now, Mason Granger. Extreme violence is no longer your default first option.'* She sent him an unusually wicked grin. *'But I very much like the fact that it can be your second and third option. Let's go CEO hunting.'*

Mason tore the door off its hinges and stormed into Richard's office.

Richard glanced up from his keyboard, put down his sandwich, and sighed. He quickly typed in a last command then stood.

'Lucky for you, I've just finished. Not a shred of evidence left in our systems.' He looked from the computer to all the empty sandwich packets on his desk, and then to his watch. 'Sadly, I only have five minutes left in my schedule, so we do need to make this quick.' Clearly there was no sadness in Richard's expression whatsoever, just a wide grin plastered all over his smug face. 'Then it's off to a nice little tax haven for a well-deserved holiday with all my money.'

He walked around the desk and casually leaned back on it, crossing his legs at the ankles in front of him and making a big show of his feet. Mason couldn't help but notice the brightly coloured, spiked combat shoes Richard had on.

'Do you like them?' asked Richard. 'The very latest from our combat wear department. I had them modelled on my favourite golf shoes. Super hardened titanium steel spikes for added grip. Works on just about any surface for fighting; concrete, carpet, open ground, you name it. Maybe a bit slippery on steel, but who has steel floors, right?'

Mason shot him in the face, the gunshot echoing around Richard's large office. The bullet pinged off Richard's forehead and he continued smiling, his skin slightly glistening in the office lights. He held up the empty vial of the Tellus third-generation prototype.

'This works a treat on the living.'

Richard held up his hands in front of him in a gesture of mock appeasement.

'I know, I know, I've done some pretty shitty things. Tellus second generation was none too pleasant. And I did rather take advantage of the undead crisis for some very large profits. But in my defence, it was my ticket to becoming the CEO and climbing on board that nice private jet.' He sighed contentedly.

Gunfire erupted as Mason unloaded half a magazine of automatic fire into Richard's chest. The man thrashed about, and the bullets flipped him over his desk, blood spraying out as one of them finally got through his armoured skin.

'Private jet that, you total bastard.' Mason leaned in to peer over the desk, then a hand reached up and grabbed the edge of it from the floor behind. The hand was followed by Richard's head and then the rest of his body.

'Third generation works even better on the dead,' he laughed at Mason. The bullet hole in his chest was now replaced with steel-glazed skin. It was even moulded into the shape of his finely tailored suit that had been shredded by the hail of bullets.

Mason stared in disbelief as Richard tweaked at his cufflinks.

'*What the hell, Nyx? I thought Nectr couldn't repair that much damage so quickly.*'

'*Tellus third generation is far more capable than we suspected,*' she whispered quietly with equal hatred and awe. '*He's able to regenerate very quickly, and he also appears to be able to defend himself further at the same time. His armour creation was fuelled by all the food he just ate. He will also now likely have a large weight advantage over you, as well as all the extra strength he has.*'

'Oh shit,' said Mason out loud.

'Oh shit, indeed, Mr Granger,' agreed Richard.

Mason fired both guns into Richard, but it only succeeded in sending ricocheting bullets all over the office, shattering the windows behind Richard, and taking a nick out of Mason's calf with a rebounding bullet. All the while, Richard stood there like an armoured tank.

'I would say the prototype has proved successful; wouldn't you agree?' stated Richard. 'The very best in military biotech augmentation; extra powerful, maximum regeneration, and kill switch resistant. All I need to do is keep it refuelled. Any food or drink will suffice.' He winked at Mason and bared a steel-like tooth with his grin. 'Even human flesh at a push; I could take a bite out of you if you'd like a quick demonstration.' He started to advance, his steps confident and sure. 'And you know what the very best thing is? It's designed to regenerate for as long as I feed it.'

'Nyx, light me up. Take the nitro as high as you can go.' Inside Mason the boost reactions kicked off and power coursed through his veins. Richard lunged, far faster than he had any right to. Mason didn't bother firing the guns, he just used them as clubs. He piled them into Richard whilst pivoting away. Richard's fingers missed his throat by millimetres.

Momentum carried them away, until Richard hit the opposite wall, and Mason crashed into the desk behind him, shattering it to pieces. Richard came at Mason again, the very best gym-trained fighting technique, slightly more cautious this time. A jab came from the right and Mason ducked aside, then a blow from the left connected and lifted Mason off his feet and slammed him into the corner of the office. Shattered windows on one side, bullet-scarred wall on the other.

'You can't win, Mr Granger.' Richard stalked towards him once more. 'You might be better trained than me, but it just doesn't matter. I simply have more power than you and I will get you in the end. You should have stayed loyal to my endeavours when you had the chance. Never mind. You live and learn.' Richard's eyes blazed with manic determination; any remainder of his slick business veneer totally gone. 'Well, live and fucking well die. Again, in your case. Nobody gets between me and my money.'

'I can't beat him,' said Nyx, pain and frustration laced through her voice. *'I want him to cease functioning more than anything on this planet, and I can't make it happen.'*

Mason stood and spat out some blood. *'Yes, we can. There's always a way. Nothing is unbeatable. What about taking the brakes off my nitro-boost and turning me into a bomb. Take him and me out with some kind of super-explosion.'*

'That would work. He couldn't survive that,' agreed Nyx. *'But neither would North London unfortunately.'*

'OK, let's skip that idea then.' Mason backed across to the window. He gave the signal to Richard. Fingers slightly curled up and waving the man towards him.

'Come on then, you tosser.'

Richard kicked off from the floor and sped towards Mason, but his angles were all wrong and he leapt in too high. Mason grabbed Richard as he hit him and pushed with his own legs to accelerate the movement. They both flew out of the sixth-floor window. Mason spun perfectly in mid-air and held on to Richard. They hit the ground together at over fifty-five miles an hour, Mason with his knees on Richard's chest. The concrete cracked as they smashed into the ground, but instead of his knees crushing Richard's ribcage like they had with Arnie, they bounced off and slammed into Mason's own chest, and he flew off the man. Richard then got back up off the ground without a care in the world.

'Oh, for god's sake.' Mason glanced at his watch as he got up off the ground, his hands on his knees for a second or so. Four fifty-two a.m. Just about time, he reckoned. '*Come on, Nyx. Let's get Richard back inside the complex for when the bombers arrive. Let's tease him in there.*'

'*How do you tease a superhuman, egotistical madman?*' asked Nyx, eager to learn.

Mason ducked as Richard leapt back in and swung at him, then Mason let the follow-up punch hit him square in the chest. He went flying back and smashed through a ground-floor window and back into the complex. '*Let him beat the crap out of me, of course.*'

'*Is that a military tactic I haven't seen yet?*'

'*Nah, it's a Mason Granger special from brawling outside the pub.*'

Richard came crunching through the debris and hit Mason with another punch. He went crashing through a door and down the corridor, finally skidding to a stop near the stairwell. He gave Richard a customary, oh-look-I'm-scared gaze, then pushed through the door and started hobbling down the stairs. '*Good old Mason pub fight speciality; lure them into a false sense of security, then bam, uppercut to the glass jaw.*'

Behind them, the doors were ripped off their hinges and thrown down the stairwell, one hitting Mason and smashing him into the wall, but he just bounced off it and kept on running down.

'*But Richard doesn't have a glass jaw,*' said Nyx, her expression all confused. '*In fact, he's much closer to steel than glass by a long way. And regrettably, Tellus third generation seems to have found a way to combine the rubber-like enhancement you have with the strength of steel enhancements that Tellus second generation gives. I don't know how; I didn't think that was possible.*'

Reaching the basement, Mason went through the doors. Once in the corridor, he ran for a bit, then waited for Richard to burst out of the stairwell. Richard took the doors off their hinges and threw them as well. Mason ducked around the corner and the doors embedded themselves in the wall beside him, digging into the plaster until they shattered against the concrete beneath it.

'He's getting good at that,' observed Nyx.

Mason peered around the corner and shouted, 'Missed me, you git.' He added a sneer for good measure, it couldn't do any harm. 'When I get out of here and tell the world what you've done. Every law enforcement agency and bounty hunter on the planet will be gunning for you. No expense spared.'

Richard sped towards Mason, running blindingly fast, his steel-spiked feet digging into the floor as he ran. Mason turned at the end of the corridor and barged through the double doors. As he heard Richard crash into the wall, then get up, Mason looked down at the floor below him and knew he had what he needed. *'Any nitro you got left, Nyx, get it ready. One last move, all the power you've got.'*

The double doors blew off their hinges, and Richard stood there grinning, Mason just twenty feet in front. He bent slightly, like a sprinter on the blocks, and dug both his spiked feet into the concrete floor under him to get an explosive start.

'No way to avoid me any more,' said Richard. 'That room is a dead end.'

Another hand gesture from Mason, this time of the middle finger variety. Then Mason grabbed at a preparation table beside him, getting his grip nice and firm.

'That won't even make a dent in me,' Richard laughed. Then he pushed off and sprinted at Mason.

Mason whipped the table around at lightning speed, putting in all the power Nyx had given him. The table missed Richard completely and sailed straight into the wall to the left of him, which meant Mason flew sideways the opposite way as Richard came racing in. Richard tried to turn, but the steel floor below his feet didn't give him enough purchase and Mason avoided Richard's charge by millimetres. Mason stuck out a foot and Richard tripped, speeding through empty air and right through the open door of the incinerator. In an instant Mason was up, he slammed the door closed on Richard and turned the thing on.

'Who has steel floors?' Mason parroted. 'A morgue and the incinerator room built next to it, that's who, you fucking idiot. Shame you never came down here to do your own dirty work, or you would have known that.'

Richard started hammering at the steel fibreglass porthole in the door with his hardened fists. *Boom, boom, boom.* Tiny cracks started to appear, and the man grinned manically from ear to ear as he worked, unheard quips coming from his lips.

Stabbing away at the controls, Mason kept going until the incinerator temperature was set to max. He slumped down in front of the door and watched the heat climb rapidly. Richard stared at Mason from within the fire and through the steel fibreglass porthole. He opened his mouth and laughed, then he started punching at the door once more. *Boom, boom, boom.*

Mason listened carefully, then he began to grin just a little.

'You hear that, Nyx?'

'*Oh yes, Mason, the blows are getting quieter.*'

He watched the temperature hit maximum and the sound of punching disappeared almost completely. Richard looked down at his blobby fists. They reformed immediately, but when he hit the door again, they just turned into half-flattened splotches once more.

'See, even I know what happens to matter when it gets very hot, it goes bloody soft.' Mason tapped at his head. 'Who's the scientist now, you Welsh tosser?' He looked down at his watch. Four fifty-seven a.m. 'Only need to keep him in there for three more minutes, then superheated, bunker-busting missiles should finish the job.'

'*What about you?*' asked Nyx quietly.

'Maybe I shouldn't be running about either. Bit of a trouble magnet me. Keep getting my friends into deep shit or killed,' answered Mason, getting comfortable for the show as the incinerator roared away. 'But you'll be OK, Nyx, there's still thirty per cent of you out there in Carter and Jane. You look after them, alright?'

'*Please don't cease to exist, Mason,*' she implored him. '*It would break my core programming.*'

'Don't you mean heart?' he said.

'*No,*' she replied, '*I don't have one.*'

'Yeah, you do, Nyx,' Mason said firmly.

A hand grabbed his shoulder, making Mason jump. He spun around to see Dan Samson looking down at him.

'Talking to yourself again, Mr Granger? A sure sign of madness that one.' Samson looked into the incinerator and saw the slightly sludgy form that was Richard Buckley, still hammering futilely away on the other side of the door. 'OK, maybe you've got good reason.'

Samson lifted Mason up effortlessly.

'We need to get your arse out of here, now.'

He dragged Mason out the door and down the corridor. By the time they got to the stairs, Mason was running too.

'I thought you didn't get your hands dirty any more?' shouted Mason as they ran up the stairs.

'This is me keeping my hands clean,' called back Samson. They burst through the stairwell doors and sped down the corridor on the ground floor towards the reception and the exit. 'I couldn't stand the thought of washing your blood off my hands for the rest of my unnatural life.'

Even from here, Mason could hear the approaching fighter jets, no doubt all of them laden with the latest bunker-busting missiles.

'Gonna be close.'

They burst out the front doors as the first missile hit the complex, tearing through the building to explode deep within its bowels. Missile after missile rained down after it, then *whomp*, the whole office complex exploded up into the air, bright fire tearing into the night sky.

With Samson alongside him, Mason watched it burn, and the fire turned them into silhouettes in the dark of the early morning. The effect was only spoiled when Mason turned and tripped on a kerb in the car park.

Carter came hobbling over and grabbed Mason by the shoulders.

'You made it,' was all the DS could think of to say.

Jane arrived behind him, just a little out of breath. She studied Mason for a beat, then put a hand on his face.

'Cora didn't make it, did she?'

Mason looked down. 'No, she didn't.' He sighed out a heavy breath. 'Should have been me left in there, not her.'

Sirens wailed in the distance and Samson turned to Jane.

'Get them out of here, now. Churchill and I will face what's coming.' A confident look eased across his face. 'But, given the crap we can expose about Richard, I reckon we can bypass all-out civil war and go straight to our legal fight in the courts.'

'*Mr Samson is right, we should leave*,' said Nyx. '*Cora wouldn't want you thrown in jail to rot, just because you're undead. She'd want us to be more than that.*'

Mason took one last look at the burning Tigris complex, then he gave the blazing remains of Richard's empire a two-fingered salute and walked away.

28 days later

Sitting on the cold, wet beach in the pouring rain, Mason looked out to sea. Everything matched his mood perfectly, howling wind, uncomfortable stones, even the bleak sunlight fading away behind the grey clouds. The dark English Channel stared right back at him. He threw another stone four hundred metres into its angry waters, just to piss it off some more.

Even the red wine was cheap and crap. He picked up the bottle and took another slug, then held it up to stare at the murky contents.

'Ugh, I really wish you hadn't grown me that extra kidney, Nyx. It takes too much of this shitty wine to get drunk now.'

'*I grew you an extra kidney as an emergency fuel source*,' said Nyx, '*not to stop you from getting inebriated. Now when are you going to get back in touch with your friends?*'

Mason threw another pebble into the sea. 'When I've filled up the Channel with stones,' he said darkly. 'The sodding world can look after itself. Not like it's done me loads of favours.'

His burner phone rang again, and he ignored it even though he recognised the number.

'*You really should answer that*,' said Nyx. '*She's been calling you all day.*'

'How the hell did she even get my number?'

Nyx gave him a look, for the seventh time. '*Mason Granger, answer your phone and find out.*'

'Fine.' He stabbed at the phone, water droplets already forming over its screen. Maybe it would short out, he hoped.

'Mum,' he answered.

'Mason.' She was quiet for a second or two, as if wondering what to say or, more likely, how to say it. 'I heard what you did, and I'm sorry about your friend.'

'Thanks, Mum.' He knew it took a lot for her to say something nice to him. 'How's Dad?'

'Happy on his new shelf,' she answered. Again, another pause. 'You've come home, I see.'

'Are you watching me?'

'Not all of the time,' she said. 'It's good that you're back near Southampton, back by the sea.' Yet again, another slightly awkward pause. 'And it's good to hear you've finally grown up and made something of yourself.'

'Ha, fat lot of good that did Cora.'

'She knew the risks,' she said, then her tone softened just a little. 'But at least you were helping others for a change, instead of just yourself. Your dad would have been proud of that.'

Mason swallowed. 'Maybe a bit,' he hoped.

'Well, I must be off. Things to do, people to deal with. You know how it is.' She took a sharp breath. 'Now, clean yourself up, Mason, and answer your phone, there's people out there who need you.'

There was dead air before Mason could ask another question.

'Great,' said Mason. 'She's watching me and my friends.'

'*I think it's sweet*,' said Nyx. '*Your mum cares enough to spy on you*.'

He went to put his phone in his pocket. Nope, it rang again. He looked at the screen, not really caring who it was, and wondered about throwing it four-hundred metres into the retreating tide.

'*Mason*,' warned Nyx.

He stabbed at the screen again and accepted the call.

'What?' he said forcefully.

'Good afternoon to you too, Mr Granger.'

'Oh great, it's you,' said Mason, instantly recognising Dan's deep voice. 'How did you get this number?'

'I have my ways,' replied Samson, without missing a beat. 'But that's not important. I'm calling because I have a favour to ask of you for a change.'

'I'm not in the mood.'

'Don't care,' replied Samson, clearly enjoying himself. 'We left you to drift about and grieve for a while, but that time has passed. Now you need to rejoin the human race, my friend, and make yourself useful again.'

'We'll see. What do you want?'

'That young man you asked me to look out for? Well, he called,' said Samson.

Mason thought for a second. 'What, the trainee security guard from the supermarket, Ben something or other?'

'The very same,' answered Samson. 'A week ago, one of the supermarket's customers found out he was undead, and they kicked up a fuss; banners in the local press and everything. Even though I've been fighting for our legal rights, and we are making progress, it's slow going. We're not all locked up by default any more, but the undead still aren't allowed to have jobs. I'm working on that one right now, but we're not there yet. So, in the end, the supermarket had to give up and let Ben go. After that, he came to me asking for something to do, like a job but without the official paperwork.'

'Fair enough,' said Mason. 'I mean, good on the lad for asking for a job, but what's that got to do with me?'

'The work I gave him finishes next week. Therefore, you need to get off your arse and find something productive for the young man to do. And yourself too.'

'I'm already busy,' said Mason, throwing another stone into the sea.

'Sure,' laughed Samson. 'Drinking crap wine and throwing stones in the sea is a full-time profession.'

Mason glanced about. 'Have you been having me watched as well?'

'I receive information from time to time.' A warm chuckle came down the line. 'I like to keep an eye on all my friends. I'll be sending Ben down to the coast next week. Get yourself presentable and make him and his girlfriend welcome. Oh, and answer your phone more often. Be seeing you, Mason.'

Before Mason could protest, the line went dead.

'Shit, has he been talking to my mum? I bloody hope not.'

He looked about to see if anyone was watching him right then. Nope, deserted beach, same as usual in the autumn rain. He stood up and decided to leave anyway. Clearly coming back to his home town was a mistake.

His phone pinged as a text came through. He felt Nyx staring at him intently, so he tapped on the message and read it.

Dear Ex-Honey,

Sorry about Nectr 37 not working on Cora, I just didn't want it bringing that bitch Sadie back if I ever got lucky enough to see her dead.

So, when I heard what happened, I thought I'd get you a divorce present to cheer you up. In the old days you'd have loved lots of money, but now I'm not so sure.

Anyway, I'm rambling. Something opportune came up, and your present is on its way. It was a little more expensive to make than I expected, so you owe me a favour for all my kindness.

Say hello to your mum for me and thank her for your number.

Your Mad Scientist, Ex-Wife,

Amanda.

'Sodding hell, she hasn't changed.' Mason slung his phone back in his pocket. 'Has everyone I know been talking to each other?' he asked Nyx, as he started to walk along the beach back to the car park; towards the battered old motorbike he'd bought for fifty quid from the scrapyard. 'Are you in on this too?' he scowled.

'*No, Mason, I'm no wiser than you in this matter,*' she replied. '*DS Carter is outside my communication range of ten miles, so just like you, I haven't spoken to our friends since you left London.*'

He let out an uncharacteristic sigh. 'Sorry, Nyx. I shouldn't take it out on you.'

There was no reply.

'Nyx? You OK?' Mason asked.

'*There's someone coming,*' she informed him.

Mason tensed as he caught movement at the edge of his vision, and he saw a figure clambering over one of the erosion prevention fences. Groynes or something they were called. Caught between walking away in the opposite direction and confronting the new arrival, something else occurred to him.

'Hold on a minute, how did Amanda know about the "*Mad Scientist*" description in my old phone?'

'*I believe we are about to find out*,' said Nyx excitedly.

'Alright, what the hell's going on?' asked Mason.

Nyx spread a smile throughout Mason's mind. '*Maybe we should ask Cora?*' she replied.

'What are you talking about, Nyx? Cora's dead.'

The figure continued determinedly along the beach; body hunched into an old parka to protect it against the driving rain, hood up and held by a hand to stop it flying back. Mason's eyes narrowed, and then he finally recognised the walk, a slight sway of the hips, a little more to the left than the right.

'Bugger me, it's Cora back from the sodding dead.' A grin spread across his face, and he strode towards the approaching figure, still holding the crappy bottle of red wine in his hand.

Cora closed the last few feet between them.

'Hello strangers,' she said. 'Long time no see.'

'How?' asked Mason simply.

Cora picked up a stone and threw it five-hundred metres into the retreating sea.

'How do you think? Nectr.'

'*But I can't work on women. How did I bring you back?*' said Nyx. When Cora didn't respond, Mason repeated the question out loud.

'It wasn't you, Nyx, your one per cent is gone, I'm afraid,' said Cora. 'It didn't survive the kill switch; there just wasn't enough of it.' Then she grinned at Mason. 'But fortunately for me, his mad scientist ex-wife cooked me up a special new strain of Tellus. She coded it just to me; that's why it took her so long to bring me back.'

'But nothing could've got out of the pile of molten rubble that was our office,' said Mason. 'What happened?'

'Richard's thugs left me where I was apparently, and one of the early-bird scientists found me when he came in. Total luck he was loyal to Amanda. So, he called his ex-boss, and she told him to get me out of there. He kept me on ice while she brewed up her magic.'

'Magic?' questioned Mason. 'I thought you didn't like that word.'

'Aye, well, I've changed a little too,' she smiled. 'You don't have a monopoly on that, Mason Granger.'

'Can I talk to her directly?' Nyx asked Mason tentatively. *'Would she mind that again?'*

'Nyx wants to talk to you directly. A lot,' said Mason. 'You OK with that?'

Cora spat on her hand and held it out. 'We'll do a swap, some Tellus for you, and one per cent of Nyx for me.' She nudged him gently in the ribs. 'Better be quick though, or it'll be all rain and no Nectr.'

Mason spat on his hand and shook hers, then they took their hands back and licked them.

Nyx rushed into Cora to re-establish her link, and Mason heard the most contented sigh in the short history of artificial intelligence.

'This is so nice,' said Nyx. She sent a quizzical expression across Mason's mind. *'It's all very odd, the sensation makes me want to laugh and cry all at the same time.'*

'Yup, more human every day,' said Mason, then he turned to Cora. 'A drink to celebrate?' He held out his bottle of wine.

'A drink sounds grand.' She took the bottle and looked at the label. 'Ew, maybe not this particular one though.' She poured the contents on to the stones and put the empty bottle in one of her parka's large pockets. 'I think we should get something nicer than that.'

'Fine by me,' said Mason. 'Where at?'

'That depends,' she replied, as she started to lead them towards the car park.

'On what?'

Cora dug out her phone and made a call. 'Hey Carter, I found him.' She paused a beat while DS Carter spoke on the other end. 'Yes, exactly where his mum told you he would be.'

'Jesus, is there no one who's not talking about me behind my back?'

'Don't be such a baby.' Cora held out her phone to Mason. 'Now talk to Carter and decide whether you're going to help him or not.'

Mason took the phone from Cora, muttering as he did so. 'What is this, phone a friend day or something?

'That sounds nice,' said Nyx. *'You humans should have one of those.'*

He ignored that and put the phone on speaker. 'Hey Carter, what's up? How's Jane?'

'She's good, thanks for asking,' said Carter, 'but that's not why we're talking. I've been working on something with Samson and Churchill. We have plans in motion.'

'Oh yeah?'

'Yes, and one of them requires you,' said Carter. 'I have a job for you.'

'Undead, remember; not allowed to work,' replied Mason. 'You only get away with it because you're a copper and your dead boss covered for you.' Mason thought about what he'd just said. 'Sorry, didn't mean to be disrespectful to Cuthbert. You get anywhere finding out how she got shot in that crap-fest at Brent Cross?'

'We're making progress. There's mounting evidence that she was deliberately targeted for sympathising with the undead. So, you need to stop making excuses, join the real world again, and help us reshape it. You know the laws are going to change and we'll be allowed to work again soon,' said Carter, getting into his stride. 'Samson's already halfway through fighting in the courts to win us the right to work officially, and he has a rather large army of lawyers on his side.'

That made Mason smile a little. 'Fair enough, I certainly wouldn't bet against that man.'

'But it's not all plain sailing though. There are plenty of bigoted people who want to bury the undead back in the ground, and quite a lot of them are in positions of power,' said Carter. 'Totally irrational prejudice, of course. Now that the anti-replication agent has been released, it's not like the undead are going to take over the world.'

'So, what's this job then?' asked Mason.

'A new law enforcement agency is being set up, and I'm heading up part of it. We're an offshoot of MI5 called Military Intelligence Undead branch. MIU for short. We'll handle serious crimes involving the undead,' said Carter. 'I want you and Cora to be my first employees. We've even purchased a base of operations for you to work out of, a bar restaurant on the Isle of Wight.'

'Not sure I'm secret agent material,' said Mason.

'It's a branch of MI5, not MI6,' corrected Cora. 'We're not spies.'

'And you are definitely not licensed to kill,' added Carter firmly.

'We're being established to keep the law in the UK, not to run around the place blowing things up. When you're not on a job, you two can run the restaurant like regular people. Cora can manage the place, and you can cook for the customers.' Carter paused for a beat. 'No doubt in between punching bad people in the face.'

'Cooking and beating up bad guys. Why didn't you just say that in the first place? Sodding well count me in.'

'Good,' said Carter. 'I'll be down to the coast next week for your first briefing. Oh, and Jane sends her love.'

A digital click and then silence from the other end followed.

'No one keeps that man down for long, do they?' said Mason, giving Cora her phone back.

'*They certainly don't*,' agreed Nyx. '*He's like a one-man police force on a quest for justice.*'

Mason grinned at that, then he looked towards the car park. 'So, what's this bar restaurant like then?' he asked Cora, as they restarted their walk to the top of the beach.

'I hear it serves a nice red wine, although sadly, it's often frequented by the local gangster wannabees.' She paused theatrically for a second, as if in thought. 'Should be right up your street,' she teased. 'Although, I'd rather you didn't pick a fight with all of them at the same time. We need to clean the place up, not level it to the ground.'

'I'll play nicely,' said Mason.

'I seriously doubt it,' laughed Cora, 'but we'll work on that bit by bit.'

'*This is exciting*,' said Nyx brightly. '*Something for Mason to do, besides throwing rocks into the sea.*'

They reached the top of the beach, Mason's mood lifting with every stride. He turned to look through the gloom at the Isle of Wight, the rain plastering his short hair flat on his head.

'Right,' he said with renewed energy. 'Let's go get a drink and slap the local tossers around until they behave.'

'*Mason*,' warned Cora and Nyx.

'OK, OK,' he said. 'I'll just throw the little wankers out the front door.'

Cora narrowed her eyes at him.

Mason let a devious grin cross his face. 'Who knows, I might even open the door first.'

ABOUT THE AUTHOR

After working in the video games industry of many years, on everything from *Resident Evil* to *PlayStation Home*, Charlie Cox now writes thrillers.

Zero point One is Charlie's first commercial novel, and a leap into the fast-paced world of Mason Granger, back from the dead and none too pleased about it.

Printed in France by Amazon
Brétigny-sur-Orge, FR

14793605R00150